W9-BSA-049

HOME
FROM THE
VINYL CAFE
A YEAR OF STORIES

STUART McLEAN

VIKING

VIKING

Published by the Penguin Group

Penguin Books Canada Ltd, 10 Alcorn Avenue, Toronto, Ontario, Canada M4V 3B2

Penguin Books Ltd, 27 Wrights Lane, London w8 5TZ, England

Penguin Putnam Inc., 375 Hudson Street, New York, New York 10014, U.S.A.

Penguin Books Australia Ltd, Ringwood, Victoria, Australia

Penguin Books (NZ) Ltd, cnr Rosedale and Airborne Roads, Albany

Auckland 1310, New Zealand

Penguin Books Ltd Registered Offices: Harmondsworth, Middlesex, England

First published 1998

10 9 8 7 6 5 4 3 2 1

Copyright © Stuart McLean, 1998

All rights reserved. Without limiting the rights under copyright reserved above, no part of this publication may be reproduced, stored in or introduced into a retrieval system, or transmitted in any form or by any means (electronic, mechanical, photocopying, recording or otherwise), without the prior written permission of both the copyright owner and the above publisher of this book.

The animals in this book were in no way mistreated and all scenes in which they appear were under strict supervision with the utmost concern for their well being.

Printed and bound in Canada on acid free paper ∞

CANADIAN CATALOGUING IN PUBLICATION DATA

McLean, Stuart, 1948–
    Home from the vinyl cafe: a year of stories

ISBN 0-670-88216-X

I. Title.

PS8575.L448H65 1998   C813'.54   C98-931719-6
PR9199.3.M34H65 1991

Visit Penguin Canada's Web site at www.penguin.ca

OTHER WORKS BY STUART MCLEAN

The Morningside World of Stuart McLean
Welcome Home: Travels in Smalltown Canada
Stories from the Vinyl Cafe
When We Were Young

For Peter Gzowski

Contents

Autumn

Winter, Again

HOME
FROM THE
VINYL CAFE

Winter

Dave Cooks the Turkey

When Carl Lowbeer bought his wife, Gerta, *Martha Stewart's Complete Christmas Planner,* he did not understand what he was doing. If Carl had known how much Gerta was going to enjoy the book, he would not have given it to her. He bought it on the afternoon of the 23rd of December. A glorious day. Carl left work at lunch and spent the afternoon drifting around downtown—window shopping and listening to carollers and falling into conversations with complete strangers. When he stopped for coffee he was shocked to see it was 5:30. Shocked because the only things he had bought were a book by Len Deighton and some shaving cream in a tube—both things he planned to wrap and give himself. That's when the Joy of Christmas, who had sat down with him and bought him a double chocolate croissant, said, I think I'll stay here and have another coffee while you finish your shopping. The next thing Carl knew, he was ripping through the mall like a prison escapee.

On Christmas Eve, Carl found himself staring at a bag full of stuff he couldn't remember buying. He wondered if he might have picked up someone else's bag by mistake, but then he found a receipt with his signature on it. Why would he have paid twenty-three dollars for a slab of metal to defrost meat when they already owned a microwave oven that would do it in half the time? Who could he possibly have been thinking of when he bought the Ab Master?

Carl did remember buying *Martha Stewart's Complete Christmas Planner*. It was the picture of Martha Stewart on the cover that had drawn him to the book—a picture of Martha striding across her front lawn with a wreath of chili peppers tucked under her arm. Carl had never heard of Martha Stewart. But she looked like she was in a hurry and that made him think of Gerta—so he bought the book— never imagining that it was something that his wife had been waiting for all her life. Carl was as surprised as anyone last May when Gerta began the neighbourhood Christmas group. Although not, perhaps, as surprised as Dave was when his wife, Morley, joined it.

"It's not about Christmas, Dave," said Morley. "It's about getting together."

The members of Gerta's group, all women, met every second Tuesday night, at a different house each time.

They drank tea, or beer, and the host baked something, and they worked on stuff. Usually until about eleven.

"But that's not the point," said Morley. "The *point* is getting together. It's about neighbourhood—not about what we are actually doing."

But there was no denying that they were doing stuff. Christmas stuff.

"It's wrapping paper," said Morley.

"You are *making* paper?" said Dave.

"*Decorating* paper," said Morley. "This is hand-printed paper. Do you know how much this would cost?"

That was in July.

In August they dipped oak leaves in gold paint and hung them in bunches from their kitchen ceilings to dry.

Then there was the stencilling weekend. The weekend Dave thought if he didn't keep moving Morley would stencil him.

In September Dave couldn't find an eraser anywhere in the house and Morley said, "That's because I took them all with me. We're making rubber stamps."

"You are MAKING rubber stamps?" said Dave.

"Out of erasers," said Morley.

"People don't even *buy* rubber stamps any more," said Dave.

"This one is going to be an angel," said Morley, reaching into her bag. "I need a metallic ink stamp pad. Do you think you could buy me a metallic ink stamp pad and some more gold paint? And we need some of those snap things that go into Christmas crackers."

"The what things?" said Dave.

"The exploding things you pull," said Morley. "We are going to make Christmas crackers. Where do you think we could get the exploding things?"

There were oranges drying in the basement on the clothes rack and blocks of wax for candles stacked on the ping-pong table.

One day in October Morley said, "Do you know there are only sixty-seven shopping days until Christmas?"

Dave did not know this. In fact he had not completely unpacked from their summer's vacation. Without thinking he said, "What are you talking about?"

And Morley said, "If we wanted to get all our shopping done by the week before Christmas we only have . . ." she shut her eyes, ". . . sixty-two days left."

Dave and Morley usually *start* their shopping the week before Christmas.

And there they were, with only sixty-seven shopping days left, standing in their bedroom staring at each other, incomprehension hanging between them.

It hung there for a good ten seconds.

Then Dave said something he had been careful not to say for weeks. He said, "I thought this thing wasn't about Christmas."

Which he immediately regretted, because Morley said, "Don't make fun of me, Dave." And left the room. And then came back. Like a locomotive.

"Uh oh," thought Dave.

"What," said Morley

"I didn't say that," said Dave.

"You said 'uh oh,'" said Morley.

"I thought 'uh oh,'" said Dave. "I didn't *say* 'uh oh.' Thinking 'uh oh' isn't like saying 'uh oh.' They don't send you to jail for *thinking* you want to strangle someone.

"What?" said Morley.

Morley slept downstairs. She didn't say a word when Dave came down and tried to talk her out of it. Didn't say a word the next morning until Sam and Stephanie had left for school. Then she said, "Do you know what my life is like, Dave?"

Dave suspected—correctly—she wasn't looking for an answer.

"My life is a train," she said. "I am a train. Dragging everyone from one place to another. To school and to dance class and to now-it's-time-to-get-up and now-it's-time-to-go-to-bed. I'm a train full of people who complain when you try to get them into a bed and fight when you try to get them out of one. That's my job. And I'm not only the train, I'm the porter and the conductor and the cook and the engineer and the maintenance man. And I print the tickets and stack the luggage and clean the dishes. And if they still had cabooses, I'd be in the caboose."

Dave didn't want to ask where the train was heading. He had the sinking feeling that somewhere up ahead someone had pulled up a section of the track.

"And you know where the train is going, Dave?" said Morley.

Yup, he thought. Off the tracks. Any moment now.

"What?" said Morley.

"No," said Dave. "I don't know where the train's going."

Morley leant forward over the table.

"The train starts at a town called First Day at School,

Dave, and goes to a village called Hallowe'en, and then through the township of Class Project, and down the spur line called Your Sister Is Visiting. And you know what's at the end of the track? You know where my train is heading?"

Dave looked around, nervously. He didn't want to get this wrong. He would have been happy to say where the train was going if he knew he could get it right. Was his wife going to leave him? Maybe the train was going to D-I-V-O-R-C-E.

"Not at Christmas," he mumbled.

"Exactly," said Morley. "To the last stop on the line—Christmas dinner. And this is supposed to be something I look forward to, Dave. This is supposed to be a heart-warming family occasion."

"Christmas dinner," said Dave tentatively. It seemed a reasonably safe thing to say. Morley nodded. Feeling encouraged Dave added, "With a turkey and stuffing and everything."

But Morley wasn't listening.

"And when we finally get through that week between Christmas and New Year, you know what they do with the train?"

Dave shook his head.

"They back it up during the night when I am asleep so they can run it through all the stations again."

Dave nodded earnestly.

"And you know who you are, Dave?"

Dave shook his head, again. No. No, he didn't know who he was. He was thinking maybe he was the engineer. Maybe he was up in the locomotive. Busy with men's work.

Morley squinted at her husband.

"You are the guy in the bar car, Dave, pushing the button to ask for another drink."

By the way Morley said that, Dave could tell that she still loved him. She could, for instance, have told him that he had to get out of the bar car. Or, for that matter, off the train. She hadn't. Dave realized it had been close, and if he was going to stay aboard, he was going to have to join the crew.

The next weekend he said, "Why don't I do some of the Christmas shopping? Why don't you give me a list, and I will get things for everyone in Cape Breton?"

Dave had never gone Christmas shopping in October. He was unloading bags onto the kitchen table when he said, "That wasn't so bad."

Morley walked across the kitchen and picked up a book that had fallen on the floor. "I'm sorry," she said. "It's just that I like Christmas so much. I *used* to like Christmas so much. I was thinking that if I got everything done early maybe I could enjoy it again. I'm trying to get control of it, Dave. I'm trying to make it fun again. That's what this is all about."

Dave said, "What else can I do?"

Morley reached out and touched his elbow and said, "On Christmas Day, after we have opened the presents, I want to take the kids to work at the Food Bank. I want you to look after the turkey."

"I can do that," said Dave.

Dave didn't understand the full meaning of what he had agreed to do until Christmas Eve, when the presents were finally wrapped and under the tree and he was snuggled, warm and safe, in bed. It was one of his favourite moments of the year. He nudged his wife's feet. She gasped.

"Did you take the turkey out of the freezer?" she said.

Dave groaned. He pulled himself out of bed and went downstairs. He couldn't find a turkey in the freezer—in either freezer—and he was about to call for help when the truth landed on him like an anvil. Looking after the turkey, something he had promised to do, meant *buying* it as well as putting it in the oven.

Dave unloaded both freezers to be sure. Then he paced around the kitchen nervously, trying to decide what to do. When he finally went upstairs, Morley was asleep. He considered waking her. Instead, he lay down and imagined, in painful detail, the chronology of the Christmas Day waiting for him. Imagined everything from the first squeal of morning, to that moment when his family came home from the Food Bank expecting a turkey dinner. He could see the dark look that would cloud his wife's face when he carried a bowl of pasta across the kitchen and placed it on the table she would have set with the home-made crackers and the gilded oak leaves.

He was still awake at 2:00 a.m., but at least he had a plan. He would wait until they left for the Food Bank. Then he would take off to some deserted Newfoundland outport and live under an assumed name. At Sam's graduation one of his friends would ask, "Why isn't your father here?" and Sam would have to explain that, "One Christmas he forgot to buy the turkey and he had to leave."

At 3:00 a.m., after rolling around for an hour, Dave got out of bed, got dressed, and slipped quietly out the back door. He was looking for a twenty-four-hour grocery store. It was either that or wait for the Food Bank to open, and though he couldn't think of anyone in the city more in need of a turkey than he was, the idea that his family might spot him in line made the Food Bank unthinkable.

At 4:00 a.m., with the help of a taxi driver named Mohammed, Dave found an open store. He bought the last turkey there: twelve pounds, frozen as tight as a cannonball, grade B—whatever that meant. He was home by 4:30 and by 6:30 had the turkey more or less thawed. He used an electric blanket and a hair dryer on the turkey, and a bottle of Scotch on himself.

As the turkey defrosted, it became clear what grade B meant. The skin on its right drumstick was ripped. Dave's turkey looked like it had made a break from the slaughterhouse and dragged itself a block or two before it was captured and beaten to death. Dave poured another Scotch and began to refer to his bird as Butch. He turned Butch over and found another slash in the carcass. Perhaps, he thought, Butch died in a knife fight.

Dave would have been happy if disfiguration was the worst thing about his turkey. Would have considered himself blessed. Would have been able to look back on this Christmas with equanimity. Might eventually have been able to laugh about it. The worst thing came later. After lunch. After Morley and the kids left for the Food Bank.

Before they left, Morley dropped pine oil on some of the living-room lamps.

"When the bulbs heat the oil up," she said, "the house will smell like a forest." Then she said, "Mother's coming. I'm trusting you with this. You have to have the turkey in the oven . . ."

Dave finished her sentence for her. "By 1:30," he said. "Don't worry. I know what I'm doing."

The worst thing began when Dave tried to turn on the oven. Morley had never had cause to explain to him about the automatic timer, and Dave had never had cause to ask about it. The oven had been set the day before to go on at 5:30. Morley had been baking a squash casserole for Christmas dinner—she always did the vegetables the day before—and now, until the oven timer was unset, nothing anybody did was going to turn it on.

At 2:00 p.m. Dave retrieved the bottle of Scotch from the basement and poured himself a drink. He knew he was in trouble.

He had to find an oven that could cook the bird quickly. But every oven he could think of already had a turkey in it. For ten years Dave had been technical director to some of the craziest acts on the rock-and-roll circuit. He wasn't going to fall to pieces over a raw turkey.

Inventors are often unable to explain where their best ideas come from. Dave is not sure where he got his. Maybe he had spent too many years in too many hotel rooms. At 2:30 p.m. he topped up his Scotch and phoned the Plaza Hotel. He was given the front desk.

"Do you cook . . . special menus for people with special dietary needs?" he asked.

"We're a first-class hotel in a world-class city, sir. We can look after any dietary needs."

"If someone brings their own food—because of a special diet—would you cook it for them?"

"Of course, sir."

Dave looked at the turkey. It was propped on a kitchen chair like a naked baby. "Come on, Butch," he said, stuffing it into a plastic bag. "We're going out."

Morley had the car. Dave called a taxi. He shoved the bottle of Scotch into the pocket of his parka on his way out the door.

"The Plaza," he said. "It's an emergency."

He took a slug from the bottle in the back of the cab.

The man at the front desk asked if Dave needed help with his suitcases.

"No suitcases," said Dave, patting the turkey, which he had dropped on the counter and which was now dripping juice onto the hotel floor. Dave turned breezily to the man behind him in line and said, only slurring slightly, "Just checking in for the afternoon with my chick."

The clerk winced. Dave wobbled. He spun around and grinned at the clerk and then around again and squinted at the man in line behind him. He was looking for approval. He found, instead, his neighbour. Jim Scoffield was standing beside an elderly woman whom Dave assumed must be Jim's visiting mother.

Jim didn't say anything, tried in fact to look away. But he was too late. Their eyes had met.

Dave straightened and said, "Turkey and the kids are at the Food Bank. I brought Morley here so they could cook her for me."

"Oh," said Jim.

"I mean the turkey," said Dave.

"Uh huh," said Jim.

"I bring it here *every* year. I'm alone."

Dave held his arms out as if he were inviting Jim to frisk him.

The man at the desk said, "Excuse me, sir," and handed Dave his key. Dave smiled. At the man behind the counter. At Jim. At Jim's Mom. He walked towards the elevators one careful foot in front of the other.

When he got to the polished brass elevator doors, he heard Jim calling him.

"You forgot your . . . chick," said Jim, pointing to the turkey Dave had left behind on the counter.

The man on the phone from room service said, "We have turkey on the *menu*, sir."

Dave said, "this is . . . uh . . . a *special* turkey. I was hoping you could cook *my* turkey."

The man from room service told Dave the manager would call. Dave looked at his watch.

When the phone rang, Dave knew this was his last chance. His only chance. The manager would either agree to cook the turkey, or he might as well book the ticket to Newfoundland.

"Excuse me, sir?" said the manager.

"I said I need to eat this *particular* turkey," said Dave.

"That *particular* turkey, sir," the manager was non-committal.

"Do you know," said Dave, "what they feed turkeys today?"

"No, sir?" said the manager. He said it like a question.
"They feed them . . ."

Dave wasn't at all sure himself. Wasn't so sure where he was going with this. He just knew that he had to keep talking.

"They feed them chemicals," he said, "and antibiotics and steroids, and . . . lard to make them juicier . . . and starch to make them crispy. I'm allergic to . . . steroids. If I eat that stuff I'll have a heart attack or at least a seizure. In the lobby of your hotel. Do you want that to happen?"

The man on the phone didn't say anything. Dave kept going.

"I have my own turkey here. I raised this turkey myself. I butchered it myself. This morning. The only thing it has eaten . . ." Dave looked frantically around the room. What did he feed the turkey?

"Tofu," he said triumphantly.

"Tofu, sir?" said the manager.

"And yoghurt," said Dave.

It was all or nothing.

The bellboy took the turkey and the twenty-dollar bill Dave handed him, without blinking an eye.

Dave said, "You have those big convection ovens. I have to have it back before 5:30 p.m."

"You must be very hungry, sir," was all he said.

Dave collapsed onto the bed. He didn't move until the phone rang half an hour later. It was the hotel manager.

He said the turkey was in the oven. Then he said, "You raised the bird yourself?" It was a question.

Dave said, yes.

There was a pause. The manager said, "The chef says the turkey looks like it was abused."

Dave said, "Ask the chef if he has ever killed a turkey. Tell him the bird was a fighter. Tell him to stitch it up."

The bellboy wheeled the turkey into Dave's room at quarter to six. They had it on a dolly covered with a silver dome. Dave removed the dome and gasped.

It didn't look like any bird he could have cooked. There were frilly paper armbands on both drumsticks, a glazed partridge made of red peppers on the breast and a small silver gravy boat with steam wafting from it.

Dave looked at his watch and ripped the paper armbands off and scooped the red pepper partridge into his mouth. He realized the bellboy was watching him and then saw the security guard standing in the corridor. The security guard was holding a carving knife. They obviously weren't about to trust Dave with a weapon.

"Would you like us to carve it, sir?"

"Just get me a taxi," said Dave.

"What?" said the guard.

"I . . . can't eat this here," said Dave. "I have to eat it . . ." Dave couldn't imagine where he had to eat it. "Outside," he said. "I have to eat it outside."

He gave the bellboy another twenty-dollar bill, and said, "I am going downstairs to check out. Bring the bird and call me a taxi." He walked by the security guard without looking at him.

"Careful with that knife," he said.

Dave got home at 6:00. He put Butch on the table.

The family was due back any minute. He poured himself a drink and sat down in the living room. The house looked beautiful—smelled beautiful—like a pine forest.

"My forest," said Dave. Then he said, "Uh oh," and jumped up. He got a ladle of the turkey gravy, and he ran around the house smearing it on light bulbs. There, he thought. He went outside and stood on the stoop and counted to twenty-five. Then he went back in and breathed deeply. The house smelled like . . . like Christmas.

He poured himself another Scotch, and looked out the window. Morley was coming up the walk with Jim Scoffield and his mother.

"We met them outside. I invited them in for a drink."

"Oh. Great," said Dave. "I'll get the drinks."

Dave went to the kitchen, then came back to see Jim sitting on the couch under the tall swinging lamp, a drop of gravy glistening on his balding forehead. Dave watched another drop fall. Saw the puzzled look cross Jim's face as he reached up, wiped his forehead and brought his fingers to his nose. Morley and Jim's mother had not noticed anything yet. Dave saw another drop about to fall. Thought, Any moment now the Humane Society is going to knock on the door. Sent by the hotel.

He took a long swig of Scotch and placed his glass by the hand-painted paper napkins that Morley had made.

"Morley, could you come here," he said softly. "There's something I have to tell you."

Holland

When you strap skis to your feet, winter skies are always blue and the temperature always crisp. When you strap a dog to your arm late on a winter night, crisp changes to cold, frosted becomes frozen, and walking up and down neighbourhood streets you can imagine yourself struggling across the Russian Steppes with a pack of wolves on your tail. There were nights in January when there wasn't much Dave wouldn't have done to get out of walking Arthur. Dave is not, by inclination, a winter person.

January, however, has always been Morley's favourite month, and she has tried to teach Dave how to enjoy it. Every

Holland

January they spend a weekend away together, usually in the outdoors. They have been skiing in Vermont and snowshoeing in Algonquin Park and once to an inn north of Montreal. One of the best weekends ever was a weekend they went to Ottawa. They stayed in a little bed-and-breakfast in the Glebe, and they skated on the canal—up to Dow's Lake to look at the ice sculptures and all the way back to the Chateau Laurier. That night they ate in a restaurant in the market and skated home.

They were planning to go back to Ottawa this year, but there was a big storm, the airport was closed, and you couldn't drive. Even the trains weren't running.

Morley said, "Too much ice for skating. Frozen out of the rink. Go figure."

Dave couldn't leave his record store the next weekend; he had been advertising a January sale for weeks. Before they knew it, the month was over, and they hadn't gone away for the first time in ten years.

When Morley was a child, her father, Roy, used to make a skating rink in their backyard—just for her. It wasn't always the easiest thing to do when you lived in Toronto. Some winters Roy had to take Morley's wagon out late at night and steal snow from yards around the neighbourhood in order to have enough for the base of her rink. He was happy to do it, because Morley loved to skate. She used to lie in bed at night while her father was out in the backyard—peeling his frozen hands off the hose—and she would imagine her ceiling was an ice-covered lake. She would fall asleep dreaming that she could sail on her ceiling forever.

Her all-time favourite book was *Hans Brinker*. Her all-time favourite dress was the burgundy chiffon costume that her mother made for her in 1959 for the Christmas Pageant on Ice. She was a sugarplum fairy. The burgundy dress had sequins. The years before, she had always had plain white dresses. She loved the burgundy dress because of the sequins and because the year she wore it was the only year that the Christmas pageant wasn't a total disaster. The worst year was the yellow dress. That was when she was twelve.

For your solo number you had to provide your own music, but those were the days before cassette tapes. So every girl would go to Mitchell's Music Store and cut her own record. Each record had two sides and because side B was a throw-away Morley had them put "The Stripper" on side B—just for fun.

The man who was playing the records that year was the father of one of the other competitors. When it was Morley's turn, he put the wrong side of her record on—"The Stripper" instead of Doris Day singing "Que Sera Sera." Morley began her program as if nothing was wrong. But then everyone started clapping along to "The Stripper." When somebody yelled, *"Take it off,"* she started to cry, and then she fell and didn't get up. She lay along the blue line until her father came and picked her up and helped her off. He said it wasn't her fault, but it didn't make her feel any better. She never skated in the pageant again. And she never again owned a yellow dress.

In fact, she didn't even put on a pair of skates for ten years, not once during her adolescence, not once. Not until the summer she left home.

It was 1972. She was working in summer stock, in a theatre in Providence, Rhode Island—eight plays, two months. She was a seamstress.

There was a 3,000-seat arena not far from the theatre. There was a free skate from eight to ten every Monday night. It was the only night that the theatre was dark. She kept meaning to go skating. She finally did—at the end of August. It was the night she met Dave.

Dave was in town with a Dick Clark *Caravan of Stars* production—eight acts in two hours, including "?" and the Mysterians, The Archies, and Bobby Goldsboro. It was a hateful tour. The musicians hated the music they were playing and they loathed the venues they were playing in. A sourness descended on the whole enterprise before the end of the first week. Dave, who began the tour as the technical director, soon realized he was presiding over the rock-and-roll equivalent of a Ford Pinto. He could count on something going wrong every day. He kept waiting for the explosion. The only salvation was the most hated moment of all—the last number of every show—when Bobby Goldsboro sang "Honey."

About two weeks into the tour one of the Mysterians bought a battery-operated megaphone, and every night a group of musicians would huddle off-stage, trying to distract Bobby Goldsboro by singing alternate lyrics during his song. They would sing just loud enough so *he* could hear them and the audience couldn't. In Saratoga Springs they rigged up a microphone behind stage. The plan was to feed their version of "Honey" through Goldsboro's monitor. Somehow the feed got rerouted—it was never clear how—and their lyrics, which involved Honey doing unspeakable things with a shaved, greased goat, got routed through the arena PA.

To the audience it appeared as if this unbelievable rewrite was actually coming out of Goldsboro's mouth. Goldsboro, who was dimly aware that something was horribly wrong, gamely finished the song. While the crowd watched in disbelief. When the tune came to an end, there was a moment of pure silence. Then, Goldsboro looked around in confusion as the audience rose as one and gave him the only standing ovation he got on the tour. After the show he kicked up such a fuss that the Mysterians had to stop their evening antics. Instead, every night, when it was time for "Honey," they would slip into the audience, where Goldsboro could see them, and put on oversized construction ear protectors, waving, smiling and making rude gestures at him while he sang.

Things got so bad that Dave left the tour and began to advance the show. This meant arriving in each town a few days ahead of everyone else to prepare the arena and then, thankfully, to leave before anyone else got there. He spent that entire summer arguing with arena managers about concession rights and electrical boards. And that is how he came to meet Morley in those last days of the summer of 1972.

When he first saw her, Dave was leaning on the arena boards waiting for the free skate to end so his crew could start laying a temporary floor over the ice. The lights were dim, and there were waltzes playing over the arena PA. Everyone was paired up, holding hands as they skated around and around. Dave suddenly felt alone. He got a coffee in a cardboard cup and watched the skaters, and as he watched he was transported back to the arena in his home town in Cape Breton—to the annual Valentine Weekend Ice Waltz. They used to put lights in the arena ceiling that weekend. The lights would twinkle like stars. There was the big face of a moon, which would wink its eye every so often. And a live orchestra suspended on a plywood platform over centre ice. The musicians would have to climb up a ladder with their instruments at the beginning of the night. Dave's mother made him promise he wouldn't skate under the platform during the polkas, because when the orchestra played polkas the platform would swing back and forth. Whenever that happened, Margaret would stand by the boards, light a Sweet Caporal and say she didn't mind if the cigarettes got her, but she was damned if she was going to become an item on the TV news because she was the only woman in the history of Cape Breton to be squashed to death by a polka band.

That's what Dave was thinking about when Morley skated into his life. She had long chestnut hair with bangs that were at least an inch below her eyebrows. She was wearing a handwoven poncho over a blue army-surplus turtleneck sweater, and bell-bottom jeans with embroidered cuffs. And granny glasses. Dave was bewitched.

She was the only person on the ice who could really skate—around and around all by herself—one leg crossing over the other in the corners. Every so often she would glide to centre ice and do a spin. Dave thought, She must be Canadian. He had to meet her.

He rented a pair of skates. But when he got onto the ice,

he couldn't catch up to her. So he slowed down to see if she would catch up to him. She did. But she just kept going.

Dave was getting frantic as he watched the clock at the far end of the arena. Then suddenly she was standing right in front of him at the blue line. But Dave was going so fast he was going to shoot right by her. Without thinking he reached out and grabbed her. She screamed, and then they were suspended in mid-air, clutching at each other, and for a horrible frozen moment, face to face. In that moment of eternity, as they hovered horizontally over the ice, Dave said, "Hi."

And Morley said, "Hi?" Like a question.

Then they landed in a heap.

Dave insisted on driving her to the hospital. She had three stitches just below her chin. Afterwards, he took her out to dinner. And then he drove her back to the arena, where she had left her car. He invited her to come to the concert the next night. It was only as she was driving away that Dave remembered which concert it was. But by then it was too late. The next evening she was sitting beside him fidgeting, he noticed glumly, as Bobby Goldsboro stepped on stage.

They didn't see each other again for six years, but they kept in touch by mail. Just occasional letters, and Dave's never said much. But he sent her quirky things. The week after they met at the rink, Dave sent her a package of Silly Putty in the mail. When she opened it, Morley knew he was the man for her.

Another time he sent her glow-in-the-dark skate laces, and once, a newspaper from Thunder Bay. Morley, who was back in Toronto by then, read every page of the Thunder Bay paper obsessively, looking for the significant article. Why had he sent it? She finally decided it was her horoscope, which said: "Your love life is on thin ice. Time to make a decision. Don't let distance cloud your judgment."

"No. No," said Dave, years later. "There was nothing special. I just thought you'd like to see it."

When they finally started to see each other, it was 1978. Dave was sick of life on the road. He wanted to come in from the cold, and Morley seemed so normal.

When he told her these things, Morley was overcome with the irony. She was tired of being polite. She didn't want to be normal. She wanted to lose control. But she loved him. And she had hope.

They got married before the summer was over and moved into an apartment near a large park. On their very first night together, when they were getting ready for bed, Dave said, "Do you want a little snack?"

Morley said, "You go ahead."

He came back from the kitchen with four pieces of bread slathered with mayonnaise. There were four slabs of cooking onion on a plate. And a glass of buttermilk. Morley stared at him, and he said, "It's OK. I haven't brushed my teeth yet."

When he had a sore throat, a week later, Morley said, "You should gargle with salt."

Dave said, "No. No. Just throw me one of those socks."

Morley said, "What?"

And Dave said, "One of those white athletic socks—the wool ones."

Morley stared in confusion at the heap of unsorted laundry

in the basket at the foot of their bed. "What are you going to do with a sock?" she asked.

Dave was pulling the covers around his chin like a small child. It seemed perfectly obvious to him. "You soak it in water and fasten it around your neck with a safety pin," he said.

Morley stared at him.

Dave said, "You wring it out first."

What Morley was thinking was, What am I doing here? But she wasn't about to quit.

She was so young. She believed what they were doing was important.

On Saturday mornings Dave got up first and made them scrambled eggs. Ever since he was a child Dave had loved scrambled eggs. Sometimes when he was a boy he could hardly wait to get to sleep on Friday nights because he knew he was going to get scrambled eggs on Saturday morning.

One Friday night as she was washing the dishes, Morley said, "I make the best scrambled eggs you've ever had."

The next morning she squeezed fresh juice and got out their matching coffee mugs. Carefully folding their one pair of linen napkins, laying them out side by side, she whisked up six eggs and brought them to the table. Dave stared at them. There were little green flecks all through his scrambled eggs. Pieces of chives Morley had snipped from the back garden. In Cape Breton you don't add anything to scrambled eggs. Except maybe ketchup. But this was his bride and she had made these eggs. Dave picked up his fork. When he had finished, he said, "I love your scrambled eggs."

The next weekend the eggs came with chopped-up mushrooms. The weekend after that it was tomatoes and onions. And then spinach. On the fifth weekend it was cheese. Dave had begun to hate Saturday mornings. He'd lie in bed, as the sound of a knife hitting a chopping board drifted upstairs. How did I get mixed up with this person, he wondered?

By the middle of that first winter they were both thinking, this marriage was a big mistake. Here it was, January of all things, and Morley was gloomy. Less than a year married and she felt like she had been sentenced to life with a stranger.

One night on television there was a news story about the canals in Holland. The reporter squinted awkwardly at the camera as he interviewed an old man smoking a meerschaum pipe at an outdoor café. The old man said it was the first time in ten years that the canals in the Netherlands had frozen. They cut from the old man to pictures of a Dutch boy lacing up his skates on a canal bank and from him to three girls in folk costume skating hand-in-hand through an unidentified village.

Morley watched the entire report with her chin cupped in her hand. When it finished, she turned to Dave and said, "I've always dreamed of doing that."

Dave, who had only been half-paying attention, said, "Really? That was your dream?"

Morley said, "Yes."

Dave stood up and walked into the kitchen. When he came back, he was carrying a half-finished beer. He looked at his wife and said, "We should go."

Morley said, "To Holland? Don't be silly."

And Dave said, "Maybe this is our only chance. Maybe the

next time it happens we'll have kids and a mortgage and we won't be able to go."

Dave had never said anything about kids before.

He smiled at her. And he went back into the kitchen and picked up the telephone. When he hung up, Morley was standing beside him. Watching. Nothing like this had ever happened to her.

"We leave tomorrow. We'll be back on Monday," said Dave. He was looking right at her.

The next morning they bought Dave a pair of hockey skates. At lunch Morley held out a present she had wrapped in newspaper. She said, "It's almost finished. I was going to give it to you for your birthday. I can finish it on the plane." It was a heavy blue wool sweater.

"This is a beautiful sweater," said Dave. "I love this sweater."

When the plane landed in Amsterdam, Morley had her face pressed to the window. She wanted to see everything. She wanted to make sure the canals were still frozen.

They went skating right away.

But the canals in Amsterdam were wide and windy and open and the ice was soft and bumpy and treacherous. It wasn't like Morley had imagined it at all. It was like skating on a freeway.

The man at the hotel said, "You have to go to Friesland."

So on Saturday they rented a car and drove into the country. They parked at the end of a road and left their boots and coats under a long row of willows that stood bare and wispy along the bank of the canal. When Morley climbed down onto the ice it was like her dream—the canal was framed by the high protective banks. She felt like she was a little girl again and she had stepped onto her ceiling. She was standing on a narrow swath of ice that kept going as far as she could see. She could start skating and she could go on forever. It was the greatest skate of her life. They sailed past farmhouses with roofs so low that they looked like great wool hats pulled almost to their eyes, past huge creaking windmills that Morley said reminded her of herons trying to take off. For an hour they saw no one, and then suddenly they went right through a village and saw an old man leading a donkey with panniers, and a dog pulling a cart, and a family pushing a baby carriage on wooden runners. Once in the middle of nowhere, an old man passed them going the other way. He was sitting on a contraption that looked like a wagon on blades and he was rowing it along the canal with what Dave swore were cross-country ski poles with toilet plungers fastened to the end. There were footbridges to duck under and frozen intersections, where smaller canals branched off towards villages and towns. At each of these icy intersections there was a sign nailed to a tree—a white arrow pointing into the grey distance—with something like "Leyden 50km" painted on it in neat black letters. There were no automobiles. No skidoos. It was like being in the nineteenth century.

They ate lunch on the ice, at a café on a boat that was frozen under a leafless elm. No one could speak English, so they ordered by gesturing with their red fingers at meals on other tables.

Instead of getting what they thought they were pointing at, they each got a large meat ball covered in gravy, a mug of thick hot chocolate and a huge square of gingerbread. The waiter smiled at them as they ate. It was delicious. Dave could have sat there for the rest of the afternoon.

But Morley wanted to keep moving. She was thinking, now I understand why people like to dance. Dave, who had been having trouble keeping up to her, laced up his skates wondering how to say "cardiac arrest" in Dutch.

An hour after they had lunch, Morley stopped for a rest. Dave was out of breath. "My feet hurt," he panted. He flopped on the bank.

Morley said, "Stand up."

Dave struggled up. Morley made him cross his arms over his chest. She skated behind him. "Lean back," she whispered. He tipped his head back.

"All of you," she said. "Trust me. I'm here."

Dave leaned back into her arms, and she caught him and pushed him along the canal as if he were a statue. It started to snow. It was like skating through a painting. The snow was on their hats, their mittens, their sweaters. Everything was white—above and below them—the white sky and the white ice. Dave leaning back. Morley pushing, pushing.

They had waffles and hot cheese for supper, and bought a wooden toy that would move in the wind on their balcony.

On the plane, Dave carried the toy in his lap. He was being so careful not to knock it as he stood up to leave that he snagged the sweater Morley had knitted him on the side of his seat. He had taken four or five steps before he realized what had happened. The sweater had begun to unravel behind him. There was a strand of blue wool hanging from his waist that almost reached the floor. When he caught up to Morley he was clutching the wooden toy and the line of wool was dangling behind him like a tail. He didn't know what to say, so he didn't say anything. He thrust the toy into her arms and turned around. They both stood in the middle of the walkway staring at the sweater. The man behind them said, "excuse me," and people started to push past them.

Morley reached down and gathered up the line of wool. They started to walk through the airport—Dave a step ahead of Morley like a kid on a line. They walked that way to the luggage carousel and out to the taxis. And they still walk like that today—attached, drifting apart sometimes, but never so far apart that one can't reel the other one back.

Valentine's Day

"There is something," said Dave, "about standing at the bottom of the stairs and yelling at your kids to come dinner that I find upsetting."

Morley was moving around the kitchen—straining potatoes, stirring beans, moving too fast for philosophy.

"Just get them," she said, dropping a frying pan in the sink.

Stephanie was the first down, her hair tied half-up, a horrifyingly yellow potion setting on her face. She was wearing a pair of Dave's boxer shorts and an oversized T-shirt that matched her face. She looked at the table, which Dave was in the process of setting, and said, "Why did you call me? It's not ready yet." Then she disappeared back upstairs.

An hour after dinner she is still at the table, chewing on a stick of celery and painting her nails, balancing the brush on the table, picking up the celery, holding her fingers out in front of her, waving them in the air. Sam is sitting across from her, in another universe, chewing on a pencil and frowning at the math book in front of him. When the phone rings, no one moves. They all look at Stephanie.

"Why are you looking at me?" she says.

Before Morley goes to bed she knocks on Stephanie's bedroom door.

Stephanie is lying on her unmade bed, books spread around her and spilling off the bed, where they merge with a pile of dirty clothes that stretches to the empty laundry hamper in the corner. Stephanie is talking on the phone, listening to music and, apparently, working on homework.

"It's time to say goodbye," says Morley.

Five minutes later she knocks again.

"Hang up," she says, sticking her head into the room. And then, spotting her hairbrush on the bedside table, Morley walks in and picks it up.

"I've got to go," says Stephanie into the phone. She lunges for the brush but she is too late.

"I need that," she says to her mother.

Her hand is out and they are both looking at the hairbrush which Morley is holding close to her chest. Morley says, "It belongs in the bathroom."

As she turns to go, Stephanie says, "There's a Valentine's Dance on Saturday. I'm going with Paul Chalmers."

"On a date?" said Morley, stopping at the door.

Stephanie is sixteen. Ever since she became a teenager, she has moved around the city—to movies, to parties, on shopping trips, even to the library, with a pack of friends. She has, as far as Morley knows, never been on a date.

She looks at her daughter and smiles. "That's wonderful, darling," she says.

Morley had begun dating when she was twelve. She was pleased when Stephanie hadn't shown any interest in boys during her early teenage years. But lately she had begun to wonder when it was going to start. It was, she had thought, time.

Stephanie said, "It's no big deal."

Morley said, "Is he a nice boy? Do you like him?" What a stupid thing to say, she thought. And she put the hairbrush down where she had found it, and she smiled. "Put it back when you're finished, OK?" Then she said, "Well, it's nice. That he'd ask you."

Stephanie shrugged, "He didn't ask me. I asked him."

"Oh," said Morley, her fingers fiddling absent-mindedly with her lips, "Great."

Morley is a child of the sixties. She believes in equality of the sexes. She thinks of herself as a feminist. Part of her was delighted her daughter was living in a world where she could do this. This powerful thing. Yet somewhere Morley felt an uneasy rumble of anxiety. *The boys ask the girls.* That was the rule she grew up with. Did her daughter have any idea how much the rules had changed? And *had* they? Was everybody else doing this? What would the boys think? Morley *knew* she shouldn't feel this way. She *knew* this could make her a traitor to her generation, to her feminism, to her very sex. But she couldn't help what she was thinking. She didn't want anyone getting the wrong idea about her daughter.

"Why am I feeling like this?" she asked Dave.

"Because it makes her vulnerable," said Dave. "You don't want her to be hurt."

It was not as if *the boys ask the girls* rule had served Morley particularly well. As a girl she had been subjected to an astounding number of doleful dates. Evenings she had spent with boys for whom the strongest emotion she felt was pity.

There was Colin, who, for weeks before he screwed up the courage to ask her out, rode his bicycle endlessly up and down the sidewalk in front of her house. This was when they were sixteen years old. When so many of them had their drivers' licences that it wasn't cool to ride a bike any more. What made it worse was that Colin used to pretend he was driving a bus: when he thought no one was looking, Colin would ring his bell and slam on his brakes, opening the bus doors to pick up passengers. He could make all the bus sounds with his mouth. And once the passengers were on, he would hiss and ride down the street. Until the bell rang and he had to let someone off again.

When Colin asked Morley out, she said yes. She was tired of being the only one who didn't go out on weekends. She thought, Surely Colin would be better than no one. She was wrong.

They went to a movie—*Carry On Doctor*. The feature had hardly begun when Morley was aware of Colin's hand, inching towards her, creeping across the armrest in the darkness. Colin was looking straight ahead as if he had no idea what his hand was doing, so Morley was able to watch its approach. She watched in dumbfounded fascination as his hand left the armrest and headed out into space—it was inching towards *her* hand which was gripping her knee.

She watched Colin's hand get closer and closer and then, as it closed in, she held out her drink, watching as Colin's hand sank into the icy Coke—up to the wrist—as if it were thirsty. Colin didn't even flinch. Just as slowly as he had sunk his hand into her cup, he pulled it out, easing it, inch by inch, back into his lap, his face never leaving the screen. Five minutes later Morley saw him wiping his fingers carefully between his knees.

And Colin wasn't even close to being the worst date in her life. There was the night she found herself sharing the sofa in Miriam Decker's basement with Charlie Casabon. To be *that close* to a face with *that look* is something that you never forget. She was sitting on the couch talking to Charlie when she noticed his glasses had begun to fog up—for no apparent reason—and he seemed to be out of breath. Which struck her as peculiar because he wasn't moving. He was just sitting there with his arm around her shoulders. She wasn't sure how it got there. Then she realized his face, with that faraway look, was moving closer and closer, and she knew what was happening and she knew that it had nothing *whatsoever* to do with her. It could have been any girl sitting there beside Charlie. She just happened to be in the wrong place at the wrong time—it was like a traffic accident. She didn't dare move, not a muscle, even though the arm of the couch was digging uncomfortably into her back. She was afraid if she even shifted, Charlie might take it as a sign of passion. And things could get worse.

Maybe the worst date in Morley's life was with a boy called Bucky who moved in next door in the summer of 1968. Bucky was two years younger than Morley. He was fourteen years old when he asked if she wanted to go roller skating. He said a whole gang was going. Morley had never roller skated in her life, but Bucky said it didn't matter. Everyone she knew was out of town and Morley thought, Why not? I can ice skate. I'll be fine.

She didn't understand that she was Bucky's *date* until she was squeezed beside him in the front seat of his family's Buick. The "whole gang" turned out to be Bucky's ten-year-old brother and *his* two friends. Bucky's older brother, Chucky, eighteen, the boy Morley *should* have been dating, was dropping them off at the roller rink.

It was one of those hot summer nights. Morley was wearing shorts and she could feel the back of her legs sticking to the vinyl of the front seat. Everyone was teasing Bucky because he had a date, cracking jokes as if Morley wasn't even in the car. All the way there she kept lifting one leg and then the other, trying to keep them free of the seat. By the time they got to the rink she was feeling sick.

When they got their skates on, Bucky said they should hold hands, and Morley, who was surprised to find how unsteady she was, had no choice. So around and around they went—Morley, against all her instincts, clutching onto this boy who was four inches shorter than she—praying that no one she knew would see her. The music stopped and the man on the PA announced a "Couples Only" contest. Bucky wanted to enter.

There were only four other couples standing on the concrete oval, waiting for the music to begin. The girls were all wearing short skating skirts. The boys all looked as if they could toss their dates between their legs.

This didn't seem to faze Bucky, but Morley drew the line and said she *wasn't going out*. When Bucky couldn't change her mind—and, Lord knows, he tried—he disappeared, abandoning Morley, who had never been downtown in her life, in this noisy roller rink.

After trying valiantly to skate around a few times alone, Morley fell and another girl landed on her and winded her. When she got her breath back, she started to cry. She couldn't phone her father—he'd have a heart attack. Instead, she glommed onto Bucky's baby brother and spent the rest of the evening with the ten-year-olds. She didn't see Bucky again until eleven o'clock—when he mysteriously reappeared—just as his father arrived to drive them home.

Stephanie has heard all these stories before. More than once. It infuriates her that her mother seems to believe that she is destined for a similar string of disasters. Stephanie doesn't intend to have the same experiences as her mother. Stephanie's goal in life is to end-run all the disasters.

But you don't learn about love from someone else. Love is experiential. You have to make your own mistakes.

If Morley knew some of the mistakes that her daughter had

already made, some of the lessons she had learned, if she had any inkling of what a great act of courage it had been for Stephanie to ask Paul Chalmers to the Valentine's Dance, and then to suggest that he *actually pick her up at home*, it would have broken her heart. And she wouldn't have felt so uptight about it.

Paul Chalmers is not the first man in Stephanie's life. Love first came to Stephanie the summer she was fourteen. It came in the form of a tall, long-haired, strong-faced, thirty-eight-year-old television producer. His name was Cameron Flemming and he lived with his wife and two children on the same street as Stephanie. That summer Stephanie would take the newspaper onto their front lawn before supper and sit on the stoop, pretending to read, so she could be there, outside, when Cameron Flemming walked by her house on his way home from work.

One afternoon, when Sam had set up a lemonade stand, Cameron Flemming stopped and bought a glass of lemonade. And as he put his glass down on the card table, he smiled at Stephanie. She felt herself flush. She was in love with him. The world was perfect because he was in it.

Then one evening he stopped and asked if she could baby-sit. Stephanie felt the bottom drop out of her stomach. It was his birthday and his wife wanted to take him out to dinner. Stephanie said "I took the baby-sitting course at school. I have a certificate." She was trying to sound sophisticated.

She arrived at his house with that month's *Reader's Digest.* "I'm going to read when the kids are in bed," she said. She thought this would impress him. She was wearing her favourite pair of faded jeans and a sweater that was too large for her—she liked the way the arms hung over her hands and covered her fingers.

His wife was upstairs. Cameron was sitting in the kitchen with his youngest boy in his arms. He threw the boy in the air and caught him over his head.

He reached out and touched her arm. "Nice sweater. It's a sweater for walking along a beach, in the wind."

She said, "I love the wind."

When the kids were in bed, she ignored the *Reader's Digest* and wandered around the house imagining what it would be like to live there with him. There was a picture in his bedroom of him standing beside his wife. They were on a beach. The wind was in her hair. Stephanie opened the frame and slid the picture out. With her heart pounding, she took her bus pass and found a pair of nail scissors in his wife's bureau. She cut her picture out and taped it over his wife's face, putting the altered photo back in the frame. Then she lay on the bed, his bed, and closed her eyes, pretending she was asleep. When she opened her eyes she saw herself, in the frame, standing beside him, the wind in *her* hair.

The phone rang. She ran to get it and then one of the children called. And Stephanie forgot about the picture until it was too late—until after they came home and were standing in the living room. She was putting her sweater back on, and he was saying, "I'll walk you home."

She didn't know what to do. She couldn't think of any reason to go up into their bedroom to retrieve her picture. So she didn't do anything. When she got home, she thought of killing herself. Instead, she stopped sitting on the lawn in the evenings. No one ever said anything about the picture. But the Flemmings never asked her to baby-sit again.

Grade Ten was Doug. Stephanie kept a Doug book in her bedroom. She wrote poems to Doug and kept a list at the back of the book of all the things that made Doug cool: his sneakers, his knapsack, the way he carried his knapsack, the things that he probably carried in his knapsack, his ski jacket, his earring, his ears, how he opened his locker, the things he probably had in his locker, his hair.

When Doug had a science project and was going to the library after school, Stephanie *made up* a project, so she would have a reason to go to the library too—but she didn't give him her work the way Melissa Aims did. Melissa gave Doug her math homework every lunchtime. Stephanie thought this was contemptible. Though she wished he would ask her.

One day at lunch, Doug said Oasis were contemptible and Stephanie panicked and prayed that no one would tell him that she used to like Oasis. Had liked them in fact until that day. It never occurred to her to defend her taste.

The Doug period of her life ended abruptly in the spring when Stephanie left her knapsack in the gym and someone found her Doug book. Whoever it was tore out the back page and taped it to her locker. It was up for two periods before she found out about it. There were eighty-four entries of Doug coolness for everyone to read.

Paul arrived this September. He sat directly in front of Stephanie in history. They were doing Canada. Again. At Hallowe'en they were at Louis Riel. Again. And Stephanie knew everything there was to know about Paul's neck.

She had memorized his neck. She would know his neck anywhere. As Riel rode towards oblivion, she thought, For the rest of my life I will know this neck.

She joined the debating team. So did Paul. She didn't even know she liked him until November when he was away one Monday and stayed away for the rest of the week. The next Monday when he was still not back, she began to worry. She was worried that he would never come back.

She couldn't ask anyone about him or they would figure out she liked him. All she could do was worry. In history she stared at the empty space in front of her where his neck should have been. She wrote his name on a piece of paper and then wrote her name below his and crossed out the letters that they had in common. She got an *e* and an *a* in their first names. When she added their last names she got an *s*, and an *n*, and a *t*, an *h*, and an *m*.

She counted off the letters left over. *Love, hate, friendship, marriage. Love, hate, friendship, marriage.* She got *friendship*. In math, she worked out that if she cheated and used his nickname and her middle name, she got *love*. She was startled by how pleased that made her. She wrote over his name . . . over and over again, *love, hate, friendship, marriage*, until it was a blue smudge. She didn't want anyone to be able to read what she had been doing.

That night she phoned his house and hung up before

anyone answered. She phoned again an hour later, and this time got his mother on the second ring and she hung up again.

Then Becky Toma had a Christmas party. Paul and Stephanie danced together all night.

On Wednesday after supper Sam and Stephanie had a huge fight.

Dave and Morley were in the kitchen. As the screaming escalated into slamming doors Dave made a move towards the stairs.

"No," said Morley. "Don't. If the audience doesn't show up, the actors go home."

She was making coffee. "They love each other. These are battles for affection."

Half an hour later, when things were quiet, she went upstairs. Both the children's doors were shut. She knocked on Sam's first.

"Hi," she said. "Do you want a cookie?" He was lying on the floor. Moving trucks around.

Stephanie was on her bed, reading a magazine.

Morley said, "Do you want to go shopping? Tomorrow after supper?"

Stephanie said, "Sam has my toothpaste."

Morley said, " Oh." She bent over and picked a white blouse off the floor and hung it on the back of a chair. She was thinking maybe they could go somewhere and get a pair of chinos and a blouse for Stephanie.

Stephanie said, "I don't want to go shopping."

Morley sat on the edge of the bed and reached out to touch her daughter's hair. "I was thinking," she said, "that you might like something for Saturday night. For the dance."

Stephanie pulled away from her mother. She rolled over. "I'm going to wear one of Dad's white shirts and my black jeans."

Morley said, "But your black jeans are ripped."

Stephanie said, "I'm going to have *long underwear* on."

It was a look that Morley hadn't considered.

When Morley was sixteen her mother had a dress made for her—for a school dance. It was made by Elsie Steppich, a seamstress who was married to the caretaker of their church. The dress was sleeveless. It had layers of mauve chiffon over purple silk. Her mother said it was a wonderful dress. It probably was—for a forty-five-year-old woman. When Morley put it on she felt as if she was playing dress-up. The material at the front was all gathered, puckering together to a centre point so it looked like she had a massive target on her chest, with a bull's eye engulfing her breasts.

Morley was so horrified that she could barely speak all night. She found the darkest corner in the gym and stayed put, sitting on a bench with Elenore Pepper, who had a huge nose. She went to the girls' room once and stared at herself in the mirror, but when she heard other girls coming down the hall, she locked herself in a stall and waited there, her feet lifted off the floor, until they had left and she could slip out without anyone seeing her. When Mickey Billingsley asked her to dance, she was so confused she said, "No, thank you" —not understanding that she was the only person he had asked, that it had taken him all night and several trips to the boys' bathroom before he managed to summon the courage to approach her.

When Paul arrived to pick Stephanie up he was holding flow-ers—a bouquet of twelve turquoise and green carnations.

"What a lovely thing," said Morley.

Paul looked at her defensively. "It's Valentine's Day," he said.

Morley had spent the night before helping Sam address forty-five Jurassic Park Valentines. Somehow she had disas-sociated that event from the actual holiday. She had forgot-ten it completely. So had Dave.

Dave looked at the flowers this boy had bought for his daughter and he winced.

Stephanie was still upstairs. Morley was struggling to make Paul feel at home while Dave stared at him.

Paul was wearing a pair of tight black jeans, a white dress shirt, a tie and a dark sports jacket. The tie was too thin, the shirt rumpled and the black shoes so big that they made his feet look enormous—but he was trying. Awkward, thought Morley, but sweet.

Dave was thinking, This boy doesn't look a bit like me. He was muscled. His hair black. His face round. Dave felt a wave of relief. He had read that if a girl didn't feel love from her father she would look for someone just like her father to love her. He felt liberated. He was trying hard to act natu-rally. He was about to ask what Paul's parents did for a living when he caught Morley sending him daggers. Paul couldn't have cared less. Because, at that moment, Stephanie came bouncing down the stairs and whatever it was Morley was saying was left hanging. Paul turned away from Morley and looked at Stephanie and smiled and said, "Hi."

They went into the living room. Sam appeared, smirking, with a photo album and said, "Do you want to see a picture of Stephanie in a bunny costume at her first ballet class?"

Stephanie glared at her brother. But five minutes later she and Paul were hunched over the album.

"This is me at Hallowe'en," she said.

Sam sighed with disappointment and headed upstairs.

Stephanie and Paul were so involved with each other that the rest of the family might as well have disappeared. Paul didn't even say goodbye to Morley, who was standing at the door as they left. He turned his back to her when Stephanie said something and walked right by her as if she were invisible.

Morley found this reassuring. It made her completely happy.

"Love's young dream," she said "What could be sweeter? That was wonderful."

Dave said, "I don't know. I don't know. I thought he was *too* sincere."

Out on the street Paul had opened the door of his father's car and Stephanie was climbing in.

Morley was watching them through the window in the front door.

"What do you call it?" she said. "That funny feeling when something nice make you sad?"

Stephanie was sitting beside her date now. As the car pulled away from the curb, she was feeling anything but sad.

Feeling excited, nervous, sophisticated, and to her great surprise—comfortable. She felt comfortable beside this boy. It was one of those nights she would always remember.

Morley lingered by the door and blessed her daughter quietly. When she turned, Dave was looking at the bouquet of carnations. Morley looked at him and laughed.

Everyone was so caught up in the moment that no one noticed Sam, who had run upstairs and was in his room. The lights were on, the window open and Sam's naked bum was sticking out into the cold night air. One last shot at his sister.

It was good enough to be alive.

But to be young and alive was very heaven.

Sourdough

Dave spent a frustrating week at the beginning of March trying to find someone who could sell him a box of the plastic discs that snap into the centre of 45 rpm records.

He had bought a lifetime supply of the discs in the early eighties from a manufacturer in Sarnia who was going out of business.

"Just send them all," said Dave, after they had haggled for a while. "I'll pay seventy-five dollars, plus the shipping."

He nearly croaked when the trucker met him in the alley behind his record store, spat, and pointed to the crate in the back of the van. The crate was as big as a refrigerator.

"Are you sure?" asked Dave.

"Sign here," said the trucker.

Dave needed the help of three friends to wrestle the box up to his second-floor storage room. This is stupid, he thought, as they humped the case up the stairs. But when he opened it, he felt pleased. The plastic discs were beautiful. Half of them were bright primary colours: reds, yellows and brilliant blues. The rest were muted tones of pink and brown with swirling tortoise-shell highlights. There were thousands. Dave dug his hands into the box and let them fall through his fingers. He felt rich.

He bought a goldfish bowl at a yard sale and filled it to the brim with the discs and kept it on the counter by the cash register. He let anyone who asked dip in and take as many as they wanted, for free—even people who hadn't bought a record. He figured he would never get rid of them all.

He wasn't figuring on Brian.

Brian is a kid from Saskatchewan who came to Toronto to study film. He collects Hawaiian guitar music, and when he stumbled on the Vinyl Cafe he started hanging around, always on the look-out for Dick Dale albums. Eventually Dave hired Brian. It was Brian who invented the game they called Ringo. The goal of Ringo was to take one of the discs out of the fish bowl and flip in across the counter so it landed on the spinning record turntable. One afternoon, after that had become too easy, Brian arrived with a catapult he had made out of a mousetrap and they took turns shooting the discs at the turntable from the far side of the store. The ultimate goal, never achieved—though not for want of trying—was to drop one onto the six-inch spindle.

The mousetrap ate up a prodigious number of the discs and one day in early March Dave went upstairs and realized he was about to run out. He phoned all over town but no one had any, and no one knew where he could get them. Dave finally found eight of them at one of the big warehouse record stores for $1.50 apiece. He was going to buy all eight until the salesman said, "When these go, there won't be any more coming in"—so Dave left four behind for whoever came looking after him. It was another nail in the coffin of vinyl and it depressed him.

The same week, Dave got a phone call from a woman who works at Sotheby's auction house in London. She calls twice a year to ask if Dave would consider selling some of his collection of rock memorabilia. He didn't want to sell anything, but after she told him some of the prices that things had brought at recent sales, Dave said he'd think about it.

"Phone in a few weeks," he said.

In the late sixties and through the seventies Dave was a technical director for a lot of big groups. Although a lot of them weren't big when he worked with them, some of the people he travelled with became famous. In the storeroom above his record store, where Dave has his now nearly empty crate of discs, is one of the largest collections of rock-and-roll memorabilia in North America.

The day the lady from Sotheby's phoned, Dave went upstairs with Brian after lunch. The storage room was dark. It smelled like a summer porch that had been closed for the winter. Dave flicked on a light switch and bent to pick up a shirt that was lying on the storeroom floor. It was purple.

"Did I ever tell you how Jimi Hendrix got kicked out of Little Richard's band?" he said, as he held up the shirt in front of him.

"He wore this on stage one night." Dave was folding the shirt absent-mindedly. "*No one* wore purple on stage except for Little Richard."

He was looking around for a place to hang the shirt. He dropped it on top of a pile of boxes.

"Little Richard made his comeback right here in Toronto —at that rock-and-roll festival where Lennon played." He wanted to look sharp for that show so he had a mirrored vest made. I have it somewhere."

Dave was standing directly under the bare lightbulb that hung from the ceiling in the middle of his storeroom.

"That's Dylan's set list from the 1965 Newport Jazz Festival," he said. He was pointing to a piece of paper with a handwritten scrawl thumbtacked to a pillar. He reached out for it and knocked a stack of cartons over.

"I don't know why I keep all this stuff. I should sell it."

"Whose guitar?" asked Brian.

"Which one?" said Dave.

"The Saturn," said Brian.

"Hound Dog Taylor's," said Dave.

Brian had the guitar around his neck.

"Did he really have six fingers?" said Brian.

Dave had picked an envelope off the floor.

"You know what this is?" he said.

Brian shook his head.

"This is the film . . . no . . . not the film. These are the negatives from Margaret Trudeau's camera from that weekend with the Rolling Stones."

"What weekend with the Rolling Stones?" said Brian.

"Look at this," said Dave. He was holding a negative up to the light. "This one will never get published."

Brian was fiddling with a cigarette case.

"That belonged to Leonard Cohen," said Dave, slipping the negative back in the envelope.

Brian opened the case.

"Love from *M*," he read. "Who is *M*?"

"Mariannne. Do you like it? You can take it if you want." Dave wanted to get out of there. He was standing by the door, his hand on the light switch.

That night Carl Lowbeer called and asked if Dave could do him a favour. Carl and Gerta live down the street. They were going to Florida for a month. Would Dave look after their sourdough starter while they were gone?

"It needs to be fed," said Carl. "A tablespoon of wheat flour. Once a week. It will only take you a minute or two—no more."

If anyone else in the neighbourhood had phoned with a request like that Dave would have assumed they were joking—but Carl Lowbeer didn't joke. And Dave knew enough about Carl to know that if he had unexpectedly developed a sense of humour it wasn't going to be about his sourdough.

Dave got the story at Polly Anderson's annual Christmas party two years ago. Carl had brought a loaf of his bread to the party and Dave—who had missed lunch and breakfast—was stuffing it, and everything he could lay his hands on, down his throat. Carl materialized out of the crowd and said, "I see you like my bread," and Dave replied, "What? Oh. Yes." And had to stand there, nodding politely, while Carl told him how he got the sourdough starter from his aunt Ola in Germany—how *she* had got the starter from *her* mother, Carl's great-aunt—it had been in the family for over thirty-two years. "My mother used it too," said Carl.

"It's very good," said Dave. And it was, although to be truthful, Dave had been thinking of the bread more as a utensil—to convey great mounds of smoked salmon into his mouth. Until Carl mentioned his bread, Dave hadn't really noticed it.

"I have a genealogy," said Carl. "I could show you if you come over. My great-aunt made the first batch in Staffhausen."

"You have a genealogy?" said Dave, swallowing a mouthful of salmon.

"Of the starter," said Carl. "Like a family tree. I have it in a frame in the den."

"Really?" mumbled Dave, reaching for the eggplant dip with another piece of the bread.

When Carl and Gerta appeared at his house this past Christmas with a loaf of bread, Dave wondered if Carl hadn't misinterpreted his enthusiasm. Dave and Morley hardly knew the Lowbeers. There was a moment of awkwardness when Dave opened the door and saw them standing there. Soon Carl and Gerta were in the kitchen slicing the bread so Morley could try it.

"Umm," said Morley—her mouth full. She was staring at Dave. Is this your fault? Dave shrugged.

The Lowbeers left as abruptly as they had come—declining to eat anything themselves.

"That was weird," said Morley after they had gone, cutting herself another piece of bread. "It's sort of sour—I don't think I like it."

"It's OK," said Dave, without great enthusiasm. Then he added: "It's better with smoked salmon."

The night before he left for Florida, Carl phoned Dave with his instructions.

"Usually," he said, "we take it with us."

"The starter?" said Dave. "On vacation?"

"We took it to Germany last March," said Carl.

"To Germany?" said Dave.

"Gerta carried it in her suitcase. She was going to take it in her purse but she didn't want it to go through the X-ray machine. She was afraid the X-rays might kill the enzymes."

"You took the starter to Germany?" said Dave.

"Last summer we took it to the cottage—but it didn't do well. We had to feed it commercial flour and when we brought it back it was pale . . . out of sorts."

"You took it to the cottage?" said Dave.

"It has done three interprovincial trips and two international ones," said Carl. "Plus a change of planes in Holland."

Carl explained why he didn't want to take the starter to Florida. "What if there's a tornado," he said. "What if the power fails? I don't want to be worrying all the time. It's supposed to be a vacation."

Sourdough

Then he told Dave what he wanted him to do. "The starter is in the fridge. In a Mason jar. There is a bag of wheat flour on the counter beside the fridge. Once a week you put a tablespoon of the flour into the Mason jar. OK?"

"OK," said Dave.

After supper Dave said, "What is starter anyway?"

Morley looked at her husband and shook her head. She said, "Why did he choose you of all people? Doesn't he understand what he is dealing with? The idiot."

Dave didn't press the point.

The next day he went to Wong's Scottish Meat Pies for lunch.

Kenny Wong said, "Making sourdough bread is like making yoghurt. You need something to get it going. When you are making sourdough, you use fermented dough from your last batch of bread. That's the starter. In the pioneer days, when you couldn't run to a corner store for a packet of yeast, sharing a starter was a true act of friendship. You should be honoured."

"He didn't give it to me," said Dave. "He asked me to look after it."

"Still," said Kenny. "If you don't feed it . . . it will . . . you know . . ."

"No," said Dave. "What?"

"It's a living thing. I don't know. If you don't feed it . . . who knows . . . it'll die or something."

Dave's first visit to Carl's house was on Friday. When he got there, he couldn't find the keys and he panicked. Had he lost them? He phoned Morley.

"You never had them," she said. "Remember? Carl was going to leave them under the garbage can."

Dave let himself into Carl's house and found the Mason jar of starter in the fridge. He pried the jar open and peered in. The starter looked like moist oatmeal. The pleasing sour aroma of fermenting yeast wafted up out of the jar and made Dave smile. He looked around for the bag of flour. The kitchen was full of ceramic knick-knacks. The walls were covered with framed sayings, scrolls, tea towels from Germany and Arizona. On the counter was a set of ceramic containers shaped like dogs. They were lined up in descending order of size, each dog with a name tag around its neck: Sugar, Cookies, Tea, Coffee. The kitchen had the feel of a roadside souvenir shop. The flour wasn't on the counter where Carl had promised. There was a brown paper bag by the telephone. It was full of white powder. Dave dumped a spoonful into the starter and put the starter back in the fridge. Then he spent half an hour snooping around the Lowbeers' house.

When Dave got home Morley was in bed, reading. He stood at the end of the bed and got undressed. "All his shirts are ordered by colour," he said as he pulled his sweater over his head. "All the blue ones together, all the white ones." Dave rolled up the sweater and tossed it towards his bureau like a basketball. It landed in the garbage can. He sighed.

Morley said, "You went through his closet?" She kept reading, but she sounded shocked.

"Of course I did," said Dave. "He has two pair of lederhosen. Can you imagine Carl in leather shorts?"

He was using his feet to push his clothes into the pile at the bottom of Morley's closet that serves as a laundry hamper.

"I can't believe you did that," said Morley. She was looking at him over the book. "Two pairs? Really?"

"You know what I found in the bathroom?" said Dave.

Morley put her book down on the bed beside her. She was sitting up. Looking at him.

The next Friday when Dave went to feed the starter he thought maybe it didn't smell quite the same as it did the week before but it was hard to tell. He didn't want to touch it with his fingers, so he got a fork and poked at it. He decided it was just his imagination. He put another spoonful of the flour into the jar like before and went into the den to look at Carl's books.

The third Friday he went directly to Carl's on his way home from work. He was feeling good—happy because on Saturday he was leaving with Morley and the kids for Montreal. They were going to St. Sauver in the Laurentian mountains for a long weekend ski trip. He was going to feed the starter and go home and pack. He fished the jar out of the fridge and gasped when he opened it.

He ran to the phone.

Morley answered on the third ring.

"The starter," said Dave. "The starter."

"Who is this?" said Morley.

"It's me," said Dave. "I'm at Carl's. Something is wrong with the starter."

Something was terribly wrong with the starter. Instead of a bowl of moist oatmeal it looked hard and dry.

"And white," said Dave. "It's all dried up. I think it's dead."

"You sound like you are reporting a murder."

"I am," said Dave. "It's dead. It smells."

"It's supposed to smell," said Morley.

"Not like this," said Dave. "It smells horrible. Like chemicals. Like a jar of solid smog. It smells like death. What am I supposed to do?"

When Morley arrived it took her less than a minute to figure out what had gone wrong.

"This is what you have been feeding it?" she said, holding up the brown paper bag Dave had found by the phone.

"Yes," said Dave.

"Polyfilla," said Morley.

"Polyfilla?" said Dave.

"That's what it says here on the bag," said Morley.

It was written neatly in Gerta's handwriting.

Dave sat down and stared out the kitchen window.

The Lowbeers were due home Sunday evening. "What am I going to do?" said Dave.

"I don't know, but it's going to be interesting," said Morley. She was standing by the counter opening the dog containers. "She has brown sugar in the Coffee dog."

Later that night Morley was standing in her bedroom trying to stuff an extra ski sweater into one of the kids' suitcases.

"You're leaving," said Dave. "No matter what—right?"

"Right," she said.

"Right," said Dave.

He went downstairs and stared at the phone. Ten minutes later he called Kenny Wong.

"I think I have a recipe for sourdough starter," said Kenny.

"I'm coming over," said Dave.

When Dave got to Kenny's restaurant, Kenny was waiting for him with a book, a bottle of buttermilk, a hair dryer and a bottle of Scotch.

"We've got to get going," he said. "I found the recipe. It takes three days to make sourdough starter."

"We've only got two," said Dave.

"That's what the hair dryer is for," said Kenny.

When they got to Carl's, Kenny rubbed his hands together and said, "First things first." He started opening cupboards until he found the glasses. He poured two big tumblers of Scotch and propped his cookbook open on the kitchen counter. It was called: *Cooking Wizardry for Kids—Learn about Food while Making Tasty Things to Eat.*

Kenny smiled and held up his Scotch.

"I get all my best stuff from this book," he said.

"You can't be serious," said Dave.

There was a moment of silence. Kenny and Dave stared deep into each other's eyes.

By three in the morning Dave and Kenny were anything but serious. They were still at step one of the recipe— waiting for a cup of buttermilk to warm and collect bacteria from the kitchen air, as the recipe called for, in the natural old-fashioned way. Kenny had the hair dryer set up to blow over the buttermilk.

"Like forcing a tulip," he said.

The bottle of Scotch was half-killed. Dave had discovered the Lowbeers' polka records. Kenny was wearing one of Gerta Lowbeer's aprons. There was a mop lying on the kitchen counter.

"Tired, my dear?" said Kenny to the mop.

"It must be time to add the flour," he said. "I figure six hours under a hair dryer is the same as three days in a warm place. What do you think?" He was still talking to the mop.

Dave was sitting on the floor. His head was in his hands. He was staring into the distance. He was remembering the disdain in Carl Lowbeer's voice when he had told him about the Rutenbergs. "We gave them some of the starter because they said they wanted to bake bread too. They killed it within six months. They are fools."

"I'm dead," said Dave.

They finished at ten on Sunday morning. Kenny had slept in the Lowbeers' bed, Dave on the living-room couch.

When they left, the sourdough was bubbling like a pot of oatmeal.

"It looks sort of the same. It smells right—but it didn't bubble like that," said Dave

"It will slow down in the fridge," said Kenny.

"And there is more than there used to be—there was only half that much," said Dave

Kenny picked up the Mason jar and scooped half of the new sourdough into the garbage.

"How's that," he said. "Does that look about right?"

The Lowbeers arrived home on Sunday as planned. Dave flew to Montreal before they arrived and joined his family in St. Sauveur. When they got home on Tuesday night there was a loaf of bread and a note from Carl on the back porch:

You certainly looked after the starter.
Thanks for everything

"He knows," said Dave. "He must."
"That's just Carl," said Morley.

Dave wasn't so sure. He gave Carl a wide berth for the next few weeks. They didn't rub shoulders again until the first neighbourhood barbecue, on the long weekend in May.

Dave was at the condiment table looking at the buns when Jim Scoffield leaned against him and whispered conspiratorially, "Aren't you going to have one of Carl's sourdough buns?"

"What do you mean?" said Dave nervously. *Did everyone know?*

Jim rolled his eyes.

"Carl just gave me his bread lecture. Do you know he has a framed genealogy in his den?"

Dave felt relief wash through him. "Did he tell you about his aunt in Germany?" he asked.

Jim nodded.

Dave smiled. "He's a bit much," he said, "but I like his bread."

Dave picked out one of Carl's buns from the bowl on the

picnic table. He wandered over to the grill, got a hamburger and then looked around the yard. Carl was standing near the fence, a hot dog in his hand. He was alone.

Dave waved and headed over.

Music Lessons

The problem of Sam's piano lessons began with his Christmas report card. The music teacher, Mrs. Crouch, wrote: "Sam has an unselfconscious sense of rhythm. It appears to come from inside him."

"What does that mean?" said Dave. He was sitting in the kitchen reading the report. 'It appears to come from inside him.' Where else would it come from? Is Mrs. Crouch the one with the crystal?"

"I think she means it's a gift," said Morley.

In February, at parent-teacher night, Mrs. Crouch sought *them* out. "Do you know he has perfect pitch?" she asked.

Morley smiled. It wasn't so much *what* Mrs. Crouch was telling her—just to have a teacher say nice things about *her* child was good enough. Morley didn't want her to stop.

"The other day in choir," said Mrs. Crouch, "he started to sing the descant quietly to himself. I just happened to catch it as I walked by. Most of the Grade Sixes can't do that."

Morley nodded earnestly.

By the time they got home, however, her joy had been sideswiped by a spasm of guilt. Sam was eight years old, and they hadn't done a thing to encourage this musical talent. When Stephanie was eight, she was taking piano *and* dance lessons. What if Sam did have a gift? Morley felt as if she had been asleep at the switch.

She knew from her years in the theatre that every time you see a great artist stand up on stage and perform, there is another person standing beside them. Usually it's a teacher or a parent. All great artists need a support system. Someone who believes in what they have to offer.

She had done absolutely nothing for Sam.

That night Morley dreamed she was in the audience at a symphony concert. In the middle of her dream the conductor abruptly snapped his baton in two and hurled it on the stage. The hall fell deadly quiet, and the conductor swivelled around and looked at Morley. *Someone*, he boomed, glancing back angrily at the orchestra, *has to leave the stage*.

Morley noticed, for the first time, that the musicians were playing vegetables. Then she saw Sam push his way through the middle of the leafy greens. He was waving a large eggplant over his head. "How do you expect me to play the eggplant," he said, "when I've only ever been given potatoes." Then he left the stage, passing the cucumbers with his head hanging down. As he went, Morley noticed that the entire root section was having dental work done as they played.

When she woke up, Morley said, "I am going to get Sam a potato—I mean piano—teacher.

She knew what had gone wrong. Stephanie had kicked up such a fuss about her piano lessons that she had worn Morley down. It wasn't fair. Sam deserved his own chance.

He started lessons at the beginning of March with the only piano teacher in the neighbourhood who had space to take him. His name was Ray Spinella, and he only had one arm. He wasn't the teacher Morley wanted, but she wanted to get Sam going. Everyone said the best teacher around was Brian Merriman. But Brian Merriman would not take Sam until September, and only if Sam could get his Grade One first. He suggested a month at a music camp. Camp Dutoit is good, he said.

The problem was that Sam didn't want to go to Camp Dutoit to get his Grade One piano. Sam wanted to go to the Lazy M Ranch and learn to ride a horse.

Dave said Sam should go to the horse camp. Summers are for fun, he said. But Morley found herself uncharacteristically muddled. She was sure Sam *would* have fun at Camp Dutoit once he got there. But she didn't want to send him against his will. Morley thought perhaps if she gave him some time, a few weeks of lessons, maybe he would change his mind. The danger was, if she gave him too much time, there wouldn't be a spot left for Sam at either camp. So she sent a deposit to both of them. She thought things would be clear by the time the bulk of the fees were due. Well the bulk of the fees were now due, and things were no clearer. The forms from both camps were sitting on Morley's desk. And if she didn't choose one and get the cheque in the mail soon, Sam would not be going to either camp. Morley thought of sending money to both camps—to give her a few more weeks. But she knew that was crazy. And if she did that, one day she would have to tell Dave. As much as you'd want to keep that sort of behaviour to yourself, it would be difficult—like having an affair—and eventually you'd just blurt it out.

On Thursday Dave's sister, Annie, phoned from the airport. She said, "I just got into town. I'm recording some sort of, I don't know, thing. Tonight. I'm flying back tomorrow morning—early. Are you free for lunch?"

Annie lives in Halifax. She plays in the string section of Symphony Nova Scotia.

Morley said, "I'd love to have lunch."

They met in a large formal dining room, on the top floor of a downtown department store.

Music has always been a big part of Dave's and his sister's lives. It is no accident that Annie plays in the symphony and that Dave owns a record store and spent all those years working in rock-and-roll.

Dave's and Annie's father, Charlie, loved music. There was no money for music lessons when Charlie was a kid—but as an adult, he taught himself to play the piano, and then, during the dark Cape Breton winter nights, the double bass. When Dave and Annie were growing up they were constantly surrounded by music. Nearly every morning, when it was time to get the kids out of bed, Charlie would sing them awake. He would make up lyrics about the day ahead, the things they were going to do. He used tunes that drove them crazy, like "Hello Dolly":

"Hello math test
This is Dave, math test
It's so nice to have a test
On Tuesday morn—

Come on Davey. Up and at 'em!"

Or, "Big Spender":

"The minute you walked in the room
I could tell you were a real cool fraction
Math-a-maction!
Numerator hangs out over the line
How'd you like to come and be reduced some time?"

What Charlie loved most were the nights when friends came over to the house and made music with him. He used to send away to a store in New York City for sheet music. He would hand out the music a week before his get-togethers so people could practise. Anyone was welcome as long as they could play something, which made for weird combinations of instruments. A trio made up of a recorder, double bass and trumpet. Charlie was inevitably the worst player in these bands because, although he loved music, he had absolutely no sense of rhythm and a very unusual sense of pitch. So the guy on the recorder and the guy on the trumpet would be playing away, and Charlie would lumber along on his bass about twenty yards behind them. Charlie was often still playing when the others got to the end of the piece. When Charlie finally played his last note, his friend Fred, who regularly showed up to play the piano, would say, "Well, we won that one, Charlie." They had a great time.

Dave and Annie both began piano lessons the autumn they turned six. They studied with the only piano teacher in Big Narrows, Sister Emilienne, at the convent of the Sisters of St. Seriah.

Sister Emilienne came from Pointe Verte on the south shore of the Baie de Chaleur. She was French, but she could speak English, and Annie thought she was the nicest, kindest woman in the world.

Sister Emilienne's studio, with the wainscoting and the two pianos, was the closest to religion that Annie and Dave ever got. It was so ordered and quiet in that room that it lent a sense of mystery and sanctity to music.

Sister Emilienne had names for all the notes on the piano. Mrs. Treble Clef with her tightly folded skirt; Mr. Bass Clef with two buttons on his shirt. When Dave was having trouble with B flat, Sister Emilienne drew little bumble bees wherever Dave was supposed to play a B flat. "Press hard," she said. "Make the Bee flat." In one lesson, the B became his best note. He became very attached to the B.

Sister Emilienne would sit on the piano bench as they played and as she listened her head would tilt to the right. She would smile and nod and tilt over—just like the nuns in *The Sound of Music*.

Annie adored her.

One spring she went on a school trip to Quebec City and she brought Sister Emilienne back a snowglobe from Ste. Anne de Beaupré. It was a little plastic globe the size of a baseball with a miniature model of the shrine inside. The globe was filled with water, and when you shook it little white flecks floated in the water and made it look like it was snowing.

"Oh, look," said Sister Emilienne, when she opened her present, "When I shake it, look how the angels fly around the shrine." She put it on a special shelf in her studio.

Every lesson Annie would head off determined to find out if Sister Emilienne had any hair under her wimple, or if, as Dave had earnestly told her, she was as bald as a bowling ball. Annie was forever touching Sister Emilienne's long graceful robes. There seemed to be so many mysterious layers. Sometimes she would reach out and touch one of the crosses that hung around her neck.

Sometimes when she came home from her lessons, Annie would dress up in her mother's skirts and put on some of her old jewellery. Margaret would sit patiently at the piano, and Annie would give her mother a piano lesson. Put your thumb on the C, she would say, and Margaret would put her thumb on the D beside middle C, and say, This one?

Piano seemed to come naturally to Annie. She was playing Bach the first year she began her lessons. And maybe

Sister Emilienne was right. Maybe she could play better than any six-year-old in the country.

Indeed, the summer after she began her lessons, Annie was chosen to play for Queen Elizabeth when she came to Halifax.

The recital was on the lawn of the citadel. They set up a stage and a yellow and white awning for shade. Annie was sitting two rows behind the Queen, and she saw her yawn while the choir was singing "Farewell to Nova Scotia." To this day Annie can remember watching the Queen yawn and deciding that playing Bach was not a really good idea. Thinking that the Queen had probably already heard Bach, Annie decided it would be better if she made something up. When they called her name, she walked onto the stage in her new smocked dress, her white socks and her black shoes. She sat at the piano, and when she began to play she was making the notes up out of her head. If someone had not come and dragged her off the stage she would have sat there for ever—entertaining the Queen—completely confident that her tune was far superior to the piece by Bach that she had been practising for weeks.

One day, when Annie was seven, Charlie invited a fiddler to the house to play with him, and when Annie saw his violin, she fell in love with it. She had never been so close to a violin before. She loved the way it looked, and the smell of the rosin and the rich colours of the wood—and she adored the sound. When they finished playing, she asked her father if she could touch the violin.

The day Annie began her violin lessons was the most exciting day of her life. She came home from her first class and ripped open her violin case. She made the whole family listen to what she could do. She could play all four open strings: E, A, D and G. She had her mother call the notes to her and she would play them. She couldn't believe how easy it was.

The next week her teacher taught her to put down her first finger, and she could play A and B on one string. That was a very big deal.

She wanted to learn how to read notes.

"Just show me where they are," she said. Pretty soon she was able to play small pieces, with the teacher playing along. She was a violinist. It was brilliant.

It made Charlie extraordinarily happy to watch his daughter. But Annie didn't notice. Because it made her happier.

Eventually she got to a whole different level and playing the violin became work. She did what lots of kids do: she pretended to practise. She would shut the door to her room and set up a book on her music stand. She would play random notes and read her book as she played—she raced through *Anne of Green Gables* this way—and when her mother called from the kitchen, "That doesn't sound like practising to me," Annie would call back, saying she was sight reading.

But she kept at it. And if you keep at anything long enough the work adds up. She went to McGill University and studied music. When she graduated, she got a job with the Montreal String Quartet. It was a wonderful honour for a young musician—playing with three great musicians, all of them at least a decade older than her—but she felt incomplete. She wasn't having fun. Everyone was so intense. And earnest.

Annie had thought that when she got out of school playing music would be fun again.

One day, a friend who knew the famous Israeli violinist Avi Stovman said, He takes students, you know. If you want to write him you can mention my name. So Annie wrote. And to her great shock Avi Stovman called her back.

She came home from a rehearsal one afternoon and her roommate said, "You are not going to believe who called today."

When she called him back, he said, "Send me a tape." So she made a tape and sent it to him. But he didn't respond. She waited for a month and never heard a word. She thought, The tape was horrible. She decided he was laughing so hard, he couldn't make it to the telephone. Her friends said, "Phone him back." And one night after a big spaghetti dinner, when they had drunk two bottles of Mateus, her boyfriend dragged her to the telephone and dialled Avi Stovman's number. He handed her the phone and held her to the wall to make her talk to the great violinist.

When Stovman answered, he said, "I've been going to the post office every day. Where is your tape?"

It had been lost in the mail.

He said, "There is nothing I can do . . . I only take seven students and already my class is full."

Annie decided he had listened to the tape and it was dreadful and he was just being polite. But her friends didn't let her quit. They said, "Go to New York and phone him when you get there. Play for him."

In April, her boyfriend forced her into a car, and they set off for New York City. They drove until after midnight, following Highway Nine along the valley of the Hudson River. The next morning when they stopped for breakfast in Hastings on the Hudson, Pete Seeger walked by them on their way to the café. Her boyfriend said, "It's an omen." They were in Manhattan just after noon. The idea was Annie would make a casual phone call and then go and play for Avi Stovman.

She called him from outside a bookstore on the corner of 52nd and 7th.

He said, "Where are you? You sound like you're around the corner." Annie said, "I am around the corner."

She was standing on one foot and then the other, not looking at her boyfriend who was watching from inside the bookstore.

Stovman said, "Come on over. I am leaving tomorrow morning at eight o'clock. But you can come tonight and play for me."

"That's OK," Annie replied. "I don't think it's a very good time." Then she said goodbye, and hung up. Her music career was over. She didn't have what it took. She broke up with her boyfriend on the way home—at a gas station in Poughkeepsie.

Three months later Annie told the whole story to the viola player in the Montreal String Quartet. It turned out that this women knew Stovman's assistant. They had studied together.

"You're crazy," she said. "I'm going to phone Ruth. You are going to play for Stovman when he comes to Montreal."

Stovman remembered the girl who didn't send the tape and didn't come to play. He was interested enough to see if she would show up on her third chance. He said, "All right. When I am in Montreal, if she wants, she can come and she can play and I will listen."

Annie went to the Ritz Carlton Hotel and knocked on his door nervously. He was playing with the Montreal Symphony that night. It was four in the afternoon, and he was sitting in his room watching *MASH* on television.

Annie warmed up in the bathroom. She thought she sounded OK. But when she came out to play for him, a strange thing happened. She put her bow on the strings and she couldn't hear anything.

She stopped, and Stovman looked at her and said, "What's wrong? Keep playing." So she started again, but she still couldn't hear the music. When she finished, she didn't have a clue what she had done. It could have been the same random notes she played for the Queen.

Stovman said, "Is that a favourite piece?"

Annie just stared at him—horrified at what had just happened. In the middle of this long silence, Annie realized Stovman was looking for a nice way to get rid of her. So she said, "Maybe it's not a good idea that I come to New York."

She was trying to help him out.

"What?" he snapped. "Do you think you won't learn anything? You think you have nothing to learn? Of course you have to come to New York. I'm just trying to think how we're going to get you started."

And that was that.

To help pay for the lessons in New York, Annie got a job playing at Radio City Music Hall. She did the *Liza Minnelli*

Show. She had to wear a sequinned gown even though the orchestra was in the pit because at every show there was a moment when the pit was raised. The orchestra would rise up above the centre of the stage. They would play a number as they hovered in the air and then they would drop out of sight again.

Some of the people had been in the pit for over a decade. They hated what they were doing, but they didn't leave because it was a good job and steady. One night Annie watched the trombone player filling out his income tax form during the show—putting down his pen and picking up his trombone without missing a cue.

Stovman had an apartment on Riverside Drive, in the same building as Pinchas Zukerman and Itzhak Perlman. Perlman lived on the top floor in the apartment where Babe Ruth used to live.

Once, while she was warming up, Annie played a reel, and Stovman screamed at her. Don't play like that in here, he said. The accompanist told Annie Stovman was harder on her than any of his other pupils. That made her happy. She stayed two years.

When she left she got a job with the Boston Symphony. She got married six months later. She thought she had everything she ever wanted.

But life with the orchestra didn't seem to suit Annie. She found the program was repetitive, and when the conductor did choose new pieces to perform, they were seldom things Annie wanted to play. After rehearsals and performances, the younger members would sometimes gather at each other's apartments for a glass of wine, but invariably the talk would return to the same tired complaints—the lousy salaries, the long hours, the lack of opportunity. Annie had the job she had always wanted, but she couldn't find any joy in it.

Then the first violinist left the orchestra and the undercurrent of rivalry that Annie had always suspected was there burst into the open. The woman in the chair beside Annie suddenly stopped talking to her, and it didn't take long for Annie to learn that the woman had tried to undercut her—had actually complained to the conductor that she was tired of carrying Annie, that Annie always played off tempo.

When her marriage began to fall apart, she decided she had had enough. She quit the orchestra and moved back to Nova Scotia with her daughter, Margot.

Stovman was furious. He wrote her a blistering three-page letter. "What are you trying to do to me?" he wrote. *To him?* thought Annie. What am I doing to him? Oddly the letter made her feel better about her decision. She took a contract with Symphony Nova Scotia. She also joined a Celtic group. Suddenly music was fun again.

Morley knew much of this, but she hadn't heard all of it before, not all at once. They were eating dessert when she told Annie about Sam's piano lessons and what his teacher, Mrs. Crouch, had said about him. She explained her plan to send Sam to music camp, so he could study with Brian Merriman.

Annie said, "Brian Merriman is a prissy snob. I thought Sam already had a music teacher? You said he is having fun with the guy."

On Thursday when Morley took Sam to his piano lesson she asked if she could stay and watch. Ray Spinella, the one-armed teacher, looked surprised but delighted. "You could sit over there," he said.

Morley did her best to disappear. She needn't have bothered. Ray and Sam were soon utterly absorbed by the music. Morley noticed that Ray obviously wasn't following a method. And he wasn't teaching the Grade One syllabus.

At the end of the lesson Ray had Sam make up a tune, then he took a trumpet off the top of the piano, stood beside her son and began to play along. Sam smiled at his teacher, Ray nodded and they both kept going.

On the way home Morley said, "When you're at camp do you think they'll give you your own horse or do you have to share it?"

Sam said, "I think you have to share. But I'm going to save up and buy my own horse. I'm going to call him Bach. Ray is going to teach me some of the cowboy songs that Bach wrote. Can I do piano next year?"

"We'll see," said Morley.

Sam had his face pressed to the car window. He was whistling the tune that he had just made up. The tune he and Ray had been playing together.

Morley smiled.

Spring

Burd

Early on a Saturday morning in May, Dave slipped out of his house while his family was still asleep. He was wearing a faded green sweatshirt, jeans with a rip at the right knee and sneakers with no laces. He hadn't shaved. He closed the door carefully behind him so he wouldn't wake anyone and surveyed his backyard. The morning light was soft and silky, lending a yellow wash to the greenery of the garden. But Dave was more interested in the hedge in the shadows than he was in the rest of the garden. He stared at the hedge for a few minutes and then he walked towards the bird feeder in the centre of his backyard. When he got to the feeder, he stood on his toes and peered over the lip. There was a yoghurt lid in the far corner. He brushed the seeds away from the edge of the lid. Then he picked it up and carried it carefully to the picnic table by the fence. He dumped the contents of the lid onto the table and sat down. He was looking at a pile of meal worms about the size of a hockey puck. He frowned as he pushed at them with his finger. He counted the worms carefully . . . thirty-three, thirty-four, thirty-five, thirty-six. The exact number he had put out the night before when he came home from work.

"Damn," he said. He shovelled the worms onto the ground with the lid. One of them landed in the V between two planks on the seat. He tried to pick it out and then, thinking he might squish it, he went back inside and got a pencil and used it to work the worm carefully along the groove. He didn't want squished worm on his hands.

He went back inside, made coffee, and took the newspaper upstairs to bed. Arthur, the dog, who was splayed out on the couch, opened one eye and watched him pass and then fell back to sleep.

Dave and Morley gave the bird feeder to Stephanie last Christmas. Who knows? They thought it might distract her—get her involved in the greater world around her. It was an unqualified failure. When she opened it on Christmas morning, Stephanie squinted at the bird feeder, frowned, then checked the gift tag to see if she had opened the wrong present.

"Is this a mistake?" she asked, without a trace of enthusiasm.

So it was Dave who ended up assembling the feeder and Dave who filled it each day. Every day through the dark mornings of January and February when the snow and ice was piled up in all the provinces, it was Dave who beat the path from the back door to the bird feeder on the pole in the centre of his backyard.

At first the only birds interested in his efforts were a thuggish gang of sparrows. They flung Dave's birdseed onto the ground, where it was pecked over by a bunch of pigeons. The pigeons had begun to hang out under the bird feeder like a squad of squeegee kids.

"It's more like a shelter for the homeless than a bird feeder," said Morley.

The only member of the family who displayed any real passion for the arrival of the feeder was the cat. Galway spent hours perched on the kitchen radiator, her face against the back window, her tail twitching in frustrated concentration. There were not only birds to lust after, but squirrels too.

The squirrels appeared on Boxing Day, an hour after Dave got the feeder up. They spent the week between Christmas and New Year trying to shinny around the squirrel guard. They would get halfway up the pole and then drop to the ground like plates of china. One by one they gave up—leaving the only squirrel who was not a quitter. If anything, its determination grew. Having failed from below, it shifted strategy and began hurling itself at the feeder from rooftops, the fence, a tree and Dave's television antenna.

Dave would be washing the dishes and there would be a blur of grey in his peripheral vision and he would turn just in time to see the squirrel ricochet off the barbecue. Galway studied each of its attempts with the intensity of a general studying military history.

One afternoon Dave and Galway watched the squirrel haul itself, upside down, along the clothesline—paw over paw to within a few feet of the feeder before it lost its grip, hung from the line for a moment by one leg like a doomed mountain climber, and let go, its tail flailing in the air as it tried to right itself for landing. As it dropped, Galway, who was sitting in Dave's lap, dug her claws into his leg. Dave flew out of the chair, unsure if Galway's reflex was in sympathy for the squirrel or out of the forlorn realization that this too was a lost opportunity.

"Wouldn't it be simpler," said Morley one lunchtime as the squirrel bounced off their compost bin, "to take the winter off? Isn't hibernation an option?"

In the new year, Dave added a blue jay and a junko, and then a gang of chickadees and some birds who seemed to be travelling with them. But the vast flocks he had imagined filling his backyard were avoiding it. Short of amusing the cat, the feeder seemed to be filling no real need in the universe—and certainly none in the bird universe.

Then on a chilly grey Saturday in the middle of the month, something came. Dave pointed it out to everyone at lunch.

"Over there," he said. "See. In the Lowbeers' pine tree."

No one was particularly interested.

It was not a big bird—not as big as a robin—with olive green above its wings and a dull yellow below. It seemed to favour the evergreen hedge that bordered their backyard. It would flick out of this thicket, and peck at the seeds in the feeder tray, then vanish into the hedge again.

Dave watched it for a week before he asked Gerta Lowbeer

if she knew what kind of bird it was. Gerta brought her three bird books and her binoculars over. She said, "It looks like a tanager. A female summer tanager. But a summer tanager is not supposed to come this far north."

Gerta's finger was moving along the small print of her bird book. "In January a summer tanager is supposed to be on a beach in Mexico or Brazil."

Dave was watching his bird through Gerta's binoculars. He had never seen it so close. It had a stubby bill, almost swollen—not pointy like a robin's.

"And it shouldn't eat seeds," said Gerta. "A tanager eats insects and wasps. It's a carnivore."

When Gerta left, Dave put out a few pieces of tangerine. The sort of thing you might expect to eat if you were used to wintering in Brazil. Then he drove to a pet store to see if he could buy his bird some insects and wasps. He settled for a bag of crickets.

The bird fell on the crickets like she hadn't seen a decent meal in months. That bird was starving, thought Dave. For two hours straight, she flicked back and forth from the hedge like windshield wipers. But as happy as she seemed with the crickets, Dave could see that they weren't going down easily. She was having trouble with the shells.

It was now quarter to six.

Dave returned to the pet store and came back with a bag of meal worms. He set them on the counter and wondered how he was going to get them to the feeder. The idea of dipping his hands into the seething bag revolted him. He tried a pair of Morley's oven mitts, but they were too large and clumsy to work with. He imagined sucking them up with the turkey baster, and experimented with the barbecue tongs. He settled on the flour scoop.

The bird didn't stop eating until 9:30 that night. She is going to be sick, thought Dave.

Then he looked at his nearly empty bag of meal worms and thought, I'm going to be eaten out of house and home by a bird.

He went back to the pet store first thing in the morning.

When he came home at supper only half the worms he had put out that morning were eaten. The rest were frozen to the feeder.

It only took a few days for the bird to train Dave.

By the end of the week they had worked out a routine they could both live with. A scoop of worms at breakfast, a scoop of fresh worms at lunch and a scoop of worms at dinner. It meant Dave had to come home at noon.

"I don't mind," he said.

And he didn't. He would fix soup and cheese, or a sandwich, and would sit at the table and watch his bird through the sliding glass doors that led out to the backyard.

She was not a spectacular bird—she didn't have the blood reds of a cardinal or the rich yellows of a fall warbler. On dull days she almost looked dingy. But in some lights, she was beautiful. If the sun was low and the light warm, she would glow, like there was a reddy hue to her. Almost gold.

Usually she spent only a moment or two on the feeder, preferring, it seemed, to eat her worms in the obscurity of the hedge, but one sunny afternoon she sat on the feeder for nearly five minutes looking around and singing softly.

Dave knew that if Gerta was right, the bird would die if he stopped feeding it. By February he had bought so many meal worms that the pet store was giving him a discount. He felt a sense of pride about what he was doing—he felt honoured that the bird had chosen him.

It was not long after Valentine's Day when Gerta mentioned the bird to her friend Nick who, she said, was a bit of a birder. She brought Nick over that evening so he could see it for himself. Nick watched for half an hour and said, "I'm not sure, do you mind if I call my friend Bob?"

Bob was there in less than an hour. He was wearing camouflage pants and a heavy sweater with a high neck. He was carrying a pair of binoculars in a canvas shoulder sack. He took one look at Dave's bird and asked if he could borrow the telephone. He didn't even use his binoculars.

"I'm phoning from Toronto," he said into the phone. He was excited, his right foot bouncing up and down.

"I'm in some guy's kitchen." He smiled at Dave, then he looked at him quizzically. "About fifteen minutes from downtown. Right?"

Dave nodded.

"You aren't going to believe this," he said into the phone. "*Summer* tanager."

When he hung up, he turned and smiled at Dave and Sam.

"That's the bird of the winter you've got there." He pulled out *his* bird book—*The National Geographic Book of Birds*—

and flipped it open and pointed at the page. Dave peered at the picture and nodded.

The man said, "There are a few of my friends who would love to see it. Would that be OK?"

Morley came home at 7:00.

"Guess what we have in the backyard," said Sam.

"What?" said Morley, throwing groceries on the kitchen counter.

Sam looked at Dave.

"What?" said Morley.

"The bird in the backyard," said Dave. "The one I've been feeding worms . . ."

"It's COSMIC," said Sam.

"It's a summer tanager," said Dave.

That night as Morley was brushing her teeth, Dave said, "Some people might drop by in the morning."

"Who?" said Morley.

"To look at the bird," said Dave.

"What bird?" said Morley.

"The bird I feed the meal worms to," said Dave. "It's supposed to winter in Brazil."

"It chose our backyard over Brazil?"

"So people want to see it," said Dave, "because it's a rarity. It'll be OK. These are birders we're talking about—nice people."

"I don't want people poking around our backyard in the morning," said Morley. "Can't they wait until the weekend?"

It was so early that the sun wasn't up the next morning when Dave heard the noise. He listened for a moment and then he thought, Raccoons. And he went back to sleep.

When he woke the second time, Arthur was beside the bed, whinging—padding to the window and back again. Raccoons aren't that noisy, thought Dave dimly. Then it dawned on him: someone was stealing the bikes. He leapt out of bed and opened the curtains and squinted into the backyard. There was a smudge of grey on the horizon. When his eyes finally focused, he gasped and stepped back from the window and said, "Sweet Jesus on a bicycle."

There were maybe fifty motionless men lined up in the shadows behind his house—strung out along the alley, leaning over his back fence and scanning his backyard with large binoculars. Dave inched forward and peeked out again. Then he pulled the curtains shut and sat on the edge of his bed.

"Houston," he said softly, "we have a problem."

Morley mumbled and rolled over. Dave said, "Don't wake up. I need a plan before you wake up."

He wasn't saying these things out loud. He was saying these things in his head. It was the closest he had come to prayer since last Christmas morning when he defrosted the turkey with the hair dryer.

He needed to wake up. Coffee, he said, prayerfully.

It was only when Dave was downstairs, standing in the middle of the brightly lit kitchen, scratching, that the enormity of his problem struck him. As far as the fifty men in his backyard were concerned, he was standing on a spot-lit stage. He stopped scratching. Then he turned the kitchen light off.

It was 6:45 a.m.

Fifteen minutes later Sam's clock radio snapped on. Here we go, thought Dave. Lift-off. He was sitting at the kitchen table, not sure what he should do. Before he could do anything the phone rang. It was Carl Lowbeer.

"Dave," he said. He was whispering. "There is something terrible going on outside."

Not as terrible, however, as what was going on at the Turlington's. Two doors down—at the Turlingtons' house—Mary, Bert and the Turlington twins were lying on the floor of Mary and Bert's bedroom, with their hands over the heads.

At 6:55 a.m. one of the twins had looked out *her* bedroom window to see if it was good snowball snow. When she saw the men with the binoculars she had run to her parents' bed and said, "The house is surrounded by police. I think it's the *swap* team."

Bert, who is not what you'd call a morning person, nearly stroked out when he saw the men in the dark jackets with their binoculars trained at his kids' window. The first thing he thought about were the carpet installers who were accidentally shot dead through their motel room door by over-zealous police in the Eastern Townships of Quebec. It was a case of mistaken identity—as this obviously was too. Bert dropped to the floor and crawled around his house, waking everyone up.

"We're surrounded," he said. "Get into our bedroom. Fast."

And now the whole family was there except for Bert's fifteen-year-old son, Adam, who had locked himself into the upstairs bathroom. Bert wormed his way into the hall and pounded on the door.

"What are you doing?" he howled.

Adam, who had never gotten up so fast in his life, was desperately trying to flush the first marijuana he had ever bought down the toilet. He had bought it three weeks ago from a kid at school. Afraid to smoke it, he had hidden it in an old pair of sneakers in the back of his cupboard. Now the marijuana kept floating to the top of the toilet. And the police were here to arrest him.

Bert inched his way back to the bedroom and pulled himself up to the window to peer over the sill. There were cars everywhere—parked on both sides of the street and pulled up onto the sidewalk. Bert's heart was pounding. There were men who looked like they were carrying telescopes running down Dave's driveway towards his backyard.

High-powered rifles, thought Bert.

The Lowbeers' dog was barking.

A man came running out of Dave's yard and pointed directly at Bert's house. Bert gasped and dropped to the floor.

"Blessed Mother of Mercy," he said. "We are going to die."

Twenty minutes later, Dave was still trying to explain things to the neighbours standing on his lawn.

"It was announced on some birders' hotline," Dave was saying, when there was a sudden commotion at the Turlingtons' house.

Dave stopped talking and everyone turned just as the Turlingtons' front door flew open and the entire Turlington family burst out of the house. They had wrapped themselves in a large white sheet and were moving down their sidewalk like a bunch of Shriners in a horse costume. They all had their heads low, even Bert, who was leading the way, waving his hands in the air and screaming at the same time.

"Don't shoot," he was saying. "Don't shoot."

Arthur, sitting at Dave's side, began to bark furiously and pull on his leash.

That night at 11:30 Dave was standing on a ladder in his kitchen—tacking a sheet over the sliding glass door in the kitchen.

"It'll be over soon," he said to Morley. "There can't be that many birders in the city."

The phone rang at midnight.

Dave and Morley stared at each other.

Dave picked it up.

"Who was it?" said Morley

"Some guy from Halifax asking if the bird is still here."

"Halifax," said Morley.

"He said he'd be up on the weekend. He said he heard it was a mega-twitch."

The next morning Arthur began barking at 6:30. When Dave opened the door to pick up the paper, two men passed him on their way down his driveway towards his backyard.

"Morning," they said, in unison.

"Morning," said Dave.

It rained on Friday. One of those unpleasant February rain-storms.

When Dave lifted the sheet in the kitchen to look outside,

there was a group of seven men standing in his driveway staring back at him balefully. They were looking at his coffee. He let the sheet drop. "It's not my fault it's raining," he muttered.

Saturday morning at 9:30 when Dave came downstairs, there were already fifteen people outside. Sam was heading out the front door with a hammer and a large piece of cardboard.

"Where are you going?" said Dave.

Sam stopped. As he flipped his sign over, he dropped the hammer. SEE THE BURD it said in large hand-painted letters. Under the writing there was an arrow which Dave assumed would soon point down his driveway.

"We're going to sell hot chocolate," said Sam.

By ten o'clock there were close to a hundred people milling around Dave's house. Arthur was beside himself. He spent the morning throwing himself around the house, barking from window to window. By eleven o'clock he was getting hoarse.

"Shut up, Arthur," said Dave for the fiftieth time.

Even though all the birders were within twenty yards of the bird feeder, they had ringed it with binoculars and telescopes, many on tripods. One man was peering through a camera with a lens as big as a toilet bowl.

At noon, when Dave stepped outside with fresh worms, he heard someone whisper, "Feeding time." He felt the crowd stir. He felt like an aquarium showman. Maybe, he thought sourly, he should climb onto the feeder and hold the worms between his fingers so the bird could pluck them out on the fly.

After lunch Dave watched a woman pushing a man up his driveway in a wheelchair. The man had an IV drip in his arm. The couple were arguing. When she got him to the end of the driveway, the woman stormed back to her car and drove away without looking back.

Early on Sunday a man arrived in an airport limousine, ran into the backyard, saw the bird, jumped back in the limousine and headed back in the direction he came from. He never even closed his door. The limousine never shut off its motor.

"Not unusual," said an older man, near the end of the day, whom Dave recognized as one of the group who had been standing in his driveway the morning it had been raining. He was wearing sneakers and a rumpled canvas hat. He gestured over his shoulder where the limousine had been.

"We call them twitchers," he said. "When they get close to whatever bird it is they're trying to add to their list, and they aren't sure if they're going to see it or not, they start to twitch."

It was getting chilly. There was only this man and Dave left in the driveway.

"They can pretty much tell as they drive up the street," said the old man. "If everyone is looking through their binoculars, then they know they're all right. They can relax. But if people are walking around . . . that's when they start to twitch. Because they know as soon as they get out of their car someone is going to say, 'She was here two minutes ago but you missed her.' "

"You watch her long enough," said Dave, "and you get to know her habits."

"She likes to fly in from the right," said the old man.

"Out of the hedge," said Dave. "I reckon she comes every fifteen minutes or so."

As they stood watching, the little bird flicked out of the hedge and landed on the feeder. She looked around rapidly, knocked back a few worms and flew off.

"She feeds more in the morning," said Dave.

The old man nodded.

The bird flew back.

"This is a crippling view," said the man.

"Would you like to come in?" said Dave. "Have a coffee?"

The man held out his hand. "My name is Bert," he said.

It was like that for three weeks. But then instead of trailing off, it got worse. Someone from one of the television stations did a feature on Dave's bird. The following weekend when Morley was coming home from grocery shopping, she was stopped by a policeman a block from her home. "You can't go down that street," said the cop. "Some idiot put signs up all over the place about a rare bird."

"But I live down there," said Morley.

The cop waved her through. As she got close to her house, there were cars parked everywhere and people walking in the middle of the road.

Sam was standing at the front door. He was wearing a pair of oven mitts that made his hands look ridiculously large.

"We dropped a pot of hot chocolate on the stove," he said. "It put the flame out, and the stove won't go on again. It smells of gas."

That was the weekend when people who weren't even interested in birds started coming. They wanted to be there because they had heard a lot of other people had been there, and they didn't want to miss anything.

One of the men, who had come in from the suburbs, chewed Dave out. "It doesn't look so special to me," he said. "I drove all the way from Brampton. It's not like it's an eagle or anything. I'll bet that bird has never killed anything in its life."

The second time *that* happened Dave called the hot line and said, "The bird has gone. Could you take it off your list, please."

Then he went outside and took down Sam's sign and put up a new one. The Bird Has Gone, it read.

That was at the end of March. The bird hadn't left, of course. Dave continued to feed her three times a day. He spent over two hundred dollars on meal worms during the winter. He came to know her well.

She was a woodland bird, in the middle of the city, way off course, and she had landed at *his* feeder. He felt proud that he had seen her through the frigid months, that he had kept her alive. He felt affection for her. He felt that she belonged to him somehow. He knew this was sentimentality. He knew the bird didn't feel anything about him. If anything, he was just another intruder in the backyard, and God knows there were enough of those.

But on that fresh, soft morning in May, when Dave slipped into his backyard and counted the worms and found none missing, he knew she was gone and he felt sad. Hell, he was heart-broken—although he realized the bird had probably migrated and that was the best thing for her.

Some of the birders told him they thought she had been blown north in a storm. But the old guy, Bert, who had come in for coffee, told him that he didn't accept that theory. He said that sometimes something just happens to a bird's wiring and they show up in the wrong place. He said that birds who show up in wrong places have a way of doing it again.

So Dave sat in bed with the unread paper beside him early on that quiet Saturday morning and wondered if maybe he would see his bird again in the fall. He imagined that whatever else she had felt, she had felt a sense of home. She could have left anytime she wanted. And now she had. Just like everyone else who has ever had a home, she had followed that universal urge to leave.

Dave picked up the paper. Then he put it down and got out of bed and stared out the window. He was thinking of the mysteries of migration. He was thinking that of all the mysteries maybe the one true thing we know and share with the animals was this sense of seeking, finding, leaving, but above all, of returning home.

Emil

It was the mulberry spring. The spring the mulberries were fatter and juicier than anyone remembered. The sidewalk under the mulberry tree on the corner was stained deep purple for weeks. The birds got fat. Morley sent Sam out with a chair and a bowl three times. Three times in two weeks she baked mulberry pie, the juices bubbling over the pie crust like wine.

It was the spring it only rained at night. The spring of damp earth and blue skies. The spring of fat worms.

It was the spring gardening became so popular that even criminals got into it.

"I don't believe it," said Morley standing on her front lawn, waving at her garden. "They took two ornamental cabbage, my hens-and-chickens and the smoke bush."

"I loved that smoke bush," she said. She was pointing at the hole between the forsythia and the Siberian iris. "It was purple. My aunt Muriel has a huge one in her backyard."

Each plant had been excised with medical precision. Morley kicked the only thing that the thief had left behind, a melon-sized pile of earth on the edge of the lawn where the roots had been shaken clean. Whoever it was had made off with everything—roots and all.

"Surely," she said, "Surely, you would notice someone walking down the street with a smoke bush. Do you think we should call the police?"

When someone you love is upset enough to suggest calling the police over a missing smoke bush, you have two choices. You can, if you don't care how the rest of the day goes, say, "The plant police? We should phone the plant police? Are you out of your mind?" Or you can muster as much affection as possible and say, as Dave did, "You stay with the plants. I'll call the police." Then you go inside and stand in the kitchen for what feels like the appropriate amount of time before you come back outside and lie. You say, "They are sending out a car. And if they see *anyone* with a smoke bush they are going to stop them. On the spot." Dave considered adding something about how they were going to check the florists in the area—but the thing about a successful lie is not going too far.

That night, as she sat in bed with gardening magazines fanned around her like playing cards, Morley said, "I'm going to get him." She meant the thief.

It took her three weeks.

She got lucky one night. She woke up at 3:15 in the morning and she couldn't get back to sleep. It was hot, and she was restless, and because she didn't want to wake Dave she got out of bed and wandered absent-mindedly to the window. It was a beautiful night. The moon was shining and the white flowers of the nicotiana held her eye. The small fragrant petals, outdone in the light of day, were radiant in the moonlight.

"To every thing," said Morley.

She frowned. Something was bothering her. Gradually she became aware of what it was. There was movement across the street. Someone was on their hands and knees in the Schellenbergers' garden. And it wasn't Betty Schellenberger.

When you witness a crime in progress in the middle of the night, the *only* thing to do is to phone the police. Unless, of course, instead of being in the hands of reason, you are in hands that control more satisfying emotions—like rage and revenge. If you are being moved by hands of rage, you grab your robe, and one of your socks, and one of your husband's socks, and you pull on the mismatched socks as you hop-skip towards the stairs, and you race out the front door in the frayed robe that you would never, under ordinary circumstances, wear outside, and you dash across the street into your neighbour's yard without stopping to think.

Morley stormed into the Schellenbergers' garden. When she saw the man on his hands and knees digging up Betty

Schellenberger's gold flame spirea she stopped dead. She thought, I should have woken Dave.

The man must have heard her, because without warning he stood up, whirled around and gasped. He looked frighteningly like Rasputin—bearded and dirty, wild and crazy. He took a step towards Morley but she stood her ground, her hands folded across her chest holding her robe closed.

"Hello, Emil," she said. "I see you're doing some gardening."

The man—Emil—began breathing rapidly, panting almost. Wringing his hands as if he were washing them.

"I am going on vacation," he panted. "I am going to . . . Greece," he said. "Have you ever been to Greece. They have castles there. I am going on a charter flight but it will be safe because they line the planes with lead. Before they didn't and the rays got you and that's how you got cancer. Did you know that? Eh? Did you know that?"

Morley met Emil three years ago. He showed up one morning in front of her husband's record store wearing a pair of ripped pants and slippers and stood on the sidewalk for two weeks.

"He's making me crazy," said Dave. "He's driving away business."

"He is *not* driving away business," said Morley.

"I've asked him to go somewhere else," said Dave. "But he's back every day. He can't just stand around on the street like that."

Morley looked at her husband carefully.

"Why not?" she said.

Emil had appeared at a bad time. He had appeared only a

week after the notorious Flick Lady had disappeared from the neighbourhood.

The Flick Lady had marched into Woodsworth's Bookstore out of the blue one day, gone to the history section, and begun flicking the covers of all the political biographies . . . snapping her finger on the jacket photos and making her disgust clear with each flick: *yech, yech, yech*. After two minutes she walked out of the store. She did this every afternoon—usually between two and three.

Dave tried to convince Dorothy, who owns Woodsworth's, that the Flick Lady was harmless. And probably politically sophisticated. He held his position until she added the Vinyl Cafe to her afternoon rounds. The Flick Lady came into Dave's record store one afternoon and picked up an album and held it to her chest as she sang a tuneless rendition of "Downtown." After three months of these daily visits she stopped as mysteriously as she had started. Disappeared. But now there was this man. Standing in front of his store like a rain cloud.

One morning at breakfast Morley said, "What is his name?"

Dave was holding up a jar of peach jam, squinting at the list of ingredients. He said, "What?"

Morley said, "The man on the sidewalk with the pants. What's his name."

Dave said, "I have no idea. What is pectin anyway?"

Morley was pouring herself a cup of coffee. "Don't worry," she said, "it's natural."

She reached out and took the jar from Dave and made him look at her. "You can't expect him to listen to you if you don't even know his name, Dave. You should introduce yourself."

And that's how Morley came to know the name of the man in the Schellenbergers' garden. Emil.

After Dave had introduced himself, Emil had moved across the street. For the past two years he has sat in the stairwell next door to the Heart of Christ Religious Supplies and Fax Services. The stairwell has become his place in the world. And slowly he has become part of Dave and Morley's world too. They don't know where he sleeps, but they know before he sleeps he goes to the Beaver Electronics store and watches television on the set in the store window. He likes baseball games. He owns a universal remote control and he can change the channels. And he can raise the volume loud enough so he can hear the games through the store window.

The first time Morley gave Emil money—she gave him five dollars—Emil said, "That's too much." And he gave her two dollars' change.

Other times he wouldn't take her money. "I don't need it," he would say. "I have enough. I have enough."

Sometimes he was too agitated to speak. Morley would see Emil standing on a corner somewhere, his shirt out, his belly showing, the bottom of his pants ripped and grubby. He would be lost in some world, staring at his feet, talking to himself. He wouldn't even notice her. Other times he would see Morley coming and he would brighten and say, "Hello," as if they were old friends, as if he had been waiting for her.

When Morley tried to give Emil food, he wouldn't take it. The first time, he said, "I can't take your sandwich."

Morley said, "Well, I'm not hungry." And she put the sandwich she had bought for him on the top of the garbage can on the corner. When she came back an hour later, it was gone.

One day Emil showed up at the Vinyl Cafe with a shopping cart full of books. They were old library books he had bought for twenty-five cents each at a library sale: math texts, novels by unknown authors, books of language instruction, romances.

"If you want to take out a book," said Emil, "you have to to take out a membership."

Dave had been spending the morning slipping 45 rpm records into plastic envelopes that said Vinyl Cafe on them in large red letters. Underneath, in blue lower case, it said, "We may not be big but we're small." Dave has thousands of 45s, and normally he doesn't pay much attention to them. He sells them like vegetables. There is a roll of plastic bags on the wall near the bin of records. You can put five 45s in a bag for ninety-nine cents. But he has been slowly working his way through the bins, pulling out the good ones, struck by the wonderful artwork on the labels: the flowing silver script on the Mercury label, the fat happy letters on the Dot.

When Emil walked in, Dave had just picked up *California Dreamin'* by the Mamas and the Papas. The moment he saw the record he remembered that he owed Denny Doherty three hundred dollars. He was wondering if Denny remembered the weekend he had lent him the money. They had gone to Jamaica with Carl Wilson. Or was it Mustique with Al Jardine? Carl or Al? That was what he was thinking when

Emil walked in and said, "If you want to take out a book, you have to take out a membership."

Dave slipped the record under the counter, separate from the others, and said, "How much? How much is a membership in your library, Emil?"

Emil shook his head back and forth and laughed. "Don't be crazy, Dave. Everyone knows libraries are free." He said it as if he were talking to a child.

Dave wrote his name and address on a piece of paper Emil tore out of his book and picked three books out of the shopping cart, and Emil said, "You can't take more than two books out at once, Dave."

Dave settled on a western and a high-protein cookbook. He put the books in a drawer under the counter—or thought he did.

He forgot all about them until Emil appeared a month later and said, "Did you know your books are overdue? You owe five dollars in fines, you know."

Emil then reached into his jacket pocket and pulled out the piece of paper Dave had signed when he had joined his library. Dave stared dumbly at the paper, wondering where Emil had kept it for the month.

He said he was still reading the books and would pay the fines when he finished them. He said, "Come back in a few days, Emil."

He looked for the books at home and again at the store and then he had to admit to himself that he had probably lost them. It bothered him that Emil could keep track of the scrap of paper, and he couldn't keep track of the books. What bothered him even more was the disturbing feeling that he had lost something else—something he couldn't even remember losing.

Emil came back two more times—each time pushing the shopping cart. The first time he told Dave his fine was up to seven dollars, on the second visit he said it was up to ten, and then just as Dave had hoped, Emil forgot about the books and the fines.

Dave doesn't believe in giving Emil money. He has argued with Morley about this.

"If he gets money," he said, "he buys cigarettes and lottery tickets. And I'm sure he loses the tickets. Why would you give someone money so they can throw it away on lottery tickets they are going to lose?"

Morley didn't have an answer to this. "I don't care what he does with the money," she said. "He doesn't take it if he doesn't need it. Sometimes he won't take it."

Dave wasn't listening. He had suddenly remembered why losing Emil's book had bothered him so much—remembered the object that had disappeared from his life that had been gnawing at the edge of his consciousness. He had bought a lottery ticket the weekend the prize had gone over ten million dollars. And he had no idea where he had put it. He had read that it was not unusual for winning tickets to go unclaimed because people lost them. In the middle of his conversation with Morley he abruptly turned and went downstairs and rummaged through the laundry hamper—knowing he was never going to find the ticket, wondering if it was one of the winners and exactly how much money he had thrown away.

And that's why Morley felt so let down last month as she stood on the Schellenbergers' lawn at 3:15 in the morning—that of all people it would be Emil standing there with the Schellenbergers' gold flame spirea at his feet.

Instead of getting angry, however, she said, "Is that for your garden, Emil?"

Emil said, "Did you know the moon is a hotbed of hostile alien activity?"

Morley wasn't falling for that. She said, "That's crazy talk, Emil. I want to know what you are going to do with that plant. Do you have a garden?"

Emil looked up at her and for an instant he was clear and she could see him—the real person.

"Yes," he said, softly.

"I want to see your garden," she said. "Will you show me your garden tomorrow?"

Emil blinked and said, "Oh." Then he hung his head and said, "Yes."

Morley drew her robe tighter around her and said, "Good night," and turned to walk across the street, noticing for the first time that she wasn't wearing shoes.

The next day at lunch Morley went to the stairwell beside the Heart of Christ Religious Supplies and Fax Services.

"I have come to see your garden, Emil," she said.

"There," Emil replied.

He was pointing to one of the large concrete boxes that line the street. Sure enough, nestled around the trunk of the stunted gingko tree that the city planted, and occasionally watered, were Morley's hens-and-chickens.

"I have another box," said Emil.

"Near the TV store," said Morley.

"At night I take the plants with me," said Emil.

"You can keep your eye on them that way," said Morley.

"So no one can touch them," said Emil.

At supper that night Morley told everyone what had happened to her plants.

"What would you do about that?" she asked.

Sam said, "Call the police. Call the police and send him to jail. He stole."

Stephanie said, "He's retarded—just take the plants back."

Dave said, "What *did* you do?"

Morley said, "The ornamental cabbages have aphids—I took him stuff for the aphids."

All June, Emil kept busy with his garden—moving his plants back and forth among various concrete boxes around the city. He moved the smoke bush twelve times—he noted each move carefully in his book.

The garden, however, was not the biggest thing that happened to Emil this spring. The biggest thing happened on the last Saturday of June, when Emil won the lottery, not the big prize, but big enough—ten thousand dollars.

Emil went to the lottery offices on Monday morning with Peter from the laundromat where he had bought his ticket. But they wouldn't give him a cheque because he didn't have two pieces of identification.

"I don't want a cheque," said Emil. "I want the money."

It took several weeks for Emil to get a social insurance

number. When he got it, he took it to the lottery office and they gave him the cheque.

When he took the cheque to the bank, the teller, Kathy, took him into the manager's office and tried to talk him into opening an account.

She said maybe it was not a wise decision to walk around with that much cash.

"Why don't you take forty dollars?" she said. "You could come here any time you wanted and get more money."

All the time Emil was in the manager's office, the assistant manager was watching warily from the door.

It took him a half an hour to convince them to give him his money—they said they were worried people would take advantage of him. He said he knew what he was going to do. He left, at noon, with ten thousand dollars in twenty-dollar bills. They put it in a vinyl burgundy pouch.

He took it to his spot in front of the Heart of Christ Religious Supplies and Fax Services and he gave seven thousand dollars away—actually he misplaced two thousand five hundred dollars, so he ended up giving four thousand five hundred dollars away. He had three thousand left at the end of the day.

He didn't just hand the money to anyone who walked by. He gave it to his regulars—people who gave *him* money. Or stopped to talk to him.

They were awkward transactions. At first Emil tried to slip them the money surreptitiously, the way you might tip a headwaiter who had led you to a good table. Most people didn't like being that close to Emil and as he tried to give them the money they would back away. When they realized what he was trying to do—*he was trying to give them money!*—every one of them tried to refuse it . . . backed away as if he were offering them a religious tract. But Emil was persistent.

He gave Morley five hundred dollars.

"It would have been patronizing not to take it," she told Dave. "It would have been an insult." They were across the street, in the record store.

"I had to take it. But I know what I'm going to do with it."

"What?" asked Dave.

"I'm going to give it back to him," said Morley, "bit by bit."

"It'll just go back to the lottery," said Dave.

"Dust to dust," said Morley. "It's his money."

As soon as Morley left, Dave phoned Dorothy.

"He gave me five hundred dollars," said Dorothy. "Kenny got seven hundred and fifty."

Dave hung up and headed across the street. He was sure Emil would offer him money too. After all, he had known him as long as anyone else. By the time he was out the door he knew what he was going to do with his share. There were still things around that paid 8 percent. If everyone did that, Emil could have fifty or sixty dollars a month.

Emil was standing in the middle of the sidewalk looking around as if he was supposed to meet someone—as if they were late.

"Congratulations, Emil," said Dave. "I hear you're a big winner. When do I get my share?"

He meant it as a joke, but Emil took him seriously.

"No share for you, Dave," he said. "You still owe your library fine."

Dave and Morley aren't sure what happened to the money Emil didn't give away. They know he had a haircut and a shave. He looked great for a week. So good that Dave didn't recognize him the first time he saw him. He bought himself a portable battery-powered television and a chair, and all July he sat on the chair in his stairwell and watched his TV. The chair was eventually stolen, and he lost the TV, or someone took it from him. Or maybe he gave it away.

Emil wasn't sure when Morley asked him about it. "It's OK," he said. "The battery was going anyway, and it only got Canadian channels. You can't get cable on those small sets."

It was all gone by the end of July. Well, not all gone. Because Morley still had four hundred and twenty-five dollars that belonged to him. She kept it in a glass in the kitchen, in the back of the cupboard behind the canned soups. She had already given him fifty dollars in cash. Spent twenty on sandwiches and coffee, which she left on the garbage can on the corner. And she bought some feverfew—a plant that looks like a daisy—and gave it to him to plant in his box. It's an herb that people say can cure fevers—a pretty little plant and the leaves smell good when you work around them, and best of all it seeds itself, which means it will grow again next summer. It will need to be tough to live in a concrete box all winter—along with the Coke bottles and the straws—but the feverfew is a tough little thing and not without dignity.

And on the last weekend in September Morley will spend another five dollars while she is grocery shopping. She'll buy a box of grape hyacinth bulbs and she will plant them one night when Emil has left—thinking as she scrapes at the hard dirt in Emil's box that they will come in the spring and surprise him.

When she finishes, she will lift the watering can she has carried all the way from home and drain the last of it onto the dry soil. Then she will button her sweater and set off down the street, savouring the thin chill of the night air, the feel of earth on her fingers.

The Birthday Party

On Thursday morning, on his way to work, Dave passed Emil standing in the doorway of the Heart of Christ Religious Supplies and Fax Services. Emil was rocking back and forth with a vacant expression on his face until Dave said, "Hello," and Emil stopped rocking and said, "Morning," cheerfully. Dave was headed across the street to his store. He was halfway there when he remembered he was supposed to buy a bottle of wine. He frowned and slowed down as he tried to remember why—there was an occasion—but he couldn't remember what it was. All he could remember was that he wanted to buy something special.

This has been happening frequently to Dave. Often in the morning as he is about to leave for work. One moment he is standing by the front door, the next, he is galloping up the stairs on some vitally important mission, the purpose of which escapes him once he is standing in his bedroom. All he can do is stand by his bureau, like one of those poor dumb moose that wander into sub-divisions, moving his eyes woefully around the room, looking for a clue.

The moose end up in the suburbs when a parasite moves into their brain. As far as Dave can figure, whatever has moved into *his* brain has been marching around with a clipboard and a ladder unscrewing light bulbs. More than once, in the evenings, Dave has stood up abruptly—right in the middle of a television commercial—and walked into the den because . . . well that's the problem. He can't remember why he is in the den. The dog follows Dave around at night—in case it might be time for a walk—so the two of them stand there, Dave and the dog, both of them staring at Dave's desk with the same perplexed expression.

It was five past ten when Dave saw Emil and remembered that he was supposed to buy the wine. He hesitated in front of his record store. He couldn't remember what the wine was for, but maybe, he thought, he should go and buy it before he forgot altogether.

It is a fifteen-minute walk to the wine store. It was a beautiful morning. The idea of staying outside pleased Dave. The walk would do him good.

There were no other customers when he got there. Just three clerks leisurely restocking the shelves and chatting among themselves.

Dave was feeling pretty leisurely himself as he wandered around the aisles. He still couldn't remember why he wanted wine, so he read a lot of labels and to be safe chose four bottles—two white and two red. Two Canadian, a Chilean cabernet and an Australian Merlot.

There were four cash registers at the front of the store, but nothing to indicate which one was open. There wasn't a clerk at any of them and no signs or gates to suggest a course of action. Dave chose the cash register nearest the door.

He put his four bottles of wine down on the counter and got out his wallet and put his credit card down beside them. Sometimes when you aren't in a hurry waiting can be a pleasant experience. An opportunity to prove how mellow you can be. Dave wasn't in a hurry. He thought of the different kinds of people who came into his record store. He was pleased that he hadn't begun tapping his credit card on the counter, or clearing his throat, or shuffling his feet, or any of the other irritating tricks customers resort to when they are trying to attract attention. By standing quietly at the counter Dave was displaying his solidarity with his fellow retail workers. After a moment, his patience was rewarded. Dave saw one of the three clerks stand up. Then he watched him languidly drift up to the farthest cash register from where he was standing.

Dave didn't move.

The clerk looked over at him and, in a voice Dave would later describe as being a combination of disinterest and aggression, said, "Over here."

Dave said, "I have four bottles of wine and my credit card. Could *you* come over to this one?"

The clerk shook his head and said, "This is the one that's open."

Dave felt all the goodness that had accrued to him during the morning evaporate. He felt his mellowness fade away. Felt himself slip into an elbows-up mood. Indignant that he, of all people, should be treated like this. Dave felt himself switching from compatriot to customer. He heard himself say, "Well, I'll come back when *this one* is open." And he walked out of the store and into the sunshine. He squinted at the men and women walking to and fro on both sides of the street, wishing they knew what he knew—knew what he had just done for them. He was feeling pretty darn good about himself. Pleased because the line had come out so fast, and pleased because he had not been rude, and pleased, most of all, because he had struck a blow for all customers looking for good service and courtesy. He didn't have the wine he had come for, but he had something else—a good feeling—and it stayed with him until he got a block and a half away from his record store.

Stayed until the little voice inside his head that had been so busy congratulating him suddenly said, I don't think you have your credit card, Dave. He froze in mid-stride.

Dave knew right away that he hadn't put the card back in his wallet. He thought perhaps he had slipped it into one of his pockets, and hope flared. He stood on the street, patting himself. He checked all of his pockets, twice, even the pocket in his shirt where he never put anything. And knowing he should turn around and go back to the liquor store, he walked, with a sinking heart, in the other direction. He knew that he should retrieve his card. But how could he face the clerk?

A few moments ago Dave had felt so sure that the clerk had been rude to him. So sure that *he* had been courteous. Now, he wasn't so certain. Had he really been courteous?

So instead of going back and claiming his card he walked to the Vinyl Cafe. When he got there, he took off his jacket and sat down behind the counter. He had to think about this. And the more he thought about it, the more he realized that he was far more tense about what awaited him at the liquor store than he was about losing his credit card. He could imagine himself standing in front of the liquor store clerk, with his baseball cap in hand. He got up and walked slowly towards the front of his store—trailing his hand along the piles of records as he walked. He gazed at the little mound of hand-written notes Scotch-taped to the back of the door. He pulled off one that read, Back in thirty minutes. And he winced. He was too proud to do it. So he did the only sensible thing he could think of doing. He picked up the telephone and called the bank.

"I would like to report a stolen credit card," he said.

He should have said lost, a lost credit card, but theft seemed to have more dignity and Dave was feeling woefully low on dignity.

If he had remembered, at that moment, that Saturday was Sam's birthday, and that the reason he had wanted the wine in the first place was so when everyone was in bed he and Morley could quietly toast the anniversary of the birth of their second child. If he had remembered these things, Dave might have acted differently.

But he had forgotten the birthday. He had forgotten that ten of Sam's friends had been invited over for supper and a sleep-over that very night. Forgotten that he had agreed to run the party, to order the pizza and buy a cake and get a video. Forgotten that Morley was going shopping for presents that very morning.

In fact, at the very moment Dave was reporting his stolen card, Morley was wheeling a shopping cart with the Bat Cave Deluxe in it towards the cash registers at a suburban toy store. Five dollars' worth of extruded plastic that was about to cost her forty.

Birthdays have always been a problem for Morley. She finds it stressful to have her house full of children expecting to be entertained. She has tried, over the years, to cope with her anxiety by careful planning. When Sam and Stephanie were little, Morley spent days preparing prizes for games, and wandering around stores, loading up on cheap but interesting things for loot bags.

But no matter how hard she tried, there was always a kid who did not want to play the games she had planned, a kid who thought the prizes were stupid, a kid who hated the food. And for all her efforts, at some point the strain of the party inevitably rendered her children, the very children she was doing this for, tearful.

Morley was a scarred birthday mom. So when Sam said that for his ninth birthday party he wanted "A major sleep-over. With all my friends. With pizza and a movie," Morley blanched. She knew there was no reason not to have ten boys ransack her house for twelve hours, but she didn't know if she was up to it.

So Dave had agreed to run the party. Morley would

organize things, but when it was time to man the battle stations she was, for the first time in sixteen years, stepping aside. She was going to go to a movie with Gerta Lowbeer while the kids had supper—this was Dave's idea—and Dave was in charge.

If Dave had remembered any of this he might have, probably would have, *certainly* would have, swallowed his pride and returned to the liquor store and retrieved his credit card. But he didn't. So he reported the card stolen, and the woman on the phone typed his report into the bank's computer.

It is amazing how fast computers work these days. Morley, who was feeling both pleased and slightly resentful about the Bat Cave, had just begun to unload her shopping cart when Dave hung up the phone.

Morley didn't notice that the clerk was having difficulty with her purchase. Didn't notice anything was amiss until a man materialized and invited her to accompany him to the security office.

It took twenty minutes and two phone calls before Morley convinced the manager that she had not stolen the credit card. After twenty minutes he apologized to her. But he didn't give her the card back. Morley had to watch him take a pair of scissors from his desk and cut up her credit card in front of her.

"Policy," he said.

When Morley got home there was a message from Dave. It said, "phone me before you use the credit card."

Because she loved her husband, Morley decided to wait until after lunch to call him.

In fact, she didn't call until the afternoon.

Dave said, "Of course, I remembered the birthday party. Why do you think I was at the liquor store?"

Then Dave said, "Of course, not for the kids. I was getting the wine for us."

And then he said, "Of course, I'll get the pizza . . . Yes and the movie . . . Yes and the Bat Cave."

Then the line went dead and he looked around and he said, "Of course, I have no money."

Which wasn't completely true. Dave had nearly twelve dollars in his wallet. And there was forty-seven dollars in the store's till.

Dave looked at his watch. It was 4:15. His bank was closed. He realized without his credit card he had no little plastic key to any more money. He had to move fast. He went outside and unlocked the six-foot wooden kangaroo that stands on the sidewalk in front of his store. Hop On In, it says on the pouch. He wrestled the kangaroo in and then carried a chair out and unscrewed the two speakers that hang over the front door. He was moving so fast that he hadn't turned off the record player. Frank Sinatra began to sing "I Get a Kick Out of You" as Dave lifted the first speaker out of its brackets. It was an odd sensation to cradle the speaker in his arms as Sinatra sang. The speaker, thought Dave, was probably about the size Sinatra's head had been.

He had both speakers stashed behind the counter and was standing in the store with his hand on the light switch when a big guy in a wool toque stuck his head in the front door. "Are you open?" he asked.

"Just closing," said Dave.

The man was wearing grey sweatpants and a Road Runner T-shirt. He had about ten albums under his arm.

"I was wondering if you wanted to buy these?" he said, holding up the records.

Dave had already flicked off the lights in the back of the store and was about to say, "I have already closed the till," when he spotted the album on the top of the pile. It was the original RCA Victor Living Stereo copy of the soundtrack from *Casino Royale*.

His hand stopped in mid-air on its way to the last light switch. He invited the guy into the store with a wave of his hand, locked the door behind him, and said, "What else have you got there?"

What the guy had was the motherlode: *Harry Belafonte Live at Carnegie Hall*. A sealed copy of Simon and Garfunkel's *Wednesday Morning Three AM*, and best of all, the *Bonanza Soundtrack* with Lorne Greene singing the theme.

Dave whistled. "Where'd you get this stuff?" he asked.

The guy pulled a crushed package of Export A out of his pants pocket and looked at Dave questioningly. Dave nodded, "Go ahead," he said.

The guy said, "My brother used to collect them. But he's been in Australia for eighteen years and I'm getting tired of having his stuff filling up my apartment. He said I should just sell them."

Dave had been looking for the Simon and Garfunkel album for a year. He had never even *dreamed* of seeing a *sealed* copy.

"How many?" Dave said. "How many records in all?"

"There are hundreds," said the guy.

Dave said, "I can give you two dollars for each album and four for Simon and Garfunkel. That's what? Ten albums? Twenty-two dollars. I'll make it twenty-five."

The guy looked disappointed.

Dave said, "Look. I'll sell these for about six dollars each. I'll come over to your place tomorrow and look at the rest. If there are five hundred albums, that's good money."

He glanced at his watch as the guy thought it over.

Dave had thirty-four dollars left in his wallet when he finally locked the store.

As he walked by Emil he considered asking for a loan. Instead, he found a toy store downtown that took a cheque for the Bat Cave.

He stopped at a phone booth and called his friend Kenny Wong. He said, "Tonight is Sam's birthday party. There are kids coming over, I need food."

Kenny said, "You got it."

He got home at five-fifteen. Stephanie was in the living room watching *The Simpsons*. Dave said, "Please turn that down."

"There's a note on the refrigerator," said Stephanie.

The note said "Birthday party instructions." Dave glanced at the note.

He said, "Stephanie, I want you to go and get a movie."

Stephanie said, "When this is over."

Dave said, "Now."

Sam emerged from under a piece of furniture and said, "I want to go and get the movie."

Dave said, "No way."

Sam started to argue.

Stephanie was still glued to the television.

Dave said, "Stephanie. Go and get a movie for the party."

His daughter stood up slowly and held out her hand. Dave said, "I don't have any money. Do you have money? I'll pay you back. Tomorrow." Stephanie rolled her eyes. Before she left she made Dave sign an IOU. On her way out the door she looked at Sam and said, "I'm going to get *The Little Mermaid*."

Sam screamed, "I hate you."

When Dave came into the room to see what was the matter, Sam screamed, "I hate you, too. I don't want a party." And he ran upstairs. His bedroom door and the front door slammed in unison.

It took Stephanie almost an hour to return with the movie. Unfortunately she didn't get *The Little Mermaid*. She got *The Night of the Zombie* instead. By the time she got home the kids had arrived and were bouncing off the basement walls.

Dave was trying to ice the cake—something he had never done before in his life. He was trying to spread icing from the fridge onto a cake he had just taken out of the microwave. He was too busy to ask about the movie. The cold icing was ripping hunks of cake the size of golf balls away from the surface. When he finished, the cake looked like it had been iced with a chain saw.

Dave stared at what he had done and poured himself a drink.

Which is when Kenny Wong arrived. Kenny was wearing a pair of green tartan pants and a bright yellow T-shirt. The red letters across the front of the T-shirt read, WONG'S SCOTTISH MEAT PIES—GOOD ENOUGH TO EAT!

He threw two plastic bags of meat pies onto the kitchen table.

Dave said, "There's only ten kids."

Kenny said, "It's a party. They'll be fine. I'll be right back. I'll have Scotch."

When he came back, Kenny was carrying a large, cardboard pastry box.

He set the box down on the table and motioned at Dave to open it.

"What do you think?" he said.

Dave peered in the box. It looked like an order of fried fish.

"What is it?" he asked.

"Deep-fried Mars bars," said Kenny. "There are two dozen. I made them myself."

Dave frowned.

Kenny pointed at the lumpy cake on the counter. It looked like a Grade Five geography project—a papier mâché model of a mountain range.

"What's that?" said Kenny.

"The cake," said Dave. "I made it myself."

The kids took one look at the meat pies and rolled their eyes.

"I thought we were having pizza," said Sam.

"They were out of pizza," said Dave.

Only Terrence was interested in the pies. Terrence, the smallest kid at the party, with a little round face and dark grubby hair hanging to his shoulders, said, "Please, can I have two?"

The other kids disappeared into the basement with hunks of cake and two Mars bars each.

Terrence was back in five minutes. He said, "Could I have two more pies please?"

Ten minutes later Terrence was back upstairs for a third helping. He had ketchup all over his hands and T-shirt. He said, "These pies are good."

Kenny reached out and rumpled Terrence's hair, "At least someone likes them," he said. When he removed his hand from Terrence's head it was streaked with ketchup.

When Morley came home at 8:30, the front door was open and the house was deadly quiet.

She walked into the kitchen and saw Kenny heading out the back door with a garbage bag.

"Be careful," said Dave from under the kitchen table. "We've had a little ketchup accident."

Morley looked at the meat pie crusts piled on the counter.

"I thought you were getting pizza," she said.

"They were out of pizza," said Dave.

Morley stared at him for a moment and then said, "What did you give Terrence?"

Dave looked at her.

Morley said, "The O'Connors are strict vegetarians—it's on the note—Terrence has never eaten meat."

Dave looked at Kenny.

Kenny grinned at Morley.

"He has now," he said.

Morley was hoping things would be cleaned up by the time she got home. However it wasn't the state of her kitchen that was bothering her. What was bothering her was the silence.

She looked at the basement stairs. "It's awfully quiet down

there," she said. "Are they watching TV? I thought they were going to play baseball."

Dave said, "We got a movie."

"What movie?' said Morley.

Dave crawled out from under the kitchen table, holding a red sponge. "I'm not sure," he said. "Stephanie got the movie."

Morley went downstairs.

The kids were on the floor—a mound of goggle-eyed nine-year-olds, their faces bathed in the eerie glow of the television set.

No one moved as she stepped into the room. Morley could see that some of them were already in their sleeping bags.

"I thought you guys were going to play baseball," she said.

"Shh," said ten boys as one.

They were on another planet. They didn't want to have anything to do with her. She was from the wrong planet. If she persisted they would turn on her. The last thing they wanted was to see was the light of day—not when they could see real life on a screen.

As she turned to go, Morley stepped on an unopened bags of chips.

"Shh," said the boys again.

Her eyes were beginning to adjust to the gloom. She noticed the floor was littered with empty chip bags, half-filled glasses of pop, candy wrappers, and popcorn. There was popcorn everywhere. Arthur, the dog, was over by the sofa licking at the floor. Morley stepped over the boys to see what he was eating. When she got within a few feet, Arthur turned and bared his teeth and growled. The basement felt like one of those abandoned warehouses full of squatters. She had only been gone for a few hours. Could things fall apart that fast? It was like an accident scene. It was bad enough that she would be pulling food out of the basement for weeks. She didn't have to stay and watch the accident in progress.

Morley wanted to leave, but she began to feel herself sucked into the movie.

It was night. A young mother was putting some children to bed. She seemed to be at a cottage.

Morley noticed some of the kids were gripping onto each other.

"What is this?" she asked.

"Shh," said Sam.

"The zombie is coming," said Terrence. "He has an axe."

There was a chilling scream.

Walter Colbath emerged from a sleeping bag and crawled over to Morley. "I'm scared," he said.

Later Dave worked out that everyone had been enjoying *The Night of the Zombie* until the zombie started losing limbs. First a finger fell off, followed by his left ear, which Walter, his eyes as big as saucers, later explained was devoured by a Jack Russell terrier before it hit the floor. Apparently every time the zombie lost a body part it left a gaping sore that began to pulse and ooze some sort of material that Sam said looked like a cross between pus and melted cheese. Within a few scenes, the zombie was transformed from a mild elementary school teacher to a waddling sore, with arm enough still for what Dave later referred to as "the knife scene."

Except it wasn't really a knife scene; it was more of a cleaver scene. It was the moment when the zombie lodged the cleaver into the skull of the dashing young scientist—the man all the kids had assumed was going to stop the zombie from doing what he did to the kindly old crossing guard.

It wasn't just the violence of the scene that had upset the kids, but the morality of it.

"Why did he do that to the crossing guard?" whimpered Scott, at midnight, as Dave tried to coax him from behind the sofa.

As Dave reached for Scott, he rested his knee in something greasy and it slid out from under him and he fell forward and hit his chin against the arm of the sofa. While he lay on the floor wondering when this was going to end, the dog began to lick his knee. Dave reached out and fingered his pants—the remnants of a half-eaten Mars bar adhered to him. When he stood up, the dog began barking.

"Excuse me," said Bill. "I have a headache. I want to go home."

Timmy said, "My tummy hurts. I want to go home too. Please could you phone my parents please?"

Phoning a family at two in the morning to ask if they would mind dropping over to pick up their child because you have just shown him *The Night of the Zombie* is not the easiest thing in the world to do. But Dave had no choice. It didn't take longer than fifteen minutes for the parents to begin to arrive. Everyone was polite, but Dave knew what they were thinking. They were thinking their kids would never come to this house again. Certainly not on a sleep-over.

When Terrence's parents came, Terrence said, "I ate meat. I ate meat. They made me do it."

"It was soya protein," said Dave glumly. "It just looked like meat."

Everyone was gone by 2:30.

All except Walter Colbath.

Walter was a thin boy with a perpetually runny nose. He was always worried that someone was breaking the rules.

Walter Colbath's parents weren't home. Or if they were, they weren't answering the phone.

"Maybe they turned the ringer off," said Dave. "You just stay. They'll be here in the morning."

Walter said, OK, and Sam and Walter, the last remaining warriors, headed off to bed together, Walter chewing his nails. Finally the house was quiet.

Dave had just drifted off to sleep when Sam appeared by his side, poking him, saying, "Walter is crying. Again. He thinks there's been a fire at his house and his parents are dead."

At 3:30 Dave agreed to drive Walter by his house so he could see that it hadn't burned to the ground.

"You don't have to get dressed," said Dave as he struggled into a raincoat. "We're not going to stop. We'll just drive by. Just put on a sweatshirt over your jammies. And your sneakers."

It was chilly outside. Dave had to turn the wipers on to clear away the dew.

"Please, God," he said quietly as they rounded the corner.

"See," he said. "Your house is still standing. No fire." He still didn't know why the Colbaths weren't picking up the phone.

"Maybe they're murdered," said Walter. "By a zombie or something."

"Your mom and dad are up north," said Morley to Walter softly. They had woken her when they got home. "They're coming home tomorrow."

"I know," said Walter. "But I'm afraid that the zombie got them."

Morley looked at Dave. She put her arm over Walter's shoulder and said, "You come here with me. You can sleep with us in here."

When Dave woke up at 6:30, it was with Walter Colbath's feet sticking into his back. Walter was sleeping diagonally across the bed, his feet drilling into Dave's kidneys, his head where Morley's should have been. Morley was nowhere to be seen.

Dave got up and went downstairs. Morley was snoring softly on the living-room couch.

Dave went into the kitchen and put some coffee on. He went to the front door and picked up the morning paper.

He looked at Arthur, who still had chocolate smeared around his mouth, and said, "What was the point of all that?"

The dog seemed to shrug.

"Pride before a fall," muttered Dave as the coffee began to sputter. If he had only gone back for his credit card. None of this would have happened. He wouldn't have had to send Stephanie for the movie . . .

Was that what he had learned? Or was it simpler than that . . . maybe the lesson was supposed to be . . . don't put your credit card down anywhere.

Arthur shook his collar. The jingle of the dog tags echoed in the quiet morning. Nothing else stirred.

Dave carried his coffee to the table.

He opened the paper.

Then got up and got a meat pie out of the fridge and dropped it in the dog's dish.

"Happy Birthday," he said.

Summer

Summer Camp

The fact that he hated his niece, and had from the moment he met her, bothered Dave. He felt it was wrong to dislike, let alone loathe, a little thing that stood no taller than three feet; and in this case, because the little thing was his sister's child, he felt it was shameful. But he loathed Margot and he had loathed her since she was four years old.

That was when they first met. She was walking down the arrivals corridor at the airport, holding a white vinyl purse in one hand and a large doll in the other. Annie had broken into a broad, toothy grin when she spotted her brother. She dropped her suitcase and held out her arms.

"It's so good to see you," she said.

Dave had hugged his sister, and then he had bent down, with love in his heart, and smiled at Margot. But before he could say anything she said, "You're late. We've been waiting. You were supposed to be here to meet us."

Annie had left her husband, whose name Dave always had difficulty recalling: Peter? Paul? It was one of the disciples—Matthew. *Matt*. Annie had left Matt that spring and was bringing Margot to Dave's for Easter.

They had stayed a week.

"We should have done this years ago," she said. "It's good to see her with the kids. It's important."

Mostly it was Margot tagging around behind Sam and Stephanie. Margot with her doll. The kind with the string in the back that you could pull when you wanted her to talk. A Chatty Cathy.

"Have you noticed," Dave said to Morley at the end of the first night, "how the doll is always interrupting me?"

Maybe they would be drinking coffee in the kitchen, talking, doing the dishes, and whenever Dave had something to say, the doll was nearby and ready to jump in:

"You could feed me now. Oh, I love you *soooo* much."

He hated the doll's whiny voice. And he hated everything it had to say—eighteen different statements. He knew them by heart by the end of Day Two.

"*Ohhhhhhh,*" he said to Morley as they went to bed. "I love you *soooo* much."

The summer he was seven, Dave sneaked one of Annie's dolls outside on a Saturday afternoon and sat it in the middle of the sidewalk in front of their house. Then he got his sister's tricycle and took a run at the doll from down the street. There was such a satisfying crunch that he set the doll up again and then again, until it was first a collection of limbs and finally just a pile of plastic. Unable to stop himself, he went upstairs and collected an armful of her dolls and began running over them, one by one. When Annie saw what he was doing, she started to cry hysterically. He calmed her down and convinced her to join in. You can be the nurse, he said. She was four. He had her stand on the lawn and throw her dolls in front of his bike as he flew by. As if they jumped, he said.

As he was putting the car in the garage, Dave imagined running over the Chatty Cathy in the driveway. "*Oh*," he said softly, "*I'm soooo sorry.*"

The next time Dave saw Margot she was six. He was in Halifax at a convention. He bought Margot a Barbie doll. He wanted to make up.

"Thank you, Uncle Dave," she said, flatly.

But she didn't play with the Barbie.

"She has gone off dolls," said Annie.

She didn't watch television either. Or do anything Dave's kids seemed to do.

"It's all dumb programs," said Margot, when Dave asked her about her favourite show.

After dinner she was working on schoolwork and she looked at Dave and said, "Why is the sky blue?" When Dave said he wasn't sure, she rolled her eyes and disappeared into her bedroom.

"It's OK," said Annie. "She can look it up."

An hour later she was out again.

"Uncle Dave," she said, "how many moons does Jupiter have?" Dave was sure she already knew the answer. He felt she was tormenting him.

He stayed three days.

He was determined not to leave without breaking through.

As he was going, he hugged Annie and then picked Margot up.

"I'm getting on an airplane," he said, grabbing her wrists, spinning her around.

"Put me down," screamed Margot.

But Dave kept spinning around and round, making airplane noises until her foot smacked the kitchen table and she yelped with pain.

As he stopped and set her down, she cried, "I hate you," and then turned to run. But she was so dizzy that she hit the kitchen counter with her forehead and fell down.

They were going to come with him to the airport.

"I'll just go," said Dave. "I'll go. You stay."

"What?" said Annie. Margot was screaming. Dave didn't bother to repeat himself.

At Christmas, Annie wrote that she was going to France for the summer. She had a six-week tour with a Gaelic group she played with.

Morley said, "Why don't we take Margot? Give Annie some time off."

Annie wrote back in a week. *Are you sure?*

Margot arrived on July 1st. She flew from Halifax by herself.

138

"You wouldn't let *me* fly to Halifax alone," said Stephanie to Dave as they drove to the airport to pick her up.

Margot, who was now ten, arrived sullen and grumpy.

"She wanted to come to Paris," said Annie to Morley on the phone. "I'm sorry. Will you be all right?"

"She'll be fine," said Morley, not knowing that at that very moment Dave was standing by a luggage carousel at the airport, trying to coax the colour of her suitcase out of his niece.

"Is it that one?" he said.

"I don't know," said Margot. "I told you. Mummy packed. I haven't the foggiest what it looks like."

Stephanie, who had refused to come into the airport, was lying in the back seat of the car when they got there. She was wearing a Walkman and had her eyes closed, her feet tapping on the passenger door window. She didn't acknowledge their arrival until Dave reached into the back seat and removed her headphones.

"Hey!" she said.

Margot watched carefully.

She was growing up to be a serious and intense little girl. Stephanie, six years her senior, was clearly the most interesting thing to have entered her universe in a long time. Here was a gateway into the world of teenage femininity. She wanted as much of it as she could get. She was attentive to everything that Stephanie did, the music she played, the way she used the telephone, what she watched on television and especially the nightly application of unguents and balms. When she learned that Stephanie and Sam were about to leave for two weeks at camp, Margot was distraught. "What about me?" she said.

When Annie had asked, Margot had rejected the idea of camp. Summer camp is for *children*, she said. Now, however, as Stephanie's departure drew closer, Margot wanted to go to camp, too.

She became increasingly difficult.

"There is nothing to do," she said. "I'm bored."

Morley gave her the Camping Association booklet and said, "Maybe there's a place you'd like."

Margot took the book to her room and came back in an hour, pointing to *The Crystal Lake Thespian Experience: Artistic Direction and Creative Encouragement for Young Actors*.

Morley phoned the camp the next morning. It was full. That night she handed the camping booklet to Dave and said, "This is your job."

These were the sort of decisions Dave normally tried to avoid. He preferred the conceptual over the practical. But the possibility of two weeks without Margot—without, in fact, any children—delighted him.

"There must be a camp with space somewhere," said Dave.

Dave only ever spent one summer at camp himself. He was hired as the Arts and Crafts Director. Before he left the city for camp he was seized by some primitive and unfamiliar wilderness spasm and he bought a book on plant identification. It had pencil sketches in the margins of flowers, trees and shrubs. Dave had the idea that he would spend his free time poking around in the forest. He believed that, if he applied himself, by the end of the summer he could become an accomplished woodsman. Maybe, by August, some kid hanging around the Hike and Trip Office would poke his buddy as Dave swung by and say, "That's Dave." The kid would say it with the same reverence he might say, "That's Pierre Radisson." Dave planned to forgo the pleasures of The Red Pine Inn, where the other counsellors went to drink at night. He would get up with the sun and go to bed at dark. Born to television, bred to the automobile, he would become Wilderness Dave.

As Arts and Crafts Director, Dave had a two-room cabin called the Wig-Wam near the hospital. He set off from his cabin at rest period on his second day at camp armed with his plant book.

Somewhere between the Chapel and the rock where the trail angled up towards the Indian Council Ring, Dave found himself staring at a shrub with three leaves and prominent veins. It looked like the first picture in his book, an Indian turnip.

The way you identify Indian turnip, said his reference, was by its white root. Dave reached out and plucked the plant from the ground. To his great astonishment he was holding something that looked like an albino carrot.

Dave still finds it difficult to understand what happened next. Perhaps the word turnip is what confused him. Perhaps he was just excited. Without pausing to think about what he was doing, he wiped the end of the root on his jeans and sank his teeth into it. He had already swallowed a large mouthful before it occurred to him that this might not have been the smartest thing he had ever done. That's when things started to happen in the back of his throat. The first thing was a mild burning sensation. The second felt more like the detonation of a small nuclear device somewhere in the vicinity of his tonsils. As Dave stood on the Chapel trail clutching the stump of the Indian turnip, wondering what would happen next, he noticed that his lips had gone numb. In fact he became aware that his entire mouth had begun to tingle and the tingling was crawling down his esophagus towards his stomach. It didn't take Dave long to realize that eating the root had been a terrible mistake.

Turnip in hand, Dave made his way back to camp.

If he was going to lapse into unconsciousness, he wanted to do it where someone might help. Once back at camp, however, Dave felt too foolish to turn himself in to the nurse. How could he go to the nurse with the turnip and say, I ate some of this.

He went back to his cabin and lay down on his bed. It occurred to him that if he passed out no one would know why. He got up and put the turnip on his desk and wrote a note. The note read: "I ate some of this." Dave figured if he made it to dinner he could destroy the note and no one would know anything. However, if he blacked out, someone would surely find him, read the note and organize the appropriate treatment. Dave lay down again and prepared to die. During the hour he spent on his bed he came as close to embracing religion as he had in his life. After the hour of prayer and wild promises it occurred to him to have another look at his plant book.

The information on the Indian turnip was continued on page two. In his original enthusiasm Dave had failed to read the whole story.

Indian turnip, he read, also a close relation of the horse radish. When cooked, it is a mild and pleasant vegetable. When eaten raw, it is the hottest plant known in the northern woods. Indians used to feed it to settlers as a joke. Painful but not poisonous.

That night Dave got drunk at The Red Pine Inn. He gave the plant book away to the Hike and Trip Director.

After the kids were in bed, Dave came downstairs with the camping booklet. "There are camps with rifle ranges," he said. "We're not sending Margot somewhere were they arm the campers."

"I knew you could handle this," said Morley.

He chose a camp that didn't have power boats. No water-skiing, he said to Margot. No horses. A small quiet camp. With a lake and sailboats. A summer place.

What Margot really wanted was to go with Stephanie.

But Stephanie was going to a teenage camp, and, for the first time ever, to a camp with boys.

They all left the same Monday morning. It was as chaotic as Christmas. Sam packed all his comics and no clothes. He was being driven to the bus by neighbours. His first time at camp and he ran out the front door without saying goodbye. "Hey!" said Dave. "Come back."

Stephanie thumped downstairs with a trunk and a suitcase and a sports bag full of stuff—including, hidden in her sleeping bag, the family's only hair dryer and a handful of make-up she had swiped off her mother's bureau.

She wasn't talking to anyone. She was mad about some-thing—mostly nervous, probably. Dave looked at her across the table, scowling into her cereal bowl, and his heart went out to the boys into whose lives his daughter was about to march. Somewhere, he thought, some poor kid, who has no idea what is heading his way, is calmly eating breakfast.

Margot was last to leave. After lunch Dave drove her to the parking lot of a suburban shopping centre. She was wearing flared blue shorts, a white T-shirt and a scarf in her hair. She left on a bus with a lot of other kids and a handful of counsellors wearing tie-dyed T-shirts—all of them too perky for Dave. The last Dave saw of her, Margot was sitting alone at the back of the bus. All of the other kids were clapping their hands and singing. Margot had her hands in her lap. She was staring dead ahead.

For the first few days the kids were gone Dave was edgy. "I don't get it," he said. "Margot's the one I'm worried about."

In the morning he'd wake up and say, "I wonder how she's doing?"

Morley would say, "She's doing fine." Strangely, this would make Dave feel better. But it didn't last. An hour later he'd be worried again.

By Thursday, however, he was enjoying an unfamiliar sense of freedom. That night he and Morley wandered out to a local restaurant for supper. Afterwards, on impulse, they went to a movie. On Friday morning they slept in.

"This is kind of nice," said Dave. "What do you want to do tonight?"

The first letter arrived at noon:

Dear Uncle Dave

This place is torture. Get me out of here. The meals are horrible. I haven't eaten anything for two days. They serve old porridge in the morning. My counsellor's name is Phyllis. She looks like Igor. Except meaner. I hate the kids in my tent who are all weird. I got bit by a weird looking bug and my arm is swelling up and turning red. I hate this camp. Why did you send me here to this place? This place is despicable. When is my mother coming home? I can't stand it. I might kill myself.

Love, your niece,
Margot

Dave was horrified.

"What are we going to do?" he asked.

"I thought we'd go to another movie," said Morley.

"About Margot," said Dave, pointing to the letter. "What are we going to do about Margot?"

"Nothing," said Morley. "She's fine. She'll be fine."

"What if she's not fine?" said Dave. "If it's such a great place why did they have spaces available in the middle of July? What if the kids *are* all weird? What if her counsellor *is* meaner than Igor?"

"Dave," said Morley "Stop it. She's fine."

At dinner Dave said, "What if they have guns and she gets a gun and shoots someone. Her counsellor. What if she shoots her counsellor? What if she shoots herself? She sounded pretty desperate. How am I going to explain that to my sister?"

"Dave," said Morley. "They *don't* have guns. Remember?"

"Maybe," said Dave, "it just wasn't in the brochure. Maybe they knew better than to put it in the brochure."

That night as he was getting undressed for bed Dave said, "What if she gets so hungry she goes into the woods and eats a poisonous plant? What if she starts eating plants that make her sick?"

Morley, who was already in bed, didn't even pretend to stop reading. "What," she said, "are you talking about?"

Dave said, "Margot. I am talking about Margot. What if she gets a book on plant identification and pulls up a poisonous plant and eats it?"

Morley closed her book carefully and looked at her husband as if she were seeing him for the first time. "Dave," she said, "only an idiot would go into the woods and pull up a plant and eat it. Your niece is not an idiot." Then she said, "Do you know how crazy that is? Maybe you need professional help."

On Monday, when he came home at lunch and saw the envelope addressed in Stephanie's handwriting, Dave's heart was filled with the milk of human kindness. Stephanie had been gone nine days and to Dave's surprise, he missed her. He carried the envelope to the kitchen table, sat down and held it up to the light. Then he got up and poured some juice. He was savouring this. He sat down, had a sip of juice, and opened the letter.

"There are boy's everywhere," it began. "Boys! Boys! Boys! This camp is boy! heaven. Mostly they

are dorks—real geeks—except this guy Larry who
is 18, and a lifeguard, and a hunk and last night . . ."

Last night?

Dave stopped reading and stared out the kitchen window.

This letter seemed to be heading to a place he didn't want
to go. He didn't want to know about *last night*.

He glanced down at the pages on the table in front of him.
He began to read it again. From the beginning.

July 7,
Dear Becky,

Becky is Stephanie's best friend.

Dave stared at the greeting as the awful truth slowly came
into focus.

His daughter had put the letter she had written to her
friend Becky into the envelope she had addressed to her parents. It was seven pages long.

I don't need to read this, thought Dave. This letter was not
meant for me. Please, Lord, give me the strength not to read
this letter. Lead me not into temptation. Stop me from reading any further. Deliver me from evil.

His eyes flicked down at the page in front of him. He
thought he saw the word tongue.

He looked away quickly. Lord, why are you testing me like
this? Why are you doing this to me?

It has been Dave's experience, over forty-seven confusing
years, that the best way to get rid of a temptation is to give
into it. He fingered the letter without looking at it and

thought of his little girl, as sweet as summer. Don't give in, darling, he thought. Please don't let bad things happen. Then, not sure at all that he was doing the right thing, he put the letter back in the envelope and carried it to the garbage can. He held it away from his body the way he might have carried a dead mouse. And he never mentioned it—not to his wife and not to his daughter. Only sure of one thing—if he was doing the right thing, he was doing it for the wrong reason—acting out of cowardice, not courage.

He drifted around the house aimlessly. Picking things up. When he got to the bathroom, he leaned on the sink and stared at himself in the mirror. Then, without thinking where he was going, or why, he wandered into Stephanie's room and sat on her bed. It was not a big room. Years ago he and Morley had framed a collection of family photos and hung them on the wall at the foot of her bed. His father and mother, Roy and Helen; Stephanie in a stroller, on skates, at Hallowe'en with her friend Becky. There were about ten pictures. They were the only things in the room that Stephanie hadn't redone. The rest of the walls were covered with pictures she had cut out of magazines. The collage, which had begun with rock stars and lately grown to include a collection of models who looked like they didn't eat enough, had begun over her desk and moved up the wall, across the ceiling, and down to where he was sitting. Three walls and half the ceiling were completely covered, but still, the wall with the photos was untouched. Like she didn't want to hurt their feelings. Or maybe because that was her, too.

Dave bent over, picked up a sneaker and looked around for its mate.

Instead he found a paper bag with the two bottles of sunscreen he had bought for her to take to camp. He picked it up and looked around for somewhere to put the bottles. He tried to clear a space on the table by her bed, but he only managed to push a bottle of lotion onto the floor. He picked up the lotion and put it back where she had left it. She would soon be seventeen. This was her room, not his. He left the sunscreen on the floor and went back to work.

That night as Morley and Dave were watching the news on television, Dave said, "You know, I'm still worried about Margot."

Morley started to say, "Margot is fine," but Dave stopped her and said, "No. Listen. We don't know anything about that camp. Maybe she is miserable. She *is* only ten. You know. That's young. And Annie is in Paris. And God knows where Ralph's gone—or whatever his name is. Why did she marry that guy anyway?"

Later Morley said, "If you're so worried about Margot, why don't you phone the camp and ask them how she's doing?" Then she rolled over, put her book on the table beside her bed and put her head under the pillow.

Dave phoned the camp from work the next day.

A woman answered.

Dave said, "I am phoning about my niece. I was wondering how she's doing. She's in Igor's tent."

The lady at the other end of the phone said, "What?"

Dave hung up.

On Wednesday Dave couldn't stand it any longer. "I'm going to drive up to see her," he said.

Morley said, "They are not allowed visitors for two weeks. It's against the rules. It makes them homesick."

"I've thought it out," said Dave. "She doesn't have to see *me*. I'm going to take a paddle. I'm going to say she forgot her paddle. I'll say I was in the neighbourhood and thought I'd drop it off. I'll see *her*. But she doesn't have to see *me*."

Morley said, "If it makes you feel better. But I'm not going to come with you."

Dave said, "That's OK. I can go myself." He didn't think she was going to let him go.

The camp was two hours north of the city. He parked his car in the visitors' parking lot at the camp gate. There were no other cars there. He got his prop, the paddle that he had just bought that morning, out of the trunk and started off down the dirt road. There was a lake beside the road on his left. There was a forest on his right. It was a beautiful summer afternoon. The sky was blue. The clouds white and cottony. And there was wind. A cool breeze off the lake. Dave felt like he was taking a wind bath. The city was so hot, so sticky. He could hear children playing ahead of him.

There was a bend in the road. As he came to the bend, Dave saw a beach and a group of girls swimming. The road he was walking on dipped down a hill and wound down to the beach. From the top of the hill Dave could see the length of the lake, the shadows of the clouds on the water. It was beautiful. More beautiful than he had imagined. Dave stood at the top of the hill and drank it all in. He was about to walk down to the beach when he recognized one of the bathing suits. It was Margot. Margot standing at the end of the diving board.

Margot laughing and pointing at a teenager in the water. That must be Igor. Margot running the length of the board and hurling herself into space, grabbing her feet and tucking herself into a cannonball, exploding into the lake a few feet from the older girl. Dave stepped off the road so no one could see him. He stood behind a tree and watched his niece play for fifteen minutes. Watched her get out of the lake all legs and arms and tighten herself into a towel and pick her barefoot way along the road Dave was standing beside.

Dave was overwhelmed by the urge to leave his tree and tell his niece he was there. He wanted to walk up to her and pick her up and say, here I am. I just drove two hours to see you. I drove all the way from the city because you're my sister's kid. I was worried about you because of the stuff you wrote in your letter. He wanted to say, I love you Margot, and if you are really unhappy here you can come with me if you want. And if you are ever unhappy anywhere else all you have to do is call me and I'll come. I love you.

He knew she wouldn't come. Knew she would want to stay. He felt stupid for coming. Knew that something important had happened. His family was growing up. His little sister's kid was doing fine at camp.

He jumped when he heard the man's voice.

"This is private property. What are you doing here?"

Dave stepped out from behind his tree.

The man was older than he was. Maybe fifty-five. Wiry. Tough looking. Like a farmer.

"God," thought Dave, "what am I doing here?"

"Hello," he said, trying to be pleasant, trying to be non-threatening.

"What are you doing here?" said the man again. Threateningly.

"I was watching the kids," said Dave.

"This is private property," said the man. Moving in front of Dave so he couldn't get by him.

Dave said, "Uh. It's not what it looks like. I'm a parent. My kid is down there." Dave thought trying to explain it was his niece would be too complicated. "I was bringing her this paddle." Dave held the paddle up. "I didn't want her to see me. They're not supposed to have visitors."

Dave held out his hand. "My name is Dave." He said.

The farmer didn't move. He didn't want to shake hands.

"You work at the camp?" said Dave.

"I'm the caretaker," said the man. "Maybe you better come to the office."

"Wait a minute," said Dave. "I really don't want to go to the office." Dave did not want a scene. He did not want his niece to know he was there. Did not want them to phone Morley.

"Have you got kids?" said Dave. "A week ago I got a letter from my kid. She's the one in the bright blue Speedo. In the letter she said she was unhappy. She said she hated it here. I needed to see if she was all right. The paddle was just an excuse." Dave held out the paddle. "Take it," he said. "The camp could probably use it somewhere. I really don't want to go to the office."

The caretaker sized Dave up and took the paddle.

"Visitors' day is on Sunday," he said.

"Yeah," said Dave. "I know. Listen, I'm sorry. Thank you."

The caretaker stood back and let Dave pass. Watched him

as he walked down the road. Dave turned around once and waved awkwardly and then didn't turn again, walking with the strange self-conscious roll that comes when you know someone is watching you.

He picked Margot up a few days later. He got her at the same parking lot where he had dropped her off. Sam was already home—minus most of the clothes he had left with, but not the comics. Stephanie was coming that evening. As they were walking into the house, Margot turned.

"Uncle Dave," she said, " do you know what it is we breathe in?"

"Oxygen?" said Dave.

She nodded and took a step and stopped again.

"And what about what we breathe out?"

"Carbon dioxide?" said Dave.

"Huh," said Margot.

"Why?" said Dave.

"I didn't think you were that smart."

Dave winced for only a second before he laughed.

The Cottage

Dave saw an ad for a cottage in the newspaper. The ad said, "Rustic Gatineau cottage on beautiful Lac de Boue." The week before the kids left for camp Morley had said, "What about a cottage? Could we get a cottage for a week in August and all go together?"

Dave called the number in the ad and a week later an envelope arrived with a schedule and five dark photocopied snapshots. Each picture had been folded randomly so there was a crease bisecting it—some on the horizontal, some on the vertical. The package had the feel of an elementary-school project.

Dave said, "There's a week free in August. Do you think we should take it?"

Morley peered at the smudgy photos. "I can't make these out," she said. "Is that a balcony? Maybe we should see it first."

Dave was thinking, If we don't go to a cottage we are going to end up on the road again. He would rather have a needle in his eye than spend another family vacation in the car. "I'm sure it will be fine," he said. "There's a beach and an indoor toilet. There's not a lot available at this time of the year. I think we should mail a deposit."

Morley pushed one of the photos across the table. "I don't think it's a balcony," she said. "I think it's a woodpile. See how it slopes."

Dave glanced at the picture. "Balcony," he said, sounding as confident as he could. "See the railing. It'll be great. What could go wrong?"

The first thing that went wrong was Stephanie. Two weeks at camp hadn't, as the brochure promised, instilled a sense of community in their daughter.

"I don't want to go away to a cottage," she said. "What am I going to do at a cottage?" She said "cottage" the way some people say "dentist."

It turned out that the week Dave had reserved the cottage was the week The Deadly Snakes were playing at the Shanghai Club.

"I already have tickets," said Stephanie.

"Sell them," said Dave.

On Thursday they drove Margot to the airport and put her on a plane. She was flying to Paris to meet her Mom.

"Margot is so lucky," said Stephanie. "If you got separated I could go to Paris for August."

They packed on Friday night and drove to the cottage on Saturday. They arrived just before supper. A six-hour drive. The trip was uneventful until Sam threw up outside of Smiths Falls.

"I told you I was going to barf," he said. Stephanie refused to sit beside him after that, so Morley had to move into the back seat. Stephanie sat in the front with Dave—the volume on her headphones just high enough to provoke him. He set his jaw. He was not going to ask her to turn it down. She could go deaf.

"Look," he said as they crossed the Ottawa River, "scenic point of interest—the river that opened Canada." No one responded.

They drove by the cabin road twice before they found it.

"This must be it here," said Dave, pointing at two narrow ruts disappearing into the forest. "There was supposed to be a sign."

The grass in the middle of the driveway was over a foot high. They could hear it brushing along the bottom of the car as they bounced along the road.

Stephanie said, "This is stupid."

Sam said, "I don't feel so good."

There were two notes waiting for them on the kitchen table. One was from the woman who had rented them the cottage. The other was from the previous week's tenants.

The owner's note said:

Welcome to Lac de Boue. This is just a note to ask you please do not clean the shower stall and the bathroom and kitchen floors. Pick everything out of the sink before you go to bed. And put the red brick on top of the garbage can in the kitchen.

Help yourself to the rhubarb in the garden and the raspberry patch. Also read the sign above the toilet. Wishing you a very peasant holiday.

Lissiane Boisclair.

"Is that what it says," said Morley. "Peasant holiday. Peasant?"

"I'm sure she meant pleasant," said Dave. "Why do you suppose she doesn't want us washing the floor?"

"I don't know," said Morley, "but I can live with it."

The note from the last tenants was more direct.

"Good luck," it said.

"That's a little cryptic," said Morley.

"They mean have fun. I am sure that's what they mean," said Dave. "I want to read the sign over the toilet. Anyone know where the bathroom is?"

The sign over the toilet said, "Only the last person flushes the toilet please."

The word "last" was underlined three times.

"What do you suppose that means?" said Morley. "The last person of the day, or the week, or what?"

"I think it means you only flush when you have to," said Dave.

"Gross," said Stephanie. "How much did you pay for this place anyway?"

Dave left his wife, his daughter and his son upstairs, staring at the toilet as if they had just lost a close relative. He went to explore the rest of the cottage.

And so Dave was the first to walk into the living room. He stood in the doorway feeling like he was about to step back into the nineteen forties.

The room was dark, like he imagined a men's club might be. The walls were unpainted tongue-and-groove pine boards— coloured a red-brown by the years. There were old couches, a rocking chair, a Fawcett wood stove, scatter rugs on the pine floor, pennants, old photographs, and in the corner, a Victrola with a hand crank. The room had the musty rich smell of butter. Dave smiled, breathed deeply and stepped into the past. A red squirrel popped up from behind the record player, jumped to the windowsill and stared at him indignantly.

"Everyone," said Dave, "come here. Look at this."

The squirrel chattered at him like an angry typist, then disappeared through a hole in the ceiling. Dave walked around like he was in a museum.

When Morley and Sam found him he was reading the pennants out loud. JUNGLE GROVE 1948. TAMARACOUTA 1947. And his favourite, at the far end of the room, a red pennant with one word in white letters . . . QUEBEC. There were two crossed flags at the fat end of the Quebec pennant . . . the Union Jack and the old Quebec flag . . . the one with the Union Jack in the corner.

"This place stinks," said Stephanie on her way past the living-room door. A minute later the toilet flushed.

"Everyone unpack," said Dave. "I'll do the food." The ice in the Styrofoam cooler had melted and there was a pound of butter floating there like a lump of Vaseline. Dave reached in and picked it up and it squirted out of his hand and bounced across the kitchen floor and disappeared under the fridge. He looked at the streak of grease across the brown and yellow tiles and wondered if Mrs. Boisclair would mind if he wiped it up.

That night, as he and Morley were lying in bed, he said, "Do you think Mrs. Boisclair would miss the Quebec pennant if I took it?"

The kids were in bunk beds upstairs. Dave and Morley were sleeping on two single beds in a room off the kitchen. They were lying on their backs reading mysteries. Their mattresses were so soft they had folded up on either side of them like wings. Dave had to prop himself up on his elbow if he wanted to see his wife. Outside there were frogs and crickets. Then there was a loon. It was the earliest they had been to bed for months.

"This is OK," said Dave, to the ceiling. "I like this."

"Me too," said Morley.

Upstairs, the pad of feet running across the room. The sound of the toilet flushing.

And Sam screaming.

"Stephanie flushed the toilet before she even used it."

"It was disgusting," said Stephanie "I'm not going to use a toilet Sam has used."

"Go to sleep you two," said Dave. "Settle down."

It began to rain the next morning after breakfast. Dave and Morley were on the balcony drinking coffee and they saw the rain coming across the lake like a grey curtain sweeping towards them. Then they could hear it on the trees. It sounded like a train coming through the yard.

"What's that," called Sam from inside. But before they could answer the rain hit the roof.

Stephanie said, "It's raining, stupid."

Sam said, "I know."

Everyone came out on the balcony and watched the rain blowing across the lake in smoky gusts, dripping off the pine trees down by the water, pouring off the roof in front of them.

"Isn't it beautiful?" said Dave.

"Now what are we going to do?" said Stephanie.

It rained all day. After lunch Sam made a tent in the living room using blankets and the kitchen chairs. He put pillows in his tent and crawled into it with a book about a vampire Rabbit called Bunnicula.

He was there for fifteen quiet minutes before his disembodied, disappointed voice floated out across the room.

"I'll never read all the Bunnicula books," he said. "There are over eight million in print."

They went shopping in town. Morley said, "All year no one cares about groceries and suddenly everybody wants to come."

They bought cookies, and pop, and she let them each choose a box of cereal she would never let them buy at home. Dave bought smoked oysters and blue cheese and bread. When he found wine in the grocery store he said, "Civilization." He felt like he was in a foreign country. In many ways he was. Swept away by the moment he said, "Everyone choose a bag of chips." Morley chose pork rinds.

"You can't get these at home," she said. "I haven't had these for years."

Sam chose potato chips—chicken flavoured.

"Those are gross," said Stephanie.

"You can have as many as you want," said Sam, smiling.

When they got home, Morley said, "All year you watch what you eat. And then we go out and get all this stuff."

"We're on vacation," said Dave. "It doesn't count."

Sam found a crokinole board behind the couch. Dave set it up after supper and explained the rules. The first time she tried to whack the checkers across the board, Stephanie nearly took the end of her finger off and the checker flew across the living room, ricocheted off a lamp, and landed in the chip dip.

"What a stupid game," she said, flouncing out of the room with her chips.

Morley caught Dave reading the ingredient label on the pork rinds.

"Don't say anything," said Morley, "I'm enjoying them."

Dave said, "I was just wondering how many varieties of edible oil there are."

What he was really wondering was whether it was dangerous to mix too many junk foods at once—was there, like with prescription drugs, a point of critical mass? He had eaten more than his share of pork rinds and chips. There were no warnings on any of the packages. He wondered how many times he would have to flush the toilet in the next twenty-four hours.

It was still raining on Tuesday when they woke up. Sam spent most of the morning in his tent until Stephanie finally persuaded him to come out and play cribbage. They played for half an hour before Stephanie realized the deck they were using was missing the jack of clubs.

"I'm not playing with a full deck," said Stephanie.

"Pardon," said Dave. "What did you just say?"

Morley was reading an interior-decorating magazine from France that was making Dave nervous. It looked like it was written for the sort of people who could afford to go to France to buy a couch.

Everything in the cottage was damp. There weren't enough lamps and the charm of the dark panelling was starting to fade. Dave was hoarding a change of clothes in his suitcase but he didn't want to wear them.

"I don't want to get them wet," he said. "I feel like I am starting to get mouldy."

"Maybe," said Morley, "you'd feel better if you shaved."

She certainly would.

That Tuesday night while they were asleep it rained so hard that the driveway washed out. When they woke up on Wednesday morning there was gravel over the lawn. Dave walked out to the road.

"There's a canyon where the driveway meets the main

road," he said. "There's no way we are getting out of here until someone comes and fixes it. I'll phone Mrs. Boisclair." He was beginning to feel trapped.

After supper Sam figured out how to work the Victrola.

"How did he do that?" said Dave to Morley after Sam had gone to bed. Dave had tried himself that afternoon and had given up after half an hour.

There were twenty-two heavy lacquered 78-rpm records in the cabinet below the turntable. They played them all. "Bad Sir Brian Botany," by Stanley Maxted, on Decca. "The Happy Fox Trot," by Boots and his Buddies on Bluebird. Bing Crosby. Most of the records had a different artist on each side. Dave and Morley danced together. Then Morley said, come here Sam, and Dave held out his arms to his daughter.

"Tonight's the night I was supposed to be going to The Deadly Snakes concert," said Stephanie. "I don't want to dance to that stuff."

On Thursday morning Morley opened the kitchen cupboard where she had put the breakfast cereals and a bat flew out of the open door and over her head. She did the only sensible thing she could think of doing. She screamed.

Dave, who was still in bed, thought his wife had disturbed a burglar.

They collided in the hallway each running towards the other.

Later Morley explained how the bat had come out of the cupboard. "It was like in that movie," she said. "The movie about the aliens. The one with with Sigourney Weaver."

"I'm not worried about bats," said Sam. "If there are any bats in my room the snake will get them."

"Snake," said Morley. "What snake?"

"The snake in my cupboard," said Sam.

"What snake in your cupboard?" asked Morley.

"There's a big snake in my cupboard," said Sam. "It's started to shed its skin."

Stephanie said, "I want to go home. Can we go home now?"

Dave said, "We're not going home."

After lunch he tried to build a fire to dry things out. But he couldn't get the logs to catch.

"I can do that," said Stephanie. It was the first thing his daughter had shown any interest in since they had arrived. Dave shrugged and handed her the matches and the newspaper.

"I don't need the paper," she said. "Paper is for sissies."

Dave had found a pile of *Sports Illustrated* from 1957. He had made it as far as the July 22nd issue. Would the rookie of the year in the American league be Frank Malzone or Roger Maris? Who had ever heard of Frank Malzone? Mostly Dave was reading the old ads. "Hey Mabel, Black Label!" "Martin's Scotch . . . that's the spirit." And on the back page of every issue, "The Marlboro Man: He gets a lot to like—filter, flavor, flip-top box."

Dave wondered if the guy in the ads was the one who got cancer and made all the anti-smoking commercials.

"There," said Stephanie. "Perfect."

And it was. A perfect little fire.

"How did you do that?" asked Dave.

"I learned at camp," said Stephanie. "You just have to be patient, Daddy."

It stopped raining on Thursday. Sam spent the last three days fishing off the dock. Dave cut the barb off his hook so he could throw back the fish he caught.

"He must have caught the same poor rock bass fifty times," said Morley as they watched Sam from the balcony. "God bless stupid fish."

"If I have to untangle his line one more time," said Dave, "I think I'll let him shoot the fish."

They went swimming for the first time on Thursday before supper. The water was chilly and they ran across the lawn to the cottage and got into their sweatpants and it felt good to be cold and dry. They swam a lot after that. Except for Stephanie. There was a spider the size of a sparrow living under the dock and after Sam helpfully pointed it out, Stephanie refused to go anywhere near the water.

But on their last night there, she built another fire. And when Dave and Morley were in the kitchen, Sam cranked up the Victrola and Stephanie taught Sam how to waltz. After dinner the two kids put on a dance show for their parents that made all the rain and all the fights melt away.

"This is the fox trot," they said. "This is the polka."

Dave and Morley clapped. Then they started dancing too.

Morley drove the car back to the city. Dave sat in the back with Sam. They bounced down the driveway to where their road joined the highway. As the car pulled onto the pavement, Sam twisted in the seat and said, "That was fun, can we come back next year?"

"Yeah," said Stephanie, "are we coming next year, Daddy?"

"Maybe," said Dave. "Maybe. We'll see."

Road Trip

By the end of August, summer had settled so lazily upon the city that it was hard to imagine a different season. It confirmed itself every night, in the clutter spilling from the sidewalk cafés, in the chatter of neighbourhood baseball games, in the night-time hiss of a thousand water sprinklers.

Across from the Vinyl Cafe two young men, both wearing beards and assorted earrings, had erected a scaffold and were painting a mural down the empty brick wall of an old theatre.

In Jim Scoffield's backyard the last of the raspberries were barely hanging onto the raspberry bush. The afternoon Dave and Morley got home from the cottage, Jim brought them a bowl of berries and they had them for breakfast the next morning. Sam spent his first morning back in the city following the water truck around the neighbourhood on his bike. He rode in the rainbow at the back of the truck—in the driver's blind spot—laughing at the spray licking at his pedals, enjoying the sweet iron smell of cold water on hot pavement. There were worse places to be, in the dog days of summer, than back in the city.

Dave was not unhappy to be home, pleased that after its stuttering start this year's vacation had been declared a success. It was a far cry from last summer when he had taken his family on a road trip—something he might not have tried if he had read the survey that said 40 percent of Canadian children claim they would rather clean their room and eat vegetables every day than go on a family holiday.

The survey hadn't been published when Dave and Morley were planning last summer's vacation. Dave had always wanted to drive west with his children, and Stephanie was almost sixteen. She would soon be too old for family trips. They were running out of summers when they could travel together.

"We could go around the Great Lakes," said Dave. "Maybe into Saskatchewan." Dave wanted to show his children the beauty of the prairies. Imagined his family in a campground in the valley of the Saskatchewan River. What could be better?

Morley said, "We are not going to put the cat in the car again, Dave. If the cat's in the car, I'm not coming."

Dave said, "We'll find someone to look after the cat."

The cat had belonged to Dave's sister, Annie.

Dave and Morley took it the spring Annie moved back to Nova Scotia from Boston.

"I don't know," she said, when Dave offered to take the cat.

"What do you mean?" said Dave.

"I feel stupid," said his sister. "I don't like to say it out loud."

"Say what?" said Dave.

"Whenever the cat is around, things seem to go wrong."

Dave said, "Don't be silly. We can look after a cat."

Annie brought the cat in a cage. As soon as she was in the house Dave kneeled down and wiggled a finger through the bars.

"Puss puss," he said.

"Galway," said Annie, "after the American poet, Galway Kinnell."

The cat was beige with black spots—lean and rangy. A female.

"I know," said Annie. "But we were big fans."

Dave started to fiddle with the latch on the cage door.

"Wait," said Annie, holding out an envelope. But she was too late. Dave had already flipped the latch open.

"Here, Puss," he said.

The cat shot out of the cage as if she had been spring loaded.

"Oh," said Annie.

"Oh," said Dave.

They were both off balance—staring at each other and

then at Galway, who had sailed over Dave's shoulder and landed in the middle of the hall with the sureness of a jazz dancer.

"It's OK," said Dave. Thinking, Maybe it was not OK at all.

"You should have read this first." Annie was gesturing with the envelope. "Before you let her out."

As Dave took the envelope, Arthur, the family dog, ambled through the dining-room door. When Galway saw Arthur, she hissed, and Arthur jerked to a stop as if someone had yanked his chain.

"Arthur," said Dave, "this is Galway. Galway is a cat."

Arthur took a cautious step forward, his tail wagging tentatively. Galway sank to the floor, and began to lower her ears—they folded towards her head like bat wings—until they were flat and she looked like she was wearing a helmet. Arthur bared his teeth and a sound that was more a rumble than a growl began to emanate from deep inside of him. The cat and the dog stared at each other for a moment and then Galway flicked her tail. Arthur abruptly stopped growling, looked pathetically at Dave as if to say, Why are you letting this happen? and slunk into the kitchen.

Annie looked defensive.

Dave said, "I'll read this later." He stuffed the instructions in his back pocket.

He forgot about the letter until that night. When he pulled it out, he wondered how his sister could have written three pages about a cat. Typical of Annie to fuss like that. He took the letter and went into the den. Arthur, who was curled up on the couch, lifted his head, furrowed his brows, slid onto the floor and mooched out of the room, throwing a doleful glance over his shoulder as he left. Dave shut the door. He had come into the den because he didn't want to read Annie's letter in front of Galway, so he was startled, when he turned around, to find she was sitting on top of the book shelf—with what Dave would later describe as a smirk on her face.

"She was threatening me," he said to Morley the next day.

Instead of reading Annie's letter he took it downstairs to put in his briefcase. Then he went to bed.

Or he was pretty sure he had put it in his briefcase.

"Maybe you threw it out," said Morley. "Last night was garbage."

"I didn't throw it out," said Dave. "The cat took it out of my briefcase."

"Probably," said Morley.

"She did," said Dave. "Look at her. That's a smirk. She's smirking." At that moment Galway turned and walked away, her tail in the air.

"See," said Dave. "She didn't want us to read the letter. It said something about the cage. About keeping her in the cage."

"Probably," said Morley. "That's probably it. The hair dryer is missing too. Do you suppose she has the hair dryer as well?"

It took Arthur and Galway about a week to work out an uneasy truce. For the first week the cat barely set foot on the floor—she moved around the house from chair back to table-top—often settling somewhere above Arthur, gazing down at him threateningly. Dave came home one night in the second week and the cat had descended. Morley said, "See. They're fine now."

Dave wasn't as sure. "Watch," he said. "Whenever Galway comes into the room, Arthur gets up and leaves."

One day Dave came home at lunch to check the mail. It was garbage day, so instead of going through the front door he picked up the empty garbage can and lugged it down the driveway. As he passed the dining-room window he saw movement in his peripheral vision. He turned just in time to see Arthur hurtling through the dining-room with Galway clinging onto his back like she was riding a bucking bronco.

A moment later they came back, heading in the other direction, Galway barely clinging to Arthur. Dave watched her slide off as Arthur spun wildly into the kitchen—watched Galway jump onto the dining-room buffet and perch there, her eyes glued to the kitchen door.

No wonder Arthur had seemed so tired.

That summer Dave made the mistake of trying to take Galway with them on a weekend trip to the Muskokas. This was what Morley was remembering when she said she would not travel with the cat again.

The car was all packed. Sam, who was two at the time, was already strapped into his car seat, and already crying, when Dave tried to put Galway back into the cage. Getting the cat into the cage was like trying to fold a large spring into a tin can. Galway kept popping free, then hiding—behind the fridge, under a bed. Dave chased her around the house, humiliated— thinking, when he was young fathers knew how to do things like change the oil in their cars, solder things together, clean fish. Surely he could put a cat into a cage. He needed to show his family he could do this thing. It was driving him wild.

Out in the car Stephanie had begun to throw a tantrum. Morley, who was feeling pretty irritable herself, said, "Stay here. I'm going to get your father."

When she found him pulling Galway through a radiator by her tail, Morley said, "What are you doing? Why do we have to use the cage? Why don't we let her free in the car?"

"That's why," said Dave five minutes later, as the family stood in the driveway beside their packed car, watching Galway disappear over the backyard fence like a burglar. There was a set of red scratches that looked like skid marks running up Dave's face and over his forehead.

"You better have those looked at," said their neighbour Jim Scoffield, who had been watching. "They can infect."

"What?" said Dave.

"Cat scratches," said Jim, "They get infected easily."

"She didn't have to do that," Dave told Morley as she wiped his face with hydrogen peroxide. "She had to go out of her way to go over my head. It was deliberate. It was malicious."

It started to rain. They never got to the cottage.

Last summer Dave said, "I'll get Kenny to look after her. We'll leave her here and Kenny can come over and feed her. It's just two weeks. Kenny can do that."

Dave knew Kenny would be delighted to have a key to his house. To a television set with cable.

Dave was prepared to leave Galway in the house by herself, but not Arthur. Jim Scoffield had offered to look after the dog.

Usually Arthur was anxious when he sensed he was being left behind and Dave felt like a traitor when he led him over to Jim's house. But when they got there Arthur seemed . . . relieved. Almost delighted. When Dave took him off the leash he bounded around Jim's house. When Jim leant over to pat him, he licked his face with enthusiasm.

"That's odd," said Dave.

They left on a glorious Monday morning in August. They drove north, stopping for hamburgers after two hours on the road. Stephanie walked into the restaurant after they had found a table and sat at the counter by herself.

They made supper in a provincial park on the shores of Georgian Bay.

"This is what Canada is all about," said Morley. "This is the heart of our country."

"It's too windy," said Stephanie. "It's just trees."

They drove aboard the ferry to Manitoulin Island in the morning. First on, first off, said Dave.

Halfway across the lake, the sky abruptly darkened and the ferry started to roll in the chop. Dave said, "I don't feel so good. I'm going to the car to fetch a sweater." Down below he had to pick his way along the length of the ship to where he had parked at the front of the line of cars. First on. First off. The rumble of the ship's engine and the greasy smell of motor oil didn't make Dave feel better. He was standing alone among the parked cars, like a wonky scarecrow, wondering what he should do if his stomach got worse, when he opened the trunk. He was preoccupied and totally unprepared for what happened next.

He squinted into the dark trunk and leaned forward, feeling for his sweater. In the darkness his hand brushed against something soft and wool-like on top of the picnic hamper. He tried to pick it up and then, with a shock of adrenaline rushing through his body, he let it go—knowing this thing he had touched wasn't a sweater-thing, but something that could breathe, it was a breathing-thing. At this point Dave lost conscious awareness of what was happening. The adrenaline hit some primal gland and he became Cro-Magnon Dave. Knowing only that the thing-that-wasn't-a-sweater, the breathing-thing, was big enough to be a life-threatening sort of thing. Not cougar, but maybe wolverine. Cro-Magnon Dave made a grunting prehistoric sound that twentieth-century Dave had never heard before, but immediately understood to mean get-me-out-of-here.

When you reach into any dark place, a place you can't see into, even an innocuous place, like under-a-sofa, when you reach under-a-sofa expecting to come up with something like a newspaper, and hit, instead, something soft, like the family guinea pig, or worse, something you can penetrate, like a piece of rotting fruit, even these innocuous objects can kick the get-me-out-of-here gland into action.

And so it is, when you reach into your trunk in the darkness of a ferry expecting to grab a sweater, and wrap your hand instead around something that can breathe, you do exactly what Dave did—you jump back and smack your head on the roof of the trunk. And a split second later, when the breathing-thing—which some part of Dave's brain noticed bore an amazing resemblance to Galway—when this *living creature* explodes out of the trunk, you instinctively grab it by the tail as it sails by you, and you swing it in the air.

Galway landed on the roof of the car. Dave stood there,

feeling the blood pounding in his ears. Heard an announcement over the speakers instructing passengers to return to their vehicles. Saw his wife and children coming towards him.

"Now, Lord," he said. "Take me now, Lord."

The family seemed more concerned, *were* more concerned, about Galway than they were about Dave.

"Is she OK, Daddy?" said Stephanie.

"What happened?" said Sam.

"How did *she* get here?" said Morley.

As the ferry docked, the kids ran to the cafeteria. They came back with a tuna salad sandwich and a pile of coffee creamers.

"She hasn't eaten all day," said Sam.

Galway spent the next half-hour in the back seat, between the kids, lapping up the tuna sandwich and innumerable creamers. By the time they reached Sault Ste. Marie, she had settled comfortably in what became her favourite car-place— curled under Dave's seat, where she could reach out whenever she felt like it, and take swipes at Dave's ankles.

"Tough," said Morley.

She didn't say, Sorry. She didn't say, We could stop and get a cage. Just "tough."

There were some nice times: an afternoon at Science North in Sudbury, the morning the truck driver took their picture beside the giant goose at Wawa.

"I was once stuck here for two days," said Dave. "Trying to hitchhike to Vancouver."

But it wasn't the vacation Dave had imagined. He had envisioned himself in the early evening, drinking a beer in a lawn chair beside the pool of some seedy motel, watching the kids swim. He had imagined baskets of fried chicken, strange television shows, roadside theme parks.

Mostly it was a dark and sorry week.

He had not considered flat tires, No-Vacancy signs, lost sun-glasses and a worn-out alternator. He left the headlights on one afternoon in a mall parking lot outside Schreiber, Manitoba. They had to phone for a boost.

Mostly it was thumping west along the Trans-Canada Highway to the constant buzz from Stephanie's Walkman. Mostly it was Morley and Dave barely talking, Sam and Stephanie only talking when they needed to point out where their side of the seat began or ended. Every night Dave locked himself into the motel bathroom and dabbed at his shredded ankles with hydrogen peroxide. There was no air-conditioning in their car and each day it seemed to get hotter.

On a Sunday when they woke up sticky and got stickier as the day progressed, Galway started to behave oddly. She moved out from under Dave's seat and began pacing around the car.

"I think Galway is sick," said Sam.

"She looks weird, Daddy," said Stephanie. "There's white stuff around her mouth."

Galway wasn't sick. She had just been heated up hotter than a cat should be heated. Dave said, "We'll get off the highway. There must be a back road."

The temperature in the car *was* unbearable. They couldn't open the windows much for fear Galway would jump out. Dave was thinking, We'll stop for ice cream first place we see.

And then, suddenly, they were in a traffic jam.

On a Sunday? thought Dave. In Atikokan?

"I need a drink," said Stephanie. "I don't feel so good."

Dave said, "Hold on," and turned abruptly onto a side street. He had no idea where he was going. He just knew that he had to keep the car moving until they got somewhere. Anywhere. He didn't want to be stuck in traffic. He drove halfway down the block and to his horror saw there was a barrier at the end of the street. He could feel the car closing in on him.

"I don't believe this," he said.

He stopped abruptly, throwing the kids against the front seat and Galway into his ankles.

"Cool," said Sam.

"Dave," said Morley, "take it easy."

But Dave was beyond easy. He pulled the car into reverse and began backing up the street faster than he should have. Swinging from side to side.

"There's an alley," he said. "I saw an alley."

He turned into the alley and too late saw that a block away, where the alley rejoined the street, there was a crowd of people standing with their backs to him, blocking his way. He honked. And when nothing happened, he honked again. He kept driving down the alley. Honking. No one moved until he was close and then a man, holding two children by their hands, turned and looked. And only then did the crowd part, parents tugging children out of the way.

Then they were out of the alley and turning onto the main street. Dave hesitated and turned right because everything seemed to be moving right. He thought, At last.

And Morley said, "Dave?" It was a question.

Dave noticed the sidewalks were lined with people—not just across his alley, but all up and down the street—on both sides.

Stephanie said, "Why is everybody waving?"

And Morley said, "Because this is a parade. We are in a parade."

And Dave started to feel sick himself.

"This is pathetic," said Stephanie as she slipped out of sight onto the seat. Then before Dave could think what to do there was an explosion, like a cannon or a rocket.

Loud and close. And another . . .

It was a bass drum. Dave looked in the rear-view mirror and saw that there was a band right behind them. He watched, as the man in the bearskin hat leading the band, about ten feet behind Dave's car, hurled a silver baton high into the air. When he caught it, the band began playing. Dave didn't know marching bands sounded so loud when you were that close to them, and then he couldn't see them any more because the mirror was suddenly filled with the image of Galway hurtling from the back seat towards Dave's head, like a jet plane. Dave ducked. The car lurched momentarily towards the sidewalk. Dave slammed on the brakes. But he had to start up again, quickly, jerkily, or the marching band was going to march right over them.

So they drove on, Galway ping-ponging around the car, over all of them. Front seat. Back seat. Ricocheting off the windows. Flecks of foam flying from her mouth. She settled abruptly in Sam's lap.

Sam said, "Cool."

He held the foaming cat up to the window, waving her paw at the crowd.

A clown suddenly appeared at the side of the car, jogging along beside them, knocking on Morley's window, waving. Morley looked straight ahead.

Sam said, "This is *really* cool."

Dave smiled weakly at the clown and waved at a little girl who was pointing at him. He was looking for a street he could turn onto.

But there were no streets to turn onto.

"Well," he said, leaning into the driver's door, trying to be comfortable with this, "it could be worse."

Which is when Galway vomited.

Into Morley's lap.

They turned around that night.

They were sitting in the parking lot of a doughnut store somewhere between Atikokan and Fort Frances. It was 8:30 at night and they couldn't find a motel.

Morley said, "Dave, do you want to go home?"

"Is this Saskatchewan?" asked Sam. "It looks just like Scarborough."

They got home three days later.

As they drove under the warm orange glow of the lights that hung over the expressway, Morley felt as though she was being wrapped in a blanket. She turned to Dave.

"If you had to," she said. "how would you categorize this holiday?"

Dave looked at his wife. She was smiling.

He felt a wave of relief wash over him.

"Catastrophe," he said.

"I thought for a while," she said, "that you were . . ."

"Catatonic?" said Dave.

She laughed.

"It's good to be home. It wasn't a complete . . ."

"Cataclysm?" said Dave.

"Next year," he said, "no car. We'll fly to the . . ."

"Catskills," said Morley

"And eat the flesh of large, dumb, slow-moving animals," said Dave. "Meat that will block our arteries and make us fat."

"What?" said Morley.

"Elephants," said Sam.

"Cattle," said Stephanie.

It was good to be home.

There was a pile of mail on the dining-room table.

"I'm going over to Jim's," said Dave. "To get Arthur. I'll be back in a minute."

It was Morley who found the note from Kenny on the kitchen counter.

> Didn't see the cat for the first day or two so I put the food on the porch and he started eating it. He finally came in after a couple of days. I didn't let him out again. I think he missed you. He's been scratching the furniture a bit.

Dave walked into the living room with Arthur the same moment Galway came pounding down the stairs with a huge orange tabby on her tail. Galway, a step ahead of the tabby, leapt onto a bookcase and spun around to face the intruder. There was an instant of perfect silence. Dave standing at the doorway with Arthur at his side, Morley on her way from the kitchen with Kenny's note in her hand, Stephanie reaching for the mail, Sam about to turn on the television. All of them frozen for a moment, their eyes on this monstrous cat they had never seen before.

Arthur was the first to react.

He growled, and as everyone turned to look at him, the growl changed to a bark and he jumped into action, his feet windmilling on the hardwood floor, barking, growling, chasing the orange cat once around the dining-room and then out the front door.

It happened so fast no one had a chance to say anything.

Before anyone moved, Arthur was back, wagging his tail.

Galway jumped down from the bookcase and Arthur wagged up to her and licked her face.

"That's so cute," said Stephanie, turning back to the mail.

"They're happy to see each other," said Morley.

It was only Dave who noticed Galway's ears flattening ever so slowly; Dave who recognized the look of despair descending on Arthur as he tucked his tail between his legs and loped towards the kitchen, his dark woeful eyes glancing back over his shoulder at Galway as he went.

Autumn

Labour Days

On the first Tuesday in September, Morley flew through the back door of her house and said, "Sorry I'm late," to whomever was in the kitchen—whomever turned out to be Arthur, the dog, sitting expectantly by his dish, his tail wagging to see her. It was 6:15. Morley had meant to be home before 5:30. She thought *everyone* would be waiting, *everyone's* tail wagging, *everyone* expecting supper.

"Dave?" she called as she kicked her shoes onto the back steps and headed for the kitchen. She hesitated in front of the refrigerator for the briefest instant, like she might hesitate at the side of a lake or a swimming pool, pushing the hair off her face and then taking a deep breath before plunging in. She was on her knees rummaging around for something fast and easy to make for supper when Dave walked in.

Before he could say hello, she said, "Potatoes or rice?" And before he could answer, she did. "Rice," she said. Kicking the fridge closed, she headed for the cupboard. "Anna Lindquist asked me to go with her to L.A. for the weekend."

Dave opened the fridge and pulled out a beer and said, "Why not? It couldn't cost more than a few thousand dollars."

"It's Emma Thompson's birthday," said Morley. "Anna invited me to go with her to Emma Thompson's birthday dinner. In L.A."

"We could put off fixing the car," said Dave, helpfully.

"She says she doesn't want to travel alone. Emma Thompson, Dave. The movie star."

Dave said, "When she invited you . . . did she mean you . . . you? Or you . . . and me?"

Morley was standing by the sink, rinsing the rice. She screwed her face up in concentration and said, "This is ridiculous. I can't afford to go to L.A. for the weekend. She knows that. That's why she asked me."

Morley and Dave had talked about Morley going back to work once the kids were grown. She never thought she would stay away from the stage so long. It was hard to believe it was almost twenty years. But she was busy and she was happy with what she was doing. But when The Century of Wind Theatre Company asked her if she would work for them as general manager, she realized it was the right time.

She was feeling defeated by the Sisyphean nature of her life—washing the same dishes, doing the same laundry, over and over again. She was jealous of Dave's engagement with the world. Even around the house, he always took on the big industrious projects—re-wiring the basement might be hard work, but she suspected it was a lot more interesting than organizing the winter clothes, again.

When they offered her the job, however, no one mentioned that the British actor Anna Lindquist had been signed to a six-week contract—due to arrive in Toronto on August 22nd to begin rehearsals for the role of Madame Arkadina in Anton Chekhov's *The Seagull*. In her darker moments Morley thought maybe someone had thought better of mentioning it. Anna Lindquist is what is known in the theatre business as "high maintenance."

As it turned out, Anna Lindquist arrived in Toronto two days early. It was Morley's first week at work.

"Darling," she said when she phoned from the airport, "surely you don't expect me to take"—her voice dropping an octave—"a taxi?"

"She did this last time," said Robert, the stage manager. "She does it to put everyone off balance. I can't stand it." And he started to cry.

As she rushed out to the airport, Morley wondered if she would be able to recognize Anna Lindquist from her publicity photos. As it turned out, she needn't have worried.

Anna was sitting in the arrivals level with a little white dog in her lap. She was holding a lit cigarette in a long tortoise-shell holder—under a No Smoking sign. She was by far the most colourful thing in sight. Her heels were high, her skirt was short, her nails were long and her hair, under the glare of the bright neon lights, was a shade of red Morley had never seen before.

Morley introduced herself and asked about luggage.

"I don't know, darling," said Anna, frowning. "I haven't the foggiest."

There was, she said, a matched set of three suitcases, and a hat box.

"In canary yellow, darling. I bought them in Mustique." While Anna stayed in the lobby, Morley found a cart and wheeled the suitcases across the airport.

"If you'll wait here," she said, "I'll get the car."

Morley had been too panicked on the way to clean out the candy wrappers, coffee cups and the stack of vinyl Dave had left in the front seat.

She rolled the baggage into the elevator and wheeled around the ramp to the parking lot. She threw the suitcases and the records into the trunk and cleaned up the car as best she could.

Ten minutes later she led Anna out the airport door to where she had parked the car illegally by the curb. She ran around to the driver's side, jumped in, and noticed Anna standing on the sidewalk looking vague. At first Morley thought Anna was looking for the limousine. Then she realized she was waiting for Morley to open the door for her.

When she finally settled into front seat she said, "I was actually expecting a car and driver."

Morley drove directly to the apartment the theatre had rented for Anna Lindquist. It was on a lovely tree-lined street.

The uniformed doorman, who had a nose for these things, immediately opened Anna Lindquist's door and led her into the foyer, leaving Morley to struggle with the luggage.

The apartment had the deep tranquillity of serious money—thick carpeting in the halls, heavy oak doors, the burnish of old brass, and a lobby mirror that really was antique.

Anna Lindquist peered in the open third-floor apartment door, her feet firmly planted in the hallway. "I can't possible stay here, darling," she said. "The walls are green. They remind me of vomit. I'll stay at a hotel until you can find something suitable. No need to drive me, darling . . . I'll call a taxi."

After supper, a week after Anna Lindquist arrived, Morley said, "The roughs for the posters came in today. Anna was upset because her name was below the title."

Dave was reading a music magazine at the kitchen table. "Gerta phoned," he said. "She's going to some new discount mall on Saturday."

Morley was spreading newspaper on the table. She was going to waterproof a pair of boots. "Chekhov is the only name above the title. I told her, 'You can't be above Chekhov.'"

Dave said, "Gerta wants to know if you want to go with her—to the mall."

Morley said, "You know what happened then? She said, 'Chekhov's been dead for ninety-three years, darling. What could he possibly care about where he is on your silly poster?'"

"Then she started talking about the size of the type. She wants her name in bigger print than Martin's."

Morley glared at her husband. "It's like working with a five-year-old. I went back to work because all I was doing was picking up after children and I end up picking up after a fifty-five-year-old."

Dave said, "You should go. It'll be fun."

"This is my life?" said Morley. "Shopping for bulk food is fun?"

Morley eventually decided she would go to the mall with Gerta Lowbeer, more to get out of the house on Saturday than anything else. Going to a bunch of discount stores in the suburbs, she decided, was the closest thing to foreign travel on the horizon.

"I'll just look," she said. "It will be a cultural experience."

She looked at the aisles of cartons, the miles of produce, and as she looked, strange and unfamiliar urges descended upon her. She came home with a camp-sized case of cereal that had to be wheeled to her car, a carton of frozen lasagna with fifty individual meals and a case of organic All-Natural Fruit Snacks—four bright new flavours: Pear, Boysenberry-Mango, Apricot and Very Berry—for the kids' lunches.

Morley prepared the lasagna for the first time the next Monday night. "This is easy," she thought coming home from work. "Frozen lasagna and a salad. No sweat."

She was feeling smug until Sam asked what was for dinner and said, "I hate frozen lasagna. Can I have spaghetti?"

Just as the water for the spaghetti was beginning to boil, Dave phoned and said, "I'm going to be late."

Instead of waiting, they started without him. When Stephanie took her first mouthful of lasagna she said, "This tastes doughy—it's not like the kind you make."

Morley didn't answer. She was watching Sam suck a piece of spaghetti up his nose. "Do that again," she said, "and I'll cut your nose off."

Sam said, "Robbie taught me."

Stephanie said, "I hate this lasagna."

And Dave came through the door and said, "Hi, everybody. Sorry I'm late."

The three of them stopped what they were doing and turned towards the door in unison—Stephanie raising her head glumly from her plate, Sam with a piece of spaghetti dangling from his nose, Morley frowning. All of them staring at this inappropriately cheerful man standing in the kitchen doorway.

At some mysterious level of Dave's brain a tiny voice was saying, Don't say anything, Dave. Just sit down and eat the lasagna. But Dave didn't hear the voice in time. So instead of sitting down he stood in the doorway. "It was great. Kenny Wong is doing renovations. *He* got *his* belt sander and *I* got *mine* and we were drag racing them—around the restaurant. I lost track of time."

No one said anything except the little voice. I told you not to say anything, it said.

So Dave sat down and took a bite of supper and said, "The lasagna is kind of doughy."

And the little voice said, Uh oh.

But Dave continued, "What's wrong? Where are you going?"

And Morley snarled, "I have to go out. Sam wants to show you something Robbie taught him."

Dave twisted around in his chair. He was talking to Morley's retreating back. "It's just frozen lasagna right? It's not like you made it. That was a compliment. You don't have to buy any more of these frozen lasagnas."

The next morning Morley got up and went into the bathroom and her toothbrush was already wet.

She said, "My toothbrush is wet. Why is my toothbrush wet?"

The family gathered solemnly around her.

"See," she said flicking the bristles. "It's wet. And I haven't brushed my teeth yet."

Sam and Dave stared glumly at the toothbrush—full of concern—it was as if she were telling them the dog had been hit by a car.

"That's *my* toothbrush," said Stephanie quietly. "The red one is *my* toothbrush."

Morley felt her heart turn cold.

"The red one," said Morley, "is mine. I use it every day. *You* are green."

"I am?" said Stephanie. "I thought I was red."

"Me too," said Sam. "I thought *I* was red."

Morley screamed and disappeared downstairs.

"What's the matter with her?" said Stephanie.

The kitty litter was Maggie's idea. Maggie's fault.

Maggie, who has three boys. It was Maggie who told Morley that she had had it with washing around the toilet.

"I told them if they planned to keep using our toilets they were going to have to sit down when they went from now on," said Maggie.

Bob, Maggie's husband Bob, said if he had to sit down every time he went to the bathroom he would leave home. He thought it was a humiliating thing to say to a man.

Maggie said OK. And then she dumped an entire bag of kitty litter around the base of the toilet.

Morley said, "You're kidding."

She didn't stop to think that the difference between her house and Maggie's house was that Maggie didn't own a cat.

When Galway saw the kitty litter around the upstairs toilet she assumed it had been put there for her.

It took Morley a day too long to figure out was happening—removing all the litter took nearly an hour.

Convincing Galway to give up on her new second-floor litter box will take even longer. It will not be until the middle of November that Morley will be able to stop reminding everyone, guests and family alike, to barricade the bathroom against the cat. Even now, whenever she sees the cat slinking down the hallway towards the bathroom, Morley shouts and rushes madly after her.

In the middle of September, the cast of *The Seagull* moved from the rehearsal space across the street into the theatre. An outline of the set had been marked off on the black stage floor with masking tape. Without flats, and with all the curtains raised, the stage looked like a empty aircraft hangar. You could see the dirty brick wall at the back of the building and the iron stairs leading to the catwalks. Standing alone on the stage Morley was struck, as she always was, by the space above her. The black bars holding the rows of lights seemed impossibly high.

Thursday afternoon was a technical run-through.

Anna Lindquist arrived carrying a large mirror. She played the entire first act holding the mirror no more than six inches from her face. Her eyes never left the mirror.

No one said a thing. Not even Martin Tidmarsh, who was playing her young lover. He leant forward and kissed her on the cheek, pushing his lips around the mirror as if she always carried it, as if it was the most normal thing in the world.

This is how crazy she had made them.

Ralph knew what she was doing. She was checking the lighting.

"She has approval of the lighting," said Ralph, the director, to Morley when she slipped into the theatre to see how things were going. "If she complains, I think Gordon is going to quit."

They were sitting in the middle of the empty theatre. Ralph had his feet jammed against the row of seats in front of them. Morley was holding a large green binder.

"Why," said Morley five minutes later, "is she facing *that* way. If she's talking to Martin shouldn't she be facing him?"

Anna Lindquist had her back to the entire cast. Everyone else was stage left except Anna, who was delivering a passionate soliloquy, to stage right.

"This way," said Ralph, "her left profile is facing the audience."

"She said my lights make her look old and crumpy," said

Gordon to Morley an hour later. "I don't have to take this, you know."

Morley was sitting in her office working on the first draft of the next season's budget.

"Come in, Ralph," she said, flipping off her computer screen. "I was just going to get a coffee. Do you want one?" She could work on the budget at home.

Thursday night at nine Morley went upstairs, announcing she was going to take a bath and go to bed early. As she passed Stephanie's room she stopped and said, "Have you hugged your mother today?"

Stephanie rolled her eyes and got up from her bed and leaned her arm around Morley's shoulders and slouched back into her room.

Dave was downstairs helping Sam with math homework when Morley screamed.

Dave said, "Stay here," and ran up the stairs. Two at a time.

Morley was standing in the bathroom. She had her bathrobe on.

"It's happening again," she said. "There are more toothbrushes in this bathroom than there are people in this house."

She assembled everyone and lined up the toothbrushes.

"Where did this *purple* toothbrush come from," she asked. Nobody would look at her.

Friday, Dave phoned Morley at lunch.

"I think I have solved the toothbrush mystery," he said. "I think that during the day, when the house is empty, there are people coming off the street and into our house to brush their teeth."

Morley said, "This isn't a joke, Dave."

On Tuesday morning Ralph came into Morley's office. He sat down beside her desk. When he began to speak, it was with uncharacteristic intensity.

He said, "She refuses to hold hands during curtain call."

It struck Morley that Ralph didn't look well.

"I am not going to tell you what she says about Martin," he said. "I am going to tell you this, instead. If you don't get her to hold Martin's hand during curtain call, then I'm leaving and I am never coming back."

He stood up, carefully. Morley noticed that the act of standing required more thought on his part than usual. He pushed the chair deliberately behind him.

He turned at the door. "One more thing," he said.

His deliberate calmness was starting to worry Morley.

"You tell her that if she slaps Melissa for real in Act Two that I am going to press charges. No more of this *heat of the moment* crap. And I don't care if she needs time off to be Rolfed. There is a rehearsal tomorrow morning and if she can't make it we'll get Joanna to play the part. And if Joanna plays tomorrow morning, Joanna opens tomorrow night."

Anna Lindquist opened Wednesday night. Gordon was on the lights, Ralph in a seat at the back beside Morley.

The next morning all three papers weighed in favourably. Two with raves. The play was a success. The mood at the theatre was buoyant.

Friday morning, Morley decided to stay at home.

The house looked like it needed bulldozing.

Morley had been so preoccupied with the theatre and Anna Lindquist that she hadn't noticed how bad the house was.

When everyone was finally off to work and school, she wandered into Sam's room. There were dirty clothes everywhere. She felt a heaviness descend upon her as she bent over to pick up a blue sweatshirt.

By eleven o'clock she had done seven loads of washing.

One more, she thought, and maybe she would have time for a load of her own things before she had to leave.

She was doing fine, thought she had broken the back of the laundry, until something made her look behind Stephanie's door. She found another pile of dirty clothes.

The relentlessness of the task overwhelmed her.

She could wash everything she could get her hands on— she could clean everything in the house—and no one would ever notice, no one would say thank you. They would just put on the clothes and get them dirty again.

The washing machine, open beside her, seemed to understand what it was doing. Seemed to be saying:

"I'm a bottomless pit. You'll never be done with me."

Morley started to cry. And then she started to struggle out of her shirt.

"Take this," she said, throwing it in the black hole at the top of the washer.

"Have more," she said, pulling off her jeans.

She was really crying now, pulling off her socks. "Have it all," she said.

At that precise moment Dave walked in the back door.

Morley quickly wiped the tears from her face, and turned slightly as Dave walked into the kitchen to find his wife standing there with no clothes on.

He had read about things like this.

A goofy, lopsided grin spread across his face.

He winked at his wife.

He started to unbutton his own shirt.

There are small moments of misunderstanding in a marriage that can be cleared up with a simple apology. There are other moments that require elaborate explanations and fast talking. And there are moments when neither an apology nor an explanation will do.

These moments require time and patience and great faith for the air to clear. Sometimes they require even more.

Morley had to get up at 5:30 the following Friday morning to take the limousine to the airport with Anna Lindquist, on their way to L.A. for Emma Thompson's birthday party.

"I left a note," she said to Dave as she got out of bed, "by the phone. The meals are all written out. They're all in the freezer."

Dave read her note an hour after she left. He was standing in the kitchen in his pyjamas, squinting at the paper, waiting for the coffee to brew.

Friday night, he read, lasagna and salad.

Saturday, lasagna and salad.

Sunday, lasagna and salad.

I'll be home at noon on Monday.

We'll go out for Chinese.

When Morley got home they went out for Chinese food. And she told them all about the impossibilities of travelling with Anna Lindquist. And about Los Angeles and the birthday dinner. She sat beside Candice Bergen. Opposite Ron Howard. She barely said a word all night.

"Those people," she said, "They don't know a thing about laundry or kids or running a house."

She seemed happy to be back.

"They've all had face lifts and tucks. You know what they served for dinner? Grilled tofu with guava relish."

She laughed out loud as she said it, and reached for another spring roll.

School Days

September is the most beguiling of the months. It is the month that won't let go of summer and it is the month that calls from the crow's nest of the year and announces, in the thinning air and morning dew, that summer is gone and autumn already here. One day September will lull you into believing that you should assemble your things and mount a picnic on a Saturday afternoon—September is made for Saturdays. But when Saturday comes, you spend the morning fumbling around in the attic, looking for sweaters, because it is raining and cold. You look at the picnic supplies you gathered and you wonder how you could have been so misguided.

September is a month for plans and a month for no plans. The month of full shelves and empty fields. A time for leave-taking and taking stock. It is the end of summer and the beginning of all that is to come. It is the month that Morley still uses to mark the progress of the years.

This September, her forty-fifth, Morley had to be at work early every morning. An American production house was using the theatre where she works to shoot scenes for a made-for-television movie. The agreement was that they would move in every night at midnight, wrap by eight and be struck and gone by ten in the morning. On their first Wednesday no one from the theatre was there at eight to lean on the director and the last lights weren't packed away until after eleven-thirty and they almost didn't have the theatre ready for a matinée of *The Seagull.*

Morley didn't mind coming in early. She likes the texture of morning—the colour of the light, the peaceful feeling of moving around the house while everyone is asleep. She bought a pastry on her way in, a chocolate croissant or a brioche. When she got to the theatre she brewed tea, walked around to let everyone know she was there, then went to her office and got a start on the day.

Although she enjoyed these early mornings, it meant she missed, for the first time ever, the kids' first giddy days of school. Dave was looking after things at home. It would have broken Morley's heart if she could have seen her husband and her son walking along the sidewalk every morning, hand in hand. Though she might have felt a pang of jealousy for the lost intimacy of this early morning ritual that had always been hers—if she could have seen them walking along together she would have also thought, I should have done this years ago. Sent them off together. Her son's canvas backpack. Her husband's leather briefcase.

The morning walks caught Dave by surprise. On Tuesday night he told Morley that walking to the schoolyard with his boy was like walking through a house of mirrors. You bump up against reflections of your past in the most unexpected places. You are hurrying your child to school and you turn a corner and look across the street and see a seven-year-old version of yourself standing on the opposite corner.

Dave grew up in the town of Big Narrows in Cape Breton, Nova Scotia, Canada, third planet from the sun, the Milky Way, the universe, et cetera.

This September the kids in Big Narrows were picked up at their doors and bused to what Dave still thinks of as the new school—only twenty-five years old and less than forty miles out of town. When Dave was a boy, he went to school in town. He went to the Big Narrows Elementary School on High Street. Which was not only, worse luck, the same school his sister attended, but also the school where his own mother—in one of the greatest treacheries that can be perpetrated on a child—worked as one of four teachers.

Dave had to walk the best part of a mile to get to school—and he can't remember ever walking with his mother, not once—even though for seven years they left the house at the same time and were heading for the same place. Dave had his own route and his mother afforded him this independence. It took him down dirt lanes, through vacant lots and along residential streets. It was a route carefully designed to pass the

Pattersons' woodshed—where kids would gather every morning to talk and scuffle and sometimes smoke, if someone had cigarettes.

Because Dave was Margaret MacNeal's son, every year, on the first day of school, he would have to endure what every other kid in the Big Narrows Elementary School still remembers and cherishes as Miss MacNeal's greatest moment. Because every year on the first day of school the entire student body—all sixty of them—was assembled in the basement lunchroom and Dave's mother climbed onto one of the six picnic tables they kept down there, and to the great amazement of the kids in kindergarten who had never seen this before, and to everyone else's delight, Miss MacNeal would burp the alphabet from A to Z.

Many of the kids in kindergarten actually stopped breathing when they witnessed this extraordinary feat. Their mothers had told them many things about school, but they hadn't told them about this *wonderful* woman. Some of them were away from their mothers for the first time ever. They would stand with their mouths hanging open and think, The world is so immense and I have so much to learn. It was a performance that would damage live theatre for many of them. It was good, they would say many years later of a play they had just watched—but, they would think quietly to themselves, not as good as the morning in September when Miss MacNeal burped the alphabet. Even Nora MacDonald, who as an adult went on to play in the woodwind section of Symphony Nova Scotia, had more than once stood squinting into the audience after a concert, bowing, thinking to herself how much better the concert would have been if Miss MacNeal could have been there. It was true art.

Every September, after she was finished, and before everyone was sent to their classrooms for the first morning of school—sent up to find their seats, to get their readers and workbooks and pencils, and to contemplate the year stretched ahead of them as fresh and full of possibility as a field of snow—every year before they went upstairs to do these things, Dave's mother would demonstrate how to burp the alphabet the way she did. They would try it in unison, the entire school together.

Most kids never got past C—although not for want of practice. It didn't in fact seem to *be* a matter of practice, it seemed to be more of a gift, that would appear every few years, usually in some kid in Grade One with a skinny neck and a large Adam's apple who could do it just like that, as if there was nothing to it.

If you were in kindergarten at Big Narrows Elementary you didn't see Miss MacNeal again for five years—until you got to Grade Five—and then you had her for three years straight: Grades Five, Six and Seven. And for three years you got to take part in the other ritual she is remembered for—the morning challenge. Every morning, before anyone was allowed in her classroom, Miss MacNeal wrote the morning challenge on the blackboard. When the bell rang she expected her students to take their seats and work quietly on the quiz. Everyone did, because everyone knew that whoever scored best on the quiz would be let out of class fifteen minutes early at lunch to ride their bike into town and buy Miss MacNeal a package of cigarettes. They got to spend the seven cents change on penny candy. It was a ritual that made children so happy that even parents who didn't approve of smoking didn't think to question it.

Dave never got to do this—even on the six mornings when he scored highest on the quiz. His mother did not want to appear to be favouring her son—so on those six occasions when she could have legitimately sent him, she sent the child who had come second. He was once, however, allowed this— the exquisite joy of drifting along Main Street when every other kid in town old enough to have a two-wheeler was still in class—when the principal, Mr. Ormiston, sent him to the hardware store to pick up a hunting rifle he had ordered.

"We were so free," said Dave to Morley one night. "Nothing was organized. There was a creek behind the school. We spent hours catching frogs. God, that was fun."

"All I remember," said Morley. "Is pain. Pain and humiliation."

On *her* first day of kindergarten Morley was made to lie down on a piece of long brown paper while the teacher traced her outline with a thick black pencil. Then Morley was given a box of crayons and told to colour the life-size outline. Morley started with the eyes. She put the first eye smack in the centre of her forehead. She knew it was the kind of mistake you couldn't come back from and she asked for another piece of brown paper. But no matter how hard she tried to explain about the eye in the middle of her forehead, her teacher wouldn't let her make a fresh start.

Instead of turning the paper over and starting again, Morley sat on her spot on the floor and refused to do anything.

At the end of the morning when everyone's pictures were put up on the wall, Morley's went up too—with no mouth, and no hair and no clothes—just one huge brown eye staring down from the middle of her forehead and her name written at the bottom of the paper in big black letters. The portrait glared down at her every day for a month before it was removed.

"It was humiliating," said Morley, "having to look at the eye every morning. I felt like it was watching everything I did."

That, thought Dave, is the essence of elementary school. You walk around the schoolyard, up and down the corridors, you sit at your desk, and wherever you go there is someone with a great big eye in the middle of their forehead staring down at you. Sometimes it's your teacher, sometimes it's your friends or your family—most often it's the quiet voice in your mind that compares you to everyone else and weighs in with its inevitable and unforgiving judgment.

Last year, when he was in Grade Three, Dave's son had his own meeting with the unflinching eye. After Christmas each student in Sam's class was assigned a pen pal from a school in the suburbs. Sam was assigned Aidan. Most of the letters written back and forth between the classes were stiff and a long way from real—but somehow the stars were aligned when Sam and Aidan were paired. They developed that most rare of modern relationships—they became correspondents.

Through the mail, Sam and Aidan learned they liked the same television shows, played the same video games, read the same books and soon discovered they felt the same way about much of it. They even had the same birthday.

"Maybe," said Sam, "Aidan is my twin brother. Maybe there was a mistake at the hospital or something."

At the end of May the two schools arranged a field day so they could bring all the pen pals together. Everyone knew the highlight was going to be the moment when Sam met Aidan. Everyone knew how excited Sam was about the meeting, and about the plans he and Aidan had made.

"I'm going up to his cottage," said Sam. A statement of fact, not a question.

They met on the sidewalk beside a large yellow school bus.

"I'm Aidan," said the skinny, freckled, eight-year-old girl holding out her hand. She had stringy, straw-coloured hair that hung down to her shoulders. She was wearing a grubby T-shirt, jeans and sneakers. She looked as if she could throw a ball. She also looked undeniably like a girl.

"I'm Aidan," she said, again.

"No, you're not," said Sam.

"Aidan is a girl," sang Lawrence Hillside. "Aidan's a girl."

It was a fact beyond Sam's comprehension—outside his realm of the possible. His friend Aidan was a boy. His friend Aidan could not be a girl.

"Yes, I could," said Aidan, holding her ground.

There was a circle of kids around them.

Sam was dumbfounded. He said, "I have to go." And he turned and pushed desperately through the crowd, pain on his face. He never mentioned Aidan again. Dave knows this much because he heard it from Sam's teacher.

"We had a fat boy in our class," said Morley. "His name was Norman Minguy. Did I ever tell you about Norman? He got along better with the girls than the boys. But he didn't get picked on. Probably because he always had lots of money. He used it to buy penny candy. The year we were in Grade Four we had Mrs. Merrill who was strict—but nice. Norman sat in the middle of the class and sometimes when Mrs. Merrill was writing on the blackboard and her back was towards the class and the room was quiet because everyone was copying what she was writing on the board into their exercise books, sometimes Norman would reach into his desk and take a handful of penny candy and toss it into the air. It was like someone had lobbed a grenade into the class—one minute dead silence and the next, bedlam. Kids on the floor, kids under desks, everybody fighting for candy. Mrs. Merrill would turn around—mystified—genuinely astonished because except for these unexpected explosions we were a well-behaved class. She would put her hands on her hips and ask what was going on, and of course no one would tell her. No one would turn Norman in because no one wanted him to stop. It was too good to be true."

In the middle of her second week of early mornings at work Morley dreamed she was sitting on a bench in a crowded waiting room.

"All the parents were there," she said to Dave on the telephone the next morning. "Everyone looked so worried. I was sitting right across from Ted and Polly Anderson. But they wouldn't look at me. No one would. Polly was wringing her hands like something awful was about to happen. It felt like we were there because we had done something terribly wrong. Do you think it means I shouldn't have gone back to work?"

Sam had never been so far out of her orbit. He was moving into a universe that soon she would hardly be allowed to visit. And he was moving so fast. She began to think more and more about her own childhood—to compare her experiences to her son's. It was dangerous ground—even the happy memories could make her sad. She was feeling guilty that she was not walking Sam to school—that he was eating lunch in the cafeteria for the first time.

She kept coming back to Norman Minguy and the utter joy of those classroom scrambles that he set in motion when he threw the penny candy in the air. Morley wanted the same thing for Sam. And that is what led her into the schoolyard at 6:00 a.m. on a Monday in September with two rolls of quarters and a roll of dimes and nickels. If she couldn't lob candy around Sam's classroom, she could scatter change around his schoolyard. Morley imagined that a schoolyard full of coins—like pirate's treasure—would create the same joy for her son as Norman Minguy's penny candy did for her.

She scattered twenty dollars in loose change around the yard. Under the play structure and in the sandbox and by the tool shed and under the stairs where the little kids gathered. She felt wonderful and light and alive. It didn't matter, she thought, if Sam got any of the money—although she was planning to head home as soon as she finished and do her best to get him to school early. But it didn't matter because schoolyards exist in stories as much as real life, and Sam would be part of the story, and the story would become a legend, and it would grow in the telling—before long it would be hundreds of dollars—they would talk about the morning there was hundreds of dollars in the schoolyard. Kids would be at school early for weeks—in the sure knowledge that it would happen again.

It did not, of course, work out like that. After she finished spreading the money, Morley went for coffee and a roll at a little place run by a Portuguese baker from Argentina—it was a happy little spot where you poured your own coffee from a pot on the counter and sat, if you felt like sitting, at one of the two tables in the rear of the store. Morley liked it there because everything was made of wood and you still got your bread in brown paper bags.

On her way home she detoured by the school to savour the sheer recklessness of what she had done. As she pulled up to the school fence she saw a tall, bony man with a goatee standing by the swings, wiping his brow. It was Floyd, the school janitor, who was never seen within an inch of the schoolyard whenever there was broken glass to be picked up. As Morley watched, Floyd bent over and began ploughing around the yard like a Zamboni, sucking up every coin she had dropped. Instead of going home and getting her son up as she had intended, Morley went to a phone booth and called her husband.

"Why didn't you stop him," asked Dave. "Why didn't you tell him it was for the kids?"

"I was too embarrassed," said Morley. "It was too silly. I am going to walk to work. The car is parked by the field. Will you pick it up when you take Sam?" And she hung up.

All morning Dave imagined, with growing regret, what might have happened had Floyd not stumbled upon Morley's money. By mid-afternoon he had worked himself into such a state that he was having trouble concentrating. He spent fifteen minutes sticking twenty-dollar price tags on a stack of albums he meant to label with two-dollar tags. It took him half an hour to peel the labels off and reprice them. When he caught himself filing *The Best of Herman's Hermits* under Soul, he knew it was time to stop. It wasn't until he was almost home that he knew what to do about Morley—he was going to finish what his wife had started. But he wasn't going to fill the schoolyard with spare change for Floyd to scoop. Dave had a better idea. He was going to fill it with frogs.

"Catching frogs," he said to Morley that night, waving his arms as he walked around the kitchen, "is the essence of childhood."

It had only taken Dave two phone calls to find frogs.

"I called a pet store first," he said, "but they only had green tree frogs. For, like, pets."

"How much," said Morley, "is a green tree frog?"

"Nine ninety-nine each," said Dave. "Fifteen dollars for two."

As she stared at her husband in trepidation Morley did the math in her mind—six frogs . . . forty-five dollars. Surely he wouldn't spend forty-five dollars on frogs. There wouldn't be more than six.

Dave was somewhere else. Going too fast to notice Morley's growing apprehension. He was full steam ahead.

"Anyway," he said. "I had a better idea."

"*Different* idea," said Morley. "You had a different idea."

"Bait store," said Dave.

"Bait store?" said Morley

"Leopard frogs," said Dave. "The frogs we caught when we were kids."

"When *you* were a kid," said Morley.

There was silence. Morley and Dave in their kitchen looking at each other. Dave holding a dripping dish towel, beaming and proud. A little nervous. A *lot* excited. Morley, her hands up to the wrists in a bowl of raw hamburger, fearful of what she had created.

"How much," said Morley "are leopard frogs?"

"Only $6.99 a dozen," said Dave.

"How many are you getting ?" said Morley, wiping meat off her fingers.

"Three dozen," said Dave.

"Three dozen," said Morley, walking towards the sink.

"Maybe four?" said Dave. He said it like it was a question. Like he was asking permission. But he wasn't asking permission. He had already been to the bait store. He had already bought the frogs. They were out in the garage in five large plastic boxes. Ten dozen of them. One hundred and twenty leopard frogs Dave intended to set loose in the morning.

Morley might have stopped him then—should have stopped him—but he hadn't stopped her. Dave imagined the schoolyard full of fast-moving children—imagined boys with frogs in their pockets—girls crouched in secret councils. If she had known how it would work out, Morley would have said something. But she didn't. She was trying to be supportive.

Neither of them imagined Rebecca Morton, five years old, kindergarten, on the sidewalk in front of the school clutching her mother's leg, screaming loudly enough that she was heard a full block away.

"Take me home," she was crying.

Certainly neither of them—Dave nor Morley—imagined Duncan Sheppel—Grade Seven—would have a Swiss Army knife in his pocket. Or that Mrs. Jenkins, on yard duty that morning, would react with what Dave later described as hysteria when confronted with a frog head.

"If she hadn't fainted," he said glumly to Morley that night, "things wouldn't have gotten out of hand." Even Dave had to admit things had gotten out of hand.

Children were running wildly over the yard, girls chasing boys, boys chasing girls, everyone chasing frogs. Rebecca Morton providing the unfortunate soundtrack for the whole sorry scene.

"What sort of idiot," Dave overheard Rebecca's mother say, "would have done this?"

"Out of hand?" said an icy Nancy Cassidy, the school principal, as Dave sat across from her desk the next morning. "It was like a prison riot." Nancy Cassidy had always struck Dave as a gentle soul. Now she was reprimanding him as if he were a child.

"What on earth did you think you were doing?" she demanded. "Perhaps you would consider some form of counselling?"

Dave had already spent an hour on his knees with Floyd, the janitor, scraping frogs off the schoolyard with a putty knife. Surely, he thought, this was enough. Clearly, it was not. And that is why on the following Monday morning the entire school gathered in the lunchroom so Dave could explain what he was thinking when he had brought the frogs. Why frogs were such a joyful memory—memories he had hoped they would capture as they went about capturing the frogs. And why it was wrong to remove a frog's head. This was his idea—to make this speech. It was one of the worst moments in his life.

The next morning when Duncan Sheppel saw Sam walking across the schoolyard he fell in beside him and said, "Your dad's pretty cool."

Sam didn't know what to say. It felt odd to have this older boy walking beside him. He wasn't sure if the boy was teasing him or not. He looked around to see if anyone was watching.

"He's all right," he said.

Then Duncan pulled out his Swiss Army knife.

"I'm not supposed to have this," he said. "I'm afraid they might take it away. Could you hold it until three o'clock?"

Sam nodded dumbly and took the knife and stuffed it into his pocket. He had never had a knife in his pocket before. All day he could feel it, hard and full of potential. He returned it to Duncan after school, by the climber, carefully.

Mostly now when they pass each other in the schoolyard, Duncan ignores Sam, but from time to time he nods and says, "Hi."

This is what Sam will remember of everything. Not the thrill of finding treasures or the joys of catching frogs. Rather, that his father came to school one day and talked about memories and that Duncan Sheppel, who was in Grade Seven, lent him his knife once, and sometimes even said 'hi' to him.

A Day Off

The Seagull was extended for two weeks, and might have been held over for two more, had Anna Lindquist not had to be back in London by mid-October.

The week before she left, Anna appeared in Morley's office and said she wanted to throw a cast party on closing night. She wanted a room at the Palazzo. And champagne. Could Morley help with the details?

Organizing the party gradually took over Morley's life during the final few days of the run. There were constant interruptions from Anna, and Morley ended up having to come in even earlier in order to keep up with her own work.

When closing night finally arrived, Morley was so fed up with Anna Lindquist, and so utterly exhausted, that she said she wasn't going to the party.

"It's her last night," said Dave. "You'll never have to see her again. Just go."

So she went. She spent most of the evening on the balcony, smoking Ralph's cigarettes and drinking too much of Anna Lindquist's white wine.

"At least she's paying," she said.

"I didn't know you smoked," said Ralph.

"I don't," said Morley, reaching for another cigarette.

At midnight, Anna Lindquist left her own party without saying goodbye to anyone. She left with Martin, who had played her young lover in *The Seagull*. Martin was not yet thirty. Anna Lindquist was fifty-five if she was a day.

"How long has *that* been going on?" asked Morley.

Anna Lindquist was standing at the door, a cigarette holder dangling in her right hand, her left hand running through Martin's hair.

"I don't even want to think about it," said Ralph. "Let me get you another drink."

It was the last time Morley saw Anna—but not the last she heard of her.

The next morning when they woke up, it was snowing. The snow turned to rain before breakfast. It was a warning shot, a whiff of winter, but it was enough of a warning that it propelled Morley to make the annual trip down into the basement. She headed into the darkness like a migrating goose, carrying a dim memory of Sam's snow boots, which might have been blue, and maybe still fit. She waved her arm in front of her in the darkness, as if she were trying to brush away a spider's web. She groped for the string that turned on the storeroom light, then she reached up amongst the pipes, praying as she did that there was a light bulb in the socket so she wouldn't stick her finger in an empty socket and die.

Morley knew she was on a fool's mission. She knew in her heart that the boots weren't down there. And if they were, she wasn't going to find them. Not in October. She would find them in June. When she was down there looking for bathing suits. Sam's boots probably spent the spring at the bottom of a lost-and-found box—at a school he never attended. And now? They weren't in the basement. They were on the back of a shelf in a Goodwill store, miles from home. Morley trudged upstairs.

"We'll have to get Sam new winter boots on the weekend," she said.

Dave nodded.

On Wednesday, two unexpected letters arrived at the theatre. The first, addressed to the accounting department, was from the Palazzo. It was a bill for Anna Lindquist's party—$4,700.

Morley threw the bill onto Ralph's desk. "I don't believe it," she said. "It was clear from the beginning. She was paying for the party, all of it."

Jennifer, who opened the mail, wasn't sure what to do with the second letter. It was a handwritten note on pale blue vellum—a heartfelt thank-you note from Anna Lindquist.

"Dear Morty," it began.

Jennifer took it to Ralph.

"We don't have a Morty," she said. "Who could she mean?"

When Dave woke up the next morning, Morley was sitting in bed drinking coffee and reading the newspaper. This wasn't part of the normal routine. Dave peered at the clock radio and then at his wife.

"I'm sick," she said.

Dave propped himself up. She didn't look sick to him.

"I am," she said.

She put the paper down and stretched languidly.

"So are you," she said. "I think you should get someone to open the store." Morley leaned forward and put her face close to Dave's. " I don't think you should go to work. Not the way you're feeling."

Dave reached up and touched his forehead. It was a reflex.

Morley nodded. "I think it has a fever."

She jumped out of bed, wandered to the window and stretched again, "We're staying home. We're taking a mental health day."

Dave said, "I can't do that."

Morley said, "Yes you can. Phone Brian. He's always looking for extra hours."

Dave said, "I've never done anything like that in my life. Ever."

Morley said, "Dave you *own* the business. If you want to stay home, you're allowed. If you really were sick, everything would work out."

Dave said, "Yeah, but . . ."

It was not that the store was so busy. Nor was it that Dave

was the kind of man who couldn't goof off once in a while. Dave had whiled away entire mornings at the Vinyl Cafe with a Rubik's Cube—ignoring dusty shelves, piles of filing and overdue accounts. Dave could goof off. It was his sense of himself that was affronted—his place in the world. Every morning, after he woke and showered and dressed and ate breakfast, Dave headed off to open his record store. If he didn't have to do this today, then he didn't have to do it tomorrow. Or, for that matter, ever. And if he didn't have do this—what did he have to do? By asking him to stay home Morley was calling into question his place in the universe.

She said, "We've been married fifteen years, Dave. It's time for some spontaneity. We are going to spend one unplanned perfect day together. I am going to go to that gourmet food store near Thea's and buy supplies. I'm going to get some videos. We are going to eat and watch movies. And other things."

It was the "other things" that got Dave.

He shoved a wad of Kleenex in his mouth and phoned Brian and said "I'm sick. Can you open up?"

Brian said, "Yeah. Sure. What are you eating anyway? It sounds like your mouth is full of Kleenex."

Morley said, "I'm going to get the food and the videos. I'll be back in an hour."

Dave is hardly ever home alone.

He made a pot of coffee, settled down with the paper. He wondered if Morley would get some of the chocolate-covered strawberries he loved. He wondered if she would get some crusty bread and smoked cold cuts. He felt deliciously guilty. He felt free.

This *was* a good idea, he thought.

He wondered if they had any wine. Maybe for lunch he would open the bottle of Bordeaux they bought at the duty-free shop two years ago.

The telephone rang. Dave stared at the phone on the counter by the door but didn't make a move to answer it.

He knew people who could do this. He had friends who could let their phone ring and ring. He couldn't.

He sat at the table and stared at the phone as if he were hypnotized. It rang two, three, four more times.

When it stopped the house felt immensely quiet.

Dave felt wonderful.

He didn't care who had called.

No one was going to bother him today.

He got up and walked across the kitchen, moving slowly and deliberately. He poured himself another cup of coffee. He read a movie review.

It was like skipping school.

The phone began to ring again.

Should have taken it off the hook, thought Dave.

Then he thought, Maybe it's Morley. Maybe she wanted to consult him about the videos. Maybe he could ask her to get some of the black olive paste.

Maybe if he didn't answer she would be worried. Or angry.

In a sudden panic, he jumped for the phone. He scooped it up on the fourth ring. He was out of breath when he said, "Hello?"

It wasn't Morley. It was Morley's mother.

"I phoned a few minutes ago," said Helen. "Then I tried the store. They told me you were sick. Are you OK?"

Dave reached into his pocket, pulled out his wad of wet Kleenex and stuffed it back in his mouth.

"Just a bit of a fever," he mumbled.

"You sound horrible," said Helen. "You sound like your mouth is full of Kleenex."

Dave said, "I'm OK."

Helen said, "I wanted to see if Morley would have lunch with me."

"Morley's sick, too," said Dave. He said it without thinking. The words just flew out of his mouth. He was trying to save the day. He was trying to head Helen off at the pass.

"Can I talk to her?" asked Helen.

"Too sick," said Dave. "She's too sick to come to the phone. She's upstairs. Asleep. I don't think I should wake her."

Dave felt like he had stepped onto a treadmill. Some part of him knew he should pull the brake and get off. He should tell Helen the truth. Should say, Helen, we're not really sick. We're taking the day off. We're going to spend it together. Alone. Instead he said, "She has fever and these little red dots." Then for good measure he added, "She threw up last night."

Helen said, "Red dots. Maybe I should come over."

It was a statement not a question.

Dave could feel perspiration gathering on his forehead. His breathing was shallow. His hands were cold and damp. He was beginning to feel . . . sick.

Dave said, "It's OK. We'll be fine."

Helen said, "I'll bring some soup for you two and fix dinner for the kids. It's no trouble. Don't worry. I'll be there in an hour."

Morley came home half an hour later carrying two large brown paper bags and two videos.

"I got *Wild Orchid* and *9½ Weeks*," she said.

Dave picked up *9½ Weeks*. "It's the original, uncut, uncensored version," said Morley. "We're going to see it the way it was meant to be seen." Dave flipped the box over. "What's it about?" he asked.

"It's the one with Kim Basinger," said Morley. "The one where Mickey Rourke feeds her the giant chili pepper." Morley reached into one of the bags and pulled out a box of chocolate-covered strawberries. Then she walked across the kitchen and put her arms around her husband's neck. "It's a steamy story of a love affair that breaks every taboo."

Dave swallowed.

Morley laughed.

"I got some of that olive paste you like. And some French bread," she said.

Dave said, "There is something I better tell you."

Morley said, "Just a second." She reached into the other bag and pulled out a handful of magazines. She was grinning.

"This is going to be great," she said.

Dave said, "Helen phoned. She's coming over."

Morley said, "You can't be serious."

Dave said, "I told her I was sick. Then I told her you were

sick." He pressed his hands against his forehead. His head was beginning to throb.

"I didn't know if I should tell her I was faking—we were faking. I felt like an idiot."

Morley said, "That's because you are an idiot.

Dave and Morley spent half an hour running through the house, madly tidying up. Then Morley went upstairs and put on her old flannel nightie, which hung off her shoulders like a sack. When Helen arrived they were both lying in bed, stiff as corpses. They weren't speaking to each other. The two brown paper bags from the food store were under the bed on Morley's side.

Helen said, "You look awful. Have you eaten? I'll make soup."

She went down to the kitchen.

Dave turned to Morley and said, "I'm sorry. Come on. This isn't my fault. She's your mother." Morley looked at him and said, "I don't believe this." Then she reached under the bed and pulled out a chocolate strawberry and ate it as if she were alone.

Dave's headache was getting worse.

"Could I have one of those?" he asked.

"I'm not stopping you," said Morley.

But she wasn't offering them around either.

Dave crawled over his wife and took two strawberries out of the bag.

He was standing by the bed in a T-shirt and a pair of boxers when Helen came back in the room.

"Everything ok?" she said.

Dave rammed the second strawberry into his mouth.

"Dave?" she said.

He covered his mouth with his hand.

"I think I'm going to be sick," he said, and ran for the bathroom.

"He doesn't look well," said Helen to Morley.

By the time Dave was back in bed, Helen was in the kitchen again and the oily smell of chicken soup was drifting upstairs.

Morley said, "This is a nightmare. I hate chicken soup. I had to eat chicken soup when I was a kid. That's what she always fed us whenever we were sick. Just the smell of chicken soup makes me ill. Do something. Get her out of here."

Dave said, "How do I get her out of here? She's trying to help."

"You invited her," said Morley. "You uninvite her."

Helen brought the bowls of soup up on a tray.

Dave's head was pounding. His mouth was dry.

He didn't want a scene. He didn't want Morley to thunder out of bed and tell Helen he had lied. He would feel too stupid. It had gone too far. Please, God, he thought. Please let us carry the soup part off.

He smiled weakly at Morley.

"Look," he said. "Dry toast. Dry toast is just what I wanted."

Morley made Dave eat her bowl of soup.

"Can't I flush it down the toilet?" he asked. "It tastes funny. I think it's off." He was starting to feel queasier with every spoonful he swallowed.

"Eat it," said Morley. "All of it." Then she got out of bed and started to get dressed.

Downstairs, Helen was sitting in front of the television.

Morley walked into the room carrying two crushed paper bags. She put them down and said, "The soup was great. I feel much better. I think it was one of those eight-hour things. I'm going to go for a walk. Can you stay for a while? What I'd really like to do is go to a movie. I haven't been to a matinée for years. Would that be wicked?"

Helen frowned. "Do you really feel better?"

Morley said, "I'm fine. Could you stay with Dave? He's not looking so good. I think he needs more soup."

Helen brightened. She was watching a documentary on the grizzly bear. She saw Morley frowning at the screen and said, "There's nothing else on."

Morley picked up the two videos she had rented and looked at them ruefully. She put them back down and gathered up the two brown paper bags.

"What's that dear?" asked Helen.

"Oh, just some dry cleaning," said Morley. "I'll drop it off on my way to the theatre."

When Helen came into the bedroom, Dave was lying under the covers staring at the ceiling. Helen was holding a bowl of soup in one hand and a video in the other. She said, "Morley thought you might like company," and then, lifting the video, she added, "I found this downstairs."

Dave's stomach began to churn. He felt like he was strapped into the passenger seat of a car that was about to be involved in an accident. Everything seemed to be moving in slow motion. He closed his eyes. This couldn't be happening.

Helen flicked the television on and bent down and stared at the video player. She slipped the movie into the machine and pressed the play button.

She straightened up and kicked off her shoes and sat down on Morley's side of the bed, arranging the pillows so she could lean against the headboard.

"It's called *9½ Weeks*," she said. "Have you heard of it?"

Dave shook his head numbly.

"Me neither," said Helen. "I hope it's not full of violence."

Dave was too ill to reply.

"This is fun," said Helen. "I don't think I've ever watched a movie in the middle of the day. I should do this more often. Eat your soup."

Winter, Again

On the Roof

Betty Schellenberger and Morley were drinking coffee.

Morley said, "They've done studies about this. Even in families where men and women do equal amounts of housework, it's always the women who organize it."

Betty nodded, her hands cradling the mug of coffee in front of her on the kitchen table.

"It's the women," said Morley, "who plan and assign. It's the women who drive the train."

Dave was washing the lunch dishes. It made him feel bad, listening to them talk. It felt personal—like they were criticizing him. No one, he thought grimly, assigned me these dishes. He considered stopping. I wouldn't want to overstep my boundaries, he thought. Since Morley had gone back to work in the fall Dave had been trying to shoulder his share of the chores. But Morley was right. There was no denying it. She was management. He was labour.

It was Saturday afternoon. The sky was grey and heavy. The wind was rippling the puddles on the driveway. It looked like it could snow.

The weather suited Dave's mood. When he finished the dishes he said, "I'm going to take Arthur out."

He put on an old blue sweater and a canvas jacket, stuffed a toque and a pair of gloves in his pocket and headed outside with the dog. He thought of loading Arthur into the car and driving to a park, or maybe taking him down to the lake. He stood on the front walk—Arthur looking up at him expectantly—then instead of getting in the car he headed north through the neighbourhood.

There was hardly anyone else out. There were some kids walking through the park, but there was no one in the playground. The abandoned swings hung on their yellow metal frame like a row of mourners.

Up ahead there was a woman walking towards Dave on the same side of the street.

"Hello," said Dave as they passed. The woman did not acknowledge him. She walked by with her jaw firmly shut, her eyes straight ahead. As if he and Arthur didn't exist.

There are lots of things that can give you the blues. The weather can give you the blues. Sometimes it is so grey out it makes you feel blue inside. Your best friends can give you the blues. In fact your friends are often better at making you feel blue than your worst enemies. Sometimes, however, it's just an overheard conversation, a stranger on the street, empty swings.

Dave had not intended to be gone long. But he kept walking. After forty-five minutes he was on a street he had never been on before, gazing into the window of a store he had never seen: Thrift Villa—"Where smart shoppers save."

He only went in to warm up, but he ended up buying two drinking glasses—sixty-nine cents each. One was a Dave Keon hockey glass with a picture of Dave on one side and a referee on the other demonstrating the signal for a holding penalty. "Holding" it said in black letters under the referee. The lady at the cash told him it was a peanut butter jar from the 1960s. She couldn't remember the brand name.

"I'm pretty sure it was a rodent," she said, as she rolled the glasses in newspaper. "Like a beaver. Or a squirrel."

When Dave was halfway home it started to snow. He pulled his toque out of his pocket and tugged it down so it covered his ears. It was 4:30 and it was getting dark. He had been gone two hours. The weather was whispering warnings: Just wanted to remind you, said the snow, that you'll be walking home from work in the dark from now on. Just wanted to let you know, said the wind, that it will probably be raining.

He was cheered by the texture of the light from the houses he passed. It reminded him of winter nights when he was a boy, of afternoon-long games of shinny. *Maybe*, he thought, *he should take everyone to Cape Breton for Christmas*. He hadn't been home at Christmas for too many years.

He thought of the disaster that befell him when he tried to

cook the turkey last year. They could do worse than spend the holidays with his mother. She would be happy to see them. The kids could cut a tree on the McCauleys' farm.

That's what started him thinking about Christmas decorations. He had been late with them last year—so late that he had ended up more or less throwing their lights over the front hedge. He had promised himself he would do better this year.

Well, it was this year now. He would get the lights up before anyone had to ask. He would beat Morley to the punch. He would be labour and management. He was feeling better when he got home.

On Tuesday Dave came home early determined to climb onto his roof and put out the Christmas lights. He wanted to be up and down before dark. But first, he had to go to Jim Scoffield's house to borrow a ladder, and they had to have a beer. Then they had to *find* the ladder. Dave had to replace all the burned-out bulbs. Suddenly it was dusk.

It was dark by the time Dave stepped gingerly onto the roof and half-walked, half-crawled across the shingles to the chimney.

It was colder than he expected. He grabbed hold of the television antenna and carefully straightened up. He could see all over the neighbourhood. He wondered why he only got up there at the worst times of the year. I should come up here more often, he thought. He sat down with his back to the chimney and began to untangle the lights that he had already untangled before he climbed the ladder.

It took him about half an hour to attach the lights to the antenna. When he was finished, he plugged them in and his roof was bathed in light—yellows, reds, greens and blues. They didn't look half bad, and miracle of miracles, no bulbs had burned out since he had checked them half an hour ago. Dave shuffled back to the ladder to get a better look.

The antenna reminded him of the clothesline in his yard when he was a child—they had the kind made from one centre pole—the kind that looks like an umbrella with the fabric removed. Dave remembered the winter mornings when his mother would push him into a snowsuit and out the back door like a blimp, remembered the swishing of all that nylon material between his legs. How he inevitably needed to pee once he was stuck outside.

He looked out over the neighbourhood rooftops and suddenly, as sure as she was standing beside him, Dave could hear his sweet mother's voice fill his head. She was warning him about something. She was saying, Dave, don't lick the clothesline.

Sometimes you do things just because someone tells you not to. Sometimes you do things because you have never done them before and you want to see what would happen if you did. Sometimes it's hard to figure out why you do some things at all.

Dave had never put his tongue against a television antenna on a cold night in November, although he had a pretty fair idea what would happen if he did. But the moment his mother's voice came into his head he could feel himself drawn to the antenna.

As he slowly crab-walked back across the roof towards the chimney to which the antenna was attached, Dave was thinking to himself—this won't happen. I won't do this. Why would I do this? I'm not stupid. I'm just trying to scare myself. Yet he felt as if he were outside of his body. It didn't seem to be him moving across the roof. It seemed to be someone else. And there didn't seem to be much he could do to stop him.

Part of Dave was saying, I don't want to put my tongue on that television antenna, but another part of him, the part that seemed to be in control—the part his tongue seemed to be listening to—was saying, Just do it, Dave. You don't have to listen to your mother any more. You're an adult. You can do whatever you want.

He was surprised by how unequivocally his tongue grabbed onto the metal. It was not at all uncertain about what it was expected to do. Dave himself was uncertain that he had even touched the metal. He thought there was still some space between him and the pole, and then suddenly he was bonded to it. At first he was intrigued by the way his tongue stuck. Almost proud of it. It hurt a bit, but it was not an excruciating pain—more the pain of melted candle wax than molten lead.

Then it hurt a bit more and Dave thought, OK, that's enough, and he tried to pull his tongue off the antenna. It didn't come. He leaned forward because it hurt when he tried to pull and then more of his tongue was stuck to the antenna and he felt a wave of panic rush through him.

His mother's voice filled his head again. She said, I told you not to do that.

And Dave said, "Why didn't you stop me?"

Except it sounded different . . . more like "MMMMUUU-

UGGGHHHH." When he said it, his top lip brushed against the antenna and then his top lip was stuck as well as his tongue and he knew he was in serious trouble.

Dave stopped moving. He was very still. Then he tried to lean back a little, but it hurt, and his tongue didn't want to let go.

He thought, Maybe it's like taking a Band-Aid off a kid. Maybe you have to be sure about it. Sure and fast.

So he counted. "One. Two."

Just as he was about to say, "Three," Dave heard his mother's voice again. She said, Have you thought that you could pull your entire tongue out of your mouth and leave it on the antenna. Have you thought of that?

Dave stopped counting.

That's impossible, he thought.

But it occurred to him that if he didn't actually lose his entire tongue, maybe he could lose a layer of it—the layer with his taste buds. He would never taste anything ever again. For the rest of his life he might as well eat tofu and it wouldn't make any difference. That scared him so much that he didn't move a muscle for a long time. He stood on the roof, sucking on his antenna without moving.

He could see his neighbours walking up and down the street. He saw the Schellenbergers stop and look up at him. When they stopped, he began to flap his arms up and down, being careful not to move his face. The Schellenbergers stood and watched him for a few moments and then they said something to each other, turned and walked inside their house.

Dave knew they weren't going to come to his rescue. They had been admiring him. They thought he was part of the display—hanging from the antenna in the middle of all the lights.

This is what happens when you do things you weren't asked to do, thought Dave.

He was filled with self-loathing. His life seemed to be a parade of similar incidents.

When his daughter was very small, Dave had taken her in the car on his way to a job interview. Morley was sick and he was going to drop Stephanie at Morley's mother's house while he went to the interview.

The interview was for a job that Dave thought he wanted at the time—a buyer for a record store chain. He had borrowed a briefcase from Carl Lowbeer as a prop.

It was not an easy drive. Stephanie cried all the way across town. Dave was desperate to calm her down. He needed to be calm for the interview. He decided that a stick of licorice might do the trick.

He pulled up in front of a corner store. As he jumped out of the car he noticed four young thugs, wearing more than their fair share of black leather, bumping up the street. He didn't want them messing with his daughter. Better lock the door, thought Dave.

He patted his pockets looking for his keys. Silly, he thought, they're still in the ignition. Dave had left the engine running so that when he came out of the store he could be on his way as quickly as possible. He wasn't exactly late for his interview, but he didn't have a lot of time to spare.

No worries. He could lock the car door without the key. Dave reached inside the car and depressed the lock button.

Then he slammed the door, carefully holding the door handle so the door would stay locked.

As he stood beside his locked car and smiled at the four thugs, Dave was vaguely troubled by a feeling that something wasn't right. But he was too uptight and in too much of a hurry to worry about it. He dashed into the store and moments later dashed out again waving the candy. When he saw his car, he stopped dead in his tracks. The doors were locked. The motor was running. His keys were in the ignition.

When Dave saw Stephanie locked in the back of the car, something inside him snapped. He was irrevocably and undeniably certain that his daughter was in danger.

He knew that people who wanted to end their lives often sat in running cars. He understood that they usually did this in garages, but he reasoned that even though his car was in the open air, fumes could still seep through the floorboards, and if they didn't kill his daughter, they could surely damage her brain.

Dave looked around for something to break a window with in case Stephanie started to nod off. He spotted a brick at a construction site and placed it on the sidewalk beside the passenger door. He sprinted to a phone booth.

Morley, who had a fever of 102, got dressed and took a taxi across town with their extra set of keys.

By the time she arrived, so had the police.

Morley still says she should have denied knowing Dave. When she tells this story she says she should have pressed charges. Look at the brick, she could have said, I think he was planning to steal my daughter.

Dave was late for the interview. He didn't get the job.

This was the life that was flashing by Dave's eyes as he hunched over his chimney—sucking on his television antenna. He could hear his family moving around the living room. He could hear their voices floating up the chimney. He heard Morley say, "Wouldn't a fire be nice?"

"No," said Dave. "No, it wouldn't."

Then he heard Sam.

"Can we put on two logs?"

Dave and Morley burn synthetic wax logs. The moment the waxy smoke hit Dave he needed to pee. He thought, The fumes are probably poisonous. I am being asphyxiated. My body is trying to clear the toxins.

It was like being trapped in the backyard in a snowsuit when he was a kid.

His mind began to race.

What if spring never came? What if there was never a thaw? What if he died there?

He couldn't remember the last time the chimney had been cleaned. What would happen to him if the chimney caught fire? The fumes were stinging his eyes. He needed to pee badly now.

What if he peed on the antenna?

Would that warm it up enough?

Enough to set him free?

And what, God help him, would happen if his penis touched the metal?

And then it came to him.

Why didn't he take one of the Christmas lights and hold it against his lip so the warmth from the light would melt his mouth free?

It took less than five minutes.

In five minutes he was down the ladder, in the house and peering into the bathroom mirror at his tongue. It was red but not too sore.

Sam and Stephanie were snuggled on the couch watching television, and Morley, his sweet wife Morley, was sticking cloves into an orange as she watched with them. Dave thought, They didn't even know I was in trouble.

There was a commercial and Sam said, "What were you doing up there? The picture was really fuzzy for a while. Then all of a sudden it got better."

Dave said, "I put up the Christmas lights. Come and see."

They all trooped outside.

Sam looked up and down the block. "We're the first. We beat everyone."

Morley was smiling. "I was thinking about the lights yesterday," she said.

The kids ran back inside.

Morley was still looking at the lights. "They always make me feel good," she said. Then she turned and put her arms around her husband. "I ordered the Christmas turkey today," she said. "I was thinking, you did such a nice job with it last year, do you think you could do it again?"

Polly Anderson's
Christmas Party

*D*ave received his new driver's licence in the mail at the beginning of October. It was accompanied by a letter that began:

> Dear Sir;
> We were pleased to note that you no are no longer required to wear corrective lenses.

Dave has never worn glasses in his life. Somewhere in the pit of his stomach he felt a queasy twinkle . . . like the birth of a star in a distant galaxy.

Before we can change the category code on your Driver's Licence, [the note continued] we must receive notification from an opthamologist of the change in your vision.

Dave's vision hadn't changed in twenty years. The star in his stomach was burning brightly now. Ahh, thought Dave, I know the name of the galaxy. It's the galaxy of bureaucratic misfortune—an abyss of swamps and labyrinths, a horror house of tunnels and mazes. Dealing with the letter would be like playing a real-life game of Snakes and Ladders. With a sinking heart Dave finished the note.

We have reissued your permit subject to the following conditions.

At the bottom of the letter it said:

Driver must wear corrective lenses.

Dave knew this wasn't going to be easy.

"Do you have any idea," he said to Morley, "how long you have to wait to get an appointment with an eye doctor?"

The next morning, when Morley woke up, Dave was lying on his back, his hands cupped behind his head. He was staring at the ceiling. "This is the sort of thing that sends people into clock towers with high-powered rifles," he said.

October, and then November, came and went. By early

December Dave still hadn't made even a half-hearted attempt to schedule a doctor's appointment.

"I'm too busy," he said, when Morley asked.

December is the busiest time of the year if you work in retail and things had been busy enough at the record store, but they both knew this was a lie. By the middle of the month Morley was ready to force the issue. Then she thought, He's an adult. Why should I be the bad guy? Instead, as he left for work on Saturday morning, she reminded Dave that they were expected at Ted and Polly Anderson's annual Christmas "At Home" that night. As he stood at the front door, his parka open, his hat askew, Dave gave Morley a look that said, Please say I can stay home and watch the hockey game?

Morley was sitting on the stairs, frowning into her open briefcase. "Don't look at me like that," she said. "We have to go."

Dave's shoulders sagged. "OK," he said. "But let's go early and leave early."

And that's how Dave came to be standing in his driveway, yelling impatiently at Sam, on Saturday evening at 5:30.

"Just come without your jacket," he said. "You don't need your jacket. The car is warmed up. Just come."

Sam bounded down the front steps, his shoelaces undone, his shirt untucked, and jumped into the car beside his father.

"Back seat," said Dave as Sam reached for the radio.

Morley was next. Slipping into the car and examining her lipstick in the mirror on the back of the sun visor.

Dave had to send Sam back to fetch Stephanie.

"What's the hurry?" she said, slumping into the back seat.

"No one will be there yet. This is stupid. There's never anyone my age. Do I have to come?"

They were, as it turns out, the first to arrive.

"Come in," said Polly Anderson, who hadn't finished setting things out. "It's good to see you." Looking as though it wasn't.

"I told you it was too early," said Stephanie.

"It's OK," said Dave. "We'll help out."

Five minutes later Dave was holding an open bottle of rum in front of two bowls of eggnog. He was helping out.

"The Lalique crystal is for the adults," called Polly Anderson from the kitchen. "The glass bowl is for the kids."

Dave took a step back and peered at the two bowls.

"Which is the Lalique?" he called.

The doorbell rang.

Polly said, "The Lalique is on the left. Can you get the door?"

Dave said, "Just a minute."

The doorbell rang again.

Dave frowned and said, to himself, Glass left and crystal right . . . or crystal left and glass right?

From the dining room Morley said, "Dave get the door."

Dave said, "Eeny meeny miny mo," poured the rum, and ran for the door. As he left, he saw Ted Anderson pick up one of the bowls and head down to the rec room where Sam had joined the Anderson kids.

Morley has always left Polly Anderson's Christmas party feeling defeated and inadequate. There was the spiral staircase, the Lalique bowls and Polly's bonsai collection in the hall—which this year she had decorated with miniature origami birds, each one no bigger than an aspirin. Morley felt defeated by these things, and by the moment at the end of each year's party—a moment that was not unpleasant, but just so perfect—when everyone gathered around the Andersons' Christmas tree (it always seemed taller and straighter than the tree Dave and Morley had found), and Ted turned off the lights, and lit the real candles and they all sang carols. Defeated by these things that the Andersons seemed to do so effortlessly. And if that wasn't enough, there were the Anderson kids—so polite and well dressed and most galling of all . . . so clean. It all made Morley feel small.

But the thing that really ground her down was the mountain of food that Polly produced. This year it was Christmas sushi—pieces of salmon twisted into the shape of fir trees, little tuna wreaths, yellowtail angels with white-radish wings, and in the middle of the table, a seaweed manger with a baby Jesus made from flying-fish roe and three wise men with pickled ginger robes and wasabi faces.

Then there were the crackers. Polly Anderson's crackers were better dressed than half the people at the party. It was as if Polly Anderson had Martha Stewart working for her in the kitchen, and any moment Martha Stewart was going to march out carrying something on a silver platter: a stencilled roast beef, Cajun fillets of peacock tongue, a roasted unicorn, or maybe quail, a flaming wreath of baby quail with cranberry and mango salsa.

The last time she had entertained the Andersons, Morley was so determined to measure up that she had gone to the library and checked out a pile of gourmet magazines. She had come home and rolled cylinders of salmon in a soft cream-cheese dip and stuck toothpicks at the end of each roll. It didn't occur to her, until Sam pointed it out, that her creation looked like a plate of miniature toilet paper rolls. She saw Polly Anderson looking at the plate quizzically, then watched in horror as Polly picked up one of the hors d'oeuvres and it slid off the toothpicks and landed in her drink. Morley hid in the kitchen until Dave forced her to join them in the living room.

As Morley stood in the Andersons' living room, staring at Polly Anderson's Christmas crackers, she thought about the week following her own party. For days she kept coming across remnants of her toilet-paper hors d'oeuvres all over the house: under the couch, in the drawer where she kept her cheque-book, in the bathroom garbage can, on a window sill. All of them had one bite missing.

Morley was so lost in these memories that when Ted Anderson came up behind her and offered her a drink she jumped.

"Are you all right?" he said.

Ted, gliding from guest to guest in a grey suit and ivory collarless shirt, buttoned to the neck.

Morley looked across the room at Dave. He was wearing the blue sweater his mother had knit last Christmas—it had a map of Cape Breton on the front with a large red dot marking the site of his home town. One side of his shirt was hanging out from under the sweater.

Morley had already had three cups of eggnog, but she just couldn't seem to relax.

"Sure," she said, holding out her cup to Ted.

Morley thought the party seemed stiffer than usual, though the kids seemed to be having a whale of a time.

Sam wound by her with a plate piled with bread and salmon mousse.

You'd never eat that at home, thought Morley.

"This is the moose," said Sam exuberantly, pointing to the orange spread. "And this," he said pointing to the gelatin, "is the moose fat."

He snorted and wheeled back towards the basement where the kids were. When he opened the basement door the sound of boisterous children singing Christmas carols came wafting up the stairs.

Dave headed back to the punch bowl and poured himself another glass of eggnog—his fifth. He couldn't seem to loosen up.

Half an hour later Bernie Schellenberger lurched by Dave on his way upstairs. Bernie looked like he was being chased by wolves. He was holding his five-month-old daughter in his arms. The baby was howling.

"Every night," said Bernie.

"When you try to put her down," said Dave.

"She screams for two hours," said Bernie.

"You ever try the car?" asked Dave.

"What?" said Bernie.

And Dave, who was looking for any excuse to leave the Andersons', said, "Get your coat."

Sam came out of the womb screaming, and every night at bedtime, for the first year of his life, he would lie in his crib and scream.

Morley and Dave would sit in the kitchen as rigid as lumber and listen to him. They would say things to each other like, "We are not going in there. Not tonight. He has to learn."

Other parents in the neighbourhood would find excuses to drop in on Dave and Morley around bedtime, because listening to Sam scream made them feel better about their own children. If mothers were becoming short-tempered with their children, fathers would say, "Could you nip over to Morley's and see how things are coming with . . ." and they'd make something up. And their wives would go, because they knew it would do them good.

People who didn't have children were horrified with the way Dave and Morley could offer them coffee and carry on a conversation while Sam raged against sleep. They would keep glancing towards the stairs. When they left they would say things like, "That was unbelievable. Our children will never do that."

On the rare nights when Sam stopped crying within an hour, Dave and Morley would glance at each other nervously and one of them would say, "Maybe I should check him."

As soon as they opened the bedroom door, he would start crying again.

Once, Dave crawled into Sam's room on his belly and pulled himself up the side of the crib, like a snake, only to come face to face with his son. They stared at each other for an awful minute. Then Dave slid back down. Sam smiled and waved. Dave had crawled halfway out of the room before Sam started to cry.

They lived like this for a long time before Dave discovered the car. He took Sam with him to the grocery store one night and Sam drifted off to sleep in his car seat. After Dave had carried him to bed, he said, "I'm going to try that again."

The next night he drove around the neighbourhood for an hour before Sam conked out—but it beat sitting at the kitchen table. So every night Dave loaded Sam into the car and drove around until Sam fell asleep. He had to drive less and less each night. Soon Sam was falling asleep within a block of the house. One night he nodded off before Dave got out of the driveway. Eventually Dave could put Sam in the back seat, start the car, and idle it in the driveway. It was something about the sound of the engine.

One night, instead of putting him in the car, Dave put Sam in his crib and said to Morley, "Watch this."

He got the vacuum cleaner and he carried it into Sam's bedroom and turned it on and left the room, shutting Sam's door behind him. Five minutes later, when they opened his door, Sam was out cold.

By the time he was fourteen months they could put him to sleep by waving the hair dryer over him a couple of times.

Bernie Schellenberger was standing on the stairs, at the Andersons' party, his screaming daughter in his arms, listening intently to Dave's story.

"Get your coat," said Dave again. "You'll see."

Then he said, "I'm going to bring Sam."

He was thinking, after all those years his son should see what he put him through.

When Dave went down the back staircase into the Andersons' basement the television was on—but none of the kids were watching it. The videos Polly Anderson had rented to keep them amused were still piled on top of the TV. The TV was flickering like a yawning grey eye at a bunch of empty chairs. The twenty kids were at the other end of the room, pressed around the upright piano. Sam, to Dave's astonishment, had his arms draped around the shoulder of a girl Dave had never seen before. Dave couldn't see who was at the keyboard, but he recognized the tune. It was "The North Atlantic Squadron":

> Away away with fife and drum
> Here we come full of rum
> Looking for women to . . .

Someone noticed Dave and the piano stopped abruptly. Sam said, "Hi, Dad."

He jumped towards his father and caught his foot on the edge of the piano stool and came down hard on middle C with his face leading. All the kids applauded, and Sam bowed, blood dripping from his nose.

He said, "Our family motto is, 'There are sewers aplenty yet to dig.' "

Then he wiped his nose, smearing blood across his face and shirt. Dave said, "I'd like you to come with me in the car. Where is your other shoe?"

Sam looked around. "Beats me," he said.

Dave held out his hand. "Forget it," he said. He picked his son up and carried him out to the car.

It only took twenty minutes before the Schellenberger baby was snoozing comfortably.

Bernie couldn't believe it. "Geez. I am going to have to buy a car," he said.

"Try a vacuum first," said Dave.

Bernie said, "We have central vac."

"Then move her crib to the basement," said Dave.

From the back of the car Sam said, "It's the physics of baseball that has always fascinated me."

Dave looked at his boy in the rear-view mirror.

Sam waved absently at his father, then he pressed his face to the window and started to sing something that sounded like opera.

Carmen? thought Dave.

Then something awful occurred to him.

Dave slammed on the brakes and squealed to the side of the road. He twisted around in his seat and stared at Sam.

"What have you been drinking?" he asked.

"Eggnog," said Sam.

"From which bowl?"

"From the bowl in the basement, of course," Sam replied.

Uh oh, thought Dave.

Bernie Schellenberger said, "Dave?"

Dave looked at Bernie, then he looked at Sam, then he looked at Bernie again. Bernie was pointing. Dave peered into the darkness and spotted three police officers standing on the edge of the road half a block away.

They were manning a roadside check for drunk drivers, and Dave had just fishtailed to a stop in front of them. The cops all had their hands on their hips. The street light shining from behind them made them look ominous. The only thing Dave could do was put his car into gear and creep towards them.

Sam pulled himself forward so his head was beside his

father's. "This," he said, "is an area of jurisprudence that has always interested me."

Dave pulled up beside the police and rolled down his window. He smiled.

Two of the cops took a step back from the car. The third was shining his flashlight in Dave's face. He didn't try to engage in small talk.

He said, "Could I please see your licence."

He peered at the licence and then he looked at Dave and said, "Where are your glasses?"

Without waiting for an answer he handed Dave a little machine and said, "Blow."

Dave is not sure who was more surprised to find there was no alcohol in his bloodstream. Dave had, after all, drunk six cups of eggnog.

Dave and the cop were both squinting at the machine when Sam joined the conversation from the back. "Can I blow too?" he asked.

Dave said, "Maybe that's not a good idea."

But the cop, who was friendlier now, said, "It's OK. I don't mind."

Dave said, "Oh, well."

Sam blew into the little machine.

The cop pointed at it and said, "See son, if you had been drinking, the arrow would be . . ." His voice trailed off. He squinted at his machine and took a step backwards. He looked at Dave, who shrugged and smiled. He opened the back door of Dave's car and looked closely at Sam, the streaks of dried blood across his face, and said, "Is that blood, son?"

Sam said, "Our family motto is, 'There are sewers aplenty yet to dig.'"

The cop frowned and said, "Son, I want you to get out of the car."

Sam slid over to the far side of the back seat and said, "Come and get me, copper."

Then he threw up.

Dave folded his head into his arms and rested it on the steering wheel.

The Schellenberger baby started to cry.

So did Dave.

Bernie Schellenberger called a taxi from the police station.

By the time Dave had explained everything and got back to the party, the Andersons' house was dark and locked up. Sam was asleep in the back seat. He didn't stir when they got him home, and Dave carried him upstairs.

Just like the old days, thought Dave.

Morley was waiting in the living room. The whole house was dark except for the coloured lights glowing on the Christmas tree.

"I love it like this," she said. She was sitting with her legs up on the sofa, an empty cognac glass beside her.

Dave sat at the other end of the couch so their feet met in the middle. They compared stories.

"It took five minutes for the police to get Sam out of the car," said Dave. "They wouldn't let me help. When they got him out, he had blood all over him, and he didn't have a winter coat, and he was missing a shoe, and he was drunk."

Morley told him what he had missed at the Andersons'. "It was like homecoming at a frat house," she said.

"Pia Cherbenofsky got herself into the Christmas tree and no one saw her until Ted Anderson began to light the candles for the carol sing. Pia was hidden in the branches, halfway up the tree, and she started blowing the candles out as fast as Ted could light them.

"At one point," said Morley, "there were ten adults trying to coax her down with candy."

Then she told him about the McCormick baby.

"He was missing for half an hour," she said. "He finally turned up asleep in a laundry hamper with the youngest Anderson boy squatting beside him."

Bobby Anderson had wrapped himself in an large green terry-cloth towel.

"I'm the three wise men," burped Bobby. "That's the baby Jesus."

Sam was never able to tell Dave the name of the girl he had his arms around in the basement. No one seemed to know who she was.

"She was in a red dress," said Dave.

"When I left," said Morley, "there was a girl in a red dress standing at the top of the spiral staircase, singing 'Don't Cry For Me Argentina.'"

Dave got up and poured himself another drink.

"What did Polly say?" he asked.

"Last I saw of Polly Anderson," said Morley, "she was in the hallway protecting her bonsai collection."

Morley stood up and hunched over.

"She looked like a football player ready to make a tackle,"

she said. "She was screaming: 'Stand back. Stand back. Don't come a step closer.'"

"Who was attacking the bonsai?" asked Dave.

"Her eldest son," said Morley. "He was trying to shoot the origami birds out of the trees with a Nerf gun."

The only child who wasn't sick, singing, or passed out was their daughter, Stephanie.

"I told her I was proud of her," said Morley.

The truth of that dawned on Dave later, when they were upstairs and Dave was in the bathroom brushing his teeth. He walked into the bedroom, holding his toothbrush at his side.

"Stephanie was the only kid drinking from the adult bowl," he said.

"Oh," said Morley. "Oh."

"Merry Christmas," said Dave.

P9-DFD-802

Starfields

Starfields

CAROLYN MARSDEN

CANDLEWICK PRESS

This is a work of fiction. Names, characters, places, and incidents are either products of the author's imagination or, if real, are used fictitiously.

Copyright © 2011 by Carolyn Marsden

All rights reserved. No part of this book may be reproduced, transmitted, or stored in an information retrieval system in any form or by any means, graphic, electronic, or mechanical, including photocopying, taping, and recording, without prior written permission from the publisher.

First edition 2011

Library of Congress Cataloging-in-Publication Data

Marsden, Carolyn.
Starfields / Carolyn Marsden. — 1st ed.
p. cm.
Summary: While big changes are coming to her Mexican village,
nine-year-old Rosalba hears that the Mayan calendar predicts the
end of the world in 2012 and she dreams of an ancient Mayan boy,
eyes bound in a shamanistic ritual, who hints at what Rosalba can do.
ISBN 978-0-7636-4820-6
[1. Mayas—Fiction. 2. Indians of Mexico—Fiction. 3. Prophecies—Fiction.
4. Mexico—Fiction.] I. Title.
PZ7.M35135Sta 2011
[Fic]—dc22

2010045791

11 12 13 14 15 16 RRC 10 9 8 7 6 5 4 3 2 1

Printed in Crawfordsville, IN, U.S.A.

This book was typeset in ITC Stone Informal.

Candlewick Press
99 Dover Street
Somerville, Massachusetts 02144

visit us at www.candlewick.com

RO432552215

For Sydney,
my first child reader

AD 600

Some might guess that I live in blackness. Others that I see vague splashes of color. But in truth I see everything.

For I am the Seer. The Shaman. The Holy Man.

As I swam in the dark waters of my mother's womb, my destiny was divined. When I emerged from the dank tunnel, holy men wrapped my eyes with thirteen layers of bandages, immersing me in sacred darkness. Thus I have been blinded for almost thirteen revolutions around the sun.

2011

Poof!

Two village dogs joined Rosalba as she walked through a forest full of birdsongs. The dark purple trills, bright red calls from one treetop to another, the golden squawks reminded her of the colors she wove into her loom.

Pine needles released their drowsy fragrance into the warm air.

Halfway to the highway the river turned, making a deep pool. In other parts of the forest men cut the trees, and even burned them, but not here. The thick trunks were covered with moss and white mushrooms. In the late afternoons, Rosalba loved to sit quietly in this spot, letting her thoughts wander loose from the tight lines she wove.

Sometimes when she was at the pool, she closed her eyes. She saw colored shapes and strange faces that she thought might be those of her ancestors. Sometimes when she was by herself, she heard soft, otherworldly flute music.

Other girls from the village wouldn't have gone to the pool alone. Certainly not her cousin Sylvia, who said things like, "You might fall in and never get out," or "Sometimes the boys from town go there."

But Rosalba didn't like to feel penned in by the village. She looked forward to being close to the water in this dusty time before the rains. She walked confidently to the deep pool, certain of the protection of the Earthlord.

Suddenly one of the white dogs barked.

"Shhh," said Rosalba, and stood motionless. Underneath the music of the birds, she heard singing.

"Los de adelante corren mucho, y los de atrás se quedarán . . ." Rosalba looked down through the trees to see a girl, dressed plainly in a tan jacket and pants. Her light hair curled like the tendrils of chayote squash. She wasn't a Mayan, but a *ladina* girl. She sat on the bank, tossing rocks into the water, singing: *"Tras, tras, tras . . ."*

2

Rosalba watched from behind a tree, her hands against the rough bark. Whenever she went with Mama to market, she saw *ladinos* and other foreigners. *Ladinos* were rich. They drove cars and watched televisions and enjoyed many different kinds of food, including ice cream. *Ladina* girls wore pretty clothes and hair ornaments.

Rosalba had always wondered about those tall, light-skinned people, but had never spoken to any. Never had she seen one so close to her village.

Just then, the girl turned and cried out, *"¡Hola!"* She raised her hand. "I see you behind the tree!"

Rosalba hesitated, then stepped out. *"Hola,"* she said.

"Sit here." The girl's voice rang over the sounds of the river. She touched the ground beside her.

As Rosalba moved forward on the soft pine needles, the dogs scampered into the trees. Reaching the edge of the pool, she settled herself near the girl. The girl looked at her with eyes as green as the moss growing on the trees.

The *ladina*'s curls were fastened with a butter-fly clip covered with sparkles. Rosalba wanted to reach out and touch that shiny barrette, those light curls. The girl's fingernails were painted bright pink. She'd been building a tiny house of twigs and pine needles.

"Don't be afraid," she said. "My name's Alicia. What's yours?"

"Rosalba."

"I'm from Mexico City," Alicia announced, throwing a stone into the pool. "I'm eight."

The girl came from the far-off big city that Rosalba had heard about. In town she'd seen pictures of that place where buildings touched the clouds. There was a market where people floated on boats filled with sweet-smelling tube-roses. In Mexico City you could get on an airplane and lift off into the sky itself. Mexico City was an important place to come from. But that this Alicia was a year younger than she made Rosalba feel braver. "What are you doing here?"

"I'm on an expedition with Papi and other scientists. They're studying frogs and I'm helping. Did you know that frogs are disappearing from the planet?" Alicia stretched her arms wide, the pink fingernails gleaming. "From everywhere. They're dying off."

Rosalba fiddled with the edge of her shawl. Sometimes her brothers caught frogs for the family cooking pot. They hadn't mentioned there being any fewer. . . . "There's a frog right there," she said as a small brown one leaped from one mossy rock to another.

"I didn't say they'd *all* disappeared. But a lot. They're sick with a fungus. Frog die-off is so important that Papi said I could miss school if I do research with him and write a report."

Rosalba, who had never written anything, changed the subject. "How do the men study frogs?"

"They catch them in traps. But not the kind

that kill them!" She shook her head and gestured, accidentally knocking over the miniature house. The twigs and pine needles fell every which way, but the girl didn't seem to mind.

"You're a real Mayan, aren't you?" she asked.

Rosalba nodded. "Of course I am." What else?

"Papi said I'd meet some real Mayan people. He said you Mayans would know all about the prophesy of the year 2012."

Rosalba wrinkled her forehead.

"You know—when the Mayan calendar ends. After thousands and thousands of years it stops just like that." Alicia snapped her fingers, her bright fingernails flashing.

"I know about the Mayans from a long time ago. Foreigners come to see their pyramids. But I don't know anything about a calendar."

"You're a Mayan, but you don't *know*?" asked the *ladina,* tilting her head, the sparkles in the barrette twinkling. "The world might stop existing. In just a little over a year. All this"—she looked around—"the trees, the sky, you and me, *poof!* All gone."

Rosalba shook her head. "I've never heard of that. Everything's always been the same."

"But everything's not going to *stay* the same."

"But the Earthlord makes sure—"

"The who?"

"The Earthlord, who lives up there." Rosalba gestured toward the cone-shaped mountain behind the trees. "He takes care of us. He'd never let such a thing happen."

Alicia peered. "Where *is* the Earthlord?"

"In his cave." Again, Rosalba gestured.

"Have you ever seen him?"

Rosalba shook her head. "Of course not. No one has seen the Earthlord. But Mama says he keeps the heavens in motion, the crops growing, and the rain falling. Without the Earthlord, the world wouldn't run right." She reached for a twig from the fallen house and laid it straight.

"He sounds like Jesus."

"A little." In the church in town the priest

talked about Jesus. But while Jesus was in heaven, the Earthlord lived close by.

Alicia set out three more twigs. Making a square, she said, "Let's build it back. Let's make it a real Mayan house this time."

"Fine," Rosalba agreed. She placed three pebbles in the middle, explaining, "This is the hearth." She dropped in bits of dried moss for pretend fire. "This is fun. I haven't played for a long time."

"What do you do instead?"

"I help Mama with real work. Don't you help your mama?"

Alicia shrugged. "I have my schoolwork."

Together they built up the walls. Each time their hands touched, happiness sparkled in Rosalba. She hadn't only *met* a *ladina;* she was making a house with her. It was like being offered a tray of sugary sweet-potato candy.

"This can be for the frogs who live here," said Alicia.

"A house for *frogs*?" Rosalba couldn't help but giggle. "Frogs are food."

"Papi told me people here eat them. But I didn't believe him. I love frogs."

Balancing pine needles for the thatched roof, Rosalba considered this. She'd never heard of anyone loving frogs except in a pot of soup. But if this Alicia loved frogs, so would she.

When the house was complete, the sun had slid behind the mountain of the Earthlord, dropping into the Underworld. In the dim light, the stream ran more quietly, the frogs sang more loudly.

"I should go home," Rosalba said reluctantly. She didn't want to part from her new friend, but neither did she want to run across the fruit bats or spooks that came out in the dusk.

"Me too. Papi will be worried."

After they'd stood up and brushed off their clothes, Alicia undid the butterfly barrette from her hair. She handed it to Rosalba.

The pretty clip lay in her palm, winking up at the trees. Rosalba thought quickly. What did she have to give? Nothing but her silver stud earrings. But she'd had those since she was a baby. They matched her little sister's. "I'll bring you something next time," she said.

"Something *Mayan.*" Alicia took the barrette from Rosalba and fastened it into Rosalba's hair.

Rosalba patted the stiff outline of the butterfly. She'd have to take the barrette out before Mama saw it. Mama didn't like her to talk to strangers. If she knew of the meeting, she might forbid her to see Alicia again.

"Meet me here tomorrow," Alicia said, "and I'll bring a book about the prophesy. I'll bring proof."

And then she was gone, walking quickly down the path.

I surrender to the will of my elders, the other shamans with whom I live.

I am cared for by the holy man, Mauruch. Every
dark moon, he changes my bandages, his fingers
rough as he unwinds the layers. Each time I count
them: thirteen. When my face is bare, he washes my
eyes with herb water, and I know not to open them.

Under pain of death, I never look at the world.

Calla Lilies

Rosalba had forgotten that the next day was market day, making a trip to the pool impossible. She and Mama left early, carrying nylon bags filled with eggs neatly wrapped in cloth.

On the way, they stopped to cut the calla lilies that grew at the edge of a small stream. The white lilies rolled up and curled back in on themselves, like soft leather. Mayans and *ladinos* alike used these flowers for their altars, but the *ladinos* paid money for them.

As Rosalba bent over the flowers, she felt the outline of Alicia's butterfly barrette. It was fastened to the waistband of her skirt, underneath her blousy *huipil*. She imagined it glittering in the darkness.

She and Mama reached among the leaves, which were like long, skinny hearts. With sharp knives, they sliced the watery flower stems. In a pine tree overhead, two birds squawked noisily.

Rosalba glanced at Mama's serious, lined face and thought of yesterday's adventure. While she herself still found gathering calla lilies fun, for Mama it was just work. To make the time pass, Mama might enjoy hearing about Alicia, seeing the barrette, and yet . . .

Rosalba didn't want to endanger her new friendship. Alicia was not a friend like her cousin Sylvia. She was someone unrelated to her, a friend she'd found herself in the forest. A *ladina* from Mexico City. Someone important.

Yet along with friendship, Alicia had brought troubling ideas. Ideas that had spun around in Rosalba's head until late into the night. She'd never thought that anything would be different from the way it always had been. The idea of change—*big* change—made her slightly dizzy.

Mama was very wise. Perhaps she would know. Moving closer to Mama on the damp bank, in a hushed voice Rosalba asked, "Is the world going to end soon?"

Mama laughed. "Why would you ask such a thing? Just look at these flowers." She gestured toward the lilies. "If the world were going to end, why would they be growing so beautifully?"

Rosalba nodded. Mama knew just what to say. Rosalba laughed, as if she'd been merely curious. She touched the bright yellow pistils of the flowers, saying, "These remind me of sunbeams."

Mama smiled. Yet as Rosalba laid the cut flowers in two piles, the worried feeling seeped back. Alicia had spoken with such authority. Rosalba wondered if there were things that Mama didn't know.

When the two piles were big enough, and after they'd been tied with lengths of rope, Rosalba knelt while Mama loaded an enormous bundle onto her head. Mama hoisted up her own mass of flowers, and they set off for market.

The path led through the forest, then over rolling hills marked by the cornfields, dry and brown, waiting for the rains. K'in, the sun, burned down with a ferocious brilliance.

When the path reached the highway, the

world changed. It was no longer the realm of the Earthlord, where life was lived in graceful order. Here, on the edge of the highway, the day turned chaotic, the air loud with the sound of traffic. Dust swirled behind the cars and buses.

Here, with the sky light all the time, people paid no attention to the movement of the sun through the thirteen layers. They were out of touch with the Earthlord, who kept everything running in an orderly fashion. Rosalba didn't like to think that this ugly place had once been peaceful forest.

"Careful!" Mama exclaimed as a dull green truck filled with soldiers drove so close that Rosalba's flowers were almost knocked off her head.

Rosalba wanted to lift her shawl against the smelly black exhaust, but one hand held the nylon bag, the other the lilies. She called out, "I'm glad we live far away, Mama."

They headed toward the high mountains that rose behind the town, along with a line of people and loaded donkeys. They walked with Mama's sister, Tía Cristina, and Papa's sisters, Tía Sonia and Tía Yolanda, with her little boy, Efrain.

Rosalba was joined by Sylvia, a cousin just her age. Whereas Rosalba had a wide, round face, Sylvia was delicate, with large eyes so dark brown they were almost black.

Sylvia mustn't know about Alicia. She'd probably be jealous of a *ladina* friend.

Efrain ran back and forth along the road in between Tía Yolanda and one of the donkeys, his sandals slapping the dirt.

Finally, the white church came into view, with its steeples rising into the sky. Bougainvillea spilled over a wall, the pink flowers reminding Rosalba of Alicia's pink fingernails.

Rosalba and Sylvia peeked into the shops selling auto parts, brooms, and plastic buckets.

"I wish we had those things in San Martín," Sylvia said.

"There's no way to get them there," Rosalba

retorted. There'd never been a road to San Martin, never would be.

The open-air market spread over the plaza next to the church. Huge tarps made everything and everyone underneath look blue: soldiers, tourists, *ladinos* who lived in the town, Mayan women with blue shawls, Mayan men wearing hats with waterfalls of colored ribbon. Even the wandering dogs looked blue.

Mama led the way past *nopales* with the spines cut off, pyramids of guavas, herbs hanging by the stems, red chilis, round green squash, and fragrant tamales.

Rosalba noticed two *ladinos* buying a bag of dried beans, joking and bargaining with the vendor. One wore a shirt with green frogs embroidered on it. Could these be the scientists?

Was Alicia here, too? Rosalba stood on tiptoe, looking through the crowd. But she saw nothing of that curly light hair.

Finding a bare patch, Mama and Rosalba's aunts squatted to lay out their blankets. Rosalba helped Mama make a neat display of the lilies, eggs, and some napkins that Nana had woven. Today Rosalba hoped that all would sell quickly so that she could return to the pool in the forest and to Alicia. If she didn't make it back in time, if she didn't fulfill her promise, would Alicia think she didn't want to be friends? Would she never again build a tiny house with her?

As Rosalba looked around the market, everyone was buying and selling as usual. No one acted as if the world was about to end. Children ran along the rows, kicking up dust. A tourist bargained over a striped shawl. A man played a flute.

Rosalba decided that there could be no such thing as Alicia's 2012 prophesy. Just as her new friend had built a pretend frog house, so she'd imagined the story of the end of the world.

As people bought eggs and lilies and even some of Nana's napkins, Rosalba pushed the remaining items to the front of the blanket. She smiled extra hard at the customers. If everything was sold quickly, she and Mama could leave. She might make it to the pool in time.

When the sun paused at the top of the sky, beating down through the blue tarp, the church bells tolled the hour. Mama opened her coin purse and gave Rosalba money for shopping.

"Let's go, Sylvia," Rosalba said, getting up, smoothing her skirt.

"Why are you in such a hurry?" Sylvia asked. "You almost knocked into that man."

"I . . . I want to make sure to get kerosene. Last time they ran out."

Rosalba filled the nylon bags with a plastic bottle of kerosene for the lamp, sugarcane beer for Papa, and salt and sugar wrapped in bits of newspaper.

As Sylvia bought sandals for her big brother, Rosalba rocked from one foot to the other.

When Sylvia giggled over a donkey painted to look like a zebra for picture-taking tourists, Rosalba pulled on her arm.

Next, Sylvia stopped to examine the displays

19

of bright yarn looped over the poles. Usually Rosalba loved to finger the yarn, imagining it glowing on her loom. But today she only glanced impatiently at the rainbows of color and sighed loudly.

With the few coins left, Rosalba bought two apple-flavored *refrescos,* one for herself and one for Sylvia.

As she was taking her first sip, Rosalba saw Catarina Sanate, surrounded by a group of American and *ladino* tourists.

"Don't go over there, Rosalba," said Sylvia. "My mama says to stay away from her."

Rosalba's mama had said the same thing. But Rosalba was fascinated by Catarina. She felt certain that Catarina, like her, wouldn't be afraid to walk alone to the pool.

Catarina had been a bit older than Rosalba when she'd taken up folk painting. Everyone had disapproved. At the river, as the women did laundry, Rosalba had overheard the gossip. *Weaving* was the job of girls and women, they'd said. Painting on canvas was for men. Just as a woman was known as lord of the house, and a man was the lord of the cornfield.

But Catarina had gone on and painted everyone in the village, whether they liked it or not. The women whispered that her paintings were more lifelike and beautiful than those done by the men.

As Rosalba drew closer, she heard Sylvia's loudly whispered warning: "But she's a *bruja,* Rosalba. When she paints people, she bewitches them."

Lots of people believed that. Just in case, no one wanted to be near Catarina. She sometimes disappeared from the Highlands. But she always came back, and now lived in town in a small house of her own.

Rosalba was now near enough to see the thick brushstrokes of Catarina's paintings.

Instead of being laid out on the ground, the paintings were set up on easels: men working in the cornfields, women kneeling to wash at the river, musicians at a fiesta, the dance of the men who pretended to be the deer and jaguar.

For a moment the figures seemed to move as if they were really laughing, dancing, or playing instruments. When Rosalba blinked, the figures became mere paintings again.

"Come on, Rosalba. Let's go!" insisted Sylvia, tugging at the edge of Rosalba's shawl.

I behold the world through senses other than sight.

I feel the prickle of shells hung in strands around my neck, looped as bracelets around my wrists. My skin warms adornments of cool jade.

I run my fingertips over Mauruch's face, pausing at the deep lines. I compare his face of many details with my own smooth one.

In our cave I press my palms onto the slippery lumps of the stalagmites and stalactites, one formation stretching to the stars, the other to the Underworld. Bathing in the water of the dzonot, *I never linger. I immerse my body quickly and pull myself out with the rope. That cold sinkhole leads straight to Xibalba.*

Outside I walk the paths, sensing direction and the time of day by the warm pulse of the sun on my face.

Mornings, the cries of the roosters wake us. Softer is the flutter of their wings. Far off, in the fringy jungle, my ear discerns the noisy calls of the howler monkeys as they move in black troops through the trees. Swimming in the river, I become one with the loud plunge of the waterfall.

Traveling sightless, I guide myself by listening to sounds bouncing off trees and rocks.

Sometimes I lie down on the ground, becoming one with it, feeling the Earth's grainy touch against my bare skin. I welcome even the sharp sensations of the insects' bites.

I breathe the cave air musky with bat guano, the smoke, the damp odor of the earth, the lightning's bitter scent.

Finally, there is always a taste on my tongue: rainwater; clear, sweet coconut milk; dark pataxte; the musky meat of the wild pig. . . .

The Flight of an Owl

By the time Rosalba and Mama arrived in San Martín, the sun had dropped into the Underworld.

On the final stretch of the path, little Adelina ran to greet them, crying out, "Nana is teaching me weaving!"

As the Mayan words reached Rosalba's ears, she relaxed. Now she was truly home.

Adelina threw her arms around Mama first, then Rosalba. "Nana, let me help her."

Nana stood smiling, surrounded by pecking chickens. Behind her, Rosalba glimpsed Papa coming down the mountain through the mist. He carried a huge load of firewood on his back. With a cry of exhausted triumph, he threw the wood down.

Anselmo, age seven, and Mateo, eleven, appeared, staggering under smaller loads. Papa helped Anselmo untie his bundle.

When Papa was tired, Rosalba knew to stay away, to say nothing. When hungry, Papa could snap like a dog.

"Help me set the table, Adelina," she said, taking her sister by the hand.

While Mama reheated the tortillas and lit the fire under the pots of beans and squash, Rosalba handed Adelina the enamel plates, then the cups. Finally, she carried out a bowl of dried chile flakes.

Once everyone had eaten, they grew quiet. One by one, the night stars popped out. Rosalba was glad to be home from the market, the highway, the town. She liked to go out, but loved even more to come back. Now she heard only the sounds of frogs and crickets, the crackle of the fire. She fingered a collection of yarn scraps in her lap.

At last Papa lit a cigarette, saying, "We passed the camp of tents the *ladinos* have set up."

"They've brought lots of boxes," added Mateo, propping his feet on a log. "They don't seem to be tourists."

26

"They've come to study us so they can write books," said Nana.

"And make a lot of money," Mateo said.

Mama said, "They must be looking for another lost city. For pyramids."

Anselmo's eyes grew wide. "*Pyramids*? Pyramids close by?"

"If they find a pyramid, many people will come," said Nana.

"I don't think it's pyramids they're looking for," said Papa. "These may be the same *ladinos* who years ago tried to grab our land."

Mama sucked in her breath.

Rosalba had heard stories of the days when land-hungry *ladinos* had come to the Highlands. The Mayans had fought back, calling themselves Zapatistas after the famous revolutionary Emiliano Zapata. Just before Rosalba's birth, both men and women had taken up guns and donned the black knit ski masks called *pasamontañas*. Papa had been the village leader. His gun still lay beside his bed.

In some places, where the Zapatistas had

lost, their land had been taken. But the villagers of San Martín had kept their cornfields.

Listening to the conversation, Rosalba braided yarn into a pretty bracelet for her new friend. She alone knew that the men weren't pyramid or land hunters, but scientists. She mustn't reveal the secret of her meeting with Alicia. Yet, in spite of Mama's reassurances, she couldn't forget what Alicia had told her.

"When I was in the market today," Rosalba said carefully, "I heard something strange. A man said that the world will end soon. In just over a year."

Papa ground his cigarette butt into the dirt. "Who told you that?"

"I overheard someone talking."

Mateo laughed very loudly. He jabbed his elbow into Anselmo's arm until he too laughed.

"But it's a *Mayan* prophesy," Rosalba persisted.

"People want to make us Mayans more exciting than we really are," said Nana.

"And I told you just this morning the lilies

would know," said Mama, pulling Rosalba close on the narrow bench.

Rosalba relaxed against Mama's shoulder. Of course Alicia's story wasn't true.

As an owl flew overhead, flapping its pale wings, everyone grew quiet.

In spite of Mama's embrace, Rosalba shivered. An owl could be a *brujo* come to steal a soul. An owl could mean death. Or, as Alicia might say, it could mean the death of the world.

I see when Mauruch decrees it.

When he brings me the bitter hot drink, I down it without question. Crouched in the back of the cave, I conquer the demon of my nausea.

With the drink circulating in my veins, I dream the world.

I surrender to visions of the king and his priests whirling in quetzal-feathered headdresses. I witness maidens wearing white dresses, armies of slaves dragging great stones to build pyramids and majestic cities, serpents with plumes on their backs. I see a great stone calendar. Rubber balls bounce across the stone ball courts of the temple-pyramids rising above the forest canopy. I behold the blue, yellow, and red macaws, and the iridescent green and gold tail feathers of the quetzal birds. In the lagoons crocodiles and caimans laze, iguanas strut over hot rocks while boa constrictors and venomous fer-de-lance slither through the tall grass. Beneath the mahogany, sapodilla, and bread-nut trees, the jaguar stalks.

Here in the heart of the world.

Frog Heaven

"You didn't come yesterday!" Alicia called out.

Rosalba waved, breathless from running. Her heart beat quickly. "I went to market with my mother." She handed the yarn bracelet to Alicia, who sat on a rock.

"How pretty!" Alicia exclaimed, examining the strand of colorful braid. "I can tell it's really Mayan." She held up her arm so that Rosalba could tie the bracelet around her wrist.

"And that looks so nice on you." She pointed to the sparkly barrette in Rosalba's hair.

At the last turn of the path, Rosalba had stopped to clip the butterfly onto one of her braids. She sat closer to Alicia than she had the first time. She was about to put an end to Alicia's end-of-the-world talk so they could just have fun together. Folding her hands in her lap, she said, "I asked my family about your prophesy. They've never heard of it."

"Well, they should have. Look at this." Alicia held up a shiny blue book. On it was a picture of a Mayan pyramid surrounded by storm clouds. "Here's the proof." She opened the book and put it in Rosalba's lap.

Rosalba stared at the black markings.

"Turn the book over, Rosalba. You've got it upside down."

Rosalba turned the book around, yet still just stared, her cheeks growing warm.

"You don't know how to read Spanish?"

Rosalba shook her head. "I don't read at all," she said in such a low voice that Alicia leaned forward.

Alicia glanced around the forest, then stated, "You don't have a school here."

"The school's in town," Rosalba said quietly. Mateo had attended when he was very small, and Anselmo, too, before Papa had needed him in the cornfield. But she, a girl, had never gone. Mama needed her too much. Who else would watch Adelina while Mama did laundry at the river? If she went to school, when would she find time for her weaving?

"Sometimes I wish I didn't have school. It's so boring." Alicia yawned. "But listen." She took the book back and began to read aloud: "'According to the ancient Mayans, the solar system rotates in cycles of 25,625 years around the center of the galaxy. Once every 5,125 years, it reaches the center. Then the whole galaxy is illuminated by a burst of light. When this spark hits the sun, it causes solar flares as well as changes in the sun's magnetic field. Because the burst changes the earth's rotation, great catastrophes can occur.

"'According to Mayan beliefs, the world is now entering the starfields.'" Here Alicia broke off to say, "The starfields is a special place at the heart of all the stars." She waved a hand at the sky, then looked down at the book again. "'The earth will meet the next burst of galactic energy on December 21, 2012, the date when the Mayan calendar ends.'"

Alicia set down the book. "Now do you believe me?"

Rosalba hadn't been listening carefully. She was awash in shame at not knowing how to read, and the words had flown past her. Alicia was obviously very good at reading. How could she want a friend who didn't know how?

To Rosalba's relief, Alicia closed the book and set it aside, saying, "Let's make a Mayan pyramid."

"For the frogs," said Rosalba.

"Yes, for the frogs."

They stood up and began to gather stones. As Rosalba worked, piling small rocks into her apron, Alicia's confusing words swarmed back into her mind. Finally, she asked, "*Which* Mayans know about the end of the calendar? No one in my family knows."

Alicia hesitated, staring up into the tall pines. At last she said, "Maybe the ancient ones."

"But the ancient ones didn't write those kinds of words," Rosalba protested. She'd seen pictures of the swirly glyphs from old temples.

Alicia brushed off her hands, saying, "What's important is that our planet is traveling with the other planets from the Milky Way. When the earth gets into the starfields, a big light is going to shoot our sun."

Rosalba glanced toward the sun dropping through the trees.

"The light will make the sun act so crazy it might kill the earth," Alicia went on.

"The earth can't die."

"Why not?"

"It just can't." A sharp rock scratched Rosalba's palm.

"The frogs are dying, aren't they?"

Rosalba shrugged. "I haven't *seen* any dying."

"Come to our camp, then."

Although Rosalba didn't want to see dying frogs, seeing the green tents up close sounded like fun.

Alicia turned to the pile of rocks they'd collected, saying, "We can make a pyramid just like on the cover of the book."

"Let's build the pyramid next to the house,"

Rosalba suggested. Though some of the sticks had been knocked out of place, perhaps by a curious animal, the little structure still stood.

They laid a solid square for the base, the rocks clattering softly. The stream murmured, and soft patches of light fell onto the forest floor.

They put down fewer rocks for the next layer, fewer still for the next, building a cone shape.

As Rosalba worked, questions still wound through her mind. Who *had* written that book? In the end, it was all just words, wasn't it? The words weren't even words spoken by a shaman. Nor were they the words of the holy Bible the priest read from in the white-steepled church in town. Was all that Alicia had read true or not?

"Ta-da!" said Alicia as Rosalba balanced one rock on the tip top of the pyramid.

Rosalba stepped back to inspect their work. When Alicia held up the book, the little pyramid looked lumpy compared to the picture on the cover.

"We should name this place," said Alicia.

"It's quiet here," said Rosalba slowly. "There's lots of frogs."

"How about Frog Land?"

"Or Frog Heaven?"

"That's it!" Alicia clapped.

Rosalba smiled. Alicia could read, but *she'd* come up with the name.

"Next time," said Alicia, tucking the book under her arm, "I'll take you to our camp. I'll show you the frogs. I'll read you more about the prophesy."

One day when Mauruch gives me a handful of dried mushrooms to chew, I vomit. Nonetheless, before my entrails can spew the potion out, the essence enters me.

This time I see the priests with their great feathered headdresses stripping a man of his clothes. The man does not resist; his eyes are dazed, as if looking within.

The priests paint his skin with pigment as blue as the winter sky. They lead him to a blue-painted stone, where they lay him face-up.

The victim is grasped by his arms and legs. His mouth opens in a wide circle, but I hear no scream. He squeezes his eyes shut. Against the merciless eye of K'in. Against the sight of the flint knife.

The priest wearing the largest headdress lifts that knife high into the air.

In spite of my drowsiness, I sit up and stare into the world behind my eyelids.

The high priest brings the knife down, dividing

the victim's chest. The man's mouth closes, and his eyes open. My breath leaves me.

The priest reaches inside to bring out the still-beating heart. He holds it high to a roaring crowd. He drinks the blood, hot red liquid oozing down his chin and onto the feathers he wears.

I wake, clutching my own heart and crying out, "Why? Why, Mauruch?"

Mauruch rouses himself from his own dreams. He stirs, then says, "The gods demand it. They gave us blood to live, and now we must give our own. Without such sacrifice, the sun won't shine. The earth will shrivel. Without the blood of life, our people will perish."

The Earthlord and His Squatting Toad

That night as Rosalba lay with Adelina breathing softly beside her, she thought again of Alicia's prophesy. It *couldn't* be true. The earth had always been the same way it was now, and always would be. As Mama had pointed out, beautiful flowers still bloomed. To ensure that sameness, men tended the corn, women wove.

Rosalba's own life was as it had always been. Inside the hut, the dampened fire glowed, the air smelled of sweet smoke. Mama's bucket of shelled corn mixed with lime water simmered gently. Outside, the night rang with the cries of crickets and frogs.

Tonight another sound wove itself in and out of the outdoor sounds. Rosalba leaned up on her elbow to listen. Were the crickets louder than usual? Or was it—she could hardly believe this—the roar of trucks on the highway? But that couldn't be. The highway was too far away.

The noise was like the buzz of a pesky mosquito. Why had she never noticed it before? Was it because in meeting Alicia, she was paying attention to new things?

Rosalba pulled the blanket over her head, but couldn't block out the sound. She'd always considered her village completely separate from the highway and its activity. The village seemed like a nest of tranquility. But it wasn't really. She'd been fooling herself.

Plugging her ears, Rosalba began to toss. Adelina cried out in her sleep and Rosalba hushed her, yet she too felt like crying out. *Be quiet!* she wanted to shout at those trucks.

Rosalba turned over so quickly, she yanked the blanket off Adelina. She wished she'd never met Alicia, had never heard her story.

The next day, Rosalba didn't go to Alicia. She didn't want to know more about the prophesy, didn't want to see the dying frogs at Alicia's camp.

Instead she carried her backstrap loom outside. She tied one end to a tall tree, then unrolled it and slipped the other end around her waist. The loom stretched in front of her, the bright-red yarn of the warp shining against the green forest.

Nearby, Adelina played at making tortillas with round leaves.

When she'd been just a little older than her sister, Rosalba had learned to weave plain blue-and-white striped cloth. At first it had been like weaving spider webs, the threads had gotten so tangled, but with practice she'd gotten good at making napkins, tablecloths, and even simple *huipiles.*

Mama and Nana had taught her more than just weaving. She was learning to brocade, using a pointed stick to insert colored yarns into the woven fabric.

She had planned a very traditional design for her *huipil:* the squarish figure of the Earthlord and his squatting toad. A line running across the bodice would show the path of the sun through the heavens and the Underworld.

The front and back of the *huipil* would be identical.

She'd started this *huipil* when the dark mornings were shrouded with mist. Every day she sat under the tall tree, little by little creating the universe.

"The gods have sacrificed parts of their precious bodies," Mauruch has said. "Therefore, blood and life must be given back."

Every crevice of the cave fills with the sweet smoke of copal incense and with the ancient words of our chanting: O Hunahpu Possum and Hunahpu Coyote, Great White Peccary and Coati, Sovereign and Quetzal Serpent, Heart of Lake and Heart of Sea, Creator of the Green Earth and Creator of the Blue Sky . . .

I hear a screech or groan or cry as an animal is sacrificed.

In the silence each shaman draws his own blood.

Mauruch comes to me and pierces my earlobes. I flinch at the sharp barb of a stingray spine, then breathe in time to the rhythmic dripping as Mauruch collects my blood.

The bloody leaves are mixed with resin and burned. The smell appeases the gods.

As the flames grow, through my bandages I see visions.

Mauruch senses this. "Tell me, Xunko," he commands.

"The smoke is rising. It's becoming a . . . a great serpent. And now . . ."

"Speak." He grips my arm.

"The serpent has a tongue," I say slowly. "On that tongue stands an ancestor."

"And what does the ancestor tell us?"

"He sends his messengers. He sends Arrow Owl, One-Leg Owl, Macaw Owl, and Skull Owl with their burden."

"And what is this burden, Xunko?"

"We are to beware. We are to step carefully. Perhaps even the Framer and Shaper of the Universe cannot prevent what lies ahead."

I Forbid You

Rosalba wove until shadows crept across the patio. After weeks of work, she had almost completed the front of the *huipil*. Soon she'd begin on the back, weaving and brocading everything in reverse, upside down.

Every now and then Nana checked the work, running her rough fingers over the threads. She pointed out areas where the work was fine and even, and places where the threads were bunched up.

When Adelina teased, darting back and forth, dancing underneath the loom where it was tied to the tree, Rosalba hardly looked up. Once the stiff, squarish figures of the Earthlord and his toad seemed to dance across the fabric. Rosalba put her hand over the threads, stilling the creatures. It was as though her weaving had brought them to life.

Close to her, Mama was brocading a new *huipil*. Like women throughout the hills, she was creating the story of the Flood. It wasn't the floodwaters themselves that Mama wove, but rather the image of the Father-Mother, the two ancestors who'd lived through the disaster. Afterward, those two beings had planted corn, making possible the survival of humans.

Rosalba squinted at the designs in Mama's *huipil*. Suddenly, she understood. The Flood was just like the disaster Alicia foretold. The Flood had destroyed the world.

"Mama! The Flood is the same as that 2012 prophesy!"

Mama smiled. "The Flood was a very long time ago, Rosalba. It has nothing to do with us today."

"But if the world was destroyed before, couldn't it happen again?"

Mama shook her head. "Don't be troubled by such things, Rosalba."

Mama was right. But still Rosalba wanted

to tell Alicia about the connection. Maybe the writer of the book knew about the Flood.

She waited until Mama and Nana went to the tiny corn patch near the orchard, preparing it for planting. Adelina tagged along, dragging a digging stick.

Rosalba rolled up the loom, untied it from the tree, and bundled it into the house.

With the sun dangling low in the sky, Rosalba ran down the path toward Frog Heaven. Her heart tumbled in her chest. Her sandals slapped the soft dirt in time to her chant, "Be there! Be there! Alicia, be there!"

She passed girls herding sheep, muzzled so they wouldn't eat holy corn on their way to pasture, their bells tinkling softly. She leaped over a small creek and continued on.

Finally, she reached the pool, where all was quiet. The water whispered soft secrets. Birds flitted in the branches of the tall pines, slowing down, getting ready to nest. Frogs sang their evening songs.

But Rosalba dashed about, peering down into the hollows, into the shadowy places where the ferns grew. "Aliciaaa!" she called. She cupped her hands around her mouth: "Aliciaaa!"

The tiny house still stood. The nubby little pyramid pointed skyward. But her new friend wasn't there. With darkness falling, there was no sense in staying.

As Rosalba ran back along the path, bats swooped over the cornfields. On a turn, she lost her sandal. She had to search on hands and knees—feeling the icy breath of a spook on the back of her neck—until she found the shoe flung into the high grass.

After running, slowing to catch her breath, then running again, she saw the huts of the village, glowing with the light of cooking fires. When she turned onto the tiny path that led to her hut, Papa suddenly blocked the way, standing with his hands on his hips.

"Rosalba! Where have you been!"

By his voice, she could tell he was still hungry, still exhausted from the cornfield. There was no chance of escaping his notice now, of lying low. "I—I . . ." What could she say?

Mama came to stand behind Papa, and, from far off, Rosalba heard Adelina's wail.

"Answer me, Rosalba!"

Rosalba stood below him on the steep path, eye level with his feet. She drew herself taller. "I went to find my friend."

"Who is this friend? Sylvia would never go into the forest at night."

"She's a *ladina*," Rosalba said in a small voice.

"A *ladina*?" echoed Papa.

Mama stirred behind him.

"Yes," said Rosalba firmly. "She came with the men."

"And you went off to see this *ladina*," Papa said the word scornfully, "in the dark, leaving us all worried?" He broke off a small branch.

Rosalba stepped back.

"Don't, Gerardo," said Mama, grasping Papa's arm. "At least let her tell us about it."

Papa turned abruptly, bumping against Mama.

51

At the patio, Adelina ran to Rosalba and clung to her, still sniffling. "You went forever!" she cried.

Mateo and Anselmo ate silently, hunched over their plates.

As Papa pulled a chair close to the fire, a log popped, sending sparks into the night.

"Tell us, Rosalba," Mama said softly.

"My friend's name is Alicia." With a sudden feeling of pride, Rosalba undid the butterfly barrette from her hair. "She gave me this."

Adelina grabbed at the clip, but Rosalba held it out of reach.

Papa took the barrette, and held it so it winked in the firelight. Suddenly, Rosalba was afraid he'd keep it. Oh, why had she called attention to it? But he passed it to Mama, muttering, "Just a cheap thing."

"Let me see, too," said Mateo. He turned the barrette this way and that.

"Alicia is the one who told me about the world ending," Rosalba went on.

Mateo handed the barrette to Anselmo.

Rosalba watched anxiously as Anselmo opened and shut the barrette many times. He mustn't break it!

Papa crossed his arms over his chest. "That prophesy is *ladino* nonsense. Those *ladinos* are always coming here to spread foolish rumors. I forbid you to see that girl again. You are not to leave the village without your mother."

Papa's words hit Rosalba like a shower of cold hailstones. Her world closed in as in a heavy storm.

Mateo brought the battery-powered radio from the hut and set it on the table, next to the kerosene lamp. He turned the dials until the scratchy voice of the news reporter from Guatemala City spoke into the night.

When Anselmo gave back the barrette, Rosalba fastened it onto her waistband, out of sight.

As she helped with the dinner tortillas, her heart was as heavy as a river stone. What would Alicia think when she never came to Frog Heaven again? Now she would never see the camp or the frogs. She wiped her tears with the edge of her shawl.

Papa hated *ladinos* because they'd once tried to seize Mayan land. But Alicia wasn't to blame for that.

The radio now played the loud *oompah, oompah* of polka music. But even that happy sound with a strong beat couldn't lift Rosalba's heavy heart.

One day when Mauruch serves me the bitter drink, strange visions parade behind my eyes.

I see what has not yet happened.

The great cities of Tikal, Palenque, of Uxmal and Chichén Itzá—empires in the four directions—appear before me, swallowed up by the jungle, by great winding vines and roots that muscle their way into the cracks between the stones, rending the temples asunder. Under the stone blades, entire forests are felled. The rain clouds withhold themselves, the cornfields die, and the masses cry out with hunger. Men war under the hot glare of K'in.

To appease the furious gods, thousands of blue-painted men, women, and children are thrown into the morning-glory–blue dzonots. Each is a gift for the gods, descending into the watery Underworld.

Even so the sky remains desiccated: the gods will not be appeased.

The cities of the empire fall silent.

⟡ ⟡ ⟡

The next time I swallow the bitter brew, I see our people living, not in their magnificent cities, but in simple huts scattered through the jungle.

This cannot be! I squint, but the same scene presents itself time and again.

"Is this all true?" I ask Mauruch. "Will this be true?" For I cannot imagine our great stone civilization falling. "Have others foreseen this calamity?"

Mauruch remains silent.

Before my eyes the codices unfold, the sacred texts of our people. In the blue, black, and red glyphs, the fall of the Great Empire is foretold.

Our rituals grow longer as we pray harder to Chac, the rain god; to Kinich Ahau, the sun god; and to Yum Cimil, the god of death. When Mauruch pierces my tongue, he draws a rope with a barb on it through the hole, releasing a plethora of blood.

Keep This Secret

As the fire grew, a pot of beans bubbled, along with a kettle of coffee flavored with lumps of brown sugar. Mama and Nana patted masa back and forth between their palms, then laid the uncooked tortillas on the hot clay griddle.

The food smelled good, but Rosalba wasn't hungry. She'd woken to the memory of Papa's harsh words. She couldn't imagine not seeing Alicia. All she had left of her was the little hair ornament.

Rosalba coughed as the sweet smoke of the pinewood filled the hut.

Mama patted her on the back, saying, "Poor little daughter!"

At Mama's kindness, Rosalba felt tears sting the backs of her eyes. Yet she still had to help, or Papa's breakfast wouldn't be ready, making things worse.

When each tortilla puffed up, Rosalba grabbed the edge and flipped it. If her fingers brushed the hot griddle, she licked them. Once both sides of a tortilla were warm and browned, she handed it to Adelina, who placed it in a hollow gourd.

As the sun lifted into the first layer of sky, Papa, Anselmo, and Mateo came out of the nearby men's hut. With their arms up under their wool tunics, the three sat at the outdoor table, Anselmo leaning against Papa's shoulder, his long hair falling over his half-closed eyes.

Rosalba had woven the blue-and-white striped tablecloth herself and usually smoothed it proudly. But that morning, she unfurled it into the air and let it land as it would, averting her eyes and biting her lip against tears.

"Not all *ladinos* are like the men who came to take our land." She directed her words to the back of Papa's head.

Papa gave no sign of having heard her.

"I just want to see my friend for a little bit. . . ."

This time Papa shook his head.

"Please," she pleaded.

"No!" Papa pounded the table so hard, Anselmo opened his eyes.

Instead of giving Papa the hottest, freshest tortillas, Rosalba gave those to the boys and offered Papa the ones from the bottom of the gourd. Tears blurred her vision. Carrying the kettle of coffee, she tripped over a pecking chicken, spilling coffee onto the ground.

"Rosalba!" Papa shouted.

Finally, Papa stood up, then the boys. Wordlessly, they put on their round, flattish straw hats and gathered their hoes. It was time to join the other villagers for the walk to the cornfields, high on the mountain of the Earthlord.

Once the group had disappeared into the mist, Rosalba let her tears flow like the season's first rain.

"Don't cry, Rosie," said Adelina. "Papa will come back."

"That's not the problem, *chica.*" Rosalba

took her little sister in her arms, crying into her shiny black hair.

During breakfast her tears slipped into the edges of her mouth along with bites of tortillas and beans. She caught Mama and Nana exchanging glances.

Afterward, as Rosalba helped Nana wash dishes, Nana hummed a little song. Before they starting the drying, Nana pulled Rosalba close and whispered, "When your mama was young, I let her do something her father disapproved of. I think she remembers that time."

When Mama and Rosalba were lifting the table and stools to hang on pegs under the eaves, Rosalba said, "Please, Mama, let me meet my friend."

Mama touched Rosalba on the shoulder. "You really like her, don't you?" Then she glanced toward the mountain and narrowed her eyes. Was she thinking of Papa working the cornfield? What would Papa do if he found out that she'd let his daughter defy him?

Or was Mama thinking of the Earthlord? What would the Earthlord do in her place?

Or was Mama remembering the way Papa sometimes said harsh things to her and wouldn't let her stay late on market day to visit her friend Rosha?

Finally Mama turned to Rosalba. "Your papa still resents the way those *ladinos* tried to take his cornfield. Who *are* the men the girl is with?"

"They're scientists, Mama. They aren't doing anything wrong. They're just studying frogs."

Mama sighed. "You may go. But promise me you won't come back late. And keep this secret from your papa."

"Oh, Mama!" Rosalba wiped her tears with the back of her hand. She kissed Mama on both cheeks.

"But don't leave until the chickens are fed."

Tonight the drink tastes sour. Like old mangoes left in the sun. Like damp cornmeal gone rotten. Like fever breath.

When the potion takes me, I behold our people still living in simple huts. They know nothing of the great lost cities, of the sacred texts, the empire of the sun. They do not lift their eyes to the heavens. They divine nothing of what transpires outside their small jungle clearings.

I drift deeper into the dream. There's an ocean with something small and white floating upon it. The objects draw closer until I can make out canoes with great white wings. But instead of soaring through the air like huge butterflies, the canoes fly over the sea, wending their way closer and closer to our shores.

When the vessels are almost upon us, I can make out the inhabitants. The men have hair on their faces like animals.

When the flying canoes scrape onto the shoreline, a door opens and strange animals—much taller than deer—step out. The hairy ones mount these beasts, becoming half man, half beast, as they step onto the sand of our shores.

He whom the others follow has hair like the sun. It flames around his head, and even over his face. When he lifts a large pole, a loud noise comes out, scattering the deer, puma, and coati.

And then I suck in my breath. Suddenly I know. This man must be Kukulcan, the feathered serpent, the golden one. He came to us from a distant land, only to disappear, transforming himself into the Green Morning Star. His return has long been promised. For this god, we have been waiting. To this god, we shall all bow down.

Your Own Big Thing

"You're here!" Alicia called, jumping up and down on the path near Frog Heaven. She wore a very short yellow skirt, and her hair was tied back with a matching ribbon.

Rosalba waved. Little did Alicia know how hard it had been to come! Not wanting to hurt her friend's feelings, she decided not to mention Papa's order.

"Let's go to the camp. The frogs are waiting," Alicia said. "And I've read another chapter in the book. There's hope, Rosalba. There's something we can do to keep the world from ending."

If it was possible to prevent disaster, how serious had the threat been to start with? Rosalba retied her hair ribbon, which had come undone in her rush. As Alicia took her by the hand, Rosalba felt for the yarn bracelet tied around her wrist. "You're still wearing it!" she declared happily.

"Of course," said Alicia.

"I have something important to tell you too," Rosalba said, fixing her eyes on Alicia's. "We Mayans *do* know about your prophesy, after all. When I saw my mama weaving, I understood. Your prophesy is the same as our story of the Flood."

"So you do believe. . . ."

Rosalba considered. She thought of Papa and his harsh words. If he *didn't* believe, then perhaps she would. "Maybe," she said. "I mean yes."

"Oh, good." Alicia slapped her palm against Rosalba's, then led the way.

At last the path leveled off, traveling along the ridge. Rosalba and Alicia paused to look out at the forest stretching away, the scar of the highway, and even the far-off town.

Several plumes of smoke unfurled in the distance.

"Who's doing all that burning?" asked Alicia.

"The farmers. They're making room for

cornfields. Last month, Papa and my brothers cut down some trees and bushes. Now that all that's dry, it's ready to burn."

"Why don't they just plant where they planted before?"

"The soil gets worn out."

Alicia gestured with her arm, taking in the landscape of fires. "Are those people all making cornfields?"

Rosalba nodded. "Lots of farmers are burning today."

"Those trees make air. In school we learned about how trees get rid of carbon dioxide and manufacture oxygen. We can't *breathe* without trees, Rosalba."

"But we have to have corn. Corn is sacred. Corn is life," Rosalba said, repeating the words she'd always heard. "By growing it, the men became part of the movement of the stars."

Alicia's eyes widened. "What does that mean?"

"It means . . . it means . . ." Rosalba floundered. What *did* those words mean?

Alicia bent down to pick up an old can from the grass.

Rosalba noticed that the can dirtied Alicia's hands with smudges of rust. She herself didn't like to touch anything unclean.

At last they arrived at a clearing with five little dwellings. They weren't made of the usual mud and pine needles, but of green canvas. *Tents,* the *ladinos* called them.

Alicia put the can into a box with other cans and bottles, explaining, "Now this old can will be made into something else."

At the market, tourists bought tiny airplanes shaped out of soda cans. But *that* rusty can? "Like what?" Rosalba asked.

"It'll get melted down with other cans. Maybe it'll become a car. Or an airplane." Alicia gestured toward the yellow sky.

Rosalba stared at the sky and then at the box of old junk.

"Come look," said Alicia, leading the way beyond the tents to wooden shelves lined with rows of clear plastic boxes.

Each box contained a frog. Some nestled in leaves; others clung to the sides of the boxes with their webbed toes. Some opened their mouths wide. One flicked its tongue at Rosalba.

Alicia strolled up and down beside the shelves. "This tan one is Fernando, and the lumpy black one is Manuela. Cesar, Cassandra, and Josue," she said pointing to three marked with squiggly green lines. "And Berenice." A green creature peered with bulging black eyes.

Rosalba giggled. Who would think to name frogs?

"And these"—Alicia tapped her pink-tipped fingernail on a box of tiny red-and-green frogs—"are so special they're going to a frog zoo to be taken care of."

Rosalba peered closely. She realized she'd once seen many of these. Mateo had caught them easily. But now she saw hardly any. Was Alicia right? Were the frogs disappearing?

"Here comes Papi," said Alicia.

A tall man emerged from a tent, then leaned

down to zip the door. He was dressed in khaki shorts and shirt. His hair, thinning at the temples, was the same light color as Alicia's.

"Papi," Alicia called out, "this is Rosalba, the friend I told you about."

"Much pleasure," said the man, smiling. "You may call me *Antonio*."

"*Señor* . . . ?" Rosalba asked hesitantly. She never called adults by their first names.

"Too formal. *Antonio* will do."

"All the frogs," Alicia continued, waving her hand, "are going to Mexico City to be tested. If they have fungus, there's medicine. Some die anyway. As the earth gets hotter, there's more fungus."

"I learned about global warming in a movie," said Rosalba, standing taller. The movie had been shown in the plaza on a large outdoor screen. Driving back in the truck that night, showers of bright stars spilling overhead, then walking the path to San Martín using flashlights, Rosalba had thought hard about what she'd seen. She felt afraid of hot times, of floods, or, worse, no rain at all. She'd lain awake considering the possibilities.

But as the days and nights passed the way they always had, the sun climbing through the thirteen layers of sky, traveling through the Underworld and reappearing again, Rosalba had convinced herself that such a thing as global warming wouldn't happen here in the Highlands. The Mayan world was different, protected by the Earthlord.

Now she noticed another row of boxes. The frogs inside weren't moving. She stepped closer.

"Those are the dead ones," said Alicia. "Patricia and Alfredo died yesterday."

Rosalba stared at the tiny stiff bodies. A sudden thought, a very unpleasant thought, came to mind. "Are toads dying, too?"

"Like I said—all amphibians."

"If *toads* are in danger, who's going to guard the Earthlord's cave? That toad has kept watch since the beginning of time, singing his songs." Rosalba looked in the direction of the Earthlord's cave.

"He sounds really special."

"He is. The toads help the Earthlord create the clouds. Without clouds, there's no rain. Without rain, there's no corn. And corn is life."

Alicia's eyes grew big. "Let's hope that toad stays alive."

Rosalba squinted at the mountain again, as if she could actually *see* the Earthlord's toad. This news about the toads was more real to her than the words in Alicia's book.

"They say frogs are the canaries in the coal mine," said Alicia.

"The *what*?"

"Papi says that miners used to send a canary underground before they went down. If the canary died, it meant the air was bad. So many frogs dying means something is really wrong with our whole planet."

Rosalba looked around. The trees and sky appeared as they always had.

"Let's go inside the tent and I'll read you the new exciting part." Alicia knelt to unzip the door.

Rosalba crawled in behind her, into the pale green light. She noticed Alicia's bottle of pink fingernail polish, a box containing more barrettes, a tangle of bright hair ribbons, and a teddy bear with the fur worn off its stomach.

Sitting cross-legged, Alicia opened her book with the pyramid on the front and began to read: "'While many view the year 2012 as the inevitable end of the world, others hold out hope for humanity. Perhaps the universe is presenting a challenge for all of us. Through our collective actions, we may avoid catastrophe and enter a golden age of increased environmental awareness.'"

Alicia laid the book on her knee. "This means we have to do something, Rosalba. Everyone has to help. I'm helping Papi with the frogs. What will *you* do?"

Rosalba glanced around the tent, then back to her own hands. The question was unexpected. What *could* she do? "I weave," she offered.

"How can *that* help?"

How could Alicia not know? "I weave for the Earthlord."

"He's the one who lives in the mountain, isn't he?"

Rosalba nodded. "He needs help from us to keep the world running just right."

"Hmm. Maybe you can do something else."

"Could I help with the frogs?"

"You can help a little with them. But you need to think of your own big thing."

Her own big thing.

Someone stepped close to the outside of the tent. A man's voice said, "Don't believe everything my daughter tells you, Rosalba."

Alicia retorted loudly, "It's all in my *book*!"

Her *papi* laughed.

"Don't any grown-ups believe?" whispered Rosalba. "My *papi* didn't laugh himself, but he made my brothers laugh."

"Lots of grown-ups believe. The author of this book believes." She held it up. "My *papi* is so wrong. The end of the world is coming. I know it."

Rosalba let her shawl slip off her shoulders, revealing her *huipil.*

"Your blouse is so pretty," Alicia said, lying back, studying Rosalba's red-and-white *huipil.* "I just love those blouses. They have such cute animals on them."

Rosalba looked down at her *huipil.* The Earthlord *cute?*

"Maybe you could weave something that makes a statement about 2012. Let people know about it."

Rosalba felt her jaw tighten. "When I weave a *huipil,* I weave the patterns that were woven by our ancestors," said Rosalba. "Doing that, I help the earth. These"—she touched the ancient designs—"are so powerful that even just *wearing* the *huipil* helps the Earthlord."

Alicia gazed at the *huipil,* nodding, but with a slight frown.

As the sun lowered itself toward the Underworld, a tree shadow fell across the tent.

"I have to get back." Rosalba reached for the zipper on the door.

"Let me come with you," said Alicia. "I'll come as far as Frog Heaven."

Outside, with the fires burning, the sky had turned a dusky yellow color. The sun had become a dull orange ball. As they descended, Rosalba noticed smoke rising in columns all over the valley, before spreading out.

"Don't people see what the smoke does to the blue sky?" Alicia asked.

For Rosalba, smoky skies were simply necessary. Otherwise, the corn couldn't be planted.

Yet the afternoon *was* unbearably hot.

When they reached Frog Heaven, Alicia turned to Rosalba, saying, "I might as well come with you the rest of the way," she said. "I want to see where you live."

"Oh, no," said Rosalba. "Not today." Alicia mustn't come. "It'll—it'll get too dark. There'll be spooks and demons. Demons with wings." She lifted her arms, making flapping movements.

"I'm not afraid of those."

"One touched me on the neck the other night."

Alicia shrugged.

"There'll be bats."

"I love bats."

Rosalba planted herself so Alicia couldn't pass. "All right, then. My papa doesn't want me to see you."

Alicia wrinkled her forehead. "Why not?"

"A long, long time ago, right before I was born, *ladinos* tried to take our cornfields. They wanted the land for themselves."

"That wasn't fair."

"It wasn't. And now Papa doesn't like *ladinos*. He won't even like you."

"Not like *me*?" Alicia flashed her biggest smile.

"It's not your fault," Rosalba said. She glanced ahead at the path, calculating how long it would take Papa to come down from the cornfield. Might he get home before her? Touching the back of Alicia's hand, she said, "Someday he may change his mind."

Alicia leaned forward to kiss Rosalba, first on one cheek, then the other. "I hope so."

76

Rosalba scrambled up the main trail, then up the tiny one to her hut. There was no sign of Papa or the boys. The patio was deserted except for the two white dogs lying under a bush.

When Rosalba pulled back the blanket over the door, she saw only girls and women: Mama, Nana, Adelina, Tía Yolanda, and Sylvia.

"Rosie!" Adelina ran to her.

"Where were you?" Sylvia asked when Rosalba had settled herself.

Rosalba glanced at Mama.

Mama gave a slight nod.

Rosalba plunged forward: "I was seeing my new friend. She's a *ladina*."

Sylvia wrapped her shawl more tightly around her, staring at Rosalba with her large black eyes.

Rosalba bit her lip. Now Sylvia was unhappy. Another girl had come between them.

Sylvia stirred the embers with a stick of green wood, asking, "What do you do together?"

Rosalba recalled how she and Sylvia had once played house, taking turns being the papa, making Anselmo be the baby. They'd cooked mud stews. One spring when Rosalba had broken her ankle, Sylvia had sat with her, telling stories. Nowadays they liked doing each other's hair, winding bright ribbons into the braids.

"We looked at frogs in boxes. Many many frogs," she finally answered. "They're sick. A fungus is killing them. . . ."

The embers popped and sparks flew.

"Dying frogs means the world is going to end," Rosalba persisted.

Sylvia rolled her eyes.

The man-beasts advance into our jungles, searching out our people in their small huts.

Believing in the return of the Blond God, our people bow down in gratitude and submission. They do not fight these hairy men, but make offerings. When they make offerings of gold, the men clench their fists tight around the yellow metal dug from our land.

But it's more than gold they seek. They want our people to make offerings to their god. And only to their god. The man-beasts defame our gods, smashing the stelae of our temples. They burn the sacred texts, the codices that the people, even living so simply in the jungle, have still guarded. Into the heavens the truth of our gods rise as smoke.

They carry their own god on two crossed sticks. He sheds blood from his palms, feet, chest, and the crown of his head. The hairy ones proclaim him to be the only god. But how can one be god of creation and of destruction? Of the moon and the sun? Both god of life and death?

This leader does not proclaim himself to be Kukulkan. Perhaps he is not. The Green Morning Star, after all, still hangs in the sky.

When the slaying of our people begins, the Golden One kills the most. He bears down on innocent women and children until the rivers run red with their blood. How could he be the long-proclaimed Feathered Serpent?

Halfway

As Rosalba completed the last row of the front of her *huipil,* she lifted her hands in triumph.

"Congratulations," said Nana. "You're halfway finished."

"It's pretty, Rosie," said Adelina, lightly touching the threads.

Mama brought out four bright red *refrescos,* saying, "I've kept these to celebrate this moment. Congratulations, Rosita."

Rosalba smiled at the way Mama had called her "Little Rose."

"Ooh, strawberry!" Adelina exclaimed when Nana handed her a bottle with the cap twisted off.

Ever since she'd begun the *huipil,* Rosalba had looked forward to this day. Now, sipping the bubbly drink, surveying her work, she felt proud of the way she'd continued the ancestral tradition, connecting herself to something larger.

Maybe Alicia was wrong in thinking that weaving couldn't be her one big thing. Alicia didn't know what it meant to be a Mayan. Rosalba lightly touched the bright threads stretched across the loom. If she kept weaving, all would be well.

In the early afternoon, Rosalba called through the door of Sylvia's hut: "Would you like to go with me to the spring?"

The spring was located uphill, on the way to the cave of the Earthlord.

For a moment, Sylvia made no response. At last she said, "Well, yes. We need water."

Rosalba and Sylvia walked up the mountain, empty clay jars on their heads. The sky was still as yellow as ripe corn. The smoke made Rosalba long for the upcoming rains.

Now that the fires had died down, the men had gone to the cornfields with gourds filled with seed. Across the slopes, Rosalba could see the tiny figures plunging their digging sticks through the layer of new ash. Others followed, dropping corn into the holes. Everyone hurried to complete the planting before the rains arrived.

Halfway to the top, pure water trickled from a limestone cliff, forming a clear pool below. Lacy ferns grew at the water's edge.

No one dirtied the spring by doing wash here or by bringing animals to drink. A white wooden cross protected the purity. And yet people left candy wrappers, crushed plastic bottles, and fruit peelings strewn over the sand.

Just before the big Festival of Santa Cruz, women would rake the sand clean. But right now it looked very messy.

Rosalba and Sylvia filled their jars, then squatted side by side, splashing their faces with cool water. After the water settled again, they looked at their reflections: two cousins who'd grown up together—one slender, the other round-faced.

They lay back on the sand. As Rosalba

closed her eyes, colors swam gently behind her eyelids. First she saw a green star glowing in the dawn sky. How pretty, she thought.

But then a disturbing vision appeared: the trickling spring, instead of running clear and fresh, was red, as if bloodied. Abruptly, the red water stopped flowing altogether.

Rosalba sat up, her heart beating quickly. The real spring was still flowing sweetly. She shook her head to clear the unsettling vision. Had it been only a bad dream from eating too many chilies?

She looked up to see clouds forming at the edges of the sky. Rain would come soon — maybe tomorrow or the next day.

She stood up. Recalling the way Alicia had picked up the rusty can, Rosalba stretched her shawl across the bank. She began to collect the trash that littered the sand, laying everything on the dark blue cloth. Cleaning up wasn't a big thing, but it was something.

"What are you doing?" Sylvia asked.

"Making the spring nicer."

"But your *shawl*, Rosalba! You're ruining it!"

"It can be washed. Besides, everything can be made into something else."

"Like what? How can you turn that watermelon rind into anything? What can anyone do with one sandal?"

"I learned about recycling from the *ladina*," Rosalba said. "All of this will be melted together to make airplanes." She tied the bundle around her back, then hoisted the jar onto her head.

"Here. You forgot this," said Sylvia, handing Rosalba an empty soda bottle.

On the dark moon, Mauruch changes my bandages. When I count the layers he winds back on, I count only twelve.

"Where is the last?" I ask.

"You are to begin your entry into the light, Xunko."

"I am to see?"

"If all goes propitiously."

I've grown accustomed to my darkness, to occasional bright visions. To my journeys into the future of the world. I lack nothing.

The next month, only eleven layers are replaced, and so on as the year of dark moons progresses.

Each month I flinch as more light arrives. What will it be like to live in the outer world? Will it correspond with what I've seen behind my eyes? Or will all be completely different?

"Will you remove them all?" I ask Mauruch.

"That depends on how you take to the light. And we shall see if you retain what you have learned in the darkness."

Now that eleven moons have passed and only one layer of bandage is left, I can make out the bright eye of the sun. I perceive the blessed darkness of our cave.

"Will you take the last layer off?" I again ask Mauruch. Listening for his response, my stomach twists.

Do I even wish it? I have been comfortable in this life, seeing far into the future of the world. I lack nothing.

Mauruch doesn't answer. His silence laps at me.

Little Skulls

An early morning downpour rattled the huge sturdy leaves of the banana trees. As Rosalba drew her shawl closely around her in the newly chilled air, she thought of how the toads, in spite of the fungus, were working their magic.

The toads had brought the rainy season. Papa and the boys had finished the planting just in time. Rosalba imagined the hard corn—"little skulls" the seeds were sometimes called—bursting open in the fertile soil.

She stayed in by the fire, fashioning a doll for Adelina. She tied rough corn husks with lengths of yarn, cinching the yarn in tight, making first a head, then a waist.

"Here, she's finished." Rosalba handed the doll to her little sister.

"I'll call her Rosita," said Adelina.

As Adelina clutched the doll close, Rosalba heard a sound beyond the snap of the fire, beyond the steady *tap-tap* of rain on the thatched roof. It was a distant sound, a strange sound like a gigantic snoring. She cupped her hand around her ear, listening, until a great crack of thunder split the sky.

I am woken before the cocks crow. The copal is burned, and our chants echo off the cave walls: "O Hunahpu Possum, Hunahpu Coyote . . ." Finally, I am washed all over. Today is the day to remove my final bandage. Today I am to witness the world at last.

But no one touches the bandage. Instead they paint what feel like circles and stripes on my face and hands. They load my bare chest with shells and jade.

And then we go out.

After a long journey over unfamiliar paths, the sounds of crowds of people reach my ears. From the soft jungle paths my feet know well, I move onto the stones, which burn my bare feet. We enter one of the sacred cities I have seen in visions.

I am given no brew to drink, no mushrooms to chew. Hence no dreams slip behind my eyelids. I see only light and dark.

As we walk, I sense people moving out of our way. I sense great numbers on either side of me.

Mauruch guides me on the stone steps as I climb upward. Toward the sun, which burns a hole in the sky. I tremble, knowing what happens at the top of temple steps.

Look What You've Done!

The next morning crisp black shadows crossed the patio. The sun bathed the world in a yellow glow. "Please, Mama," Rosalba begged, "let me go see my friend. I promise to come home before the afternoon rains."

Nana glanced at Mama, nodding slightly.

"Quickly, then," said Mama.

Water dripped from the pine needles, catching the sunlight, and the birds sang loudly as Rosalba went down the path to the pool, to Frog Heaven. Her heart sang as always when the rainy season began. The Earthlord and his toads had done their jobs.

Alicia had been wrong. The rain was proof that all was right with the world. The prophesy of 2012 had been written just to scare people. Global warming might happen elsewhere, but not here in the Highlands.

Suddenly Rosalba heard a tumbling, rumbling, tearing sound. It was the snoring sound she'd heard the day before.

From a high point, she looked down. Far below, a large gray bulldozer moved back and forth on the forest path. Yet no road led from the highway. How had the bulldozer gotten there? Whatever could it be doing?

And then she knew. In the wake of the bulldozer lay a wide brown gash. The big machine had cut its own road!

Flying down the rocky path, Rosalba stumbled twice, righted herself, and went on.

When she arrived, the machine stood parked next to the trail that led down to Frog Heaven. Freshly cut brush rose on all sides.

Rosalba closed her eyes. This had to be a bad dream!

But the bulldozer was real—idling, spitting black smoke, while two men busily sawed away at a young pine tree.

Rosalba shouted, "No!" and ran toward the

men, her looped-up braids slapping the sides of her neck.

The buzz of the saw drowned out her words.

"No!" she shouted again.

The saw stopped, and both men looked up.

"You can't!" Rosalba cried.

"Slow down, little one," said the man with the red cap. "You live in the village, don't you? This road will make your life easier."

The other man mopped his face with a kerchief. "You won't have to walk so much. You can ride in a truck."

"I don't want to ride in a truck!" she declared.

The men laughed. Then they turned the power saw back on, preparing to cut the fallen tree into pieces.

Rosalba ran down into Frog Heaven, knowing she wouldn't find Alicia. If her friend had been nearby, she'd have stopped those men.

At the sight of the pool, Rosalba froze. Several white objects floated on the surface. She stepped closer, then covered her mouth, stifling a scream.

The objects were frogs, lying belly up.

She ran to the water's edge and lifted out a dead frog. The little brown body lay on her palm, the eyes staring at her as if to say *You could have done something!*

Where the pool narrowed and emptied into the streambed, instead of flowing water, there were hills of dirt. The bulldozer had filled in the stream. No wonder the frogs had died!

As the saw whined, tearing at the tree, Rosalba cradled the frog. She noticed that the little house and pyramid were undamaged. But what did they matter now? They hadn't helped the frogs. She and Alicia had played such silly games. Rosalba kicked at the tiny structures.

She ran back up the path, past the two men, who were lugging a piece of the tree out of the way.

"Look what you've done!" Rosalba cried, holding out the frog.

The red-hatted man and the other stared.

Tears running down her cheeks, Rosalba took the steep fork to the right instead of the path to San Martín. Everything had changed. Everything! Not only were the frogs dead, but now trucks, buses, and cars would invade her quiet village. Clouds gathered as she ran along the ridge.

When she arrived at the camp, all was silent, the doors and windows of the green tents zipped shut.

I wait for hands to rip the jewelry from my neck, to smear my body with the blue paint of sacrifice.

Here at the pinnacle, immense clouds of sweet copal rise into the sky, along with the thin whine of a flute. The priests chant. Sounds of drums, rattles, and conch-shell trumpets arrive from all directions. Far below, the crazed crowd shouts.

The hot sun makes me dizzy. My heart panting, I wait for the hands.

The crowd grows silent and a loud, clear voice rings out. "Great people of the banner of the sun! You are the ones destined to be nearest to the gods!"

Is this the voice of the masked king I have seen in my dreams?

The voice stops and the silence continues.

Then footsteps pass us. A small scuffle.

A breathless pause. A man's cry.

Silence again.

I am fortunate not to see.

And then the crowd roars, waves of sound pounding my ears.

I hear the sound of something—a head?—thrown down the steps. And then a larger sound following.

The instruments start up again. The king and priests dance, their jewelry clattering.

The first sacrifice is over.

Government Seals

Rosalba sat down on a big rock and wept. She dried her eyes and wept again. Why wasn't anyone here? Where *were* they? Why hadn't Alicia been at Frog Heaven?

Rosalba looked up at the sun, balanced overhead, ready to roll toward the horizon. She'd been gone a long time—the dead frog, wrapped in her shawl, was growing stiff—but Mama would have to understand. The men with the bulldozer were ruining everything!

A wind came up, carrying clouds from the edges of the sky.

The frogs at Frog Heaven wouldn't enjoy this rain, Rosalba thought, crying harder.

As the clouds cast the first shadows, she heard voices from the trail above. She stopped crying and listened. Whoever was coming spoke Spanish.

Rosalba stood up.

Antonio appeared first, carrying a burlap sack with something wiggling inside.

Alicia burst out from behind him, crying out, "You're here! What a surprise! Roberto found a kind of frog we haven't seen before, so we all had to go." Then she stopped. "What's wrong? Why are you crying?"

Rosalba held out the dead frog.

The skin around Alicia's eyes crinkled, as if she too would cry.

Through fresh sobs, Rosalba managed, "Some men are making a road. They've killed lots of frogs."

Antonio and the others gathered close, handing Rosalba's frog from one to another.

"Where did you find this?" the man called Roberto asked.

"At Frog Heaven."

"She means the big pool at the bottom of the mountain," said Alicia. She gestured toward the burlap bag.

Antonio opened the burlap sack and placed

a living frog—black with red stripes—in one of the plastic boxes.

Rosalba watched as Alicia shut the latch. It was good that they'd found the new frog. But with so many dead ones, what did that rescue matter now?

With lightning illuminating a distant peak, the group headed down, the men leading the way, Alicia and Rosalba following. The sky boiled with dark gray clouds.

"Can your *papi* stop them?" Rosalba asked Alicia.

"He'll have to," Alicia called over her shoulder. "He'll just have to."

Rosalba hoped Alicia was as sure as she sounded.

When they arrived, the bulldozer had moved forward, creating new destruction behind it. More trees lay fallen, sap oozing from the stumps. Alicia scooped up a nest.

Antonio ran toward the bulldozer, waving at the man in the red hat. The bulldozer stopped moving, but the man didn't turn the engine off.

The other man, who'd been slashing the bushes with a machete, let his long knife dangle.

The thunderheads closed over the last bit of blue sky.

"Do you have a permit for this work?" Antonio called up. "Nobody told *us* about this. And we have legitimate scientific business here." Even though Antonio shouted, his voice sounded faint over the bulldozer's roar. He looked small against the big machine, his wispy hair blowing.

Saying nothing, the man pulled a paper from his pocket. As he handed it down to Antonio, Rosalba saw that it bore the seal of the government of Mexico — an eagle wrestling with a snake. "We have an order to make this road to the village of San Martín, and perhaps higher into the mountains," he said.

Rosalba's legs suddenly felt as weak as blades of grass. These men had official orders. They weren't acting on their own.

The man with the machete began to hack again.

Antonio opened his wallet and produced his own paper, also stamped with the government seal.

"Oh, yes!" whispered Alicia.

The other scientists moved close, forming a group against the big machine and its driver. As Antonio held the paper up, the first raindrops splattered it.

The man on the bulldozer reached out, then drew his hand back.

"It says," explained Antonio, "that the amphibian population is dying at an alarming rate from chytrid, a deadly fungus. My expedition is here to preserve amphibians from further harm. And this"—he gestured toward the newly cut road—"causes harm."

"If any frogs died today," said the man, glancing at Rosalba, "it wasn't because of fungus. We have nothing to do with that."

The rain began to fall steadily, as if trying to wash away the words.

"Habitat destruction," said Antonio, water running off his forehead, "also kills amphibians. The government wants the animals protected."

"And the villagers of San Martín will want this road," the man insisted.

"More than they want a few frogs," added the other.

"Have you asked the villagers?" asked Antonio.

"Everyone wants convenience. And if a few animals die . . ." The red-hatted man spread his hands, palms up.

Oh! How could he say such a thing! Rosalba took a step forward. "San Martín *doesn't* want the road," she said. She surprised herself, speaking out among these *ladinos*.

"She's right!" Alicia called out. "Ask them!"

"Let the villagers take it up with the government, then!" said the man with the machete, lifting it into the sky.

The clouds released a great drenching downpour, bringing the argument to an end. Everyone dashed for the shelter of the big trees—the road builders under one, the others under another. As rain spilled from the sky in great sheets, lighting zigzagged and thunder growled.

Sitting close to Alicia on the soft pine needles, Rosalba spoke loudly, raising her voice against the pounding rain. "Don't worry. Now that the rains have started, we're going to have the big Festival of Santa Cruz. The shaman can fix anything. Señor Tulán will know what to do. This year the festival will be different."

Even now, the shaman and the other old men might be gathered in their hut in the village.

Alicia sighed. "I hope so. That man had the government's permission. . . ."

Rosalba shivered with more than the damp cold. "Don't worry. I'll go tell everyone in San Martín. They'll be really upset. They'll stop the road."

After the cries of the crowd die down, the high priest comes to me. His feathered headdress stirs the air. While Mauruch holds my arm, the priest says prayers over me. Is sacrifice what I have trained for? Has Mauruch withheld this secret from me? Have I lived thirteen years only to be offered to the gods?

My heart still beats in my chest. But if the gods desire me, I am theirs.

After the prayers, Mauruch leads me, not to the blue stone of sacrifice, but down the stone steps.

"You're shaking, Xunko," he says.

"I thought I was to be sacrificed."

After a short silence, he laughs. "Not you, Xunko. You're too valuable. This is your special day."

He means I will see. But when? Many events have passed. The hour grows late.

Our line of shamans walks the long way back under the dark moon. I, accustomed to the Underworld, lead the way.

In the cave a feast awaits us—deer and wild

pig sweetened with mango, spiced with chili peppers. I grow sleepy. Perhaps tomorrow Mauruch will remove the bandage.

But when we finish eating, Mauruch clears his throat and the others grow silent.

"Today, Xunko," he says, "is your thirteenth birthday. Thirteen years ago, you entered the world. You have become an adept seer of the world within and of the unseen world, both present and future. Tonight you will behold the outer world as well. Tonight we shall remove the final layer."

Copal is thrown into the fire, and our chanting drones into the air.

As with all the other times, Mauruch removes the bandage as if he is going to merely wash my face. "Don't open your eyes yet, Xunko." His voice is firm.

He washes my face, my eyes, with a fragrant hot towel.

"And now," he commands.

I open my eyes for the first time. Colors swirl before me. Instead of being flat, the world surrounds me. I can make no sense of it. Someone grips the back of my head.

"Focus here. Only here," orders Mauruch.

My gaze falls on a sacred text, a codex linked to the heavens. My fingers close around the cover of jaguar skin.

As Mauruch fans open the codex, my eyes marvel at the thick red frames of the pages, at the red, black, and blue glyphs—pictures that tell the story of the world.

At last Mauruch stops unfolding. He points to one section. A symbol like an eye and the bars and circles of the Long Count march across the page. Having seen these symbols behind my eyes, with ease I now read the numbers they represent. These symbols indicate the number 13.0.0.0.0. The date is the end of the final Big Cycle. The day the world will end.

I shiver in horror.

"This you must know, Xunko," says Mauruch. "Now you may gaze upon all that has been hidden."

Instead of being confined to the small space of my head, the world blooms around me. I see Mauruch's lined face and the others with their painted faces, their jewelry. The oil lamps, the fires, the cave, the turquoise waters of the dzonot.

When I reach to touch what I see, often my fingers meet with nothingness. The world extends in every direction, larger than I expected.

To my astonishment, people and objects grow larger and smaller, then larger again. As though by sorcery.

I want to study this place forever, home for my small lifetime.

But Mauruch says, "Prepare to leave."

A Sharp Tug

As the thunder rolled on down the valley and the downpour let up, Rosalba made her way home, her shawl wrapped tightly around her head. Her thoughts turned to her papa, who would have come down from the cornfield long ago. This time, Mama might not be able to stop him from punishing her. Rosalba could almost feel the sting of the branch across her bare legs.

As she ran, a new thought came to her: the bulldozer man had said that perhaps the road would go all the way into the mountains. She glanced toward the Earthlord's cave, shrouded in mist. If the men built a road up there, they might kill the singing toad. Then the Earthlord wouldn't want to live there anymore. And without him, everything would change.

She couldn't afford to be afraid of Papa or of anyone else. Rosalba strode over to the men's hut, where the firelight seeped through the cracks. She called through the blanket: "Papa!"

She heard footsteps, and Papa drew back the blanket. He stood in the doorway, lit from behind by the fire. He held a sandal in one hand and a large needle and thread in the other.

On the other side of the fire, Mateo and Anselmo whittled sticks with pocketknives, the shavings drifting into the flames.

Papa squinted at her. "Where—?"

Rosalba held up a hand, saying, "Wait, Papa! A terrible thing is happening!" She held his eyes, refusing to look away.

Papa hesitated, then gestured for her to step into the hut. The air smelled of sweet pine smoke.

As Rosalba moved into the light of the fire, she said, "The *ladinos* are making a road from the highway to San Martín."

At those words, the boys looked up.

Papa plunged the needle into the strap of his sandal. "How do you know this?"

"I saw it. I saw the bulldozer working. I

heard the men say so." The rain picked up, drumming on the thatched roof. "The road is killing frogs."

Papa gave a sharp tug to the thread. "Those *ladinos* are trying to take our land again. The road will help them do that."

Rosalba hadn't thought of that possibility. She glanced at the photograph of Papa and Mama with the black *pasamontañas* worn across their faces, and at Papa's gun from the Zapatista days tucked under the blankets.

"Ouch!" Anselmo cried out. He'd nicked his finger with the pocketknife.

Was Papa right? Would the *ladino* soldiers and their green helicopters really come again? She had no idea, but if Papa believed such a thing, he might make a good ally. "We have to stop them, Papa!"

"But wouldn't a road be good?" asked Mateo. "We could buy a truck and ride back and forth to town. . . ."

Anselmo sucked his finger.

"They're building a road right to the Earthlord's cave!"

Mateo shrugged. "Easier to get to the festivals."

"Your sister's right," muttered Papa. "A road wouldn't be good."

"If you want stupid roads," said Rosalba, glaring at her brother, "you should go live in town." With that, she slipped out into the rain, letting the blanket drop behind her.

We shamans walk out of the cave into the night.

The visible world, even in the darkness of a moon-dark night, is too much to bear. As I walk, objects loom larger. When I look behind me, they have grown small again. This shape-shifting unsettles me. I shut my eyes and walk blind, as I have done my whole life.

The night surrounds us with the husky croaks of frogs, with the long, slippery hoots of the owls. Each of us carries his own silence.

Hearing the slap of water against a shore, I open my eyes to the bottomless lake that has manifested in my dreams. Our group draws closer.

At one with our ritual silence, others greet us by starlight. By their painted faces, I know them to be fellow shamans. From a hiding place in the tree roots, two bring a canoe.

Mauruch climbs into the canoe, and beckons

me until I join him. He dips the oars into the water, propelling us forward into the lake. All on the shore grows tiny.

When we arrive in the middle, Mauruch stops rowing and sits motionless. The boat stills.

I look up into the blazing starfields. They are hotter, sharper, whiter than what I have seen behind my eyes. Each tiny point streams through my eyes, filling my body with light.

Some say the wide band of stars is the road along which souls walk to the Underworld. Others call it the World Tree—roots in the Underworld, branches in the heavens—or the White-Boned Serpent.

For the first time, I look upon the three stars that form the Hearth of the Heavens: the Jaguar Throne, the Snake Throne, and the Water Throne.

From his bag, Mauruch pulls a young coconut, cupping it in both hands. A small hole is drilled in the firm green husk. He hands this husk to me.

I shake my head. With eyes to see the world, I don't need the drink.

"You need to witness more than this world, Xunko," Mauruch says softly, uttering the night's first words. "Much more."

I take his drink to honor his wish. I find it sweet and cool, pleasant on my tongue. I feel no need to retch, and the potion moves into me quickly, powerfully. I lose contact with the wooden canoe, the water around us. Above me the starfields swirl, forming a great whirlpool in the sky.

The whirlpool darkens, a funnel of black in the black night. The tunnel stretches down to the earth, down to the lake, the base hovering over our canoe.

The head of a serpent, eyes glittering, emerges from the tunnel. It stretches its head down to the lake, as if to drink, unfurling its black tongue.

When the tongue comes looking for me, I cringe backward in the canoe.

"Sit up, Xunko," Mauruch commands. "Not sacrifice, but this serpent is your destiny."

I think of the ancestors astride the tongues of the smoke serpents. Am I to become an ancestor tonight?

"Go into him, Xunko," says Mauruch.

And those are the last words I hear.

Pink Geraniums

The next night after supper, Papi invited his brothers to join him around the fire. Tío Miguel, with his fat little stomach, and Tío Josue, his hair cut in a straight line across his forehead, had both been Zapatistas along with Papa.

Sitting at the edge of the firelight, Rosalba tried to imagine the three men in black ski masks, marching down the pine-needled trails, shouldering rifles. Surely, these three could defeat the new enemy of the bulldozer.

They passed a gourd of sugarcane beer among them.

"We have to stop those men!" said Papa, lighting a cigarette.

"But how?" asked Tío Miguel. "They have all the power."

"Not *all* the power. I have an idea." Smiling, Papa lifted the gourd.

Rosalba cupped her hands around her ears. What clever plan had Papa devised?

"I'll pour sugar in the gas tank of their bulldozer," he declared. "That'll ruin the engine."

The fire crackled in response, sending up a spray of orange sparks. Rosalba felt her own heart spark as well. What a great idea! So simple! There would be no more arguing with those men. A little bit of sugar and the piece of government paper would be useless.

Tío Josue handed Papa the gourd, saying, "That would be foolish, Gerardo."

"You'll be caught and put in jail," added Tío Miguel.

"I'm willing to take the risk." Papa flicked his cigarette. The red ash made a wide arc before falling.

Papa in jail! Rosalba almost stood in protest.

"Maybe it wouldn't be you," objected Tío Miguel. "Maybe they'd pin the blame on one of the rest of us. On someone innocent."

"Besides, they'll just bring another bulldozer," said Tío Josue.

And another and another, Rosalba thought. Those people probably had lots.

"They're not trying to take our land, Gerardo. They're just trying to modernize us."

"They want us to be like them."

All three men laughed. The fire was getting smaller, but no one put on another log.

"They want to get rich off us." Tío Miguel drained the last of the beer. "They'll bring in businesses where we'll spend our money."

"But they don't know we don't have any!" said Papa, and the three laughed again. He laid the empty gourd facedown on the table.

The three made their way to the nearby hammocks and grew quiet. At the sound of their snoring, Rosalba stood up and threw a pinecone into the fire. It popped loudly as the seeds burst in the heat. Papa had had just one idea, a silly idea it seemed. The Earthlord was in danger. And Papa had given up.

"The *ladinos* are building a road to our village, Sylvia," Rosalba said as they lowered bundles of flowers onto the sandy shore of the lime-stone spring. "You don't want a road, do you?"

Sylvia remained silent, and Rosalba thought of Sylvia's desire for auto parts, brooms, and buckets.

"The road is making a huge scar," Rosalba persisted. "The trees have been cut down. The frogs are dead."

Sylvia said, "I don't like frogs anyway. With a road, we can get everything brought here. We won't have to walk. We might even get a store in San Martín."

A store *would* be nice, Rosalba thought as they wove the spicy-smelling geraniums into the pine boughs, decorating the white cross. She could buy candies and *refrescos*. But still a road would bring such changes. "The road will make everything change. If our village doesn't want a road, the government won't build it. Please, Sylvia."

"They'll build it no matter what."

Rosalba's fingers had grown sticky with pine sap. "What if they build a road all the way to the Earthlord's cave?" She gestured toward the peak above them.

A faint shadow passed over Sylvia's face.

"What if they do, Sylvia? Then what?"

A group of women arrived with bamboo rakes and plastic bags. They busied themselves with cleaning trash out from under the bushes and rocks, raking the sand clean, all the while gossiping.

"She loves his brother instead . . ."

"And I've heard her husband consulted a *bruja* . . ."

"For a love spell?"

"And one for money. If he had more, she might love him."

Normally, Rosalba listened carefully to such talk. But now she was thinking only of the words she was about to utter.

The night before, when she'd described the bulldozer, Nana had said it would be sad to bring all the bustle of a town to little San Martín. And Mama had said they couldn't afford a truck in any case, so what good would a road do them?

When she'd brought up the possibility of

122

a road to the very threshold of the Earthlord's cave, Mama had said the government didn't have money to go that far.

Rosalba wasn't so sure about that.

After Rosalba plunged the last geranium into the pine boughs, she stood up and approached her aunties.

She explained what was happening with the road, concluding her speech by saying that the scientists who'd been studying frogs thought the road was a really bad idea.

"The scientists are *ladinos* themselves," said Tía Merced, leaning on her bamboo rake. "The *ladinos* want to keep us quaint. They don't realize how hard our lives are without the conveniences they enjoy."

Rosalba thought of Alicia's tent with the fingernail polish, the hair clips and ribbons, and the teddy bear nestled inside. Did Alicia want to keep her from having things like that?

Tía Socorro said, "My husband could have an auto repair business like his uncle does in town."

"But the road will make it easy for the *ladinos* to take our cornfields," Rosalba protested.

Tía Sandra waved a hand, as though swatting away a fly. "No *ladino* would try that now."

"We'll get electricity at last."

"Maybe even telephones."

"What if," Rosalba said, stepping forward, her hands on her hips, "what if the Earthlord doesn't like the road?"

Tía Sandra and Tía Socorro stared up at the cone-shaped peak.

Tía Merced said, "The Earthlord would get used to it."

"What if he *doesn't* get used to it?" Rosalba persisted. "What if he leaves? What if he leaves and the world can't go on without him and it ends? What then?"

Tía Merced laughed and shook her head.

Sylvia stepped up. "The trucks might run over our chickens," she said, tossing a small smile at Rosalba.

I surrender as I have been taught, abandoning myself to the will of the universe. I let myself be sucked into the serpent's jaws. Into his foul black breath. Into the tunnel of his body.

The journey takes me. It takes my breath. It crushes my bones. It takes my heart as a priest would take it. I have been sacrificed after all.

Suddenly I am out of the tunnel. I rest in a silence so complete it stills my heart.

I am above the stars, floating in ceaseless blackness. I look down onto the fate I have been born to.

I sit first upon the Jaguar Throne, gaining the ferocity of a wild cat. I sit upon the Snake Throne, learning a viper's agility. And finally, the Water Throne teaches me to flow like the rivers.

I stand upon the floor of the heavens. As if commanded, I stretch out my arms, the palms raised.

I receive the blue-green gem of the earth in one hand. I cup my fingers around that sphere, with its precious mountains and valleys, its cloud shapes and jags of lightning.

The glorious hot jewel of the sun is placed in my other hand. It is the Fifth Sun, for this is the Fifth Era.

Suddenly, the sun is torn open. The fiery flesh is ripped as if by a giant hand. A great bolt of fire escapes.

The flames travel the distance of darkness. They travel from one of my hands toward the other. Although I try to hurl the earth-sphere out of harm's way, it stays in my palm, fatally attracted. The conflagration flames from orb to orb, licking the blue-green planet.

The oceans boil. The land burns. The jungle-covered empires heave as the earth is wrenched apart.

Then all is quiet.

I look down the tunnel. The Green Morning Star, Icoquih, has appeared. Dawn is breaking and the canoe drifts.

Mauruch is bending over my body. I lie, pale, as if dead.

And then I am sucked down again. With a soft clap, I become one with my flesh, yet lie as if a flame has been blown out.

"Tell me what you saw, Xunko," Mauruch commands.

But I have sunk far away. I sense Mauruch inside my mind now, sorting through its memories. I hear his soft gasp.

The Cave of the Earthlord

From a large wooden trunk, Rosalba took her ceremonial *huipil* as well as Adelina's. This brocaded clothing, passed down to them from their great-grandmother, was different from the everyday *huipiles;* it was feathered, the iridescent green of the quetzal bird woven into the fabric.

Adelina stood, her eyes bright, ready for the moment.

As Rosalba lifted the special *huipil* over her head, she said, "Remember that when you wear this, you place yourself at the center of the world."

"I know! I know!" Adelina said impatiently, tugging the hem down to her waist, stroking the feathers.

Rosalba lifted the feathered garment over her own head. In doing so, she suddenly entered an unexpected darkness, as if in a tunnel.

"Where are you, Rosie?" Adelina asked. "Are you stuck in there?"

With a jerk, Rosalba wrested the *huipil* down, emerging at last into the light.

"Are you all right, Rosalba?"

"Of course," she replied, resting a hand on her *pit-patting* heart.

As Adelina dashed up and down the trail in her feathered *huipil,* pretending to fly, Rosalba watched the procession winding up the mountain, which had grown green during the few days of rain.

Tall trees, their needles shining with light, gave way to cornfields perched precariously on the mountainside.

When the trail made a sharp turn, Rosalba looked back to see people from town, including some *ladinos,* joining the procession. The Mayan women used shawls tied across their backs to carry bright, sweet flowers. The men hauled bundles of fireworks and food.

The ceremonial *huipiles,* the bright shirts

and ribboned hats, shone like rainbows against the green hillsides.

Rosalba waved at Sylvia, who walked behind, then waited for her to catch up.

"Only this ceremony can make the world right again," Rosalba said to her. "We have to stop that road."

"That's what *you* think," Sylvia said. "Others have other opinions."

"Well, *others* don't know," Rosalba retorted, wishing she hadn't waited for Sylvia.

When the procession arrived at the limestone spring, halfway up the mountain, the scientists in their khaki clothes and broad-brimmed hats were already waiting. They stood with their hands clasped in front of them, as if not sure what to expect.

Alicia came darting through the crowd.

Rosalba was surprised to see her wearing, not her *ladino* clothes, but a blue-and-white *huipil.*

"Papi got this for me at the market," Alicia said, looking down at the bright threads.

"I thought of what you said about helping the Earthlord. I want to help too. But, oh!" she exclaimed, laying a fingertip on a green feather. "*Your huipil* is extra beautiful."

Rosalba rose up on tiptoe, making sure Papa wasn't watching this meeting with the *ladina*. She spotted him, under his hat with the water-fall of ribbons, on the far side of the spring.

"The terrible thing," Rosalba said to Alicia, lowering her voice, "is that so many people want the road."

"They may want it now. But they're not thinking of all that will be lost."

"Sylvia wants it," Rosalba said, betraying her cousin. "Tell her why, Sylvia. Tell Alicia why."

Sylvia spoke softly—her large eyes lowered. "It would be nice not to have to walk so far. Especially when it's cold or hot."

"But what about the frogs?" Alicia asked. "What about the way they're dying?"

Sylvia opened her mouth as if to speak, then closed it.

"My papa doesn't want the road," said Rosalba. She didn't mention his silliness of the other night.

Rosalba turned to see Sylvia slipping into the crowd.

"You'll have to change their minds, Rosalba."

"I don't know how. Can't your father do something?"

"He went to town and called Mexico City. He ended up on hold for two hours. He'll try again in person when we go back. . . ."

At that, a little shadow passed over Rosalba. How could she fight the road with her friend gone?

A group of musicians settled close to the spring, tuning up a violin, guitar, and harp. When the ceremonial music filled the air, the crowd hushed.

"The musicians keep the water happy," Rosalba said into Alicia's ear. "If the water isn't happy, the spring might dry up."

Yet not everyone hushed. Rosalba noticed the town boys talking on their cell phones. Some had on earphones, listening to other music. They didn't care if a road was built to San Martín.

When the music ended, Señor Tulán stood over the spring. Lifting his bamboo staff, he recited the usual Mayan prayer in his singsong voice: *Yea, pleasing is the day, you, Huracan, and you, Heart of Sky and Earth, you who give abundance and new life, and you who give daughters and sons . . .*

The crowd listened with bowed heads.

"What's he saying?" Alicia asked.

"He prays that the water will be preserved for the health and prosperity of all." She wished that the shaman had added something about the dying frogs. About the road. About the end of the world itself. But perhaps he was saving those messages for the Earthlord himself.

The shaman turned away from the spring, leading the procession upward, higher onto the cone-shaped peak of the Earthlord. Tall pines swayed and fragrant needles covered the forest floor.

Usually, Rosalba felt happy on this festival

133

day that celebrated the rain and the new crops. But today she felt twisted, at odds with Sylvia and her aunties.

As the procession moved up the mountain, the air grew cooler and small clouds drifted across the sun. Just before the peak, a meadow spread in front of the Earthlord's cave. A collection of wooden crosses stood propped up by piles of stones. Sheltered from the breeze, candles burned in small pits.

Christians said that the crosses stood for the cross where Jesus died. But in San Martín people believed they stood for the sacred tree of life.

As Tía Mirsa and other women knelt to tie three branches of geranium flowers to the crosses, Rosalba whispered to Alicia, "They're opening the gate to the sacred world."

Men were busy lighting numerous fire altars, throwing gourdfuls of grainy copal incense into the flames, releasing clouds of sweetness.

At an altar in front of the cave, people

laid offerings of cigarettes and corn seed, bowing slightly with palms pressed together. The women added offerings of calla lilies and sweet-smelling tuberoses. The men offered gourds of sugarcane liquor, then passed the gourds among themselves.

Alicia looked on, wide-eyed.

The boys from town tapped away on their cell phones.

A woman handed Rosalba a box of matches, saying, "Please light those candles over there."

Rosalba and Sylvia took turns lowering the lighted matches into the tall glasses, touching the flame to the wicks.

When they'd finished, the same woman gave them a basket filled with herbs.

Alicia fingered the leaves and seeds.

"Sprinkle them like this," Rosalba said, casting a handful onto the ground. "The Earth-lord likes the sweet smell."

As the men lit the ends of pieces of sugarcane, rockets took off into the air, leaving behind a smell of gunpowder. The musicians once again set up—this time joined by a slit drum player—their music punctuated by the explosions of these fireworks.

Holding a sharp knife in one hand, the shaman lifted a black chicken toward the sky. It flapped its wings briefly, then cried out.

Alicia turned her head away and covered her ears.

"It's no problem," Rosalba reassured her. "There's plenty of chickens. They're not dying of fungus."

As Señor Tulán began his prayer, Rosalba moved close, listening carefully. Maybe instead of speaking to the villagers about the road, he'd talk directly to the Earthlord. He'd talk about the dying frogs, the bulldozer at the bottom of the mountain. He'd even talk about 2012. The Earthlord would do something about those things.

At the prayer's end, Alicia looked at Rosalba, her eyebrows raised in question.

"He only said the usual things. You know—asking the gods for rain and good crops."

"That's all?"

"That's all," answered Rosalba. For once, she understood more than Alicia did.

Alicia scuffed at the grass with the toe of her sandal.

Now that the ceremony was over, the women set out the feast, balancing the dishes on large rocks at the edge of the meadow.

Rosalba and Alicia carried their plates to a spot overlooking the forest below.

"It looks so small from up here," Alicia said, pointing to the scar cut by the bulldozer.

"But it's going to my village. . . . And it might come all the way here," said Rosalba, looking around, trying to picture cars and trucks parked here in the lovely green meadow. Suddenly, she didn't feel hungry for the bean-paste tamales.

Alicia sighed. "Then it's really going to be up to us. Have you thought of what you'll do?"

Rosalba shook her head. *Her own big thing.*

"Well, before I go, I'm going to make posters and put them all over. Even in town."

"What will they say?"

"Don't burn trees. Pick up trash. Don't make roads and kill frogs."

Rosalba set aside her plate of food. She didn't want to think about Alicia leaving. And she couldn't write words to make posters.

"You have to decide on something, Rosalba. I'm leaving in a few days."

"You *can't!*" Rosalba scooted closer to her friend.

"Papi has his job at the university. And I have school."

"But what will I do without you?"

Alicia put an arm around Rosalba's shoulder. "You'll be all right. You were fine before I came."

As clouds began to cover the blue sky, blotting out the sunshine, Rosalba shivered.

Just then she saw Catarina Sanate, sitting alone, overlooking the valley.

"See that woman over there?" Rosalba said. "No one likes her because she does folk paintings."

"Why?"

"Only men are supposed to paint."

"In Mexico City, lots of women paint."

"In our culture, men are supposed to do their things and women theirs."

"Is that why she's sitting alone?"

"She doesn't fit in," Rosalba explained.

As a light drizzle began, people started to pack up.

Rosalba stood and brushed off her skirt, saying, "The Earthlord has had enough of the festival. He's asking everyone to leave his mountain."

She noticed that Catarina remained seated, her shawl pulled over her head. She wondered if she felt lonely on this feast day when everyone was celebrating together.

"Stay here," Rosalba said to Alicia, then took a square of candied watermelon squash from her plate. With only one dish of the sugary treats, not everyone had gotten some.

She walked hesitantly down the green slope. When she reached Catarina, she touched her lightly on the shoulder.

Catarina started, but on looking up, she smiled.

"Would you like this?" Rosalba held out the candy.

Catarina gave a quick laugh, then lifted her open palm. "Of course. How thoughtful of you."

For what feels like many passages of the Long Count, I lie still in our dark cave. My bones cannot hold me. They are ground like fine cornmeal. Sometimes I sink through the blanket, passing through the floor of the cave and into the Underworld.

Mauruch brings me nourishing liquids, whispering, "I am sorry, Xunko. I didn't know. . . ."

My return was not guaranteed. I almost did not come back from the great Underworld of the night sky.

I want to see nothing. I want to sleep and forget all that I have witnessed. But, as if my eyes were still bandaged, behind them I see the codices. Codex after codex foretelling death, destruction, chaos, annihilation, obliteration. . . .

My fellow shamans increase their rituals, bleeding themselves, chanting, begging the gods for the lives of all Mayans. For the life of the earth itself. "O Heart of Sky! O Youngest Thunderbolt and Sudden Thunderbolt!"

The shamans burn offerings. They eat only the fruits of zapotes, matasanos, and jocotes. They deprive themselves of corn, the food of life. They lift their faces to the sky, pleading before the gods.

Do they beg for my life, too?

No one comes to me for blood.

I meet One Death and Seven Death. I meet them both and sometimes do not know if I survive on this earth or have already drifted to Xibalba. Perhaps I have been sacrificed after all.

I instruct the ants to bring me flowers from the garden of One Death and Seven Death. These I offer back to them, hoping to appease those who would steal me.

One night during the chanting, a vision of a young girl appears to me. Her braids are looped close to her ears. She wears the traditional huipil of those who live in the jungle after the empire's fall.

But around her I see animals that shine with the brilliance of gold. They have round feet that roll, traveling quickly down wide black pathways. I see gleaming animals—or are they temples?—moving through the sky.

This girl is not of my time. Nor of any I have foreseen.

She lives close to the end of the Fifth Sun. The calendar year of 13.0.0.0.0 fast approaches.

Perhaps that is why her face is sad. Why she is worried. She is alone. I am sad with her, worried with her, alone with her. Her flesh is my flesh, her blood my own.

Keeping this vision a secret from Mauruch, I gather my strength. I must become more than I have ever been.

Don't Build Roads

That night a strange dream came to Rosalba. A boy, just a little older than Mateo, appeared before her. His cheeks were painted with blue stripes. A heavy shell necklace encircled his throat. Pointed bones dangled from his earlobes.

He squinted at her as if the light hurt his eyes. And then he passed a hand over his forehead—the hand shaking—and disappeared.

All morning Rosalba had relived the dream. Who was this boy? What did his coming to her mean?

Hearing the fluttering and squawking of chickens, Rosalba turned to see Alicia entering the patio. She stood with her light hair shining, wearing a pale-blue dress.

"Alicia! How did you find the way here?"

"I followed the trail. I asked people."

Rosalba glanced toward the path that led from the cornfields. But it was too early for Papa to come down and find Alicia here. Mama and Nana were again tending the small cornfield near the orchard.

Adelina peeked around the door of the hut, then darted back inside.

"Look what I've made." Alicia unrolled a big piece of paper. The poster had a picture of a frog lying on its back. "This says," Alicia said, pointing to each word, "don't build roads."

Rosalba looked away, a blush of shame rising into her cheeks.

Alicia rolled up the poster, saying, "Don't worry. Someday you'll learn to read. It's not hard. In any case, the designs you weave are like a language. Instead of a pen, you use thread."

Rosalba smiled. It was true that each design told a story. Stories that she, not Alicia, could write. Stories that she, not Alicia, could read.

"You could weave a kind of poster." Alicia tapped her rolled-up paper. "You can weave designs that say what my words say. That way when you wear the *huipil,* everyone will get the message."

What Alicia said was wrong. It wouldn't be right to weave a *huipil* that said anything different from what *huipiles* always said: *This is the way the universe is ordered.*

"Last night I had a dream," Rosalba said, changing the subject. "A boy came to me. I think he was a shaman. I think he was from the old times."

Alicia's eyes grew wide. "From the time of the pyramids?"

Rosalba glanced at Alicia, then at the chickens hunting for bugs in the damp soil. Had the boy really come to her from such a far-off time?

Alicia fished in her pocket, then held out two tiny blue eggs. They matched her dress. "I found these near a tree those men had just cut. They'll never hatch now."

Normally, Rosalba would have thought of the eggs as food. She'd have been glad to find them on the ground. But now she saw the delicate ovals through Alicia's eyes.

"We have to hurry," Alicia said. "The road is getting closer."

Rosalba stared at the white cylinder of Alicia's rolled-up poster. "But what can *I* do?" she asked.

Alicia shrugged. "Listen to your dreams?"

I enter the House of Cold. Thick with hail, it freezes my bones.

"Drink this, Xunko," says Mauruch.

I push the gourd away.

He shoves it close again. "This is not a potion, Xunko. This is a healing tonic. You have lain too long. Your skin is cold to the touch. Come into your power. See the world that is now yours."

But I do not want to see. The outer world is only my Second World. I cannot go there yet. The very dance of the firelight stirs what needs to be quiet in me.

"Bandage my eyes again, Mauruch!" I plead.

But he refuses.

When I wrap my eyes myself with strips of cloth, he tears the strips off. "Open your eyes, Xunko! Your apprenticeship is at an end."

I keep my eyes shut, defying my master. I guard my darkness.

I come to the gods bearing quetzal feathers. I come to them bearing tribute. "O Quetzal Serpent! Show me what I must do!"

Though I have partaken of no potion, I am swept far away from this cave, from this earth. I hang in curtains of blackness.

Like the Hero Twins, Hunahpu and Xbalanque, I meet Bloody Teeth, Skull Staff, Jaundice Demon, and Flying Scab. But I hold no conversations with those demons. It is not they who hold my answer.

"O Heart of Heaven!" I implore.

The path I walk upon is dim, but wide. A pathway through the reaches of time. When I meet 13.0.0.0.0, I find myself at a juncture. One way leads to oblivion, a great abyss where not even stars can live. Gone from that place are even the bloodletters and the sacrificers, the strife makers, traitors, and tempters to chaos.

Quetzal Serpent appears before me. Writhing, with his plumes fluttering, he extends his clawed hand. He invites me to journey down the juncture's other side.

Instead of a void, I find a dominion of green cornfields, stalks climbing toward the skies. Here the people, children of the light, begotten in light, smile. The very clouds rise from the mountains singing. The sun, moon, and stars truly appear. Everything on the face of the earth has its dawn.

Like the Hero Twins, these people have defeated the gods of the Underworld. They have done battle with One Death and Seven Death, with Hun Came and Vicub Came. They have gone into Xibalba and they have triumphed.

To take the way toward abundance and harmony, this, then, the girl must do. She must declare her name before Xibalba.

A Good-bye

Rosalba waded into the shallows, wetting the hem of her skirt. Today Alicia would go home, flowing away like this river. And she, Rosalba, would be unmoved, like one of these pale-yellow river stones.

Mama and the other women already squatted by the river, pounding clothes against flat stones, scrubbing them until the white cloth sparkled. Pants and blouses, shawls and woolen tunics, rippled across the grass and shrubs, drying in the warm sun.

Rosalba returned to the bank and took up a shirt to wash. Just as she plunged it into the cool water, she heard a clatter of rocks on the path above. She looked up to see Antonio and Roberto descending the trail, followed by Alicia. In their khaki clothes, they almost blended with the forest.

Rosalba stood, the ball of wet cloth in her hands. Alicia had obviously come to say good-bye—she'd promised she'd find a way—but why had the men accompanied her?

"Greetings!" Antonio called out, lifting a hand.

The women stared. Mama and Tía Sandra rose to their feet.

Alicia scrambled down the last bit of trail and crossed the sandy shore. She greeted Rosalba with a kiss on each cheek, then took her hand.

Rosalba squeezed Alicia's fingers hard, as if she could hold her here.

"As you know," Antonio began, his voice rising over the sound of the rushing water, "a road is being built from the main highway."

A few women nodded.

"If the road is cut all the way to your village, it will change the environment forever. With vehicles coming in, you'll have pollution. Your children will breathe dirty air. Already the road building has dumped soil downriver, interrupting the flow."

The women stopped washing as the *señor* talked. They listened with respect. But Rosalba guessed they were remembering the days of the Zapatistas when they'd been in conflict with *ladinos* like these. Surely, they were concerned. But they didn't want to hear this news from Antonio and Robert.

"Your sacred peak will be degraded," declared Roberto. "You could sign a petition. . . . I can give you some phone numbers of people in Mexico City. . . ."

No one spoke.

At the scientists' camp, the tents had been folded neatly on the backs of donkeys. The donkeys were owned by Martín Xicay, who was busy making sure that the loads were securely fastened. Even the plastic boxes of frogs had been tied on, a thin rope looped through the handles.

The clearing, once full of activity, was barren.

When Antonio gave the word, the group followed the donkeys, accompanied by the metallic clattering of pots and pans and the softer sounds of plastic boxes knocking against each other. As if the day were a happy one, white butterflies danced back and forth in grass grown high with the rains.

At the edges of the sky, clouds formed like the wool of sheep at shearing time.

When they approached the bulldozer, still growling its way through the brush, Rosalba couldn't bear to look. She hurried along, ignoring the driver and the other man hacking at the bushes.

"Your *papi* and Roberto didn't change the women's minds," she said to Alicia when they reached the other side of the bulldozer, walking along the wide gash of the newly turned earth. "They didn't listen."

"Not today, maybe. But maybe they'll think it over."

But Rosalba knew the women could be

stubborn. It would take more than the words of two *ladinos* to get them to see things differently.

At the trail that led to Frog Heaven, Rosalba and Alicia paused. Looking down onto what had been the pool, now filled with rocks and dirt, Rosalba wiped away tears. "We used to come here. And now it's gone."

Alicia slipped an arm around Rosalba's waist. "Don't cry, Rosalba. Maybe someday the bulldozer will dig all that dirt out. Then it'll be just like before."

But Frog Heaven would never be as it had been. Rosalba dried her face with the edge of her shawl and moved on.

At the highway, the men unloaded the donkeys' burdens. They stacked the boxes of frogs inside the cabs of the trucks and threw the tents and other bundles into the back, the cookware clattering.

"Maybe Papi can talk to someone about the road," said Alicia.

Rosalba nodded, knowing that Antonio had already called Mexico City.

"Don't cry, Rosalba," Alicia said again. "We'll come back next year."

"If there are any frogs left," Rosalba said glumly. But then a thought startled her. "The world may not be *here* next year! *We* may not be here!"

Alicia's eyebrows pinched together, as if she too might cry. But then she smiled and patted Rosalba's arm. "The world will be here. We will be, too. Because we're going to do our big things." She walked over to a large black duffle bag, rummaged inside a moment, then pulled out the book with the pyramid on the cover, the book of prophesy. "This is for you."

"But I can't read," Rosalba protested.

"You should have this anyway. You're the one who's Mayan."

Rosalba tucked the book under her arm. Even if she couldn't read, it would remind her of Alicia.

After Antonio handed Martín Xicay a stack

of pesos, Martín roped together his donkeys and led them away.

"It's time," said Antonio to Alicia, climbing into one of the trucks.

Rosalba hugged Alicia with all her might.

Alicia hugged her back, just as hard, then let go, holding Rosalba at arm's length. "I'll be here next year."

As Rosalba waved with both arms, Alicia got into the truck beside her *papi*. As she turned to wave good-bye from the back window, Rosalba noticed that Alicia still wore the yarn bracelet. She herself reached up to touch her friend's pretty butterfly sparkling in her hair.

Floating along the river of life, the girl fast approaches a waterfall. She is soon to drop off into the Great Destruction. She is a blink of the eye away from the End of the World.

But she can prevent that end from being oblivion. Instead of succumbing to One Death and Seven Death, she can bring forth a dominion of holy corn, fragrant and heavy on multitudes of stalks.

I crawl deep into the cave. Alone I must heal myself. I summon the strength of the ancestors, of all shamans who have come before me, of those whose flesh is my flesh.

I crawl inward, descending to the four crossroads of Xibalba: the Black Road, the White Road, the Red Road, and the Blue-Green Road.

I enter my familiar House of Darkness. I am accustomed to its black passages. There, like the Hero Twins, I plant an ear of unripe corn. The corn may die. Or it may sprout, indicating true life.

From there I pass into the Shivering House, where a howling wind clatters. With my very body, I warm that cold, emanating the heat of the sun itself.

In the Jaguar House, the cats gnash and snap their teeth. I manifest bones to feed them. I breathe the strength of the jaguars into my heart.

At the Bat House, multitudes await me. They fly at my head, shrieking, their snouts like knives. I transmute the din of their flapping wings into the great stillness that I am.

This I do to save her.

Dead Cornfields

That night the shaman came to Rosalba again with his painted face, his heavy jewelry, the eyes that looked as if sunlight hurt them.

He stared at her, as if to make sure he had her full attention.

Then he lifted his hands. When he drew them apart, an image of a cornfield appeared. But it wasn't a healthy cornfield, flourishing with green life. Instead it lay dried and brown.

Rosalba didn't want to look at that cornfield. Dead, it represented all that everyone worked to avoid. Everyone guarded against such bad luck through ritual and prayer, by weaving, by planting according to the sun and stars.

The boy showed her another cornfield and then another. He showed her a mountain-side covered with dead cornfields. And then many more mountains, brown and desiccated, crackling with death.

Rosalba wished she could close her eyes against these visions.

"Show your people," the boy commanded, his voice flat and stern. "Warn them."

He pressed his palms together, waited a moment, and spread them wide again. A *huipil* appeared, stretched flat as if it had just come off a loom.

With a start, Rosalba recognized this *huipil* as her own. The designs were those she'd already woven.

But when she looked at the back panel, she couldn't believe her eyes. Instead of the careful designs, the *huipil* was brocaded with cross-hatchings of ugly black and brown.

Like a dying cornfield.

The boy stood silently before her. His eyes no longer blinked against the light, but commanded her.

And then the boy swayed. He grew white, then translucent. He was gone. Rosalba reached out for him. What had happened? Had he died?

When the dream faded, Rosalba woke up, her blood pounding.

It took her a few moments to realize she'd been dreaming. Everything in the hut was normal: Adelina lay curled beside her. Mama and Nana slept on the other side of the hut, Nana gently snoring.

The embers released puffs of sweet smoke, and a light rain drizzled softly on the thatched roof.

Rosalba lay recalling the dream. Dead cornfields were a sign of global warming. Yet how could the boy request that she brocade such a design—no design at all? How could he ask her to create such a picture of destruction? There could be nothing worse than dead cornfields. For corn was life.

To brocade a *huipil* picturing death, destruction, and ill health would be taboo.

Rosalba pulled the blanket over her head and closed her eyes tight. It had been only a dream, after all. Not a real thing.

Not a real thing like the way Alicia had left.

162

What could a mere dream matter compared to that? As a tear slipped down her cheek, Rosalba wondered if Alicia was still riding in the truck with her *papi*. Perhaps she'd arrived home at a place Rosalba couldn't imagine, perhaps in one of the sky-touching buildings. Would she ever see her friend again?

Dawn broke with the cries of the roosters. Water dripped from the eaves. Rosalba listened to the soft *pat-pat-pat* as Mama and Nana slapped masa into tortillas.

This would be her first day without Alicia.

In my apprenticeship I have transformed myself into an eagle soaring among the clouds, into a serpent slithering in oneness with the earth, and into the jaguar who rules all. In my enchantments, I have become even a lowly pool of blood lying warm and sticky under the blinding gaze of the sun.

There is nothing of me that cannot become other than myself.

I will become a crow for her. A lowly crow that only she shall notice. For a dream is only a dream. A manifestation bears more power.

In my transformation, I first become nothing but my head. The rest of my body vanishes. I wink until my head shrinks to the size of a crow's body. From my chin grow wobbly crow legs. I hop back and forth until I lose my stiffness.

The tail extends from my neck like a fan, sweeping the floor of the cave. Long and beautiful wings unfold from my cheeks. In growing the beak, my breath diminishes.

Finally, I must see as a crow sees. I look out of one eye, shake my head down, and look through the other.

I am ready for sacred flight.

The Crow

Rosalba tied the loom carefully to the tree, the other end around her waist. She straightened her skirt and placed herself in front of her half-finished *huipil.*

In spite of herself, Rosalba couldn't forget the dream. The shaman's instructions had been so clear. Yet she'd be called a *bruja* if she did as he requested. She'd be shunned like Catarina Sanate.

Rosalba decided to weave the back side of the *huipil* exactly like the front, just as she'd planned. She wouldn't think of anything but the work ahead.

Just when she started to insert the red yarn into the tight threads, a large black bird swooped down onto the loom. Staring at Rosalba with bright eyes, the crow tugged at the weaving with its sharp beak.

"Go away!" Rosalba shouted.

But the bird refused to leave. It kept tugging until it flew off, a red thread dangling from its beak.

Rosalba stared at the spot in the blue sky where the bird had disappeared. And then she began to shake: loose ends of red yarn poked out of her beautiful *huipil.* It was ruined! She wiped at tears with the back of her hand.

A lizard darted onto the patio, stopped to study Rosalba with its black eyes, then slipped into the bushes. A dog roamed close to the house, sniffing for scraps.

Just as Rosalba began to relax, a new thought quickened her breath. Had the attacker been a bird at all? Shamans were known to take animal shapes. Like the mysterious boy in her dreams, the bird had given her an unmistakable sign.

Rosalba sighed. There was only one thing to do.

She looked down into her basket of bright yarns, pulled out the ball of black, then shoved the basket to the side. She'd have no use for the rest of the colors. Yet she still needed brown, and didn't have any.

She retrieved the skein of white yarn, then cut long strands of white. She dipped the strands into cold coffee, letting the yarn absorb varying amounts of color, then hung the lengths over a tree branch.

When the brown yarn was dry, Rosalba brocaded it, along with a little black, onto her white background.

By weaving the traditional patterns, Rosalba had always assisted the Earthlord. By manifesting these designs, she made sure that the world moved properly. With her help, the sun traveled across the sky, down to the Underworld, and back up to shine all day.

Now every time she inserted her pointed stick, she created disorder. She went against all she'd been taught, against all good sense. How could it be right to weave the colors of a dead cornfield?

She sensed the Earthlord looking down on

her. Was he filled with displeasure or merely puzzled?

Some said the Earthlord took those who angered him to labor in the Underworld.

Because Rosalba created no pattern, the work went quickly. With trembling fingers, she worked until her neck ached and her shoulders were sore.

When the shadows stretched long, she heard Nana's gentle footsteps behind her.

"What are you *doing*, Rosalba?" Nana asked, bending to examine the *huipil*. "Your colors . . ."

"An ancestor told me to weave this," Rosalba said quietly. "I had a dream."

"A dream . . ." Nana mused, looking up into the tree. Then she shook her head, as though shaking away a memory. "Hide your work, Rosalba," she cautioned.

Yet when Sylvia slipped into the patio, Rosalba couldn't roll up her loom fast enough.

"Oh!" Sylvia exclaimed, then stepped closer, her huge eyes growing even larger.

"I don't like it, but an ancestor came to me in a dream." Rosalba raised her face to look straight at Sylvia. "He showed me this design."

"That's no design, Rosalba. It's . . . it's the opposite of a design. It wasn't an ancestor but a demon who sent you that dream," said Sylvia. "If you keep going, bad things will happen."

Rosalba didn't answer, but wondered if Sylvia was right. By her rash actions, was she hastening the end of the world?

Coming back, I find one arm still a glittering black wing. It takes me until Icoquih rises to transform it, to find myself completely human again.

Traveling out of the cave, back to the place where we shamans live, I pause in the House of Darkness. I check on the ear of corn planted. It is not yet dead.

Mauruch did not notice my absence. For in truth, I have not been gone for any earthly time. I sit against the wall of the cave, listening to the stalactites form.

Sometimes I am strong enough to glimpse that girl at her loom. She is a wise girl. One who listens.

I sink into rest. Or am I falling into the Underworld? Am I to be trapped forever in Xibalba?

Parching Winds

The next day, thunderheads formed, heavy with moisture. Surely it would rain. Yet as Rosalba set up her weaving inside the hut, the clouds drifted away. When the sky should have been washed with rain, bright yellow sunshine streaked across the patio.

That night the wide band of stars seen only in winter paraded across the black sky.

No rain fell the next day, or the next. By the end of the week, the sky remained a clear azure from one horizon to the other. Hot winds parched the air.

Papa complained that the new corn shoots were shriveling. For a few days, he and the boys carried jars of water on their heads to the plants. But that did little good. Soon it was no use at all going to the cornfield.

"There's no corn to eat. No corn to trade. No seeds to plant next year," Papa declared to Mama one day.

Rosalba looked down at her dusty sandals, at her dusty brown toes. She thought of Sylvia's warning. Had her ugly weaving brought on the drought?

"Maybe I should go to the *fincas* to find work," Papa went on.

The *fincas* were the coffee plantations in the Lowlands. Only men without cornfields went down there to work for the *ladinos*. Men without cornfields were men without true connection to life.

Throughout San Martín, the men swung in hammocks, sleeping, smoking, talking of the *fincas*.

Rosalba continued her weaving. Instead of tying the loom across the open space of the patio, she retreated to the side of the hut where she couldn't be easily seen.

The drought *wasn't* her fault, she kept telling herself. The Earthlord's toads were dying of fungus. They'd died because of the road. She knew this, yet with every new line she wove, she trembled.

"You can't keep this up, Rosalba," said Mama. "You'll bring a bad name to our family."

"That's such an ugly *huipil*!" Adelina declared.

Nana remained silent.

Rosalba heard the voices of Sylvia and Tía Yolanda in the patio. They were asking Nana if they could borrow some salt. She heard Sylvia and Tía Yolanda moving behind her. She sensed their gaze on her *huipil*.

The next day, as she was doing laundry at the river, Rosalba noticed glances, heard whispers. She heard the dreaded word *bruja*.

Mauruch speaks to the shamans: "In his weakened state, hovering perilously between life and the Underworld, Xunko engages in a battle I know nothing of."

He begins a slow chant: "You, Bundled Glory, and you as well, Tohil, Auilix, and Hacavitz, Womb of Sky and Womb of Earth, the Four Sides and the Four Corners . . ."

I breathe in the incense of copal.

Later Mauruch comes to me. "Open your eyes, Xunko. You are young yet. You are to live in this world."

But I cannot. Fate urges itself upon me.

If I fail, if the girl fails, the world will veer toward the Black End.

What You Need to Do

At the market, Rosalba helped Mama lay out the calla lilies, the eggs, and Nana's woven cloths. K'in, instead of hiding behind a gray blanket of moisture, showed his bright face. Instead of being a friend, the sun was now an enemy. When the hot breeze stirred the dust, women covered their faces with their shawls, grumbling.

"The rains should never have begun if they were going to stop like this."

"It must be evildoing."

Some of the women flashed looks in Rosalba's direction. It seemed the gossip of her weaving had spread beyond San Martín.

When Mama had sold some of the lilies and a basket of eggs, she gave Rosalba a few pesos.

For once Rosalba didn't look forward to going out into the market. She wished she could sit quietly, pretending to study the woven lines of her skirt.

"Go on, Rosalba," said Mama.

"But they'll look at me. They'll talk about me."

"They're doing that anyway. Plus most of that is your imagination."

Reluctantly, Rosalba stood up. With the coins heavy in her hand, she entered the crowd of sellers and shoppers. She held her head high in spite of the looks, the conversations that stopped when she drew close.

She bought the things Mama had asked for—matches, a handful of limes, coffee, chili flakes, more kerosene—loading up the nylon bag. Then she made her way to Catarina's stall, where the usual tourists clustered.

Rosalba studied a painting of men working a cornfield. Bean vines climbed the corn stalks, sprouting new leaves and red flowers. Squash vines stretched their wide, flat leaves, shading the ground so that herbs and wild greens grew underneath.

But there was something at odds with this fertile scene. Around the border, Rosalba noticed the tiny monkeys and vultures who represented the chaotic world. Sometimes women wove them to remind people of the destruction that would come if they acted badly. Then she peered more closely—in the background, high on the mountain, Catarina had painted a small brown square. It was a dead cornfield.

She shivered.

Rosalba felt a hand on her shoulder and turned to see Catarina.

"I've heard about what you're doing," Catarina whispered in Mayan. "Don't worry about what others say. Do what *you* need to do."

"Even that . . . ?" Rosalba nodded toward the tiny dead cornfield.

"Yes, even that."

"It's so hard," said Rosalba.

"Very." For a moment, Catarina locked Rosalba's eyes with her own large, dark ones, then said, "Such work makes us sisters."

Rosalba smiled, but shivered nonetheless. She had now joined herself with Catarina, the outsider. But at least she wouldn't be alone, as Catarina had always been. "Did a shaman come to you in a vision?" Rosalba asked in a whisper.

Catarina's eyes darted over the crowd, and she put a finger to her lips. "Shhh. Later." She patted Rosalba's shoulder. "Come see me any-time." Then she turned back to her customers.

The girl and I stand at the crossroads, in need of the holy power of the gods.

May there be only light within your mouths and before your faces, O gods.

I send precious gems and glittering stones. I send cotinga feathers, oriole feathers, and the feathers of red birds. I bring tribute to the enchanted lords Cucumatz and Co Tuha and also before the faces of Quicab and Cauizimah, the Ah Pop of the Reception House, Magistrate and Herald.

May there be only light within your mouths and before your faces, O gods.

Hot Stars

When Rosalba and Mama got home that night, Papa was sitting in the patio drinking sugar-cane beer. He called out, "Come here, daughter," and she went to stand on the opposite side of the fire with its thin ribbon of smoke.

"Tonight the elders are gathering," Papa announced, lifting his gourd high. "They'll talk about the drought. They'll talk about you." He looked hard at Rosalba. "You know what people are saying."

"Yes, Papa." Standing there, she suddenly felt as formless as the smoke, as though she might fade into the air. She tried to focus on Catarina's words of comfort, her offer of sisterhood.

Nana had prepared the meal, setting the table with the enamel cups and plates.

Everyone ate in silence, Papa scooping up chili flakes with his tortillas, the boys hungrily downing one bean-filled tortilla after another.

As Rosalba picked at her food, she wondered if the elders would banish her from San Martín that very evening. Would she be forced to wander the Highlands alone, as Catarina had been? At least Catarina had folk painting to sell. She, Rosalba, had nothing.

Sparks flew up from the fire, as if to join the hot stars overhead.

A small figure appeared out of the darkness, coming to stand in the circle of firelight. It was the boy Efrain. He announced, "The elders want Rosalba. Rosalba Nicho. They want her to bring her loom."

Mama and Nana looked at each other, then lowered their eyes.

Rosalba went into the hut. Somehow she had to prepare, to do something special. She put on her best everyday *huipil,* hoping the powerful designs would protect her. For extra luck, she clipped Alicia's sparkly barrette into her hair.

Outside, Mama and Nana busied themselves with cleaning the table, acting as though nothing was wrong. The boys tended the fire, while

Papa lit a cigarette and stared into the star-bright night. Adelina clung to Rosalba. "Come back soon, Rosie. Don't let the spooks get you!"

Just as Rosalba turned to leave, Nana tucked a large white carnation behind Rosalba's ear, whispering, "For good luck."

Rosalba followed Efrain through the darkness, passing the huts where firelight leaked through the twig walls. Might she soon live, like Catarina Sanate, on the other side of the village fence of stones, cornstalks, and bricks?

For courage, she imagined herself as a Zapatista going to war with the loom as her rifle. She pretended that Efrain was the leader of the revolt and that she was following him into battle.

At last, Efrain stopped in front of the elders' hut. He stepped close to the blanket and gave a low whistle.

Smelling the sweet copal, Rosalba knew the elders had already been consulting the ancestors.

A voice called out, and Efrain pulled the blanket aside. He beckoned to Rosalba.

At the sight of Tío Mariano, Tío Jorge, and Señor Tulán, a red kerchief tied across his forehead, and three other old men sitting on wooden chairs, Rosalba's heart beat hard against her ribs. Yet she drew herself tall. The unusual weaving, she reminded herself, had not been her idea.

In spite of the heat, firelight danced along the walls. The men didn't greet her, but sat silently, their hands folded, beads of sweat rolling down their faces. No one smiled. Outside, the crickets sang their rickety songs.

Señor Tulán unfolded his hands and gestured toward an empty chair.

Rosalba wondered if they'd allow her to say good-bye to her family. Maybe she could get to Mexico City and find Alicia. Cradling the loom in the crook of her arm, she decided that if she had to go, she would hold her head high. The chair rocked on the uneven ground, first closer to the men, then away.

More silence. Rosalba thought of the sun far below them, slipping through the nine layers of the Underworld.

Señor Tulán finally spoke, his voice as deep and slow as far-off thunder. "We have heard of the unusual nature of your weaving. Please show us your loom."

Rosalba stood up.

Tío Mariano also rose and held out his hands, ready to receive one end.

As Rosalba unrolled the weaving, the traditional designs appeared first: the Earthlord and his toad, the sun traveling through the thirteen layers of sky.

The men paid little attention.

When she revealed the patternless browns and blacks, each of the elders studied the weaving. None spoke. Rosalba imagined the Earthlord also looking on, peering over the shoulders of these old men.

"You may roll the loom up again," said Señor Tulán.

Rosalba did so, and sat back down. Her nostrils were full of the clove-like scent of the carnation behind her ear, grown fragrant in the heat.

"As you know, drought has struck," said the old shaman. "Not for many years have we had such a disastrous rainy season. The cornfields are dying."

Rosalba nodded slightly. He was about to say the lack of rain was all her fault.

Instead he surprised her, saying, "Obviously, one girl's weaving couldn't cause such drought."

Rosalba shifted her loom from one arm to the other.

"And yet," the shaman went on, "the people of San Martín are talking."

The embers popped. The old men sat with folded hands.

"Do you have anything to say, Rosalba Nicho?" asked Señor Tulán.

Rosalba stared at the dirt floor. Now was the moment to save herself. She hoped her words would be just right. "The other night I had an ancestor dream," she said slowly, "A young shaman came to me."

"How do you know it was a shaman?"

"By the way he spoke. His painted face. His jewelry."

Señor Tulán nodded.

Rosalba went on, her voice steady: "He instructed me to weave dead cornfields."

Tío Mariano leaned forward.

"He *clearly* instructed this," Rosalba added. "Somehow this"—she nodded toward the loom in her lap—"will help us all."

"But the drought . . ." Señor Tulán murmured.

"There's no rain not because of my weaving, but because the Earthlord's toads are dying."

All the old men looked puzzled. Señor Tulán tilted his head to the side.

Rosalba explained about the scientists, the fungus that was killing amphibians, including the toads.

"I know of that," Tío Jorge said. "It's called amphibian die-off. I too met the scientific team from Mexico City."

"But that's not all," said Rosalba, feeling emboldened. "The road those men are building is also killing frogs and probably toads. When the bulldozer filled in the stream with dirt, lots of frogs died."

She could hear the night birds rustling in the trees outside.

"We have been debating the road," said Tío Jorge. "It would bring prosperity to San Martín. Many here are poor. Many older people don't even get out. The school is far away. A road could be a good thing."

Rosalba glanced at Señor Tulán to see if he agreed. But his eyes were closed.

This was the moment to do the young shaman's will. It was a precarious moment, time to do her *one big thing,* as Alicia would have said.

Taking a deep breath, Rosalba set her loom on the ground. She sat tall, saying, "Maybe the *road* is causing the drought."

For the first time, Señor Tulán smiled. "Not a little road like that."

"Maybe not, Señor, but you never know." Rosalba could hardly believe her own daring.

"My friend Alicia—her *papi* is one of the scientists—says the sun is going to get hit by a big beam of light when it gets to the center of the galaxy. And she says that could be either really bad—the world could end—or really good. It can only be good if we take care of the planet."

"Are you talking about the 2012 prophesy?" another elder asked.

Rosalba nodded. "It's like the Flood. It's the next destruction."

And then she stood, rising to stand above the seated elders. The next words weren't her own, but those of the boy talking through her. "If the road is built, we will become less Mayan. We here in San Martín will become like those in the town. People there do not dwell in the blossoming of the Earth or in the Earthlord, who guides us. They do not dwell in the sacred movement of the stars. If we do not live as Mayans, there is no hope of maintaining the order of the universe."

Señor Tulán stared at her in surprise. Then he lowered his gaze and stirred the dirt with the toe of his sandal. "I have thought of that." He drew a circle, first one way, then the other.

"What if the road goes all the way to the cave of the Earthlord?" Rosalba asked.

All three men stared at her.

After a time in which the sun had dropped another notch into the Underworld, Señor Tulán said, "Please step outside, Rosalba Nicho, and wait."

The stars pulsed in time to the crickets' songs. As a warm wind blew, Rosalba rocked from one foot to the other, clutching her loom. Were the elders discussing her fate? Were they deciding where to send her? If they only *knew*! She needed them to *help* her, not push her out of the village. The elders had to help her! They *had* to!

She heard a flute in the distance, sweet notes like a trickle of refreshing water.

Just as a group of fireflies appeared, twinkling in the bushes, Rosalba felt a light touch on the carnation tucked behind her ear. A touch as if in reassurance, a touch that passed through her like a soft breeze.

The curtain was drawn back, and one of the elders beckoned.

When Rosalba reentered the hut, the fire had grown smaller. The light flickered, not on the walls, but on the faces of the elders. She took a seat on the chair that rocked forward, then backward.

A large log, mostly burnt, balanced on another log. Rosalba watched it, wondering when it would tumble.

When at last the log fell, Señor Tulán said, "I have felt the lightning in my blood. The lightning tells me what to do."

Another log crashed into the hot red coals.

Señor Tulán continued: "Tomorrow I will go down to the bulldozer. I will talk to the man driving it. I will tell him that I am going to talk to the government."

"Oh!" exclaimed Rosalba. "Thank you!" She took the carnation from her hair and handed it to Señor Tulán. "Thank you."

One of the men tossed a handful of copal onto the embers, and the whole room grew sweet.

I am learning to see the small things first. Inside the cave, I watch water slipping over the nodules of the stalactites. I watch until I understand how each drop adds infinitesimally to that lumpy formation.

Outside I gather the dropped tail feathers of birds. I study the iridescence in the sunlight, the webbing between each of the parts, the attachment to the central quill.

Last night, when I touched the flower in the girl's hair, passing my fingertips over its complicated form, I wanted to behold such a thing completely with my eyes. And all things like it.

For now I gather only the tiny things into myself, preparing to enter the visible world.

Today I allowed the very largest. At dawn and just past sunset I lifted my eyes to the empty sky. The light fell into me, filling me, healing me.

My eyes avoided Icoquih in the morning. I retreated before the evening stars appeared. There will come a time when Mauruch commands me to return to the Great Sky Serpent, but that time is not yet.

From large to small, my vision oscillates. And thus I absorb gradually the glories of sight.

Tonight when I crawl into the House of Darkness, I find that my ear of unripe corn has sprouted.

I burn copal before that corn because I shall live. I do the dance of the Whippoorwill and the dance of the Weasel because I shall live. I abandon my heart to the dances of the Armadillo and the Centipede.

All the great animals and small animals rejoice in the sprouting of my new life. I look upon them as they come up from the rivers and from the canyons. I see them on the mountain peak. As one we turn our faces to the coming forth of the sun. The first to sing is the parrot. The pumas and jaguars cry out. The eagles and the white vultures spread their wings as we rejoice.

Thus I live until Mauruch shall decree that I drink the bitter potion. Until I return to my duties as the Seer, the Shaman, the Holy Man. Whether the world end or not end, I do not know. But I will continue to extend my being into the vast stretches of the Long Count, transforming into bird and beast and the Great Emptiness, transporting myself, traveling through eternity.

The Hens Are Happy Today

Rosalba lifted her face to the sunshine as Mama combed her hair. She felt the comb making a neat part, front to back. She felt Mama separating her hair, making two braids, winding in the blue and pink ribbons.

When Mama had looped the braids up, tying them close to Rosalba's ears, Rosalba laid her hands over the tight plaits, saying, "Thank you, Mamacita." She beckoned to her little sister. "Adelina, do you want to help me feed the chickens?"

Reaching into the basket of dried corn, Adelina grabbed a handful. Together they walked across the patio, singing out, *"T'ikt'ike,"* to mimic the sound of a hen. In short leaps, the chickens came running and flying.

While the chickens were busy eating, Rosalba searched the broken cooking pots tied under the eaves. She handed the eggs down to Adelina, who cradled them in her shawl.

"The hens are happy today," Rosalba proclaimed.

Harmony had returned. Rosalba knew that all over the hillsides her aunts, great aunts, and cousins were also braiding each other's hair, tending to the chickens, hanging balls of ground corn out of reach of the animals. Everyone helped the Earthlord do his job of running the world just right.

She too must do those things. Whether the Earth would die, she couldn't know. The shaman hadn't made any promises. But she could do those things. And she could do more. She'd helped stop the road, hadn't she?

Maybe Alicia would come back. And now there was Catarina.

That night the shaman came again to Rosalba. He showed her the *huipil,* once again stretched out. This time, both sides were identical, brocaded with the traditional designs of the ancestors.

He showed her a sky filled with clouds, their gray bellies heavy with moisture. He showed her a green cornfield, its stalks loaded with ears of golden corn.

This he wanted her to manifest.

When he looked back at her, his eyes were unblinking, as if the sunlight no longer troubled them.

"These are for you," Sylvia said, holding up several lengths of hair ribbon. "I heard what you did," she said. "That was brave."

Rosalba slipped the ribbons through her fingers. Bright yellow was her favorite color. "There won't be a road now," she said. "Are you happy about that?"

Sylvia sighed. "I'll get used to the idea."

"Later on you'll be glad."

"Maybe."

"You can help me." Rosalba fastened one end of her loom to the tree. Today she'd work in the open instead of hidden on the side of the hut. "Tie this end around your waist and sit down."

With the loom stretched out, Rosalba gently plucked the brown and black colors from the *huipil.* As she laid the loose threads in a small basket, she thought of how each had been like a word sending a message to the elders. "My friend wrote her message with words," she said to Sylvia, "and I wrote with this yarn."

Sylvia giggled.

Rosalba wondered if she'd ever tell her cousin about the shaman. A wide smile crossed her face at the thought of him.

Tomorrow she'd do his will. She'd start on the identical back panel, weaving the patterns of creation. She'd weave the design of the universe line by line, cornfield by starfield, bringing, for now, the rain of life to Earth.

Glossary

brujo/a — (Spanish) witch

chico/a — (Spanish) child, "little one"

chytrid — a type of fungus that causes chytridiomycosis, an infectious disease found in amphibians

coati — an animal related to a raccoon

codex/codices — sacred Mayan texts

copal — a tree resin

cotinga — a dovelike tropical bird with turquoise plumage and a purple breast and throat

dzonot — (Mayan) a limestone sinkhole, also called a cenote

finca — (Spanish) a lowland coffee plantation

hola — (Spanish) hello

huipil — (from Nahuati) a woven blouse made by indigenous women in central and southern Mexico

Hunahpu and Xbalanque, the Hero Twins—mythical twins who defeated the gods of Xibalba in a ball game

Icoquih—(Mayan) a star that appears before sunrise

jocote—(Spanish) a sour yellow plum

K'in—(Mayan) the sun

Kukulcan—(Mayan) the feathered serpent god, also known as Quetzalcoatl

ladino/a—(Spanish) the term for those of mixed Spanish and Indian blood, used in Guatemala and southern Mexico

Long Count—the Mayan way of counting time. 13.0.0.0.0 is the Mayan equivalent of 12/21/2012. The number 13 refers to the number of *baktun*s, or 144,000-day periods.

"Los de adelante corren mucho, y los de atrás se quedarán, tras, tras, tras, tras."—(Spanish) part of a Mexican nursery rhyme that accompanies a game like "London Bridge Is Falling Down" and that roughly translates as "Those in front run fast while those behind will have to wait."

Mamacita—a diminutive form of *Mama,* an endearment

masa—cornmeal dough

matasano—(Spanish) a sour tropical fruit

nopal—(Spanish) prickly-pear cactus; its pads can be cooked like green beans

pasamontaña—(Spanish) ski mask worn by the guerilla group the Zapatistas

pataxte—(Mayan) a type of cacao

refresco—(Spanish) soda

stela/stelae—an inscribed stone pillar

tía—(Spanish) aunt

tío—(Spanish) uncle

Xibalba—(Mayan) the Underworld

zapote—(Spanish) a sweet tropical fruit, also called sapodilla

Acknowledgments

I'd like to acknowledge those who've spent time among the modern Mayans, inspiring me with words and photographs; my agent, Kelly Sonnack, who had the idea of adding the 2012 element to a discarded manuscript about the Zapatistas; and Deborah Wayshak for her writerly intuition in guiding this story to its truest expression.

Author's Note

Decades prior to the arrival of Christopher Columbus in the New World, an ancient civilization flourished in the dense jungles of Central America. These people, known as the Mayans, developed a written language and a calendar. They built grandiose stone cities and made significant astronomical discoveries.

In spite of the Mayans' achievements, between the eighth and ninth centuries AD their civilization abruptly fell. No one knows exactly why the great metropolises were abandoned, why the people scattered to live modest lives in the jungle. The collapse may have been due to a combination of drought, misuse of land, and overpopulation.

While the descendents of the pre-Columbian Mayans live on, they have lost almost all the cultural knowledge of their ancestors. In order to study the ancient civilization, anthropologists have had to decipher the Mayans' writing, known as glyphs. Glyphs remain on the stone walls of ruins, on fragments of pottery, and in the sacred texts known as codices. These beautifully illustrated accordion books speak of ancient kings, gods, the calendar, the history of the world, and predictions for the future. Because the Spaniards burned the codices, only four remain in existence.

Through the glyphs, anthropologists have learned that centuries before Galileo invented the telescope and Copernicus discovered that the earth revolves around the sun, the ancient Mayans accurately calculated the 26,000-year trip of the solar system through the Milky Way galaxy, recognizing that instead of spinning in place, our sun and group of planets whirl in a gigantic loop through space. The Mayans kept track of this span of time with a precise calendar, using a numerical system called the Long Count.

The Long Count documents four previous journeys of the solar system through the galaxy.

The Mayans believed that each time the earth reaches the epicenter of the galaxy, it encounters a burst of cosmic energy and suffers a cataclysmic destruction.

On December 21, 2012, our solar system is again due to pass through the heart of the Milky Way.

On this date, the Mayan calendar mysteriously ends.

This termination has been the subject of much speculation. There is terrific power in predictions of doom. Most recently, the world saw this during the Y2K scare. It was predicted that computers hadn't been programmed to recognize the year 2000, and would therefore stop functioning at the stroke of midnight. Because our world is so dependent on computers, civilization, including the delivery of food and water, would come to an end. Happily, that did not happen. On January 1, 2000, everyone woke up to find the world functioning normally.

Today, recent books like *Apocalypse 2012,*

by Lawrence E. Joseph, have made an explicit connection between the Mayan prophecy and environmental destruction.

However, Mayan scholars agree that the prophesy merely speaks to the closing of a natural cycle. According to the Mayan calendar, the Solar System has visited the center of the Milky Way four times previously and has survived. Why would this time be any different?

The story of *Starfields* explores a little of both perspectives, trying to imagine how two young girls from very different backgrounds might interpret the prophesy in relation to their own lives.

In the sixteenth century, an anonymous group of Mayan nobility re-created some of what the ancient codices had contained. They called this sacred text the *Popol Vuh*. The *Popol Vuh* is roughly equivalent to the Bible in Christianity, the Koran in Islam, or the sutras in Buddhism. It brings to life several important myths, including that of the Mayan creation.

In writing Xunko's sections, I relied heavily on the beautiful language and mythical accounts of the *Popol Vuh*.

For Rosalba's story, I gathered information from the photographs and accounts of those who've spent time among the contemporary Mayans. Having spent time in Mexico and Belize, I also called upon my own personal experience of Mayan culture.